Dear Reader:

Homecoming weekends are extremely popular among historically black colleges and universities (HBCUs) where alumni converge to celebrate with parties, football games, step shows and even steamy affairs. In *Homecoming Weekend*, Curtis Bunn visits his real-life alma mater, Norfolk State University, where characters throughout the country arrive in Norfolk, Virginia to connect with friends for good old-fashioned fun times.

The novel's annual fall tradition features a colorful cast of characters who are anxious to encounter their former crushes, check out their classmates' new looks or offer advice about life. I'm sure you will enjoy how Curtis uses humor to depict a behind-the-scenes weekend of college alumni and camaraderie.

As always, thanks for supporting the efforts of Strebor Books. We strive to bring you fresh, talented and ground-breaking authors that will help you escape reality when the daily stressors of life seem overwhelming. We appreciate the love and dedication of our readers. You can find all of our titles on the Internet at www.zanestore.com and you can find me on Eroticanoir.com (my personal site), Facebook.com/AuthorZane, or my online social network, PlanetZane.org

Blessings,

Zane

Publisher
Strebor Books International
www.simonandschuster.com/streborbooks

ALSO BY CURTIS BUNN

A Cold Piece of Work

ZANE PRESENTS

Homecoming WEEKEND

A NOVEL

CURTIS BUNN

STREBOR BOOKS

NEW YORK LONDON TORONTO SYDNEY

Strebor Books
P.O. Box 6505
Largo, MD 20792
http://www.streborbooks.com

ISBN 978-1-59309-429-4
ISBN 978-1-4516-5952-8 (ebook)
LCCN 2011938446

First Strebor Books trade paperback edition September 2012

Cover design: www.mariondesigns.com
Cover photograph: © Keith Saunders/Marion Designs

10   9   8   7   6   5   4   3   2   1

Manufactured in the United States of America

For information regarding special discounts for bulk purchases, please contact Simon & Schuster Special Sales at 1-866-506-1949 or business@simonandschuster.com

The Simon & Schuster Speakers Bureau can bring authors to your live event. For more information or to book an event, contact the Simon & Schuster Speakers Bureau at 1-866-248-3049 or visit our website at www.simonspeakers.com.

This book is dedicated to historically black colleges and universities in general and my beloved Norfolk State University in particular. The nurturing of young minds and dispensing of knowledge and esteem HBCUs provide have laid and continue to lay the foundation of countless productive lives. Say it with me, *NSU Spartans:* Behold: The Green & Gold!!!

ACKNOWLEDGMENTS

Nowhere. That's where I would be without God. I know He protects me, delivers me and inspires me in everything I do. And He surely provided the uplifting needed for me to complete this work. Thank you, Lord.

I have family that I covet, and I always start with my late father, Edward Earl Bunn, Sr.; he was the ultimate example of a hard-working family man that put family first in every case. My mother, Julia Bunn, has been the most supportive, giving, loving mom around. I love my brothers, Billy and Eddie and my sister, Tammy. My grandmother, Nettie Royster, remains our spiritual foundation.

Curtis Jr. and Gwendolyn (Bunny) are my talented and smart children that make me proud. My nephew, Gordon, has always been like a second son. And my niece, Tamayah (Bink Bink) and nephew Eddie Jr. are blessings that I love so much. My cousins, Greg Agnew and Warren Eggleston, are like my brothers, as well as my brother-in-law Deryk. And I am grateful for cousin Carolyn Keener and uncle Al and aunts Thelma and Barbara and Ms. Brenda Brown, who has been like an aunt/second mom much of my life.

So much love and respect go to Zane, Charmaine Roberts and the entire Strebor Books/Atria/Simon & Schuster family for the support and opportunity to make this book a joyful reality. I'm proud to be a part of the Strebor family.

There are not enough pages to document by name all the people who mean something to me. But I will start with my Norfolk State family that I love: Felita Sisco Rascoe, my NSU classmate and super-duper close friend I rediscovered last year; Kerry Muldrow, Keith Gibson, Randy Brown, Sam Myers, Tony (Kilroy) Hall, Tony Starks, Marc Davenport, Greg Willis, Ronnie Bagley, Brian White, Ronnie Akers, Jacques Walden, Dennis Wade, Julian Jackson, Mark Webb, Kelvin Lloyd, Frank Nelson, Hayward Horton, Mark Bartlett, Marvin Burch, Derrick (Nick Lambert), Gerald Mason, Charles E. Johnson, Harry Sykes, Kim Mosley, Patricia Easley, Gina Dorsey, Shelia Harrison, Demetress Graves, Leslie LeGrande, Bob White, Laura Carpenter, Erika and Tony Sisco, Kevin and Hope Jones, Sybil and Leroy Savage, Avis Easley, David A. Brown, Yvonne Young, Linda Vestal, Sharon Foster, Bruce Lee, Kent Davis, Kevin Davis, Rev. Hank Davis, Judge Susan Davis Widgenton, Kevin Widgenton, Donna Robinson, Sheila Wilson, Ramona Palmer, Derek T. Dingle, Leon H. Carter, Val Guilford, Curtis West, Darryl Robinson, Zack Withers, Joe Cosby, Warren Jones, Joe Alston, Deberah (Sparkle) Williams, Barbara Ray-Jackson, Anna Burch and Gail Patterson. Also, we lost some Spartans I really cared about and miss: Madinah Aziz, Ladina Stevens and Donnie Ebanks. RIP, friends.

I have been blessed with a vast and diverse group of friends that are important to me, including Najah Aziz, Trevor Nigel Lawrence, Wayne Ferguson, Darryl (DJ) Johnson, Betty Roby, Rick Eley, Christine Rudolph, Monica Harris Wade, Yetta Gipson, Denise Bethea, Betty Roby, Tara Ford Payne, Diana Joseph, Monya Bunch, Shelia Bryant, George Hughes, Serena Knight, Marty McNeal, Tamitrice Mitchell, Edward (Bat) Lewis, Kathy Brown, Angela Norwood, Angela Bass, Angie Jones, Carla Griffin, Darryl K. Washington, Lateefah Aziz, Jeff Stevenson, Derrick (Tinee) Muldrow,

Lyle V. Harris, Brad Corbin, J.B. Hill, William Mitchell, Carmen Carter, Lesley Hanesworth, Mary Knatt, Sonya Perry, E. Franklin Dudley, Skip Grimes, Sherline Tavernier, Denise Taylor, Jeri Byrom, Hadjii Hand, Laurie Hunt, Karen Shepherd, Clifford Benton, Rob Parker, Cliff Brown, Stephen A. Smith, Zain, D. Orlando Ledbetter, Michele Ship, Francine McCarley, Emma Harris, Garry Howard, Cindy Jackson, Billy Robinson, Jay Nichols, Ralph Howard, Paul Spencer, Jai Wilson, Garry Raines, Glen Robinson, Dwayne Gray, Jessica Ferguson, Carolyn Glover, David R. Squires, Kim Royster, Keela Starr, Mike Dean, Veda McNeal, Alvin Whitney, Pam Oliver, Kimberly Frelow, Karen Elaine Jones, Keisha Hutchinson, Penny Payne, Erin Sherrod, Tawana Turner-Green, Joan Hyatt, Joe Lewis, John Hughes, Sonji Robinson, Vonda Henderson, Natanyi Carter, Mark Lassiter, Shauna Tisdale, Quinn & Teeairra Motton, Tony Carter, Tamaira Thompson, LaToya Tokley, Necole Bobb, Claire Batiste, Olivia Alston, Brenda O'Bryant, Sheryl Williams Jones, Karen Faddis, Leticia McCoy, Dorothy (Dot) Harrell, John Hollis, Elaine Richardson, Aggie Nteta, Danny Anderson, Lakesha Williams, Leah Wilcox, Andre Aldridge, Ursula Renee, Marilyn Bibby, Brad Turner, Desyre Morgan, Billy Robinson, Denise Thomas, Camille York, D.D. Turner, Judith Greer, Anita Wilson, Tim Lewis, Carrie Haley, Dexter Santos, Ron Thomas, April Tarver, Michelle Lemon, Sandra Velazquez, Patricia Hale, Pam Cooper, Pargeet Wright, Regina Collins, Michelle Hixon, Sherrie Green, Jay Nichols, Regina Troy, Karen Turner, Deborah Tinsley, Christine Beatty, Angela Paige, Roland Louis, Dr. Yvonne Sanders-Butler, Deborah R. Johnson, Toni Tyrell, Tanecia Raphael, Tracie Andrews, Deborah Sharpe, Sheila Powe, Tammy Grier, Sid Tutani, Mike Christian and The Osagyefuo Amoatia Ofori Panin, King of Akyem Abuakwa Eastern Region of Ghana, West Africa.

Special thanks and love to my great alma mater, Norfolk State University (Class of 1983); the brothers of Alpha Phi Alpha (especially the Notorious E Pi of Norfolk State); Ballou High School (Class of '79), ALL of Washington, D.C., especially Southeast.

I am also grateful to all the readers and book clubs that have supported my work over the years and to my many literary friends Nathan McCall, Carol Mackey, Linda Duggins, Karen Hunter, Troy Johnson and Terrie Williams.

I'm sure I left off some names; I ask your forgiveness. If you know me you know I'm getting older and subject to forgetfulness. J, I appreciate and am grateful for you.

Peace and blessings,
CURTIS

CHAPTER ONE
BUMPY ROAD

Jimmy and Monica

Sometimes Jimmy hated his wife. Well, maybe not hated, but on occasion he certainly resented her and how she made him feel. At worst, she had a way of reducing their marriage, an institution he honored, to a prison stint—or some forsaken place he did not want to visit, like hell or the lingerie department at JCPenney.

In those times, he felt like getting into his car and driving off to no place in particular, just away from her, never bothering to look back.

After a while, those feelings would subside. But his anguish was not unfamiliar to any married person, some of whom had even more dramatic emotions than Jimmy's. Still, he believed being a loyal husband and committed father entitled him to some under-standing and not the blow-torch heat Monica spewed.

On this day in particular, it ate at Jimmy like termites through damp wood.

He had waited an entire decade for this weekend.

It was homecoming.

Monica knew how excited he was about the trip—he talked incessantly about how much he looked forward to going back to his old college—but that did not stop her from filling Jimmy's head with exactly what it did not welcome.

He had the trip all planned. He was trying to get onto Interstate 95 South by noon so he could arrive before traffic built up at the tunnel between Hampton and Norfolk, Virginia around 3 o'clock. It was a solid three-hour, fifteen-minute drive from their home in Southeast Washington, D.C.—and that included time for him to stop downtown to get his customary road food: a half-smoke (a D.C. signature sausage) with mustard and onions, a box of Boston Baked Beans candy, pumpkin seeds and a Welch's grape soda.

Monica had other notions. She was sweet on occasion, needy at times and overbearing too often. This was one of her patented meltdowns that bothered Jimmy like that sound of the old record needle screeching across an album. When she acted as she did on this day—standing over him as he packed his bags, arms folded, mouth going, attitude funky—it was a miserable existence for Jimmy. He didn't do drama well, and Monica was in straight Drama Queen mode.

While she was dramatic, and even over the top, she believed she had a valid argument. She wondered why her husband was going back to Norfolk State University's homecoming without her?

Jimmy was so frustrated because of what he deemed her last-minute sinister objective: To pressure and nag him into not going or to bring her along, even as he was moments from departing. At worst, she wanted to put him in a foul mood so he would not enjoy himself. *Selfish*, he thought.

Why else would she go into her histrionics now? he surmised. *She knew I was going to homecoming for several months.* To act a fool just as he was about to leave frustrated him.

"I can't believe this is happening," he said. He had much more to say, but he worked hard on controlling his fly-off-the-handle temper, and the best way to manage that moment was to shut it down as best he could.

"Believe it," she said with much attitude.

Monica was not cute when she was this way. Ordinarily, she was a good-looking woman, not breathtaking but certainly attractive enough for Jimmy to be proud to call her his wife. When she was this way, though, she didn't look the same. In his eyes, she resembled something awkward and distorted, totally unappealing.

Her eyes seemed to darken and to fall back into the sockets, and she held a perceptible amount of saliva in her mouth. *Some creature overtook her physical being and the devil owned her mind,* Jimmy thought.

Still, he loved his wife. She could be worse; their marriage could be worse. He could have been like one of his close friends, Lonnie, who simply had been emasculated by his spouse. She controlled everything from what he did (or didn't do) to whom among his "friends" he communicated. He became a joke among their friends.

Monica was not *that* bad. This level of discord was not regular behavior; Jimmy would not have been able to take it if it were the norm. Other times she got on his nerves (what woman didn't?) for one thing or another, and he would often acquiesce, mumbling to himself: *Keep the peace.*

She figured that if she griped enough, Jimmy would again look to keep the peace and give in. She was wrong. No amount of badgering was going to turn his position. For the most part, she was a responsible and fun wife. But something about him going back to his alma mater for homecoming turned her paranoid. Jimmy remained calm, but he would not budge.

"Baby," he said, trying his best to not sound condescending, "why must we go through this now? You knew about this trip for months. I'm about to leave. This makes no sense."

"Why is it that you *have* to go *and* that I can't go with you?" Monica said.

She had traveled with Jimmy, a lieutenant in the Army, a few places across the country and the world. They moved back to D.C. from California less than a year before, which was good and bad in this situation. It was good because he was back home and it was much easier to get to Norfolk from D.C. than the West Coast or the foreign stops they made. It was bad because he could not fall back on the excuse that it was not "cost-efficient" for both of them to make the cross-country trip for a two-day weekend, as he had in the past.

Jimmy's reality was that his wife did not go to Norfolk State. She did not go to an historically black college at all, which meant, to Jimmy, she didn't understand the value of the weekend—or that there was sort of a "no-spouse code" among most alumni, at least among those he knew well from school.

She went to the "University of Something or Other in Ohio," he liked to say, where the brothers and sisters there were in the vast minority. So, while homecoming there surely was fun, it did not include all the elements that make homecoming at an HBCU a special experience and sort of family reunion. In fact, African-Americans who went to a "majority" college hardly ever went back to their school's homecoming because it lacked that welcoming theme.

Jimmy had been in touch with classmates who talked about how impressed and proud they were to see how much their school had grown. They talked about there being fifty thousand people there, all black, all caught up in the pride and celebratory spirit that homecoming raises. At a non-HBCU, the homecoming weekend was about the football game mostly and a whole bunch of stuff that did not measure up to the cultural experience of an HBCU.

"And there's nothing wrong with that," he had told Monica. "It's just different. Our weekend is about us, the fellowshipping, the tailgate (before, during and after the game), the band, the parties and, above all, the pride of being at a place that essentially raised us from teenagers to adults. It's the place, really, where we were nurtured and grew up. That's what the black college experience gives you. That school put its arms around us and hugged us when we were hungry or scared or uncertain.

"Homecoming," he said, "is a celebration of all that."

"So what are you saying? Your homecoming means more to you than mine because you went to a black college?" Monica argued. "That's crazy."

"I'm not saying your homecoming isn't as important to you or that it isn't fun and great," Jimmy said. "But the mere fact that you have asked me to come with you to yours tells me you're not having that much fun.

"Listen, honey, it's not like I'm going there and meeting with some woman," he went on. "I feel funny about even having to say that. But that's what it comes down to, doesn't it?"

Jimmy lived mostly on the West Coast in the years after he graduated with honors as a commissioned officer. He had not made it back to a single homecoming since graduation. For the three years they had been married, Jimmy hardly even talked of homecoming because attending did not seem reasonable, as they lived on the West Coast and work responsibilities always arose. He either could not take leave because he had duty he could not abandon—or he was deployed to the Middle East. Surviving both Iraq and Afghanistan and moving back to D.C. allowed him to get excited about making homecoming, especially after he went online and read about all the growth around the school.

"Monica, I told you a while ago that I was going to homecoming," he said, placing the last of his clothes in his luggage. "Don't act like you don't remember."

He zipped his bag and lifted it onto its wheels and headed to the garage door so he could dump it in the trunk and keep it moving.

"This is the only weekend I get all year to myself," he said. He was calm even though he was furious to have to go through such explanation. He somehow mastered the art—and it was an art—of composing himself in his most heated moments. Jimmy, in fact, smiled as he explained his position although he was percolating inside.

"I go hard as a husband and father," he said. "I don't golf, so I don't do golf trips. I don't run off to visit my family without you. I don't go to the Super Bowl or NBA All-Star Weekend. I don't go visiting one of my boys for the weekend. This is it. I deserve this break."

The most important reason of all...he had to explain to her again just before he got into his car.

He said: "Even if I did take an occasional trip, this should not be a problem. I have earned it. Plus, you didn't go to school there. So, you'd be standing around bored, looking for me to entertain you. To be honest, I couldn't have the same kind of fun I normally would have with my old friends. It's innocent fun, but we use harsh language and tell jokes that are not always, uh, politically correct. It's part of what we do. I'm not comfortable doing that around you and you'd be monitoring how much I drink, what I say, what I eat, who I hug. I can hear you now: 'Who was that? An old girlfriend? Did you sleep with her?' That's not how it should be.

"Also, I would feel like I had to keep you from being miserable. I can hear you now complaining at the tailgate about needing to sit down and not wanting to go to the bathroom in the Port-A-Potty or not wanting the food. All that would not be fair to me at my homecoming.

"I have heard about people—men and women—bringing their spouses and having a miserable time because they were restricted. If you had an interest in going to your homecoming, I wouldn't even think about going. I know you and your girlfriends would want to talk freely and me being there would prevent that. And I wouldn't know those people, so I wouldn't want to be there, putting you in the awkward position of trying to keep me entertained. It wouldn't be fair."

Monica was unfazed. "But that's the difference between you and me," she said. "I would enjoy my friends meeting my husband. But you'd prefer to run off like you're single."

Jimmy's patience was diminishing.

"You know, you're about to piss me off," he started. "All that I said and that's what you come back with? First of all, if they were really your friends, I would have met them by now. This isn't a family vacation. When you go on your book club trip to Atlanta, I know it's not a family trip. It's for you and your girls. I don't know what the hell y'all do down there and I don't really care. I trust that you understand you're married and will act like it. But you don't invite me on that trip and you shouldn't. That's how my homecoming is. It's not about acting like I'm single. Act like you know me."

With that, he knew he needed to leave before the scene turned ugly. He was a thirty-two-year-old man and she was making him feel like he was a kid asking for permission, which did not sit well with him—especially since it had been established long before that he was going alone.

"Monica," he said, hugging her—she did not hug him back—"I love you and I will call you when I get to Norfolk. Stop pouting and wish me a safe trip and a good time."

She simply looked at him. They had a stare-down for a few

seconds before Jimmy turned, opened the garage door, deposited his luggage into the trunk and jumped into his car.

Monica stood there with her arms folded and a look of disgust on her face.

He honked his horn as he backed out. Jimmy did not like that his wife was being so sour about his homecoming trip. But he couldn't worry about it, either. If he did, it would put a cloud over his weekend. The forecast called for seventy-two degrees and lots of sun, meaning there was no room for clouds.

So instead of feeling awkward about leaving her there pissed at him, he felt reinvigorated, relieved and ready.

To really put that nonsense behind him, he called one of his boys, Carter, who was flying into Norfolk from New York. He was a fun and level-headed friend who graduated a year before Jimmy.

"Yo, I'm in a cab headed to LaGuardia," he said. "I can't wait to get down there. I got some work to do."

"Work to do" meant he had women to pursue. Homecoming was like a free-for-all for Carter.

"I don't think I'm going to make the parties," he said.

"What? How you gonna come to homecoming and miss the parties?" Jimmy asked.

"Oh, that's right; we haven't really talked," he said. "Well, you gotta keep this under your hat. You can't tell anyone."

"I know what 'keep it under my hat' means," Jimmy said.

"All right," Carter said. "Well, homecoming is a time for me to reconnect with Barbara. I should never have let her go back in the day. It's the biggest mistake I ever made."

At least Carter was divorced, which allowed him to do whatever he liked.

"But hold up—isn't Barbara married?" Jimmy asked.

"With three kids, too," Carter said. It was strange the way he said it, like he was proud.

"I know that was your girl about a decade ago," Jimmy said. "But, man, she has a family now. And Barbara was a good girl. You think she's coming to homecoming to get with you?"

"You don't understand, Jim," Carter said. "What she and I have is not ordinary. Why you think she's coming all the way from San Diego? We both tried to move on with our lives. And we have moved on, to a degree. But we still have that connection. Actually, it's even stronger now than ever. It's crazy."

"I wonder if she had the same issue I had—leaving her husband behind," Jimmy said. "Monica gave me the business."

"Well, when hasn't she?" Carter said, laughing. "She's just being herself, I guess. I don't know if Barbara had any issues. I didn't ask. I just know she's coming.

"Listen, I'm not proud of this situation. And I've only told you and my brother about this. And I think she's only told Donna. You remember Donna Scott, right? The Delta who went to ODU?"

"Delta from Old Dominion?" Jimmy asked. "Oh, yeah. Yeah. Wow, forgot all about her. OK, I remember Donna."

"Well, they ended up going to grad school together and becoming close friends," Carter said. "She'll be in Norfolk, too. Anyway, I really understand what the power of love means because I would've never imagined myself feeling this way about any woman, especially a married woman."

They chopped it up for a few more minutes before hanging up. Jimmy was headed to Norfolk to get the whole nostalgic feeling of seeing old friends and visiting the place that really made him—and really, to get away from the daily grind at home.

Carter was headed there for love.

And neither reason was more important than the other.

CHAPTER TWO
BRAND NEW

Tranise and Mary

"Wow. Look at Norfolk State. All grown up," Tranise Knight said, surveying the grounds on Friday morning of homecoming.

She had not been on campus in the four years after graduating and was proud to see the new buildings, including the beautiful Student Union Center and the new Lyman Beecher Brooks Library, which was so huge it had the look of a football stadium. She always thought the NSU campus was as nice as any other black college. Now…wow, she knew it.

She had not come back before now because she wasn't ready. She did not get the job in public relations with the big Chicago firm she wanted, and it made her feel like a failure. She was home-coming queen as a sophomore, president of her sorority as a junior and vice president of the Student Government Association as a senior.

Tranise was looked at as a shining star that would represent Norfolk State so well. It turned out that she had to become a middle school teacher just to have a job after graduation.

Because she had such specific dreams and ambitions, she did not realize how noble and rewarding being a teacher was, especially in an inner city area in Atlanta. It took her a while to get to that point, but in her third year, she got the perspective-altering sensation from a thirteen-year-old boy who had a troubled house-hold. He was talkative and ambitious, despite his family struggles, and Tranise identified something good in the kid.

"Miss Knight," the boy said one Monday morning, smiling, "you're my favorite teacher of all time."

"Aww, that's so sweet," she said. "Why do you say that?"

"All the things you told me about being responsible and watching who I hang out with was right," he said. "One of my friends went to jail Saturday: Tommy. You told me to stay away from him. He asked me to go to the mall with him and get some money stealing ladies' purses. I thought about what you said and I told him I couldn't come with him. If you didn't always tell me to make good choices and tell me about what happened to people who made bad choices, I probably would have been with him and been in trouble, too."

She knew then her career path, while not what she expected it to be, was far more rewarding than any PR work she could do for some big company. She impacted young lives. The job took on a new, more powerful meaning.

Because she was always good with money, which really meant she was cheap, and because she didn't have any kids and no student loans to repay, she was able to live relatively comfortably on a teacher's salary in Atlanta.

So, finally understanding that she was not a failure, but, indeed, a sort of public servant, Tranise believed it was okay to go back to homecoming and see many of her friends she missed after so many years. She found peace with who she was and her mother told her that was far more than what most people could say.

Standing on The Yard again, in front of the Twin Tower dorm-itories, brought Tranise back to some of the most fun times she'd ever had. She could not wait to see many people she had forgotten over the years that would be there for the weekend. None of them had heard from her in almost five years.

She was anxious to see the step show in the gym and to see the Mighty Spartan Legion, the nationally underrated NSU band. And she wanted to see her Chicago homegirl Trina and old roommates, Tammy and Mary.

But she also wanted to see Brandon Barksdale, the school's former basketball star she'd had a serious crush on in school. With all she'd accomplished while at Norfolk State, she did not think she was worthy of Brandon to even know who she was. He was that impressive and she was that insecure, despite her accolades.

He was tall, but not gawky-tall: six-foot-three and about two hundred-fifteen pounds. His body was lean and defined and his deep brown complexion matched Tranise's. He was an honor student and fun-loving guy, friendly and likeable, definitely the big man on campus, in stature, not size.

And yet he hardly knew Tranise existed. In deciding to return to homecoming, she decided that her time was now. She was at the best point of her young life. Her slim little figure had filled out over the years. So instead of the slender size four, from back in the day, she was a solid eight. Her breasts had blown up somehow from a 34B to a 36C. Hips sprung below her waist and her butt protruded as if injected with air. Her hair—*her* hair, not a weave—flowed like water.

In the vernacular of the streets…homegirl was a dimepiece.

She reasoned it was probably all that Southern food she ate in Georgia—especially the grits, gravy and peach cobbler—that added to her size. But the extra pounds, even she allowed, looked good on her. She was so comfortable with it, that she wore clothes that accentuated her curves—not too-short skirts and cleavage-busting blouses, but tasteful attire that was fitting, sexy and classy.

And she even dabbed on a little makeup to bring out her features, something she rarely did as a college student.

So, Tranise Knight was very much a different person than she was when she graduated from Norfolk State—different in comfort level with herself and different in how she looked. Some people were going to be shocked by this Tranise, especially Brandon, she hoped.

She knew friends would be there because they had confirmed on an NSU Homecoming Facebook event page. A week before, she had signed on to the social media site. When she checked into the Marriott at Waterside, she saw many alums, old and young, but no one she recognized. But there was a feeling of celebration in the lobby.

She headed for campus and literally received a chill when she saw all the signage and decorations welcoming back alumni. She parked in the lot in front of the campus landmarks—the Twin Tower dormitories.

She got out of her rental car and looked up at the buildings as a tourist would the skyscrapers in New York. Her mind raced through a medley of events that happened in the towers, from the all-night games of spades and backgammon to the sister from Virginia Beach who set up a makeshift salon in her room, providing everything from affordable relaxers to shampoos to braids; to having her first-ever college date, Michael Jennings, in the lobby. Neither of them had money to go anywhere, so he bought takeout from Charlie Wong's Chinese Restaurant around the corner and they spent two hours on a couch in the lobby eating and talking.

"I miss this place," she said to herself.

When she walked down to the prodigious Student Union building, site of the homecoming pep rally, she expected to see many friends and familiar faces. It was a nostalgic walk. Along the way she had images of herself as a teenager, a student, taking the same walk. She recalled thinking she knew everything back then when, in reality, she didn't know much at all. She also recalled how liberated she felt; there were no parents to tell her what to do, when to do it or where to go. She was on her own for the first time in her life. It was scary, in a sense. But that comfort of being around myriad people who looked like her made it feel like family, easing the trepidation.

She stopped at the site of the old library and remembered the many days she and her sorority sisters would gather there. It was their meeting spot. They would convene there for photos or use it as a launching point to move on to the next thing. And on a few occasions they actually went inside and studied.

Watching a group of Deltas meet at the enormous new Lyman Beecher Brooks Library made her smile. *But they looked so young*, she thought.

She strolled through a portion of Brown Hall, the oldest building on campus, just because she took so many classes there and because it was the first place she ever saw Brandon. He actually picked up her books when she bumped into him and they fell to the floor. It wasn't the classic eyes-meet-and-they-fall-in-love event, though. Instead, it was more like her eyes met his and his eyes said "bye."

When she exited a side door of Brown Hall, between the library and the old gym, she could hear the music from the pep rally, which was winding down up ahead at the Student Center. She could see in the distance a huge gathering of people and it made her pride swell even more.

"Tranise?" she heard to her right. When she turned, there was her old roommate, Mary Cotton, who was from Baltimore, but worked closer to D.C.

"Oh my God, girl," she said, and Tranise hugged her as one does her pillow at night.

"Mary," she said, "so good to see you."

When they let go, they both wiped away tears.

"I'm so mad at you," Mary said. "I've been trying to reach you for years, girl. Where the hell have you been?"

"I know," Tranise said. "I'm sorry. I had a sort of challenging time after graduation. I'll tell you about it later. But I ended up moving to Atlanta and becoming a schoolteacher."

"Really? That's great," Mary said.

As she spoke, Tranise actually stopped listening and stared at Mary. She looked great. Her short, jazzy hairstyle was just like in college, only updated. Her tight, slim physique was as tight and slim. And she wore the most fashionable clothes, like the last time she'd seen her. She was one of the few kids in college whose parents were able to supply her with steady doses of money.

Mary was a talker and Tranise couldn't wait for her to stop, so she interrupted her. "Girl, you look so good," she said. "Where are you?"

"Thanks. And so do you. That extra weight looks great on you," Mary said. "I come to Atlanta all the time. I live in northern Virginia. I work for the FCC in D.C. It's expensive up there, but everything is fine.

"I was talking about you to Charlene last night; she should be here any minute," Mary went on. "I'm going to meet her at the airport in about thirty minutes. Charlene lives in Charlotte, working for Bank of America. You know her and numbers."

"How could I forget?" Tranise said. "She was a walking calculator."

"You should go with me to the airport to surprise her," Mary said. "She will shit a brick when she sees you."

"Okay, let's do that," Tranise said. "I don't have any other plans. But you know, Mary, this is so exciting. I have not been on campus in four years. Don't you feel proud?"

"I've come back every year for homecoming and I still feel the pride you're talking about," Mary said. "It's like this is the place where we grew up."

Suddenly, another of their old classmates came up behind Mary and lifted her off of the ground.

"Yeah, who is this? Who is this?" he said. "I could kidnap you and you'd never know who did it."

"Put me down," Mary said, laughing. "Whoever it is needs some deodorant and a breath mint."

"Ah, that's cold," the guy said, letting her free.

She turned around to see Cedric Collins, one of the biggest guys on campus who did not play football.

"Ced, you're so crazy," Mary said, and they hugged. "Ced, you remember Tranise?"

He looked at Tranise with a smile and extended his hand.

"I don't, but happy homecoming," he said. "You sort of look like Tranise…Knight, I think her last name was."

"I *am* Tranise Knight," I said. She remembered Cedric; fun-loving, loud guy who did not mind being in the spotlight.

"Oh, wow," he said. "It *is* you. Tranise, you look great."

They hugged.

"Nobody's seen you since graduation," he said. "Looks like you're doing great, as everyone expected."

"Thanks, Cedric," she said. "What are you up to?"

"You know, keeping it moving," he said. His voice was booming. It almost sounded as if he spoke with a megaphone. "Lawyer in Chicago. Just passed the bar. Loving Chicago, not loving the job. But, hey, it's just good to have a job these days, you know?"

The three of them chatted for a few minutes as the pep rally wound down. The last of the fraternities and sororities put on a prelude to the step show that night at Joe Echols Arena and the band cranked hip-hop songs that made the huge crowd dance.

"How great is this?" Tranise said. "I remember being over there, in that crowd of students, having a ball. This is almost like an out-of-body experience."

The Student Government Association president, a strong-talking young man named David Allen Brown from New Jersey, ended the pep rally with these words: "It is so great to see so many alumni back to our beloved Norfolk State University. This still is *your* school as much as it is ours. You have helped make this university what it is. You have laid the groundwork and been an example for us to follow. When we graduate, it will be an exciting and a sad day. But it's good to know that when we come back for homecoming, we'll be welcomed as you all are this weekend… Happy Homecoming."

Mary, Tranise and Cedric hugged each other. The band blared the school song and Tranise felt overly nostalgic. "I feel like a fool that I have not been back here in four years," she said, her eyes watering.

Neither Mary nor Cedric responded. They sang the school song and offered smiles as wide as the building.

"Oh, check it out," Cedric said. "The homecoming drama has already started."

"Homecoming drama?" Tranise asked.

"Hell, yeah, girl," Mary informed her. "There's a whole lot of it. What happened, Ced?"

"Well, you remember Teresa and Moe, right? They dated for almost three years," he said. "Well, if you recall, Moe left her when she told him she was pregnant. They were all lovey-dovey and as soon as she gets pregnant, he bounced on her and his baby.

Well, she never saw him again—until about thirty minutes ago in the bookstore.

"I was there buying some stuff. Have you been there yet? It's awesome… Anyway, so he's looking at T-shirts and she's looking at women's T-shirts and they almost literally bumped into each other. I was standing there with my mouth open because I saw both of them come into the store. So, here's the kicker: She has their daughter with her!!! She looks like she's six or seven and looks just like Moe. I'm like, 'Ah, shit.' So, Moe says something— I couldn't hear him—and leans in to hug her.

"Teresa leans back, like, 'Don't touch me.' Then she looks at her daughter, who doesn't know what the hell is going on. Teresa tells the girl to go look at books or something because the little girl walks off. When she gets out of earshot, she turns to Moe and lets him have it. She had her finger in his face for a minute and her neck was rocking. Moe—you know how light-skinned his ass is—turned as red as a stop sign. I was like, 'Damn.'

"Teresa started crying and then quickly got herself together. She wiped her face. She pointed over toward their kid. I had to hear something, so I acted like I was shopping and I moved closer. I heard her say, 'I'm ashamed that you are her father.' And she walked away. Moe put down the T-shirt he was holding and walked toward the door. But before he left, he turned back around to get another look at his daughter. And then he left."

"Oh, hell," Mary said. "I knew both of them so well. I just knew they were going to get married."

"Me, too," Tranise said. "I can't even believe Moe did her like that. That didn't seem to be something he would do."

"I know," Mary said, "But Ced, we've got to go pick up Charlene. We'll see you later, maybe at the step show."

As they walked to the parking lot, Tranise asked the question:

"Have you seen Brandon Barksdale?"

"Oh, my God," Mary said. "All these years later, you're still hooked on that man?"

"Well, he wasn't exactly the one that got away," Tranise said. "But he was the one I wanted to get."

They laughed.

"Girl, Brandon looks even better," she said. "I saw him earlier. He said he was going to lunch at MacArthur Mall downtown. But I must tell you: He's married."

Tranise's heart sunk. "What?" she said. She heard her clearly but she couldn't muster another reaction.

"And guess who he married?" Mary said.

"Oh, goodness. Who?" Tranise said.

"Felicia Waters."

"Stop playing, Mary," she said. Felicia was Tranise's archenemy. "Not that bitch."

Felicia and Tranise had intense animus. Okay, they hated each other. The animosity stemmed from someone telling Felicia that Tranise was not going to pledge her sorority, Alpha Kappa Alpha, because Tranise did not like Felicia. At the same time, someone else told Tranise that Felicia said Tranise was not AKA material. Tranise pledged Delta Sigma Theta, which was her first choice anyway, making the rivalry that much more intense.

From there, they would scowl at each other, compete against each other and generally hate each other from a distance. They never spoke to each other about the origin of the hatred.

"Not that bitch," Tranise repeated. She was surprised she used that word because she didn't like it, but she considered Felicia the personification of the slight, in every negative way: conceited, envious, selfish, mean.

Tranise had rejoiced so much when she won the homecoming queen crown mostly because she beat Felicia.

"Might as well give you the whole scoop," Mary said. "And she's pregnant."

Tranise put her hand over her mouth.

"Come on, girl," Mary said. "Let's go. You can't worry about that. She obviously fooled him, which means he wasn't that smart after all."

Tranise nodded her head, but was not really listening. She was plotting. All these years later, she could get back at Felicia. Normally, Tranise wasn't the scandalous type. She actually kind of wanted to be that way a little in college, but she'd built a reputation and couldn't afford to lose it by sleeping around. Men run their mouths more than women about stuff like that, and the word would have spread the campus that she was a "freak." She could not have afforded that.

So she held it together. But she was out of college and she actually had grown beyond being overly concerned about what people thought of her. She wondered how it would feel to conquer Felicia one more time after all these years, especially considering the rumors about her and Tranise's first boyfriend, Michael Jennings, killed that relationship.

She got even more excited about seeing Brandon. Felicia did her dirty. But this weekend was Tranise's opportunity to do some dirt herself.

CHAPTER THREE
ON THE ROAD AGAIN

Jesse, Don and Venita

As soon as the car hit Interstate 64 East, about ninety minutes from Norfolk, Jesse Jessup, Don Anthony and Venita Daniels broke open the cooler that rested on the backseat.

It had been there, untouched, since Jesse departed Philadelphia almost four hours earlier. He stopped in Fredericksburg, Virginia to pick up Venita and then they rode down to scoop up Don in Richmond. This was how they'd traveled to homecoming for the previous six years—Jesse driving down and picking up his two close friends along the way.

Don's seat was in the back, next to the cooler, and he passed Jesse a Heineken and poured Grey Goose and cranberry juice with a twist of lime for he and Venita in see-through plastic cups. They had stopped at a Burger King drive-thru and devoured the food. It was more a coating for their stomachs than a hearty meal.

They had not seen each other in about a year—or last homecoming. But they were used to road trips together; they took countless weekend excursions home during their college days.

Each of them was from Richmond but they did not meet until they were sophomores at Norfolk State. During a party at Spartan Village, the townhouse development across from campus on Corprew Avenue, the deejay named The Controller yelled, "Where Richmond at?" into the microphone.

Venita, Don and Jesse, dancing near each other, thrust their hands in the air and yelled. They were proud to be from the state capital, and they noticed each other's enthusiasm. They stopped dancing, introduced themselves and were surprised they were from the same city but had not met. They became nearly inseparable friends from that night on.

And so here they were again headed back to Norfolk, starting their traditional pre-homecoming drinking.

"This never gets old," Venita said. "But every year we talk about getting together other than homecoming. And it never happens. We've got to do better. Y'all are my boys. This is crazy."

"I know," Don said. "But life keeps getting in the way. Plus, I'm not sure your husband wants us hanging out so much."

"What about your wife?" Venita said. "She told me she was suspect of our friendship."

"What? When?" Don asked.

"Last year when we picked you up," she answered. "I told her, 'I hope you're joking because we've been friends for years.' But I didn't say anything to you about it because I was hoping that was it."

"Plus, Don can't beat his wife," Jesse said. "If he said something to her, she'd kick his ass."

Don nearly choked on his drink, laughing. "Whatever, Jesse," he said. "Just keep the car between the white lines."

They cruised along the highway, reminiscing and joking and generally leaving behind the trials of their everyday lives. Venita's cousin died of kidney failure at forty-eight. Jesse was recently divorced and troubled by his sister's recent marriage to a drug dealer. Don had financial concerns about the survival of his business.

None of that mattered homecoming weekend; well, not as much, anyway. This was the escape of all escapes.

"You know, my little niece, Diamond, is a junior at Norfolk State; she transferred from William & Mary," Venita said. "I really want to see her. It was her uncle who was sick and passed away, as if she's not already dealing with enough family drama."

"Diamond?" Don said.

"Don't you start, Don," Venita jumped in.

"Okay," he said, smiling. "But I'm just saying. Diamond? What's she majoring in? Pole-dancing?"

Venita could not hold back her laughter. Neither could Jesse. "I was wondering when it would start—I guess it's now," Jesse said. "Okay. Cool. It's on."

"Man, I couldn't help it," Don said. "My bad. My bad."

"Too late now," Venita said. "It's been put in motion."

"Well, you knew it was going to start at some point. I'm surprised it took ten minutes," Jesse said.

"It's okay," Venita said. "Diamond is an honor student, thank you very much. As I said, she transferred from William & Mary. But she's enjoying being a Spartan."

"Lily-white William & Mary? I bet NSU is a shock to her system," Jesse said. "She probably doesn't know how to act with all those black folks. She's probably the most popular girl on campus."

"Hey, wait," Venita said. "So now you saying my little niece is a whore? I know you don't want to start fighting in this car."

"Like cousin, like cousin," Jesse chimed in and even Venita laughed and slapped him on the arm.

"Excuse me," she added, pushing aside the bangs that covered her oval-shaped face, "but ain't nobody get this at Norfolk State, thank you very much."

"'Cause ain't nobody want it," Don said, laughing.

"Oh, so the hate is everywhere; that's fine," Venita said. "You know I was fine back in school. And I ain't bad now, either."

"I'm just messing with you," Jesse said, glancing over at her. "You know you were cute. You still are cute. You just weigh a pound or two more."

"Yeah," Don said, "a pound or two more in ten different places on your body."

Venita laughed with her friends. She could take a joke—and deliver one, too. "That's okay. Wait until next Homecoming. This weight will be gone," she said. "I already started my program. Cutting back on carbs and sweets and drinking more water—and I'm walking every night. And I don't eat after seven anymore. Nothing. You probably can't tell a difference, but I can.

"And it's not like I'm the only one in this car who needs to drop a few...am I, Don? You look like the Pillsbury Doughboy's overweight brother."

Don had a thick frame in college and he gradually added on weight over the years after school. He looked like an out-of-shape football player—relatively short and round, bald-headed with a thick goatee.

"At least you don't wear clothes that are too tight," Don said, after laughing at Venita's crack about him. "I feel like throwing up every time I see a big woman in tight clothes, accentuating their rolls and rolls of fat.

"Now, don't get me wrong—I know I'm big and need to lose some weight. A lot of people have weight issues. I'm not criticizing us for that. But to be big and put on super-tight leggings and tops that hug the body and have their blubber spilling all over the place...I don't get that."

"Wait," Venita said. "Are you saying I'm a big girl?"

"Nothing wrong with big girls," Jesse said, smiling. "They are warm and cuddly."

"No, I'm not saying that, Venita," Don answered. "Relax and eat a doughnut."

"Kiss my big ass," Venita said, laughing.

"Pull those big pants down; I'll smack it and kiss it," Don said.

Their laughter was broken by the sound of state trooper sirens.

"Oh, shit," Jesse said. "Was I speeding?"

"No, you weren't speeding," Venita said. "You know I was monitoring it. But we're in New Kent County."

"Oh, hell. We got stopped in this stupid-ass county before," Don said. "They're notorious."

"Put those empty bottles in the bottom of the cooler, under the ice," Jesse said, pulling over.

Venita slipped everyone a few mints.

"Okay, everybody be quiet. Let me handle this shit," Jesse said.

He depressed the button to lower the driver side window. He placed both hands on the steering wheel to make it clear to the trooper he was not a threat.

"How you doing, sir?" the trooper said.

"Fine. How can I help you?" Jesse said.

"You can give me your license, registration and insurance card," he said.

"Can you tell me why you stopped us?" Jesse asked as delicately as he could.

"I can tell you again to give me the information I asked for," he said, as he looked over Venita and Don. He then fixated on the cooler.

"What's in there?" he said.

"Drinks," Don said from the back.

"I wasn't talking to you," the trooper said with attitude. "You—what's in there?"

"Drinks," Jesse answered.

"Oh, so you're a smart guy, huh?" the trooper said. His pale complexion turned pink. He was angry.

"Everyone out of the car," he said.

"Officer, hold on," Jesse said, handing over the information he requested. "I wasn't getting smart with you. I was just answering you."

"Wait right here," he said and retreated to his car to check Jesse's credentials.

"This is some bullshit," Don said.

"I know," Venita added. "I was checking your speed. He had no reason to stop us."

"Don," Jesse said, looking in the rearview mirror, "make sure those beers and liquor tops are on secure."

"I buried the vodka at the bottom of the ice and the empty beer bottles. We're good."

"This Robocop has nothing better to do than mess with us?" Venita said. "This is why no one likes cops these days."

"He ain't a cop; he's a trooper," Don said.

"Same difference," Jesse interjected. "He has a badge and a gun and thinks he can fuck with us anytime he pleases. I mean, why was he trying to get us out of the car? This shit is dumb."

After a few minutes of back-and-forth, the trooper came back to the car.

"Mr. Hill, your license is suspended in Virginia," he said.

"What?" Jesse said. "Sir, that's not true. As you can see by my license, I live in Philadelphia."

"Have you ever lived at 1564 Gabriel Drive in Norfolk?"

"No, I haven't. I went to college in Norfolk, but I lived on campus and then on Monticello."

"That's not what's in the system and that's what I have to go by," the trooper said. "I'm going to have to ticket you. And you must step out of the car; in fact, everyone out."

Jesse was angry and confused. "If you're giving me a ticket, why do we need to get out of the car?" he asked.

"Just do what I say or this will be even worse for you," he snapped back.

Venita placed her hand on Jesse's shoulder. "It's okay. It's okay," she said. "Come on." She knew Jesse had an explosive temper when wronged. She was there when, as a junior in college, he initiated a brawl on the basketball courts with some locals on Brambleton Avenue, near campus, after a guy he didn't like fouled him into the fence. The police came but even that did not temper his rage. Luckily, the police were more interested in controlling the situation than arresting him.

This trooper seemed to have a different objective. So Venita tried to make sure Jesse remained poised. One by one, the trooper had them lean against the car and patted them down, a humiliating act that they had seen happen to other people but were dismayed it was happening to them.

He talked into the microphone on his shoulder as he had them stand back a certain distance away from the car, in the grass beyond the gravel on which the car was parked.

"Stay right here," he ordered them through his dark sunglasses. "Don't move."

Within a minute, another trooper pulled up with his lights flashing. The two of them whispered to each other before they began searching Jesse's car.

"Don't you need a search warrant for that?" Jesse asked.

"You're driving with a suspended license in my state; that gives me reason to wonder why—and to search your vehicle," he said, his nose a few inches from Jesse's. "You got a problem with that?"

"I do have a problem with that," Jesse said. "I'm an attorney and I know we have done nothing for us to be standing on the side of the highway or for you to be searching my car."

"You're gonna need a lawyer to get you out of jail if you keep talking," the trooper said.

"Jesse," Venita said.

"You'd better listen to her," the trooper said before turning away.

Jesse was seething. When he was fifteen, he had the scare of his life. While standing in line for a cheesesteak one day, he was approached by two Philadelphia cops. They pulled him out of line and slapped handcuffs on him.

In the police car, they explained that he fit the description of someone accused of robbing a woman at gunpoint several blocks away as she exited her car.

"What? I didn't do anything," he said.

"We will see," one cop told him. "If this women identifies you, you're going to jail."

Jesse's heart pounded. He had heard of men being mistakenly identified, yet jailed nonetheless. "Oh, God. Please help this woman see I'm not the person that robbed her," he prayed to himself. He had plans for the future that included college and law school, and even that young, he knew going to jail could derail his ambitions.

When they arrived to the woman's house, she was standing in front of her brownstone on Bainbridge. The Philadelphia skyline was in the not too distant background.

One officer pulled Jesse out of the car. The other officer brought the woman over. He stood there, shaking, understanding that his fate rested in the word of a woman he had never before seen.

She was old, he quickly surmised; in her seventies, meaning her vision had to be suspect. That made him even more scared.

The woman looked him over, pulled down the glasses that hung near the tip of her nose and made a face that Jesse could not read.

"So, is this the boy that snatched your purse, ma'am?" one officer asked.

She didn't answer. She looked him up and down and focused on his eyes.

"No," she said finally. "This is not the young man."

"You sure," one cop said.

"That is not him," she said. Then she turned and slowly made her way toward her home.

Jesse was placed in the rear of the police car, where he wept. His tears were from relief that the woman was honest but also because he had no control over his life. It was then he knew for sure he would become a lawyer to defend the rights of the unprotected, the vulnerable. His parents moved to Richmond that summer.

Those troopers reminded him of the officers that randomly pulled him out of line when he was a teenager. And it made him angry. He and his friends watched one trooper pull the cooler out of the back and go through it, tossing aside items as if they were debris. Finally, he pulled out a few empty beer bottles.

"Who drank these?" the trooper said.

"They were in there from the last time I used the cooler," Don offered. "I put ice over them."

"Why wouldn't you throw the bottles away if they were old?" he asked.

"Because I bought the ice and put it in the car. I opened the cooler to put the ice in it as we were driving and saw the empty bottles in there. So, I just left them at the bottom and poured the ice over them."

The trooper was not buying it, but he couldn't prove him wrong, either. And he was so aggravated that he did not notice the vodka in the cooler. "I think we should test them," one trooper said to the other.

"Let's see what's in the trunk," he answered.

They then went into the rear of Jesse's BMW and pulled out their luggage.

"I can't even believe this," Venita said.

They searched the sides of the trunk and underneath, where the spare tire was kept, apparently searched for drugs or weapons. Several minutes later, they came over to them.

"You," he said, pointing at Jesse, "cannot operate a vehicle in my state. So, unless one of you two have a valid driver's license, I'm impounding the car."

"What?" Jesse said.

"It's okay" Don said. "I can drive."

The first trooper took his license and went to the car to run it through DMV. The second trooper stood with them.

"Where you all going?" he asked.

"What difference does it make?" Venita said. "We can go wherever we want, right? We're free, you know?"

"Hey, don't be a wise-ass with me," he said sharply.

"Nobody's being a wise-ass," Jesse said. "What if you were riding with your friends and get pulled over for no reason. You wouldn't be happy, either."

"But we know it wouldn't happen to you, would it?" Don said.

The trooper approached Don. "I don't know what you're insinuating, but I don't like it," he said. "Now, you should get out of here with just a ticket—if you keep your mouth shut."

"Excuse me, but why can't we talk?" Jesse said. "And I should be happy to get a ticket I don't deserve after being stopped for no reason and now standing on the side of the highway as I watch you go through our private property? I should be happy to receive a ticket?"

The other trooper came up. "You should be happy this man has a valid Virginia driver's license," he said.

He went over to Jesse. "This is your citation. And here's your court date," he said, circling the piece of paper. "I look forward to seeing you then. In the meantime, if I catch you driving in my state, I'm going to haul your ass off to jail. You got that?"

Jesse did not answer. They stared at each other.

The second trooper interceded. "Now you all go on and have a nice day," he said.

Jesse stepped around the trooper and opened the door for Venita. He and Don put their belongings back in the trunk and Don took over the driving duties.

In the car, the anger was palpable; no one said a word for a few miles.

Finally, Don broke the silence. "It was my time to drive, anyway," he said. "And give me a beer, Jesse. To hell with those guys. We're going to homecoming."

"For a minute," Jesse said, "I thought we weren't going to make it. I was a half-second from jumping on that dude's neck and strangling him."

"I could tell," Venita said. "And you know what? I would have helped you."

"How can I have a suspended license in Virginia from an address I never lived? That's crazy," Jesse said.

"You know they mess that stuff up all the time," Don said, reaching for the beer Jesse handed him. "The best thing to do is pay the ticket and be done with it—but also call the motor vehicles office to figure out how they have you at an address you never lived."

"Uh, bartender," Venita said. She had turned in her seat to face Don. "Can I have a Cosmopolitan, please? And not too heavy on the cranberry juice."

"Coming right up," Jesse said. "But how about a shot of Grey Goose to take the edge off. On the house."

"Well, since they're complimentary, I say pour them," Don said, smiling into the rearview mirror. Venita high-fived Jesse.

And just like that, they were back on track. Their roadside experience flustered and angered them. But it did not diminish the purpose of their journey. They were almost at homecoming, and soon that little incident would be a small but memorable part of their fascinating 2012 experience.

CHAPTER FOUR
OLD FRIENDS, NEW RELATIONSHIP

Catherine and Earl

F our months before homecoming, Earl Manning received
a surprising e-mail from Catherine Harmon, widely considered the finest woman on campus by the men of their
era at Norfolk State. Physically, Catherine was a gem, an elegant,
curvaceous, five-foot-six presence that commanded any room
without even attempting to do so. Her cheekbones seemingly
were carved perfectly by God to bring out the radiant eyes and
sexily contoured lips. Her hair was mid-length, black and flowing,
like a calm stream.

Her teeth were like a string of pearls, making her smile practically
hypnotic. Indeed, Catherine was like a delicately sculpted mannequin,
ideal in every physical sense—only she had blood running through
her veins and moved about campus like everyone else. Best of all
about her was that, for all her beauty, it did not define her. It was
hard to not notice her, but she was as smart and congenial as she
was beautiful, so much so that any woman that had a problem
with her was all about "hate." It was nearly impossible, especially
in college, to be so well-liked, especially as envious as young
women were. But Catherine did not display a strand of arrogance
or pretense. She was as close to ideal as Earl—or anyone—could
perceive.

Guys expected her to marry Michael Jordan or some other

superstar-level man—she was *that* bad. But she didn't. She married a nice guy and had an ordinary marriage for almost twenty-five years before having enough. Five years after her divorce and four months before Homecoming, she e-mailed Earl, a fellow Business major she knew but did not really *know*.

To receive an e-mail from Catherine stunned him. They had not seen each other in a decade, and even that encounter at a homecoming party was brief.

"This can't be *Catherine Harmon*," he said to himself when he read her name in his Inbox.

But it was. Turned out that Earl's name came up when she and friends gathered at the Capital Jazz Festival outside of D.C. the previous weekend, and her friends encouraged her to reach out to him. She always harbored a curiosity about Earl, and so her friends' support made it easier for her to make the first move, however subtle.

"Why is she e-mailing me?" Earl said to himself. Then he figured she must have heard that he had his own technology company and she wanted a job. Or that she was so thoughtful to just say "hello" to him. He could not make himself believe that Catherine Harmon actually had an interest in him.

When he opened the e-mail, there was no mention or intimation of a job. She talked about getting his e-mail address from a girl-friend and wanting to say hello, to reconnect.

Earl responded immediately. He had grown exponentially since college. He was considered among the more well-rounded guys on campus: athletic, funny, intelligent. But he was shy. Not to those who knew him well, but certainly to those who were not in his vast circle.

He was tall, dark and thin, considered attractive by some because of how he comported himself more than how he looked. He had a way about him, a humble and gentlemanly way. He was respected and liked by many.

Earl had friends from many factions of student life: his hometown of Washington, D.C., his fraternity, his roommates, his classmates, his floor mates when he stayed in what was called the New Men's Dorm back then as a freshman, and just about anyone he came in contact with in a more than casual way. And he treated them all the same—with respect and fondness. When it was learned he was considering pledging a fraternity, brothers from each organization recruited him—he was the guy everyone wanted.

Still, he did not even consider approaching Catherine in college. By his own admission, he was not ready for her. She was a woman—poised and self-assured. He was growing into his manhood.

More than two decades later, Earl's growth was evident. He was a man of supreme confidence and relative success in Charlotte, N.C. He was completely comfortable with who he was and believed he could hold the interest of most any woman. He kept his body in shape and looked less than his fifty years. Still, he could not conceive that Catherine would reach out to him.

But that initial e-mail put in motion a reconnection that shocked them both. Their communications grew to multiple text messages a day and infrequent but in-depth phone calls. Each contact expanded in substance and detail, advancing their knowledge of and comfort with each other and their feelings. Incredibly, the two distant friends who had not seen each other in ten years blossomed into friends that came to rely on each other.

It was the text-messaging that got them there. Their expressions in the missives ranged from how their day was going to how much they enjoyed each other to music and movie recommendations to sexual innuendo to falling in "like" to anticipating seeing each other.

"How can this happen?" Catherine wrote to Earl in a text about six weeks into their reconnection. She was on the couch in her condo in Virginia Beach. "I miss you and I haven't even seen you."

Earl sent back a smiley face and this: "This whole thing, reconnecting with you, is amazing. I knew you in school but I didn't REALLY know you. I had an idea about how you were as a person. Turns out, you're even better than I imagined. You're wonderful."

The frequency and intensity of the text messages increased by the day, and before long, they were sharing romantic feelings.

"I have NEVER felt like this before," Catherine said. "Is this crazy, considering we have really gotten to know each other for real for real through text messages?"

Earl assured her she was not alone in her surprise or delight. They earmarked a visit to Norfolk in September as an opportunity to see each other and test their connection born of phone calls and lots of text messages. Catherine bought tickets to a Sade concert and invited Earl. Even though they had really become close through the distance, her invitation still surprised him— but not so much that he did not immediately accept.

This would be their first face-to-face in ten years. There was no hiding anything. They were excited and anxious about the meeting, but mostly excited about the possibilities. This was the test.

Catherine took off work on Friday to pick up Earl from the airport. Instead of pulling up to the curve, she parked in the closest lot to the terminal and greeted him as he entered the atrium area.

He noticed her instantly and walked slowly toward her, his smile increasing in size with each step. She smiled back broadly, illuminating the entire area, at least to Earl. When they reached arms' distance apart, Earl extended his and Catherine walked right into them.

Earl wrapped her firmly but lovingly, and she could feel the affection he had for her in how he handled her. She closed her eyes and enjoyed his embrace. She took in his cologne and exhaled deeply.

He noticed how soft she was and how youthful she looked. Having her in his embrace felt like something special, like he needed her to be there. And so the hug lasted a full minute, as he inhaled her Chanel No. 5 perfume and enjoyed having her close to him.

Finally, they reluctantly let go, and pulled back so they could look into each other's eyes. They saw the same thing from the other: joy.

"I knew from the photos you sent that you look great," he said. "But you look even better in person. You're beautiful."

"Thanks—and so do you, Mr. Manning," she said. "I'm really glad I finally get to hang out with you."

After her divorce, she dealt with men who either smothered her or were not affectionate enough or who were simply not interesting. Catherine, a marketing executive, had an active mind and bored easily. Earl was anything but boring.

They headed to Earl's hotel, the Sheraton Waterside, and chatted and smiled at each other the entire time. Catherine took the streets—down Princess Anne Boulevard, across to Virginia Beach Boulevard, up to Park Avenue and then up Brambleton Avenue into downtown—so Earl could refamiliarize himself and reminisce. They passed the campus on Park and Earl immediately could see himself back on campus as a student.

She waited in the car as Earl checked into the Sheraton and dropped off his bags.

"I have this place I like in Virginia Beach I want to take you for lunch," Catherine said. "It's called Chicks. Nice view of the bay, good food."

And so they drove to the beach, which was ideal because it was a hot and sunny September afternoon. There, they put on their sunglasses and sat outside on the deck. A helicopter flew by and landed on a pad across the bay, next to music producer Pharell's house.

"I'm not saying this to flatter you, but you look as good as you did in college," Earl said. "Actually, better."

Catherine blushed. "Thank you," she said. "And I'm not just saying this, but you look great yourself."

The compliments flowed another few minutes when the server came over and took the orders. The food was tasty, the scene calming and the moment pure.

"I must say that I feel totally comfortable with you, Earl. I think our communicating as we have over the last four months has really made a big difference."

"I agree," Earl said. "I feel closer to you. I feel like I really have known you for nearly thirty years."

There was some tension in the air, though. Earl wanted to kiss Catherine; his affection for her was that intense. But he knew she was the ultimate woman and would not dare offend her. So he suppressed his feelings and enjoyed the conversation, her laugh and learning even more about her.

Forever the thoughtful person, Catherine suggested they return to the hotel so "you can rest, handle some business and get organized before the concert," she said.

Earl was too energized to rest, but he appreciated her thoughtfulness. In the room, he ironed his shirt tor the night, took a hot shower, checked e-mails and lay in bed somewhat amazed that he was going on a first date with Catherine Harmon.

This was a woman he did not even fantasize about in college. He admired her character and her curves, and even though he was relatively popular with some beautiful women, he considered Catherine out of his league—plus, she had a boyfriend the entire time he knew her.

He measured his growth by her sincere interest in him and his confidence that he was primed for her.

In her condo, Catherine's heart smiled. She loved the connection she felt being in Earl's presence. Just as she suspected, he was warm and friendly and gentlemanly. He made her feel secure and totally comfortable, which was important to her. She had recently come out of a smothering relationship with someone she realized she did not connect with. Earl being there actually made her think of the song, "How Did You Get Here" by Deborah Cox.

She had planned to take a "relationship break" and enjoy the peace and tranquility that came with it. But there was a connection with Earl that surprised her. She was not prepared to care about him so much and think about him so often and even desire his presence so fast. But she did.

And her fondness of him—and his of her—grew at the Sade concert. The Scope in downtown Norfolk was packed, and Earl was proud to return to the site of his Norfolk State graduation with Catherine. He was grateful for her purchasing the tickets and gave her a token gift of three Sade CDs as a show of appreciation.

She was surprised and grateful.

Her closest friend, Starr, and her husband, Dwayne, joined them. Starr was lively and friendly, happy to see her girl happy. Dwayne was more reserved, almost cold toward Earl, probably because he viewed Catherine as a sister who needed to be protected. Earl figured if Dwayne was married to Starr—who was cute and wonderful—then he had to be good people, so he did not take it personally.

Besides, he was there for Catherine. That was his focus, which she clearly appreciated. Many times during Sade's one-of-a-kind show, he glanced over at her, almost as reassurance that he actually was there with her. When she put her hand on his leg, his entire body warmed up.

As Sade performed sultry songs, one after another, Earl and Catherine hugged, held hands and generally looked like a true couple. And that's how they felt, too. When Sade smoothly serenaded the crowd to "Soldier of Love," Catherine looked up at Earl and asked, "Are you a soldier of love?"

He responded: "I can be." And they smiled at each other—one of many times throughout the concert.

When it was over, they went to a restaurant in downtown Norfolk, Scottie Quixx, and shared barbeque wings and French fries, all the while further establishing a strong connection.

"This has been the best first date," Catherine said as they were leaving the restaurant. It was about one-thirty a.m. and she had to work the next day.

"For me, too," Earl said.

She pulled up in front of the Sheraton and turned the car off. She was not going up to his room; she didn't want to give the wrong impression. But she wanted to spend a little more time with Earl, even though they had much of the next day to be together. Not wanting to let him go only confirmed all the feelings that were developed before he arrived and strengthened through the night.

"Think of You" by Ledisi played on the radio, which was a song they had discussed because the lyrics so matched how they felt about each other. Earl found it the proper time to lean over to kiss Catherine good night. A hug and kiss on her cheek turned into a peck on the lips and then a prolonged wet, tongue-in-mouth kiss that almost made them both lightheaded when their lips finally parted.

Catherine thought to herself: *I'm in trouble—he's a good kisser.*

Earl thought: *I'd better get out of this car right now.* And so he did. "It was a beautiful day with you, Catherine," he said. "You're more wonderful than I even thought, and I already thought you were pretty wonderful."

Her shyness showed as she looked down while thanking him. "Well, I feel the same way about you," she said. "You told me we were connected and I'm believing you more and more."

They talked about meeting the next day on the Norfolk State campus before he made his way out of her BMW and into the hotel. At the door, though, he looked back to get one more glimpse of her. They waved at each other and he watched her pull off. A feeling of wonderment overwhelmed Earl. He was falling in love.

CHAPTER FIVE

LET THE PARTIES BEGIN

Jimmy, Carter and Barbara

The day parties were the jumpoff point for homecoming weekend. The pep rally was cool, but it was more about the students still in school—and nostalgia. The day parties were for alums, and it was particularly a good idea because usually the afternoon was spent chilling until the events of the evening or in the bookstore purchasing school paraphernalia. Getting the party underway earlier made perfect sense, considering most of the people came back to socialize.

Jimmy called his wife three times after he arrived in Norfolk, the last time just before he and Carter walked into The Mansion. She finally answered.

"What do you want?" was her greeting to him.

"Excuse me?" he said. "That's how you answer the phone?"

Monica did not respond.

"Okay, well, I'm just letting you know I made it here okay," he answered. "And I'm trying to see if you've calmed down some."

"I'm fine," she said, with no emotion and obvious disdain.

Jimmy took a deep breath. "Well, for what it's worth, I love you and I hope you eventually understand why I'm here."

"Oh, I do understand why you're there, James," she said. Jimmy was alarmed; when she called him "James," she was at her most angry.

"What I don't understand," Monica added, "is why *I'm* not there."

"Yo, you coming in or what?" Carter yelled to Jimmy. Monica heard him.

"Where are you? Some strip club or something?" she said.

"Strip club? That's what you think happens at Homecoming? Come on, now," Jimmy said. "We're going into an alumni event, a day party."

"Whatever, James," she said.

"Okay, well, I'll talk to you later," he said.

"No, don't call me. Why you calling me but don't want me there?" she said. "Calling me does nothing for me."

Jimmy thought for a second about trying to assuage his wife's feelings. Then it hit him: Why?

"Okay," he said. "See you Sunday."

Then he hung up and joined the huge crowd in the elegant venue.

"You all right, man?" Carter asked. "You look like someone stole your wagon and didn't give it back."

"What?" Jimmy said. Carter had a way of butchering clichés like few people. "Whatever. I'm good. Where's the bar?"

There, Carter ordered shots of Herradura tequila—he was a self-described "tequila snob" and was pleasantly surprised that the bar had his favorite brand. "Black people go crazy over Patron," he said, handing the shot to Jimmy. "That's like drinking cologne. Cheap cologne. Here. This is some good stuff. Smooth… Happy Homecoming."

They tapped glasses and Jimmy downed his without hesitation.

"One more," Jimmy said, pulling out a twenty-dollar bill. "Might as well get a buzz if I'm gonna drink."

"Order me a Cosmo for Barbara. She and Donna are on their way," Carter said.

Almost on cue, Barbara and Donna entered the spot. Carter

waved to her to get their attention, which he did. On their way over, they stopped twice to engage old friends. Carter watched Barbara with admiration, like he was hypnotized. With heels, she was almost taller than Carter, who was five-foot-ten. But she made graceful strides in those five-inch heels, so much so that it almost looked as if she was gliding across the room.

She had an innocent look and demeanor, which is why Jimmy had trouble believing Barbara was having an extramarital affair. It just did not fit her profile.

"Hi, baby," he said as he hugged her. The embrace was long and tight—unlike of one between casual friends who had not seen each other in a while. It was intimate, just as Carter had indicated about their relationship.

Barbara's wedding ring was ostentatious, a 2.7-carat emerald cut that sparked reflections like a disco light. She was married, all right. But as much as she tried to play coy, she was in love with Carter. The way she looked at him told that story.

"Good to see you, Barbara," Jimmy said. "It's been a long time."

"I know," she said after they hugged. "It's great to see you. Looks like the decade has been good to you. I heard you're married. Where's your wife?"

"Same place as your husband," he said. Jimmy did not mean to be flippant with Barbara. But the two shots of tequila quickly made an impact. His tongue was a bit loose.

Carter snapped his head around and glared at Jimmy. "I'm sorry," Jimmy said. "I didn't mean it the way it sounded. I was just trying to say what's the point of bringing your spouse to Homecoming?"

Barbara held an awkward look for a second and moved on by introducing Donna to the men. Carter handed Barbara the Cosmo. "We would have ordered a cocktail for you, but we weren't sure what you'd like," Jimmy said to Donna, who went to Old Dominion University, about fifteen minutes from Norfolk State. She was a commissioned officer in the Army, something she had in common with Jimmy.

Donna smiled a lot but said little, making her hard to read. She ordered a Cosmo, too, and stood by patiently as Jimmy, Carter and Barbara shared stories of their college days and greeted many other old friends they had not seen in some time.

Finally, after about thirty minutes and another shot of tequila, Jimmy asked Donna to dance. The DJ was playing a head-bopping mixture of current hits and old tracks that had the dance floor pumping. But when he got to "Let Me Clear My Throat" by DJ Kool with Biz Markie and Doug E Fresh, Jimmy was ready to transform into Jimbo, the life of the party.

"It's pretty cool to be partying like this at three in the afternoon, isn't it?" Jimmy said into Donna's ear as they danced. Sweat was developing on his forehead.

She smiled. "Why didn't you bring your wife?"

"If I did, I wouldn't be able to dance with you," he answered. And that was Jimbo—Jimbo liked to flirt. Even if he was with his wife and caught a buzz, he'd flirt with her. In this case, he was away for the weekend and decided it would not hurt to have some fun—as long as he did not cross the line.

They left the dance floor smiling and returned to the bar area. More and more of their old friends emerged. Jimmy saw his old intramural basketball teammates, Bruce and Westbrook, and they reminisced about playing Spades all night and stealing bread, bologna and French fries late at night from the 7-Eleven near their apartment.

"What about all the times we went to Pizza Hut at Military Circle," Bruce started.

"Oh, yeah," Westbrook jumped in. "We put two dollars' worth of gas in Jimmy's car and that left us with about six dollars between us."

"Six dollars?" Donna said. "How could you eat off six dollars at Pizza Hut?"

"Easy," Jimmy explained. "What we did was this: We got a table and ordered a pitcher of beer, a salad and two large pizzas with sausage and pepperoni. So, the waitress gives us the bill. It's about five or six times more than what we have."

"But we went in knowing that would be the case," Bruce said. "That's why we parked over by the main entrance to the mall and not in the Pizza Hut lot. So, we take the bill and ball it up. We leave about three dollars on the table as a tip to the waitress and then one-by-one walk right past the cash register where you pay and run to the car."

"Y'all were bold to go in there and eat like that when you didn't have the money to pay for it," Stephanie said.

"We were tired of eating Steak-umms and fries," Westbrook said. "When you're young, dumb and hungry, you take those kind of chances."

"The sad part," Jimmy said, "is that you *still* try to walk out of Pizza Hut without paying today, ten years later."

Everyone laughed and Jimmy felt as free and loose as he had since he was a college student. He envisioned Monica there telling him "don't be mean" to his friends.

His buzz was intensifying—and it was just about four thirty. But that did not stop him from leaving the group and heading to the bar. That's how he was as Jimbo; he didn't like the party to stop.

Carter and Barbara slipped away, too. They had held it together for almost ninety minutes. They needed a few private moments. So, when Jimmy came back from the bar, Barbara checked with

Donna to make sure she was okay, and she and Carter left The Mansion and went to his car in the parking lot.

Without saying a word, Carter leaned over from the driver's seat and initiated a long, passionate kiss that was so hot he had to turn on the air conditioner when their lips finally parted.

Barbara wiped her face and took in a large amount of air. "Carter," she said, "we have to talk."

That alarmed him. That was not Barbara's way; she just said what she had to say. That was one of the qualities about her that he admired; she was decisive. Although morally he knew it ate at her that she was unfaithful to her husband, she made the tough decision to be involved with Carter and acted on it.

"What's wrong?" Carter said. He was trying to find a CD with soothing music but stopped his search.

"I really wanted to come to Homecoming for two reasons," she started. "One to see you. You know how I feel about you. I love you. I hate the situation I'm in—being in love with you while married to someone who really doesn't deserve this. Most days I'm able to ignore the conflict and go on with my life. But I know that's because I'm in California and you're in New York."

"What are you saying, Barbara? That you want to stop communicating with me," Carter said. "You think that's going to miraculously make your marriage turn into what you want it to be?"

"Carter, I wasn't finished," she said. Barbara sat up in the passenger seat, as if what she had to say was so important she needed to change her posture.

"What I'm saying," she went on, "is that what you and I have been doing for the last five years is wrong. My husband is a good man and if he ever found out, he would be devastated. My whole family would be. His whole family would be, too. He doesn't deserve this."

Carter's heart sank. He got what Barbara was getting at. He

always worried about Barbara eventually not being able to continue with the adultery. She was not some hoochie who decided to fool around on her husband with her college boyfriend at homecoming. That's what she did, but it was not that simple.

She could not deny five years ago that the relationship they'd had at twenty years old actually was the best and most rewarding relationship she'd ever had. She felt alive with Carter. They enjoyed each other's presence and challenged each other and brought a youthful joy that remained in their souls all this time later.

They broke up because that's what most young couples do after graduation. His career path took him to New York, hers to California. They tried to maintain their romance, but the distance was too vast to overcome. So, it faded and they eventually lost touch. Three years passed before they reconnected at the Best of Friends homecoming party five years ago at Lake Wright.

Almost instantly, they realized the flame that had burned as college students had not extinguished. They danced and laughed and caught up on each other's lives after three years of no communication. Both were married at the time and content—but not happy. And their reconnection that night was powerful.

They sealed their night with a peck on the lips that turned into a long, sloppy, passionate kiss like the ones they used to share late at night in Carter's 1973 Duster he would park in the lot in front of the Twin Towers. Their affair began then with once-a-year meetings at Homecoming.

"I can't believe I'm doing this," Barbara said the next year, as they lay in bed at the Renaissance Hotel in Portsmouth, across the river from downtown Norfolk. "But the truth is that I never stopped loving you."

"Same here, baby," Carter said back then. "I'm even jealous that you're married with kids. That was supposed to be us."

"You're married, too, and I don't like it—even though I'm

married," she said. "This is crazy. This is not me. But…my heart is with you. It kills me to say that as someone who is married with a family. But I can't lie to myself."

Carter's marriage was more unsteady than Barbara's. He did not have any children and his wife, a flight attendant, was attractive and smart. But she was not Barbara. They divorced after the third Homecoming rendezvous, when Carter's guilt overcame him.

He told Barbara, "I didn't get divorced because of you. I got divorced because I love you. I thought it was too unfair to my wife that I had another woman on my mind in everything we did. It was the hardest thing I've ever done, but it was the right thing to do."

That act—and his reasoning—made Barbara love him even more. And it increased her guilt. So, in the car outside the day party, she was prepared to give Carter the news that would make his Homecoming weekend far more dramatic than he anticipated.

"Carter," Barbara said, "I left my husband three months ago. The marriage had to be not what I needed for me to be doing what I've been doing with you for five years. I know it was only once a year, but I broke my vows. Going back home after those homecomings was awful. It took me a week to get back to normal, to try to forget how I wronged my husband."

Carter did not hear anything after she said, "I left my husband…" In that instant, he thought he was dreaming. He loved Barbara, yes. But he liked her married. It meant there was a limitation on how far they could go, how much time they could spend together, even how often they could talk. That was fine with him because he learned in his marriage that he was not the settling-down type.

Her being divorced meant she would have more time to communicate with him, more time to see him, more time to infringe on his time. All that made him uneasy.

"What?" Carter said. He tried to control his shock and dismay. "Are you serious?"

"Yes," she said. "I thought you would be happy, Carter. You said you didn't get your divorce because of me. Well, I got mine because of you, because of us."

Carter's head spun. He was conflicted. The reality of Barbara's divorce struck him like lightning. While he did love her, he was especially attracted to Barbara because she was available only on a limited basis. Having her at homecoming was enough. Her being divorced meant her free time opened up, and he was not sure how to feel about that as it related to him and spending more than a Homecoming weekend with her.

"I'm surprised," he said. "We talked and exchanged e-mails a lot in the last three months. You never said anything. And you're still wearing your wedding ring."

"Well, I didn't want a bunch of questions from people this weekend, so I put it back on," she explained. "But I received the divorce decree in August. It's over."

Carter looked off, away from Barbara.

"What's wrong?" she asked. "Please don't tell me you're not happy."

"Of course, I'm happy," he lied. "If you're happy, I'm definitely happy. I'm just surprised because you never said anything."

"I was going to tell you my plans earlier this year," she said. "I decided it was something I should tell you in person. I didn't want to freak you out over the phone. But it seems like that's what's happening now anyway."

"You should have told me—but I'm not freaking out," he said. His mind had settled. He figured that with her in California and him in New York, they could not see each other but so often anyway, married or not. He could still live his bachelor's life and enjoy his love affair with Barbara once or twice a year.

"Well, I hope *this* doesn't freak you out," she said. Carter's head snapped toward her.

"What now?" he said.

"I accepted a job in New York with the company I was with in San Diego," she said. "I needed a clean break. I needed to get out of California. So, I made an inquiry and ended up getting the position.

"So, if you really want me, as you have said, then this is your time to have me, to have me the right way, as we always talked about."

Carter had no retort. He was dumbfounded.

"You're moving to New York? When?" he managed to get out.

"In my mind, the way this played out was you smiling and hugging me and telling me you love me," she said.

He wanted to tell her that he lived in reality and this new reality was not what he expected—or wanted. But he leaned over and hugged her. It was not a sincere hug. It was a comforting hug. Barbara had made moves that dramatically changed her life—and they could change his, too. But he could not act as if he did not welcome her news.

"You know how to bring it, don't you?" he said, pulling back and with a smile. He could see that his show of teeth eased Barbara some. "You've made some big moves. I guess we have a lot to talk about."

"We do, Carter," Barbara said. "But I want you to be happy about this. I know this is a lot to handle. And now I wish we had talked about this throughout the whole process. I was thinking it would be such a good surprise and I love surprises."

"Oh, you accomplished that mission 'cause my ass *is* surprised," he said, again smiling.

Barbara managed a grin. And then silence fell over the car. She was not comfortable with Carter's reaction (no matter how hard he tried to play off his discomfort), and he was not comfortable knowing she would be moving with her kids to his city.

Finally, Carter said, "Well, I think we should go back in and have a drink. I need one."

"Oh, I thought we were going to talk," she said. "But okay, I guess we can talk later."

Sensing her anxiety, he reached over and put his hand on hers and then gave her a kiss on the face. "You could use a drink, too," he said.

CHAPTER SIX
THE OLD WITH THE NEW

Tranise, Mary and Charlene

At Norfolk International Airport, Tranise stood off to the side as Mary greeted their old roommate, Charlene, outside baggage claim. After they put her bag in the trunk, Tranise came up from behind and tapped Charlene on the shoulder.

Charlene turned around and was confused by the person in front of her. She leaned back and studied her friend that she had lived with for four years.

"Tranise?" she finally let out. "Tranise?"

"Yeah, girl," Tranise said. "I know it's been some years but come on now."

"Oh, my God. Where the hell you been, girl?" Charlene said as they hugged. Charlene was five-foot-ten and burly, more than two hundred pounds. She engulfed Tranise with a bear hug so tight Mary had to intercede. "Wait, Charlene. Don't smother the girl," she said. "Damn."

"I can't believe this," Charlene said, turning to Mary. "Where you find this heffa?"

"This heffa found me," Mary said. "She just shows up at Homecoming after disappearing for years. I thought you were one of those chicks who went to Aruba and never came back."

They jumped into Mary's rental car and drove off. "I heard you're in Charlotte, doing your thing," Tranise said to Charlene. "You look good."

"Okay, don't even start," she said. "I don't look good. Not right now. But I'm working on it. I'm back down to the size I was when I was in school. Tell her how I looked last year, Mary. I was a house."

"Well, you're a small house now," Tranise cracked.

"Then I was a mansion last year," Charlene said, and the women laughed. It was all so familiar. Although they had not been together in five years, in five minutes, they renewed their connection. It felt like old times that fast.

On their way to Pizzeria Uno at Virginia Beach Boulevard and Military Highway, Tranise gave Charlene details about her living and career situations since college and then got to the matter that hung over her like a mistletoe: Brandon Barksdale.

"How can someone so smart be married to someone like Felicia?" Tranise asked.

"Maybe he wasn't as smart as we thought," Charlene said.

"That's what I said," Mary chimed in. "Whatever the case, I think you have more hatred for Felicia than you have interest in Brandon."

"You know what? I can't even say which is stronger," Tranise said. "I don't hate Felicia. But I don't like her, that's for sure. As for Brandon—"

"You don't even know Brandon," Charlene said. "You never had a conversation with him. He could be silly and immature and totally not what you like. But at this point, what does it matter? He's married."

"I don't care," Tranise said.

"You look great. You seemed to be the same person. But to hear you say that…no, that's not the Tranise I know," Charlene said. "Mary, you hear this? The Tranise I know has never done anything amoral in her life."

"Well, maybe it's a new Tranise," Tranise said. "I don't know. Maybe I wouldn't be able to do it—if I got the chance. But I feel like I owe Felicia something."

"You're a grown-ass woman," Mary said. "Let it go."

"Okay, okay," Tranise said. "Y'all know me too well... But I would still like to see him."

"Well, I'd like to see that tall glass of sweet tea myself," Charlene said.

"I already saw him—and the man has held it together," Mary said.

The three of them looked off at no place in particular for a few seconds.

"Look at us," Tranise said. "We all are sitting here daydreaming about a married man."

They parked the car, took a few photos of each other outside the restaurant and went in. Just as they got seated, a guy wearing an Alpha Phi Alpha Fraternity jacket came over. He was excited about seeing the ladies. They hugged and smiled and shared small talk for a few minutes.

"Over at The Broadway—the club that used to be The Big Apple back in the day—is a day party that's free and should be good," he said. "My frat brothers and I are going over there after we leave here. You all should come over."

"Isn't there a day party in Portsmouth at The Mansion?" Mary asked.

"It is, and it's pretty nice, too, according to one of my boys who called me from over there," the guy said. "But since The Broadway is across the street, we're going there to see what's up. I hope you come by."

With that, he left.

He was tall and handsome and a gentleman and had the ladies' attention. One problem.

"Who the hell was that?" Tranise asked.

"I have no idea," Mary said.

"He knew our names; we obviously went to school with him," Charlene said. "How come we don't remember him?"

"We sat here and had a conversation with him like we were old friends," Tranise said. "He must have changed since we were in school. I don't have any inkling who he is.

"I figured that might happen with people not remembering me because I look a little different. But in a few minutes they would recognize me. But I was looking at this guy and I had no connection, like I never saw him before."

"Well, trust me, girl, it won't be the last time you don't know who you're talking to," Mary said. "That's just how it is. Some people change a lot in five years. I've been to every Homecoming and I see the change in some people from year-to-year. It's kind of remarkable."

"I think that's part of it that's kind of fascinating," Charlene said. "Who's going to be the same as college? Who's going to look different—better or otherwise. See, you look better, I think, Tranise, because you've kind of grown into your body and it looks good.

"Me? I've grown out of my body."

She and her friends laughed. "I'm actually about the size I was at school," Charlene continued. "But I had already grown out of my body. You ever heard of a poor college student gaining weight? Well, that's what I did."

"Charlene, you look much better this year than last year," Mary said. "I can see you're doing something differently."

Their conversation was interrupted by the arrival of the food. Charlene had a salad and mixed vegetables, a serious departure from the piles of food she would ingest three or four times a day.

"This is what I'm doing differently—I'm eating differently, smarter," she said. "And I wish I could say it was a lifestyle change that came because I wanted to do better."

"Well, what was it then?" Tranise asked.

A sad look came over Charlene. "This girl I grew up with, Toya Simpson, died right after I got back from Homecoming last year," she explained. "She had a stroke that really was about high blood pressure and high cholesterol. Bad eating habits. She was around my age, twenty-six or twenty-seven, and we looked a lot alike. People used to ask if we were sisters. Twins. We looked that much alike—in the face and in size.

"You might think I'm crazy, but when I went to her funeral, I stood over her lying there and I saw myself in that casket. I know my mind was playing tricks on me, but that was the moment for me. It was like that was the message I needed to get myself together. Then Heavy D died a few weeks later. I was like, their deaths will not be in vain, at least in how I live my life."

"I'm proud of you," Mary said.

"Me, too," Tranise added. "It really is a lifestyle choice. So, keep it going. We want you around for when we have our ten-year reunion."

"I want to be there more than you want me there," Charlene said, laughing.

Just then, the server came over with three glasses of champagne.

"We didn't order that," Mary said.

"I know. The gentleman in the black and gold jacket did. He said, 'Happy Homecoming,'" the server explained.

The women all looked over at the Alpha with grateful smiles. He smiled, nodded his head and lifted his drink. They raised their glasses and had a long distance toast.

"Miss," Tranise said to the server, "did he say what his name is?"

"He didn't," she said.

"Now we really have to find out who this guy is," Tranise said.

"I'd like to know who he is for sure," Charlene said. "He's handsome."

"He is," Mary said. "And a gentleman."

"And he isn't pushy," Tranise added. "I like his style. I just wish we knew who the hell he is."

They all laughed. But his chivalrous act sparked conversation about the most popular subject of all: men.

"So, Tranise, you talking about Brandon Barksdale, who is married—what about what you have going in Atlanta?" Charlene said. "I heard about the men in Atlanta. Is it true?"

"Is what true?" Tranise asked. "That there are a lot of gay men in Atlanta? Well, yes. I can't lie. I've seen a lot of it, to the point where sometimes I'm almost depressed about it.

"But the reality is that they have to live their lives as they see fit. I don't begrudge them that. Where I have a problem is when they're on the down low, trying to talk to me and at the same time they have a butt buddy."

The women laughed.

"I know," Mary said. "What's going on? I don't even recall any obviously gay guys when we were in school. But apparently they waited to graduate, move to Atlanta and bust out."

"We're laughing, but it's really not funny," Tranise said. "I meet guys in Atlanta now and I examine them like I never did before. I look at all their mannerisms. If I see any broke wrists, I'm gone. I pay attention to their language; I hear words like 'fierce,' I'm gone. The crazy part is that you never know. And, again, that's what disturbs me. Don't get married, have kids, meet heterosexual women…knowing you like men. That's just wrong."

"So you aren't seeing anybody down there?" Mary asked.

"No, not really," Tranise answered.

"No wonder you talking about getting with married-ass Brandon," Charlene cracked.

"Can't even lie—it's been too long," Tranise said. "If he acts right, I just might break my streak."

"And how long is this streak?" Mary asked.

"Well, let me see…"

"Damn, it's been that long that you have to think that hard?" Charlene said.

"Actually, you won't believe this, but my last was Michael Jennings," Tranise revealed.

"No way," Mary said. "You were with Michael in college."

"Shit, you got cobwebs down there, girl," Charlene said.

Tranise laughed hard and loud. "No, let me explain," she said. "About a year ago, I called him. He lives in Northern Virginia. We kept in touch a little bit and he came to Atlanta for work earlier this year. Let's just say we had a good night."

"So you let go the fact that he was running around with Felicia and you at the same time back in the day?" Charlene said.

"I didn't think I did—until I saw him," she said. "I was going to bring it up, but after a while I didn't see the point."

"Good for you—that's growth," Mary said.

"*Excuse me,*" Tranise said, feigning being insulted.

"Come on, you know how you were in school?" Mary explained. "You would analyze everything up and down, round and round, in and out. You got hold of something and you wouldn't let go, like the dog that grabs hold to your pants leg."

"Whatever," Tranise said. "Excuse me for growing."

They laughed and talked and reminisced for another half-hour before Charlene suggested they go across Virginia Beach Boulevard to The Broadway for the day party. They spent several minutes dividing the bill before finally leaving for the party.

They headed out looking for the Alpha who had sent them

champagne to thank him and finally find out who he was, but he
had gone. "Well, he told us about the party, so he's probably over
there," Charlene said.

And sure enough, when they made the three-minute trek to
The Broadway, there he was, standing among brothers of Omega
Psi Phi, who hosted the event. They were clearly enjoying each
other, laughing and recalling their college days.

"Now how is it that I know those Ques he's talking to, but not
him," Charlene said. "That's Bootsy, Darryl Ferguson, and
Conrad—they are old heads we met last year when Bootsy said
something crazy to us. Remember that, Mary? But how do they
know him, but we don't? This is crazy."

The ladies made their way through the packed building, stopping
to engage old friends along the way.

"I can't believe I have not been back before now," Tranise said.
"I forgot about most of these people. But it's great to see these
old faces. Folks are looking good—for the most part."

"Yeah, for the most part," Mary stressed. "Look over there, the
girl in the jean jacket. That's Diane Luckett."

"No way," Charlene said.

"Look at her; look hard," Mary said.

Charlene and Tranise tried not to stare. But then it hit them at
once: It was Diane Luckett, all right. Once petite with a body to
envy, she had added so much weight that she was practically
unrecognizable.

"OMG," they both said in unison, making all of them laugh.

"What happened to her?" Tranise said. "I'm not judging, but
damn."

"She probably had a kid or two and it just got out of control,"
Charlene surmised.

"She ain't had no kids," Mary said. "She married that guy she dated that went to Hampton. Remember him? He used to always be on our campus."

"I do remember him; so they got married? Good. If I remember correctly, he was a buffed guy, a workout freak," Tranise said. "He can't be happy about his wife looking like *that*."

As if she could hear them speaking about her over the loud music, Diane walked in their direction.

"Diane, how are you?" Tranise said, as they embraced.

"Tranise, you look so good," Diane said.

Tranise wanted to say the same to her, but she could not bring herself to do so. Lying was something she was taught never to do as a kid, and it stuck with her.

"I'm glad to see you," she said instead. "I heard you got married. Where's your husband?"

"Well, you know, he went to Hampton, so he wasn't really trying to come to ours, which is good because I didn't go to his. It's better this way."

When Diane walked away, the ladies stared at her in shock. Her size four frame had spread into double figures. It looked awkward, especially because she still wore form-fitting clothes that were so hot when she was forty or fifty pounds lighter.

"I never would have guessed she would blow up like that," Mary said.

"You never know what's going on in people's lives," Tranise said. "She's all smiles now, but it could be health reasons or stress or something else. We can't judge."

"I know I can't," Charlene said. "And I'm not. I think we're all just saying that it's surprising to see her carrying that much weight."

Tranise did not hear Charlene's comment because the Alpha who had bought them champagne was approaching. She tried hard to figure where she knew him from, but nothing came to mind.

"So you all made it?" he said as he approached Tranise. "If the floor wasn't so packed, I would ask you to dance."

"Really? Well, it has to clear up at some point," she said.

He smiled, and Tranise was a sucker for a glistening smile.

"Can I ask you something?" she said.

"I already know the question," he said.

"You do? What is it then?" she asked.

"My name is Kwame," he said, his smile even brighter.

"So you knew we didn't know your name?" Tranise asked.

"I did," he answered. "It didn't bother me at all. It's been a long time. Plus, if you remembered me, it would have been a miracle."

"Really?" Tranise said. "But how is it that you remember us?"

"I remember because I was enamored with you when I met you," he answered. "I was in high school and I came over to your apartment."

"You did? When?" Tranise said. "And who were you with?"

"It was about five, six years ago," Kwame said. "I was so impressed that I was in the apartment of some college women. I was actually smitten with you—you looked good and you were so nice."

"But how did you get there?" she asked.

"I was with my cousin," he said.

"Who is your cousin?" Tranise wanted to know.

"Michael," he said.

"Jennings?" she finished.

"Yes," Kwame went on. "It actually was around this time of year, homecoming. Michael brought me over on our way to the game. He said he wanted me to see what a college homecoming was like. You called him when he was at my house and asked him to bring you something.

"So, we stopped over there on our way to campus and ended up staying for a while because you and Charlene cooked some food and other people came over and it was just a party before the party.

"You don't remember that?"

"I *do* remember that," she said. "You were a little skinny kid, about as tall as me then. You've grown up. So how old are you now?"

"I'm twenty-two, graduated from Norfolk State in May," he said. "This is my first homecoming as an alum. When I saw you I knew it was you. You are the first college woman I ever met. And I gotta tell you, you look great."

The way he said that last sentence was flirtatious, and Tranise quickly picked up on it.

"Well, I'm not a cougar," she said, smiling.

"You're not old enough to be a cougar and the age difference between us isn't that big to make you a cougar, either," he said.

"Well, maybe not, but what about the fact that I dated your cousin?" she said.

"Mike was my man," Kwame said. "But I haven't talked to or seen in a few years. He didn't even come to my graduation. On top of that, we were related through marriage. My cousin married his cousin, or something like that. So, we wouldn't be crossing any bloodlines."

"You're getting way ahead of yourself, don't you think?" Tranise said.

"Maybe a little bit," Kwame answered. "Then again, you never can tell."

He smiled. And then he walked away, leaving Tranise standing there a bit ruffled.

She turned to her friends.

"So?" Charlene said.

"Who is he?" Mary added.

Tranise shook her head. "You remember homecoming back

when we were juniors, I believe, and Michael Jennings brought his little cousin over to our apartment? Well, that's his little cousin, although he's not little anymore."

"I remember him; he was a cute, little, shy kid," Mary said. "He just sat there quiet, like he was intimidated. That's *him*?"

"That's him," Tranise said. "I should have asked him how he could remember our names after so many years. We only met him that one time."

"That's pretty incredible," Charlene said. "I couldn't hear him, but it looked like he was shooting game at you."

"He was," Tranise said. "I told him I'm not a cougar."

"He's got to be twenty-one by now, right?" Mary said.

"He's actually twenty-two," Tranise informed them.

"Well, that's only a three-year age difference," Mary said. "That's nothing."

"Girl, please," Tranise said. "Guys my age aren't mature enough for me. So how you think that would work with him? And it's a four-year gap."

"I don't know, but he seems pretty mature to me—I'm just saying," Charlene said. "I mean, your ass talking about hooking up with Brandon, who is married, but you can't give a nice young man who remembered you from years ago a chance? Come on, now."

Her girls made her think. "But what about the fact that he's Michael's cousin?" Tranise asked. Then she added: "But they were related through marriage, not blood. Still, they're cousins." She did not think that held much weight, but she felt compelled to sling it out there.

"Didn't you just say they were cousins by marriage? Didn't you say they haven't been in contact in years?" Mary reasoned. "So what's the dilemma?"

"OMG," Tranise said. "*That's* the dilemma."

She stared off, between the shoulders of her friends who had her blocked in. They turned around to see where she was looking and spotted Brandon Barksdale off in the distance. He was just as they remembered: tall, distinguished, attractive in a classic way—square jaw bone, dimples, thick eyebrows, teeth as white as a golf ball.

Neither of them said anything: They watched as he maneuvered through the crowd, greeting his admirers with grace. He seemed as happy to see his old classmates as they were to see him. That humility always distinguished him as someone considered "real" and not full of himself.

It took about ten minutes for Brandon to negotiate through the mass of folks to get near the bar area, where Mary, Tranise and Charlene had posted up. When he got close enough, he made eye contact with Mary and smiled. She smiled back.

"I see you're out to get your party on," he said.

"You, too, huh?" she responded.

"No doubt," Brandon said. "It's homecoming. If you can't party now, then when can you?"

Before Mary could respond, he extended his hand to Charlene. "How are you? You were at Norfolk State when I was there, weren't you?" he said.

"We actually met a few times," she said, shaking his hand and blushing at the same time.

"I remember," he said. "You were friends with Max Johnson, the basketball team's trainer, right?"

"How could you remember that?" Charlene said.

"Well, I'm only twenty-six; dementia has not set in yet," he said, and everyone laughed.

"I'm really impressed," Charlene said. She turned to Tranise, who looked at Brandon as if he were a rib eye. "Do you remember her?"

Brandon reached to shake Tranise's hand. She was so glued into his face that she did not see his hand.

"Oh, so you gonna leave me hanging?" he said, flashing that smile that was mesmerizing.

"Oh, I'm sorry," Tranise said. "Hi. I'm Tranise. I know you don't remember me."

Brandon studied her. She looked familiar.

"I met you, too," he said. "As a matter of fact, I met you in Brown Hall. You dropped your books and I picked them up."

"How in the world could you possibly remember that?" Tranise asked. "We didn't even speak."

"Well, one, I have a good memory," he said. "And, two, I remember seeing an article about you in *The Spartan Echo* a few days later. I said, 'That's the girl from Brown Hall.' You look almost exactly the same, but different. Better."

"Wow, that's amazing you remember that," she said. "Why didn't you ever say anything to me after that?"

"I guess our paths didn't really cross like that again, although I recall seeing you at the games and at step shows," he said. "Where are you now?"

Tranise felt perspiration build up under her arms and on her forehead—a first. Brandon Barksdale was engaging her in conversation. Married or not, it was something she had wanted for nearly eight years. To get it was so satisfying.

She gave him an abbreviated version of her post-college life, calling her move to Atlanta and transition to teaching "one of those blessings you just don't expect to be a blessing."

"I understand what you mean," Brandon said. "I have been a head basketball coach at Franklin High School for the last three years. There were some overtures about pro ball overseas, but I didn't want to play that badly to go that far away. So when I got an offer to coach, I took it.

"And...wait, I'm going to order a glass of wine. Can I get you one?"

"Sure," Tranise said.

Brandon looked behind him to ask Mary and Charlene if they wanted a glass as well, but they had given Tranise her space and moved to the other side of the room.

He ordered the drinks and turned back to Tranise. "I had no idea it would be so gratifying to coach young men," he continued. "I have their attention and it amazed me at first that they listened to what I said. I saw pretty quickly that many of them are looking for guidance and leadership in their lives. Forget about basketball. I want to win as much as the next guy. But I talk to them all the time about having a victorious life. And to see the growth in maturity and responsibility in many of them from month-to-month gives you some purpose in life—or gives you more purpose. It's pretty amazing to me."

Tranise was amazed. Brandon was style *and* substance. He also was married. Married to her arch-nemesis, but married nonetheless.

Before a lull in the conversation could settle in, Tranise put it out there. "I heard you are married now."

"I am," he said without hesitation. "We met at Norfolk State, late in my senior year. Got married last year. And I have a kid on the way. So, it's an exciting time. And I'm a little nervous, too."

"Nervous? Why?" Tranise wanted to know.

"Well, you know, a new kid in the house. We've only been married a year," he said. "Changes."

"Change can be good, especially this kind of change," Tranise said. She wanted say, "You need to change wives."

He nodded his head and stared into her eyes so long that Tranise turned away. Was he trying to seduce her? Was her mind telling her that? If it was, it was working.

"So, uh, Brandon, where's your wife?" she asked.

"You know, I get to Atlanta every so often. I have family down there," he said, ignoring her question. "We should connect on my next visit."

That let her know for sure that he was flirting. She wasn't sure how to proceed. The drinks were kicking in and the flattery warmed her.

"With a new baby you're going to be needed around the house," Tranise said.

"That's true, to a degree," Brandon countered. "My mother-in-law will be staying with us, so I'll have some relief."

He had an answer for everything. And the answers came out so effortlessly, so smoothly, that Tranise was not offended that a married man was hitting on her. Any other time, she would eventually get insulted and let the guy know. The combination of it being Brandon and his wife being her enemy—and the alcohol—kept her from firing off on him.

"Well, I guess we have to figure that out when the time comes," she said.

Brandon nodded his head. "Fair enough," he said. Then he extended his hand. She put hers in his and he led her to the packed dance floor. The partygoers made room and while he had his back turned, Tranise turned to Mary and Charlene and flashed a broad smile.

"I know she's not going to go through with sleeping with that man," Mary said.

"Maybe she's just enjoying the attention," Charlene said. "But then, that's how it all starts."

They danced a few songs and made their way over to Charlene and Mary, who were smiling like children.

"I'm glad I got to see you all," he said. "If I don't see you later, I'll see you at the tailgate."

Brandon smiled and walked off.

"Where is his wife?" Charlene asked.

"I have no idea. When I asked him, he asked me something, as if he didn't hear me or didn't want to even talk about her," Tranise said. "And to be honest, it didn't matter where she was. She wasn't here."

"Now listen, heffa, I know you're not thinking about doing something with him," Mary said.

"No, I'm not thinking about doing something with him," she said. "I'm thinking about *fucking* him."

"OMG," Mary responded. "You got to Atlanta and turned into a little slut, huh?"

Tranise laughed, knowing her girl was joking.

"But even if I would, why would I be a slut?" she said. "And what would you call him? He's the married one. I'm single and can do whatever the hell I want to do."

"That's not a license to demean yourself," Charlene said.

"You heffas are no fun," Tranise said. "It's homecoming. Loosen up. I've been the straight-and-narrow one all my life. If I want to get wild for one day, I should be able to do it and not feel like I'm some whore."

"You're grown and you've always done what you wanted to do," Mary said. "I'm sure you'll do the right thing…and keep your bloomers on."

The ladies laughed again, with Tranise falling into Charlene.

"Okay, no more drinks for this one," Charlene said.

"Really? I was just about to order a round for everyone," said Kwame, who seemingly popped up from nowhere.

"Oh, uh, Kwame, right?" Tranise said. "My girls are trying to slow me down. Can you believe that?"

"I guess they're just looking out for you," he said. "That's what your girls are for, right?""

Tranise immediately sobered up. Not that she was drunk, but her buzz evaporated with Kwame's words. They seemed sincere. The men of her past were far less thoughtful and far more opportunistic. She liked his come-from.

"How about water for everyone?" he said.

"Well, you can get that heffa some water," Mary said. "Me? I'd like a Ciroc and cranberry juice."

"Make that two, if you don't mind, Kwame," Charlene said.

"Tranise, want to go with me to help me carry the drinks?"

"I'll meet you over at the bar," she said. When Kwame turned away, Tranise turned to her friends. "I'm on a roll. What do you think of Kwame?"

"It's not about what we think; it's what *you* think," Charlene said. "And if you don't think he's fine enough for you to get to know, then I'm gonna believe that you are drunk... But that's just me."

"No, it's not just you," Mary said. "It's me, too. I don't care how old he is— wait, that didn't sound right. I meant to say that I don't care if you're a few years older than him. He's legal, apparently available and definitely interested in you."

"Okay, okay, y'all blowing my little buzz," Tranise said. "Let me see what's on this man's mind. I'll be back. Then we can leave and go to the other day party."

"Not so fast," Mary said. "Look over there. That's Rodney Mercer, my old boyfriend. And he looks good."

"Rodney Mercer?" Tranise said. "Oh, that was the guy from our junior year. He left and transferred somewhere."

"To North Carolina A&T," Mary recalled. "His father died

and he went back home to be close to his family... Damn, I haven't seen him in six or seven years."

"Well," Charlene said, "looks like it's time to get reacquainted. I can see from here he's not wearing a wedding band."

"Ole Hawk Eye Charlene at work," Mary said. "Some things never change."

"Hey, don't hate on it," Charlene said. "If I recall correctly, I saw Rodney coming toward us at a step show one night when you were with that other guy, uh, Brett. I gave you the heads-up and you got rid of Brett, which, as they say, averted a disaster. So, don't act like my vision isn't used for good."

"Girl, you're crazy," Tranise said. "Okay, I gotta go. I'll be back."

"Charlene, I hate to leave you, but I've got to go see Rodney," Mary said.

"I'm coming with you," Charlene said. "You ain't on no date. We're at a club."

Mary smiled and grabbed Charlene's hand, leading her toward Rodney. On the way, however, they ran into Marissa Shaw, the best friend of Felicia, Brandon Barksdale's wife. Because Tranise and Felicia had beef, their best friends did, too. So it was not a cordial greeting when Mary and Charlene encountered Marissa.

But because they virtually bumped into each other, they could not help but speak.

"Marissa," Mary said. "Hi."

"Hi," Marissa responded. But the "greetings" were flat and unemotional.

Charlene did not utter a word. She just gave her a toothless smile and gave Mary a gentle push for her to continue walking.

"She's still the same," Mary said to Charlene. "A deadbeat."

Before Charlene could contribute to the conversation, Rodney noticed Mary and came rushing over, bumping into classmates

Troy Brown and Dee Graves on the way. That was Rodney, aggressive to the point of being obnoxious at times. Charlene used to question whether he was on steroids because his behavior was occasionally erratic.

His and Mary's eyes met and they smiled the brightest smiles. She opened her arms to hug him and he was classic Rodney: He lifted her off the ground.

"Rodney, put me down," Mary said, slapping him on his shoulders.

He finally obliged and put her down—but then hugged her tightly. "Girl, I was in love with your ass," he said so loudly that those near them could hear what he yelled, even over the bumping music.

"Yeah, I know you were in love with my ass," Mary said. "But you weren't in love with me."

Charlene laughed, and Rodney turned to her.

"Don't encourage her, Charlene," he said, then he stepped over and hugged her. "She thinks she has an audience and she's liable to say anything for a laugh."

"Rodney, forget that," Mary said. "What's going on? Where have you been? And isn't A&T's Homecoming this weekend, too?"

"I'm good, as you can see," he said, looking down at his muscular body. "I've been in living in Raleigh, working at Cisco since I graduated. All is good. Yeah, it's GHOE this weekend—Greatest Homecoming On Earth—but I feel like I'm as much or even more connected to Norfolk State. So, my boy who graduated with me at A&T came up so I can show him how we do it at NSU.

"But it had better be off the chain because A&T's homecoming is crazy. I was drunk for two days straight."

"I heard homecoming at A&T was awesome," Charlene said. "But so is ours. And it's the same at South Carolina State, Hampton, Virginia State, Morgan State, Morehouse, Florida A&M, Southern,

Tuskegee, North Carolina Central, Grambling, Virginia Union, Winston-Salem...Need I go on?"

"That's true," Rodney said. "But you won't even believe this, but I chose Norfolk State because I was hoping you would be here."

"Stop, Rodney," Mary said. "There you go with your lying."

"Wait, hold up. Wait a damn minute," Rodney said. "First, when did I lie to you about anything? And second, when did you catch me in a lie?"

He burst out laughing at his own joke as Mary and Charlene looked at him.

"Okay, look, I might have lied about some things back then," he said. "But I was nineteen years old, maybe twenty. Lying is part of all of our DNAs at that age. I've outgrown that nonsense and I'm telling you, I really wanted to see you. No bullshit."

"On that note, I will go to the bar," Charlene said.

"Come here, Mary," Rodney said. "I have a seat over here. Let's talk."

There was something in the way Rodney spoke that got Mary's attention. He was serious. More than that, he seemed sincere. And so she followed him to a table near the back and away from the action. He introduced her to his friend, who was sitting and holding a seat next to him. He excused himself and Rodney and Mary sat.

They complimented each other on how they looked and caught up on each other's lives. After ten minutes of that chatter, Rodney got down to it.

"You know me; I come with it," he said. His forehead was doused in sweat although he had been sitting the entire time. "I left here because I had to, for my family. And I, you know, buried myself in my pain and my family and didn't really deal with having to leave you like I did.

"I was in love with you, Mary. A choice had to be made and it was easy—my mom and little brother and sisters needed me to be there. I wish I had handled it better with you. I was so messed up in the head, losing my father suddenly like that. I recall us communicating a few times after I left, but somehow we just lost touch. And when I came to a place where I thought I had it together, we had totally lost touch."

Mary listened with amazement. She and Rodney had been in a relationship, but it was more a physical thing than an emotional thing. At least for her it was. Hearing this from Rodney seven years later was quite surprising.

"How many drinks have you had?" she asked him sarcastically.

"See, you still don't take me seriously."

"Rodney, I didn't expect this," Mary said. "Hell, I didn't expect to see you. I never forgot you, though. You were a good friend and we had fun. But it's been a long time. No one could have told me I would see you here and then that you'd have this to say to me."

"Well, surprises happen," he said. "And they're good for you. You don't look like you're married. You—"

"I don't look like I'm married?" Mary said.

"No. You look happy; married people don't look like you look," he said.

And Mary blushed, which was an accomplishment because she wore a protective shield of armor ever since her parents had divorced when she was in ninth grade. She witnessed her mom's pain and vowed to never experience it herself, which is why she took Rodney in college as something less than serious. She did not want it to be serious.

Now here he was, as a mature man, professing something strong toward her. This time, it had more power, as the years of being unfulfilled started to catch up with Mary.

"Remember the big snowstorm and we walked from campus across the Campostella Bridge to Giant Open Air Market to get some food?" Rodney said. "We were about the only people out there walking. It was freezing, but it was fun."

"Yeah, and I remember what happened when we found that little nook in the Wilder Building, too," Mary said, blushing.

"I remember, too. Very well," Rodney said. "I had my pants down by my ankles in the snow. My ass was freezing. But that didn't stop us."

"We must have been crazy to do that outside in a damn blizzard," Mary said, shaking her head. "Just crazy."

"I think we should take a walk to the Wilder Building tonight to revisit the scene of the…"

"The crime," Mary said. "Go ahead and say it."

They both laughed and before she knew it, her hand was on his leg. She was not the touchy-feely type, but she found herself being drawn closer to her old boyfriend by the minute.

"Don't you have a woman at home?" she asked, mostly as a defense mechanism. Maybe if he told her he was in a serious relationship, she would be less attracted to him. Maybe.

"I had a woman; you know how that goes," he said. "Good and bad until finally bad is too bad to keep dealing with. So…"

"I do know how it is," Mary said. "I have to tell you, Rodney, that I have been in a committed relationship for almost three years. He's a good man. He adores me."

Rodney did not say anything. He just admired her dark chocolate complexion and the full lips that he used to kiss when he really was not that good of a kisser.

"We need some drinks, don't you think?" he said.

"I've already had a few and it's not even five o'clock," Mary said. "How am I going to hang out tonight if I keep drinking like this?"

"You're still young," Rodney said.

"But I'm not on steroids, like you," she said.

"You really believe that, don't you? I remember you saying that to me when I was nineteen," he responded. "I don't do drugs; well, not anymore. And I never did steroids. For the record, I'm just a high-energy guy. You should know that better than anyone."

Mary laughed knowingly.

"Anyway," Rodney added, "I'm very serious about what I've said to you, Mary. You were my girl. I think we should at least see if what we had is still there."

"I don't know what to say, Rod. That was a long time ago. We were teenagers, kids," Mary said. "I don't see what harm it will do to spend some time together this weekend. But I don't think it should be about trying to rekindle the past."

"That's fine," he said. "And you're right. The past is done. It's really about who we are now. I'm cool with that."

He leaned over and hugged Mary and she hugged him back.

"Ahem," Tranise said, standing over them. "Get a room already."

"Well, look at you," Rodney said, standing up.

"Don't pick me up, Rodney," Tranise said. She recalled his unbridled enthusiasm.

He did as she asked and hugged her. "Wow, you look great, Tranise," he said. "Mary told me you were here."

"You look great, too," she said. "I see you trying to pick up where you left off."

"Definitely," he said.

Tranise introduced him to Kwame, who stood patiently by as they exchanged greetings.

"Man, this is a great woman right here," Rodney said.

"I'm learning that," Kwame responded while looking at Tranise.

"Where is Charlene?" Mary asked.

"Right there," Tranise said, pointing toward the dance floor.

Charlene was on the floor, having a ball. She could dance with the best of them and enjoyed dancing. "We'll never be able to leave now," Mary said. "She's in her element."

"Well, since we're going to be here a while, I say let's get more drinks," Rodney said.

"Yes, Rodney, I'm with you," Kwame said. "Let's make it happen."

CHAPTER SEVEN

THE REUNION

Catherine and Earl

I n the month after the Sade concert and before homecoming, Earl and Catherine connected twice: once when she flew to Charlotte to participate in a cousin's wedding, and again when they had a one-day rendezvous in Richmond. Homecoming was only a few weeks away, but Catherine suggested meeting at a neutral destination to continue the get-to-know process.

Each occasion was easy and fun—and romantic. In Charlotte, they'd had an intimate dinner at Mimoso Grille downtown. Earl had offered to cook dinner at his house, but Catherine did not trust herself in that amount of privacy. She actually, as attracted as she was to Earl, told herself she would not have sex with him until the following year—another few two months. So she had stayed at the Westin. When the night was over, they had groped each other and kissed in his car like teenagers until the windows were too foggy to see through.

It was hard to resist Earl, but Catherine did. "I just want to get it right. We'll know when it's time," she had told him.

He impressed Catherine by not trying to turn her convictions. "You're right, baby," he had said. "Things will happen when they should happen."

Two weeks later they had met in Richmond—and had separate hotel rooms. Earl figured they could share the same room and not be intimate. Catherine did not want to chance it. So, they had rooms on the same floor of the Marriott.

"Come on, man, you're joking," one of Earl's good friends, Thornell, had said. "What's the point? You know it's going to happen one day. Why not that day?"

"I hear you, but I'm not looking to force anything," he had said. "That's my girl. I'm good. The reality is that we've already made love to each other's mind. The physical will come. I'm not sweating it."

Catherine could feel Earl's disposition about the sex thing, and it only drew her closer to him. In fact, one day he texted her: *"I have been fantasizing about you all day. I miss your lips and covet feeling your body. I miss seeing you, laughing with you, being around you. Forces are pulling me toward you, our connection is so strong."*

And she texted him back: *"You just made love to me."*

By the time they got to Richmond, Catherine's comfort level and willpower elevated so much that she hung out in Earl's room after a nice dinner and cocktails. They sat together in a lounge chair and engaged in a protracted, heated session of kissing and touching and basically getting each other so hot and bothered that they actually were sweating.

Finally, around two thirty in the morning, Catherine pulled herself away from Earl. They gathered themselves and Earl walked her down the hall to her room and kissed her good night. Earl knew then he had the willpower of ten men—and that he, indeed, was in love with Catherine.

The two weeks leading to homecoming were long and torturous for two people who were in love but had not yet expressed it to each other. Earl arrived that Thursday so he could play in the alumni golf outing on Friday morning, but really so he could spend an extra day with Catherine.

And that day started as all of their previous days had: with them firmly embracing and kissing passionately at the Norfolk Airport. She took him from there straight to Terrapin restaurant for dinner in Virginia Beach. The dining room was elegant, the mood romantic. They laughed and talked and kissed and ate each other up. Before the food arrived, Earl slid his seat next to Catherine's.

"I love you and I'm in love with you," he said, looking into her eyes. "I have wanted to tell you this for a while now, but I wanted to tell you in person, not over the phone. I wanted you to see it in my eyes."

Earl's eyes actually watered, surprising him. But that's how deeply he felt for Catherine. She could feel through Earl's words and consistent actions that he loved her. To hear him say it made her heart rate increase. She loved him, too, and said so. Hearing it from Earl freed her to express her heart.

"I love you, Earl. I do," she said. They kissed and hugged and there was a relief for both of them that came with finally getting it out.

Still, Catherine remained steadfast in not consummating their relationship just yet by making love, but she did want Earl to come over to her place for cocktails after dinner to sort of kick off the weekend. After Richmond, she knew they both were strong enough to resist their ever-growing urges.

She drove to her condo after the fantastic meal, then up the ramp in the parking deck to the third floor. But instead of parking, she kept going.

"Baby," she said, "remember the guy I told you about that I stopped dating several months ago?"

"How could I forget?" Earl said.

"Well, I just saw his car parked in my visitor space," she said. He had never heard her voice sound so distressed.

"What?" Earl said. "Do I need to talk to this guy?"

"No. But I don't understand," she said.

"Well, do you want to go in or go to my hotel?" he said.

"Let's go to the hotel," she said. "I am so sorry, Earl. When I got off from work today, he was at my car in the parking lot. I told him exactly the deal. He seemed to want some form of closure because I told him a while ago that I wanted to take a break and didn't want to be in a relationship. But then I told him about you and he's saying he's confused."

"Look, you can't account for other people's actions," Earl said. He put his hand on her shoulder as she drove along. "I'm good. Relax. At some point, he's going to have to be dealt with since he showed up at your job and now at your home. That's crazy to me. I'd love to deal with him. But it'll be all right. He can't ruin our day."

The plan was for Earl to make drinks at Catherine's place; he had packed the ingredients in a bag and placed it in her trunk. And when they got to the Marriott Waterside, he immediately washed his hands and began making cocktails.

"I definitely can use one," she said. "Earl, I'm so sorry. I—"

"Catherine, it's okay. We're still together, right?" he said. "Do you want me to give you some time to call him? I can go to the lobby for a few."

"No. I have nothing to say to him," she said.

"Okay, well, here's a drink," he said, handing over a margarita. "Let's toast."

He held up his glass. "To a wonderful homecoming weekend, stalker or no stalker."

That drew a smile from Catherine, the first since she had seen her old friend in her parking garage. "I don't understand," she repeated. "I thought we could still be friends. I think he's a good person. But I guess we can't be friends."

Earl set his drink down and hugged Catherine. She hugged him back. Then they kissed. He lit a candle and found a nice playlist on iTunes on his laptop. The drapes were open and revealing the tall buildings of downtown. Catherine began to relax and the talk of anything unpleasant ceased.

After a second drink, they rolled around Earl's bed, kissing and groping each other in a fury. Suddenly, all that passion stopped. Earl stopped it. He looked into Catherine's eyes.

The music played, but they could not hear it.

"It's time," he said softly but firmly.

Those words ran through Catherine's body and settled in her heart. It was as if Earl had touched the perfect chord with her—in what he said, how he said it, and when he said it.

She sat up on the bed and then stood on it. "You want to see me out of my dress?" Catherine asked, looking down on Earl, who lay on his back. He did not have to answer; she knew the deal, and unzipped the back of the dress and pulled it over her head, revealing a curvy, sensual body that defied her age. Earl admired it as he pulled off his shirt and pulled down his pants.

Their unclothed bodies met and the passion in them was unleashed in a fury of deep kisses and caressing that lasted nearly a half-hour. Finally, they separated enough for Earl to admire her body through kisses, on her lips and face and her shoulders. He advanced down to her breasts, where he gave each the proper attention.

Catherine threw her head back and relaxed herself to enjoy the affection. Earl vowed to appreciate her entire body, and he did. He slowly kissed her down her stomach to the inside of her thighs. Her breathing turned into panting as his lips moved from one thigh to the other.

He then settled directly between her legs and used his tongue to please Catherine to climactic heights. Her body shook and she screamed in ecstasy. They spent the next hour making sweet, passionate, intense love. There were no awkward moments. Their movements and emotions were synchronized.

When Catherine rested in his arms, she cried. She was in love with Earl, and their consummation of that love drew out all the emotion in her. He did not cry, but his heart was open. He believed he had found all he needed in a woman in Catherine.

"You're my soldier of love," he said to her.

"You're my beacon of hope," she responded.

They kissed and cradled each other before eventually drifting off to sleep, punctuating an exhilarating start to their homecoming weekend.

CHAPTER EIGHT

MAKING MOVES

Jimmy and Carter

Something clearly was bothering Carter when he returned to The Mansion—he and Barbara hardly looked at each other. She and Donna went directly to the bathroom; Carter to the bar.

"Dude, you okay?" What happened?" Jimmy asked.

Carter just stared off, not bothering to answer.

"Yo, Carter," Jimmy said louder.

Carter turned to his boy. "She just told me some wild shit," he said.

Jimmy looked at him as if to say, *And…*

"She's getting a divorce and moving to New York," he said.

"Holy shit," Jimmy said. "*Really*? But you look like that's a problem. You told me you all are in love. Why isn't that good news?"

"Man, I do love her, Carter said. "But I wasn't trying to have her live in New York. That changes everything."

"What? Why?" Jimmy said. "Just yesterday—yesterday—you talked about how into her you were, how you all have been in love since college. So help me out here: How can you not like her moving where she'll be close to you?"

"There's a lot I have going on in New York," he said, which was code for he had another woman.

"Did you tell Barbara you were seeing someone else? Or did you let her believe you were waiting on her?" Jimmy asked.

"Neither," Carter said. "She never really asked me if I was in a relationship. She knew I dated."

"Do you love the girl or not?" Jimmy asked. "You told me you're in love and now she's available to you and you have a problem."

"Forget it, man," Carter answered. "You don't understand."

Jimmy smiled to himself. He knew Carter too well to believe that would be the last he heard about the situation.

But his attention shifted quickly to one of his Maurice Roper, who had the look of a man headed to the gas chamber. They hadn't seen each other in ten years. Through the expanded waistline, glasses and gray hair, Jimmy was still able to place him.

"Mo, what's happening?" he said with a broad smile.

"Jimmy!!! Damn," Maurice responded.

The two men hugged. "Damn, boy, you look just about the same," Maurice said to Jimmy. "You look good."

"You look different, like you've been living a good life," Jimmy said to Maurice, laughing, patting his protruding stomach.

"Yeah, well, you know," he said. "Married life can do that."

Then he turned to his right to introduce his wife, Eula, who was not smiling. In fact, she stood with her arms folded, like there was someplace else she'd rather be.

"Eula, this is one of my good friends from college, Jimmy," he said.

"Hi, Eula. Nice to meet you. Your husband and I had some good times together," Jimmy said.

Eula gave Jimmy a meek handshake and a faint smile. She did not say a word.

Jimmy kept his smile and turned to Maurice. "So, catch me up on what's been going on with you," he said.

Eula rolled her eyes and told Maurice she was going to find the bathroom.

"Yo, everything okay?" Jimmy asked when she walked away.

"Man, I could hurt that woman right now," Maurice said. "But it's my fault. My instincts told me to leave her ass at home. But she really wanted to come, so I gave in. We got married six months ago. She went to NYU. She's smart as hell. But she doesn't get the black college homecoming thing.

"I met her in New York, at the play *The Mountaintop* on Broadway. We were both waiting afterward for Samuel L. Jackson and Angela Bassett to come out after the show. She was holding her program up in the crowd to get it signed and I volunteered to do it for her because I was taller and could reach closer to the actors. We started a conversation from there and here we are.

"But she's had attitude ever since we got to town and I ran into some honeys from school in the bookstore—Gina Dorsey, Terry Hodge and Deberah 'Sparkle' Williams. They were looking great and, of course, we hugged and chatted for a few minutes. They actually told me about this day party. When they left, Eula starts going in about how disrespectful it was for me to hug women in her presence and all this bull."

"What did she expect you to do?" Jimmy asked. "They're your friends from college."

"That's what I said," Maurice added. "Then she said, 'I know you slept with one of them.' And I was like, 'No, I didn't. How did you get that? And if I had, what difference does it make? That would have been ten or twelve years ago. I had a life before you. We're married.' But that didn't seem to matter. So, we get here and I ran into Carter and Barbara and her friend and she starts the same stuff."

"Man, I hear you," Jimmy said. "But I felt like that would be me if I brought my wife with me to homecoming. I've been married for a few years, but something about me coming back to Norfolk

State made her feel like she needed to be here, like I was going to be screwing old girlfriends or something. But I told her I was coming alone, and you can believe she is pissed at me right now. I just want to have a good time, see my school, see old friends and go back home. I didn't need her telling me it's time to go or asking me about everyone woman I hug."

"I wish like hell I had done the same thing you did," Maurice said. "I'm really shocked by her attitude. I never would have expected it. I thought she was more secure than this. But she's making this trip hell—and we just got here about three hours ago."

"Well, it will get better once she sees how everyone is interacting and sees how innocent it is," Jimmy said. "I know some people do come back to hook up like old times or whatever. But that doesn't mean that's what you do.

"How's she going to be at the game tomorrow? She like football? She like to hang out at the tailgate?"

"Shit, that's going to be worse than today," Maurice said. "You see her in those high-ass heels? That's all she wears. I told her the tailgate is awesome and that a lot of standing is involved—and walking. But I don't think she brought any really comfortable shoes. She thinks she needs to look glamorous to impress people for me.

"But that's where she still doesn't know me. I never tried to impress anybody."

Maurice was unlike Alex Ervin, another guy from their time in college who seemed to return every year to homecoming to boast about his accomplishments. He was successful in his own right—he owned a brokerage firm that was ranked in the Top 100 businesses by *Black Enterprise* magazine. Everyone knew it; he was featured in *Behold*, the NSU alumni magazine. But that did not stop him from yearly parading around spreading the word—and exaggerating his success—at homecoming, which was the ideal time because many of his classmates that did not think very highly of him were there.

"What's up, Maurice? What's up, Jimmy?" Alex said when he showed up at the party at The Mansion. "What's happening?"

They had small talk for about a minute when Alex started in. "Listen, I'm going to have some people over in my suite at the Sheraton Waterside tonight around seven," he said. "Nothing heavy, just some good food and an open bar. Something intimate for people I'm cool with. A couple of doctors I know in Hampton Roads and a few other business associates will come through, too.

"Let me know if you need a ride. I have a limo for the weekend. You know, in New York, I don't drive. I have a driver most of the time. It's just too hectic to be behind the wheel when I have to be wheeling and dealing. Things are going great for me, man. You should come up to New York for a weekend. I have a lot of connections up there—and you know New York is the center of the world.

"Lot of people wouldn't be able to make it up there. It's a beast. But my thing has just taken off. Shoot, I have forty-seven employees now and I opened an office in Atlanta. I picked Atlanta because I have a loft down there and it's a good place to do business. I thought of doing something in Norfolk, but not enough is happening here."

Alex said all that seemingly without taking a pause to breathe. He was short in college, grew some as he got older; enough to be considered a small guy with small-man syndrome. But apparently when the Napoleon complex sets in, it does not leave, even if you grow to average height.

"Yeah, I'm happy for you, Alex," Jimmy said. "One of the great things about homecoming is to learn how people are doing. And the way I see it, the way things are in this world, if you are em-ployed, have solid mental and physical health and some values, you're successful—no matter how much money you make."

"Yeah, because you can't judge happiness with money," Maurice added. "We've got to do what we've got to do to be happy. But we're all proud of what you've done with your life. It's good stuff, great stuff."

"Yeah, man, you're right," Alex said. "I try to tell people that all the time. I might be a millionaire, but it's not the money that makes me."

Maurice and Jimmy glanced at each other.

"I have flown around the world probably seven times," Alex went on. "I have three houses and the loft in Atlanta and three cars—even though I hardly drive anymore because I have a driver. But what makes me happy is my family. My brothers, son, nephew, niece and uncle all work for me. Through my company I'm able to provide jobs for my family. That's what I feel good about."

Jimmy wanted to say, *Get away from me*. Instead, he asked, "Are you married?"

"Hell, no," Alex said. "Married? Man, the one girl I was inter-ested in marrying—and she was *bad*, too, a dime—didn't want to sign a prenup. She must have been crazy to think I was gonna put her in a position to get half of my company, what I have built, my millions? NO way. She said it was unromantic to ask her to sign a prenup. I said look at some of these celebrities and how much they end up losing in divorce.

"So, I'm just doing me. I really don't know if a woman is interested in me or interested in my money. So I've got to be careful."

Before leaving to bore others from his college days, Alex hit Jimmy and Maurice with the bombshell.

"Listen, I haven't announced it yet, but I'm thinking about running for president," he said.

"Of what?" Jimmy cracked.

"The United States," Alex answered.

"What political experience do you have?" Maurice said.

"Donald Trump was thinking about running; he didn't have any political experience," Alex answered. "Ross Perot ran and he didn't have any experience. Look at Herman Cain. He was leading before all his dirty laundry got exposed. He's like my blueprint. He led a large company to financial success. That's all his credentials consisted of. I did the same thing. You don't have to have experience in the political arena. You have to have ideas and knowledge and money—and I have all that."

It was bad enough that he bragged about his success and exaggerated his wealth. But to think Jimmy and Maurice were foolish enough to believe he was even capable of running a campaign for the Presidency was downright insulting.

"I gotta be honest," Jimmy said to Maurice and Eula, who had returned from the bathroom, "if this guy thinks I believe he would run for President, then he's even more fucked up than I thought—excuse my language, Eula. I mean, he can't speak intelligently about himself, so how can he possibly... I don't even want to say it, it's so damn dumb. He's insulting our intelligence by saying something so preposterous."

"What's wrong with him?" Maurice said.

"Why can't he run for President if he wants to, if he's capable?" Eula chimed in.

"Baby, you have to know the guy," Maurice said. "Think about your friend Lucy from Long Island. She's successful, but many times you've told me she's hardly a genius. She reminds me of him. So, if I told you there was nothing wrong with Lucy running for president, you would cuss me out."

"I might, but maybe they would surprise us. Look at George W. Bush. He wasn't the sharpest knife in the drawer," Eula said.

"There's no comparison. Bush was governor of Texas. He had a pedigree," Maurice said. "On top of that, I know this guy. And *you* know Lucy. They belong in the same egotistical, inferiority complex camp. Plus, he's just talking, trying to impress. I actually believe he's smart enough to know his limitations. He just doesn't think *we* know his limitations."

"Maybe you're hating on him," Eula said.

Jimmy looked at Maurice and could sense the tension building up in him. He had seen that look before. Maurice actually got suspended from school for being at the center of a brawl in the cafeteria. It seemed someone challenged his manhood by suggesting his girlfriend was sleeping around on him with some guy who was considered a geek. Maurice and his roommate took on three guys, knocking over tables, sending girls screaming.

This wasn't the infamous food fight in the café that left dozens of people doused in mashed potatoes and gravy. This was a straight-up brawl. Jimmy found himself pulling Maurice off one guy whose nose was bloodied in the skirmish. When the campus police arrived on the scene, Maurice admitted he threw the first punch to start the fracas.

All that came to mind when he saw the expression on his face following his wife's comment. So he did the smart thing. He excused himself.

"I'm going to the bar," he said. "Can I get you all something?"

"Yes," Maurice said. "Please get me some 'Hater-ade.' And get Eula some Kool-Aid."

He smiled and wrapped his arms around his wife, showing growth and an ability to laugh at himself that was not there in college. Jimmy had not seen his classmates in so long that he did not realize that most people—while they are the same at the core—grew into different people.

He was expecting an eruption from Maurice but instead got a touching moment that showed his sense of humor and love for his wife. His act even drew a smile from her, her first showing of teeth since arriving. It was a beautiful smile, one that reminded Jimmy of his wife Monica's smile.

And for a brief moment, he wished she were there. She would have appreciated the nice venue and the great music. She also might even have appreciated seeing him so excited about seeing old friends—some he had even forgotten about over the years.

But that moment was fleeting. He knew Monica well enough to know that her trust issues would arise when they need not. In Eula's case, Maurice explained that she had been married before to a creep, a man who had taken her kindness as the green light to break her trust. More than twice information was revealed to her that he had been with other women. It tarnished her outlook on men in particular, people in general. In one case, his mistress was an old girlfriend. Her ex-husband told her it was "nothing. We're just comfortable with each other. It was just sex." She was astonished he did not see the gravity of his actions.

But she was in love and wanted her marriage, so she gave him another chance. With it, he eventually got involved with one of her friends. Amazingly, she told Eula, "It was just sex. He loves you."

She could not get beyond the betrayal and moved forward with the idea that anyone is capable of anything. Maurice caught hell proving his commitment to her, to the point where his friends hardly saw him—unless he was with her.

"I'm just trying to keep the peace," he said.

His peace-keeping showed a strength he had not displayed in college. And it impressed Jimmy.

"You're better than me," he said when they connected just before leaving the party. "You handled that situation well. Even bringing her with you, although I know it hasn't been good so far, that says a lot about you. I hope she appreciates that."

"No, she doesn't," he said. "But she won't be coming again. I can see this will be the weekend from hell. I'll survive it. We'll survive it. But I feel like any move I make, she's examining and trying to put together stuff that's not even there. I haven't even seen anyone I messed with in college."

"Well, at least she's talking to you," Jimmy said. "My wife, Monica, won't even answer the phone when I call. The one time she did, she basically hung up on me. So I'm in the doghouse. But that's for when I get back. While I'm here, I'm going to have a good time."

"I bet you are because I saw Regina—your old girl—just a minute ago," Maurice said.

"Carter told me the same thing," Jimmy said. "Where is she?"

"And she looked damn good, too," Maurice said, looking around. "She has on an orange top… Look, over there, on the dance floor. That's her."

Jimmy focused in as if he had telescopic vision. That was his college sweetheart, all right. Regina Anderson.

Carter came over just as Maurice and Eula departed. "Where are they going?" Carter asked Jimmy.

"Probably back to the room so she could kick Maurice's ass," Jimmy joked. "Can't believe how calm he is. That's good to see."

"It's because he was a damn wild man back in the day," Carter said. "But we all grow up. Well, some of us do."

"So, how is Barbara?" Jimmy asked.

"I don't know," Carter said. "I mean, she's cool. But she's looking for me to make her feel better about her situation and I can't do that."

"Why not?" Jimmy said. "You made her feel like she had a

future with you. Now that she's set it up, you go left on her? How you think she's supposed to feel?"

"She should have asked me or at least told me what was on her mind," Carter said. "I would have discouraged her from doing it."

"I understand her getting a divorce if she's not happy. And knowing her, the guilt was too much," Jimmy said. "But I don't get her moving across country, moving her kids away from their father. That's the really tough thing about a divorce. Not just going through it, but when there are kids involved, how that plays out."

"It's probably too late, because she's already taken a new job," Carter said. "But I will bring that up to her. From what she said, he was a bad husband but a good dad. So those kids need to be around him. And he needs to be around them."

"She probably just did it because she believed you might try to talk her out of it," Jimmy said. "You never know. Women are crafty. They are manipulators by trade. They have mastered that.

"Look, you told me you loved the woman. You told me it was real. You told me that was the main reason you came down here to homecoming. So if it is all that, then why all the bitching right now?"

"I ain't bitching," he said. "I'm just not ready for her to be in New York while I'm there. I feel like she left for me, and that makes me responsible for her happiness."

"Who you think you fooling?" Jimmy said. "You have a girlfriend and you don't want things to get messy with Barbara there. At some point soon, you're going to have to figure it all out. But it doesn't have to be this weekend. It's homecoming. Have some fun."

"Yeah, you're right," Carter said. "My head has been messed up ever since she told me that. But I'm cool. I—we—will figure it out."

"Good. Go get the girl a drink—damn, we've been drinking a lot—and make her feel good," Jimmy said. "I'm gonna wait here for Regina to get off the dance floor."

"And what you gonna do with that?" Carter wanted to know.

"Nothing," Jimmy said quickly but with a devilish look on his face. "I'm a happily married man. Well, I'm not so happy right now, but in general, I'm happy."

"Yeah, well, if I'm not mistaken, someone said Regina has been divorced for about two years," Carter said.

"Damn, everyone we've been to school with has been divorced," Jimmy said. "That's a trip."

"Man, that's a reality of life," Carter said. "I learned that from just looking at my family. Now I see it in my friends. As much as I knew Barbara was in love with me, I believed she would stay in her marriage. And that made me want her—because I just knew I couldn't get her."

"Well, seems like now you don't want the woman you always wanted," Jimmy said. "And that's crazy."

CHAPTER NINE

SMOKEY AND THE BANDITS

Jesse, Venita and Don

"The Richmond Three," as they called themselves, did as they always did when they got to homecoming. They checked into their hotel, the Courtyard by Marriott in downtown Norfolk: Jesse and Don in one room; Venita in her own on the same floor. They liked the nice rooms, the good rate and its central location.

After getting settled in their room, Don and Jesse made their way to Venita's. There, she pulled out a Ziploc bag half-full of marijuana. It was time to get their smoke on.

"Dumb-ass cops," Don said.

"They were troopers," Jesse said.

"Whatever, they were some dumb-ass racists who were looking for weed but couldn't find it," Don said.

They had hidden the drugs in the side panel of the passenger door, like always. As veterans of the road and as those know-ledgeable of cops or troopers, they knew to save their smoking until they reached their destination. And they knew to hide it some place that was not obvious to a police officer pulling them over on a traffic stop.

Jesse knew that if they were suspected major drug dealers, the officials would have stripped the car down to its bare minimum to find what they believed was hidden there. But state troopers—

even ones with no real reason to stop drivers—would not go so deep as unscrewing the bolts on the doors of the car.

Once, when stopped, they were petrified because the troopers had one of those sniffing dogs in the backseat. Luckily for them, they did not call on him at that time. The dog would have gone straight to the passenger side door and they would have been arrested for possession of marijuana.

They rationalized their pot smoking as something done purely to free their minds. The everyday demands of work, home life, and family took its toll, and marijuana, they contended, allowed them to safely escape all that drama.

And every time they got high during homecoming, they felt a need to express why—or why everyone should be, too.

"If we were in California," Jesse said, after receiving the first joint from Venita. He took a puff, held it in and finally let it out, and then continued. "We could go to a store, a depository, and purchase it. All you have to do is get permission from a doctor to say you need it for medicinal purposes.

"Listen, it's a whole new, multimillion-dollar industry. Marijuana is legal in fifteen states. In Cali, it's crazy right now. What you get from the depositories is the purest form of weed. It has to have a certain amount of strands and basically pass a bunch of FDA standards before they put it on the shelves.

"I learned this from my cousin out there in Oakland. He has permission to grow marijuana. Don't know how he got it, but he does. He gave me the whole scoop on it. He told me they produce marijuana to attack all kinds of ailments, like cataracts, high blood pressure, heart conditions; you name it."

"Well, I need to move out there, then. I'll never understand why alcohol is legal but weed isn't in most places," Venita said. "Think about it: people get DUIs because of consuming too much liquor. When have you heard of someone speeding or crashing or even driving recklessly because of marijuana?"

"Exactly," Don interjected. "You don't have to speed when you're already high. You're so relaxed and mellow, you're not looking for some speed trip. I'm not sure the lawmakers understand. Weed puts you in a better place sometimes."

"Shit, they understand that," Jesse said. "You think I'm the only lawyer that gets high? You don't think judges and police officers get high? And schoolteachers and politicians? Well, just in case you didn't know, they do. Their jobs require them to do one thing. But outside of work, they getting their smoke on, too. Lots and lots of them."

The joint made its way to Don, who practically made love to it. Meanwhile, Venita rolled a second one.

"Well, after we're done here, I'm going to take a nap," Jesse said. "There's a jazz concert tonight as part of homecoming at the Wilder Center on campus. The lineup looks great."

"I'm getting with my friend Bert. He lost his girlfriend, Ladina Stevens, after last year's homecoming," Don said. "We hung out that Friday night, had drinks, laughs. She seemed great. Then, a few months later, she was gone. Breast cancer. It's amazing. A good girl. Never even knew she was sick."

"I remember Ladina," Venita said. "I liked her. She used to work at the bank when we were in school. She was young, probably forty-five or so. I was really sorry to hear that. It really scares me that people I know are dying so young. Burying my cousin two months ago at thirty-one for kidney failure was just horrible."

"I know it was, but please, don't start crying," Don said. "You get a buzz and the next thing are tears. Whether happy or sad, but tears will flow."

"Forget you, Don," Venita said. "That ain't even true."

"Actually, it is," Jesse said. "Last year, remember you cried when we saw an accident on 264?"

"It was a bad accident, Jesse," she said. "I think someone died."

"You don't even know that," Don said. "The weed just took you there. Some people can't handle their liquor and get all rowdy and loud. You get high and everything makes you cry."

"Don't be mad because I'm connected to my emotional side, Don," she said. "You are so detached from anything that requires you to tap into your feelings. So you can't relate."

"You're right," he said. "I ain't into all the crying. A man has nothing to cry about other than death. That's it. Movies, a sad story, tears of joy? *Please.*"

"That's real cave man talk, Don," Venita said. "You're telling me that you should only cry because of death?"

"Yes," Don said immediately. "Other than that, you've got to go on and do what you've got to do. Am I right, Jess?"

Jesse wanted to back him up, the way women do other women all the time, no matter what the argument. And if they were in a big group, he would have. But he was with two of his closest friends. So he gave it to his boy raw.

"Not only are you not right, but you're dead wrong," Jesse said.

"Thank you!" Venita yelled.

"What?" Don said.

"Let me explain, D," Jesse added. "I'm as manly and macho as the next guy. And I know that shedding a tear about something does not make or break my manhood. You've got to get beyond thinking not crying makes you a man."

"Preach," Venita chimed in.

Jesse puffed on the joint and passed it to Don. "I don't necessarily cry at movies or anything off the cuff," Jesse continued. "But I know I have a heart and some things move me more than others.

This is funny. I don't know why, but when I got my first job after graduating, when I lived in Dumfries, I used to watch *Little House on the Prairie* on one of those cable channels. And I'll be damned if the calamities that happened to little Laura Ingalls didn't make me cry. I don't know why, but it did. I was at home alone watching. If someone else, especially a woman, was with me I would have fought those tears back. But, at home alone, I let them flow."

"Hey, I don't mean no harm, but you might be wearing pink thongs," Don joked and they all laughed.

"Okay, you like movies, Don," Jesse said. "And I know you recently rented *Hotel Rwanda*. Are you telling me that the scene when Don Cheadle falls out of the van at night and discovers dozens and dozens of bodies on the roadside didn't move you? If you didn't cry, you fought back the tears. No way any human who has a heart could watch that scene and not be horrified."

"I was horrified," Don said. "It was a very moving scene. But there was no need to cry. Why?"

"Because you related to that moment and felt bad that something so awful could happen to someone," Venita said. "That's why. I saw that scene and I was bawling."

"Well, we know you were—and, as a woman, that's okay. It's expected," Don said. "But as a man, you take the scene for what it's worth and you move on."

"That's pretty cold, Don," she said. "I never knew that about you, that you were not in touch with your emotions."

"That's just it—I *am* in touch with my emotions," Don said. "And my emotions are to feel a certain way about something, but I don't have to cry about it. Real men don't cry."

"What, you saying I ain't a real man?" Jesse said.

"I'm saying you probably have some lipstick in your pocket," Don answered, and they again burst into laughter.

"Yeah, well, I bet you'd cry if someone you consider not to be a real man kicks your ass," Jesse said.

"What you gonna do? Scratch my eyes out? Hit me upside the head with your purse?" Don cracked.

"See, you're stupid," Jesse said.

"And hopeless," Venita said. "And Jesse, I'm proud of you for admitting that. It takes a real man to do that."

"Yeah, well, say what you want," Don said. "I know me and I know I'm a man."

"No one said you aren't a man," Jesse said. "I'm saying don't put silly boundaries on what a man is. If you think you can't be considered a real man because you can get emotional about something, that's just stupid."

"Just pass the joint," Don said.

"Forget him, Jesse," Venita said. "I wanted to go to one of the day parties. But I guess I'll just get with Charles for a late lunch/early dinner."

"Charles White? Your old boyfriend?" Don asked. "Now that's not something your husband would be happy with."

"Well, my husband ain't here," she said. "And we're just going to eat and talk. Ain't nothing else going down."

"Yeah, right," Jesse said. "Really, you could talk to him on the phone and see him on the Yard. You don't have to have dinner with him. I'm just saying. If someone you know saw you and him having dinner, what do you think they would think? What would your husband think if he walked in and saw you?"

"My husband is at home," Venita said. "And I understand what you're saying. But friends should be able to get together—especially old friends—and have a meal and that's it. Since I control what I do, that will be it."

"I hear you and I believe you," Jesse said. "But here's my question:

Would you be okay with your husband going out tonight for dinner with an old girlfriend? Even if he planned to just eat and talk?"

"Well, if I didn't know about it, then fine," she said. "I don't know what else to say. If I knew about it, then there'd be a problem. If he called me and said, 'Baby, I'm going to dinner tonight with Alice, my ex-girlfriend from college.' I wouldn't be comfortable with that."

"But you're doing the same thing," Don interjected. "If it's good for you, it should be good for him."

"It actually should be good for both of them—if they trust each other," Jesse said.

"Ah, hell—Jesse is high, so he's about to become the great philosopher," Don said.

"Listen up and you might learn something," Jesse said. "Here's my thing: If you all are in a trusting relationship, you should be able to connect with an old friend and it not be that big a deal. But you don't trust your husband, Venita, and he doesn't trust you, based on what you said.

"And please don't give me that nonsense, 'I trust him, but I don't trust the woman.' It's all about what he wants to do. If he's gonna honor your marriage, that chick can get butt-naked and he would throw her a towel and walk out the door. It shouldn't matter what she wants. What he does—or you do—is all it's about."

"Yeah, well, in theory, that sounds good," Venita said. "But we know the reality: If I woman wants to get a man in bed, he's going to get weak. He might fight it a little. But the bottom line is that he'll be right there doing what he knows he shouldn't be doing."

"And women are more disciplined than men?" Jesse said. "You might believe that based on what women tell you. But I know of women that you know who have been quietly doing their dirt.

They just don't tell you they are. They do it like the commando team that killed Bin Laden. They go under the cover of darkness, quiet like a stealth and do their damage."

Jesse was six months from divorce of his wife of less than three years. His friends avoided bringing that up as long as they could.

"So, since you're Mr. Sensitivity and Mr. Morals," Don said, "let me ask you a few questions: Did you cry when your wife left you? And did she leave you because she didn't trust you?"

Jesse was still bruised by the divorce. He had dated Nadine six months and then reunited with her two years later. They'd had a whirlwind courtship, traveling often and generally enjoying each other. After a year, they were married, but Jesse went in hoping the trust issues that floated in the back of his mind would dissolve.

He had trust issues because Nadine was married when they had dated the second time around. Unhappily married, but married nonetheless. She explained her position and he made a decision to date her because he believed she would do as she said and leave her husband. And she did.

But before leaving, she was deceitful to her husband to spend time with him. She would say she was one place, but be with him. She would call or text-message him while he was in her presence or nearby. She would come by his house, cook him dinner, have sex with him and then rush home to her husband—all the while her cell phone would be constantly ringing.

At first, it made Jesse feel good. He really enjoyed Nadine and her willingness to jeopardize her marriage showed him that she was serious about a relationship with him.

Then, late one night, around two, as he and Nadine lay in his bed, Jesse's doorbell rang. Then there was loud knocking. She looked out the window to see her husband's car. He had gotten her phone bill and noticed the inordinate amount of calls to Jesse's number. Through some Internet system, he was able to get an address to that number—Jesse's house. When he pulled up to see his wife's car in his driveway, he was furious.

Jesse's chest swelled and he wanted to confront Nadine's husband. But she pleaded for him to not go to the door. "Nothing good can come from that," she had said.

It was that scenario that Jesse began to understand the magnitude of dealing with someone else's wife. He started to feel less enthusiastic about his future with Nadine. Worse, he began to question the person she was. After all, she was married, and yet she spent so much time with him that he almost forgot she had a husband.

She was so bold that she went out of town with Jesse—twice—and even demanded that he not see any other women. He did date, but his heart was with Nadine.

Soon after the doubts crept in, she moved out of the house with her husband and filed for divorce, easing Jesse's mind about her commitment to him. Though there were various other trust concerns—from both sides—they married nonetheless. But love could not hold them together.

Simply, Jesse did not trust Nadine. He told his friends that they divorced because "there was just too much drama. Every other day there was something. I couldn't please her," he said. "All the little drama situations added up to one big problem that I didn't want to deal with anymore."

And while that was the truth, he could not bring himself to share with his boys the biggest factor: he did not trust her. He witnessed too many occasions where she was corresponding with men, inappropriate things that made him question himself as to why he did not walk away at the first sight of infidelity.

Love was his answer. And hope. But those elements could not override the continual dishonoring of him and the marriage. So he did the strong thing. He left.

"Did I cry when I left my wife—let's get that part straight," Jesse said. "No, I didn't. I was hurt. It was a bad time for me. But I've never cried over a woman. I don't think there's anything wrong with you if that's where you go with it. I just felt deflated.

"And, no, I would not trust her to go to dinner with an ex-boyfriend. Would I trust any woman to see an ex; I would hope so. It's really about the person I'm dealing with at that time. My ex-wife is a great person, but she is not trustworthy. So I couldn't and wouldn't cry over someone who didn't understand the value I brought to her life or who would disrespect me as she did with other men.

"To be honest, I have had to forgive myself for continuing to deal with her after learning some things. She says she didn't sleep with anyone. But I didn't believe her. And there were two ex-boyfriends who she'd never take a call from while I was around and I saw comments from her to various men that were out of line."

Don handed Jesse a Heineken. "I didn't know it was that bad," Venita said. "When you don't have trust, you can't have a relationship. I do trust my husband. I do. But I ain't stupid, either. While I'm here for homecoming, he'll be at home doing whatever it is he does when I ain't there. I guess all you can really ask is that he's responsible, don't bring any drama into our house, no diseases—and that I don't find out."

They laughed.

"But here's the thing," Venita added. "When your wife did what she did, it was the end of your world, right? You were devastated. *Men.* I'm not saying it wasn't horrible or anything. It was. But women have had to deal with y'all's crap forever. And you men just expect it to run off our backs and for us to keep moving, forgive you and be okay with it. Not all men, but it still amazes me that when I woman does what men have been doing since the beginning of time that the woman is looked at as this awful person unworthy of you.

"There's something wrong with that. That's what's been the norm in how people look at that; that's how men look at it. And I hate that double standard."

"It never fails," Don said. "We get here for homecoming and start tooting and the next thing you know we're in some really deep conversations. I thought we're here to have a good time."

"Nah, this is a good time," Jesse said. "We're going to get our drink and our party on; you know that. It's good to exercise your brain a little bit, too, with people you love and respect."

"Oh, boy, Jesse's getting ready to cry," Don joked.

"Kiss my ass, fat boy," Jesse said.

Venita laughed. "Okay, get out of my room—the both of you. I will catch up with you later at the jazz concert. You behave between now and then."

"We will if you will," Don said, with a smile and raised eyebrow.

CHAPTER TEN
MAY I HAVE YOUR ATTENTION, PLEASE?

Tranise, Brandon and Kwame

Tranise received more attention in an afternoon than she'd had in the last year in Atlanta. It made her feel good—and conflicted.

She only fantasized about one unattainable man in her life; Denzel didn't count. Brandon Barksdale aroused her interest not just because he was a good-looking man (although that certainly helped). She admired the way he was with people. She did not know him, but she certainly paid close attention to him and his actions and demeanor whenever they were in the same room.

"I like the way he makes everyone around him feel good," she had told Mary back when they were in school.

Other men might have sparked an interest; Brandon struck a chord.

Even as she socialized at the bar with Kwame, she occasionally glanced across the room to see Brandon mingling or dancing. Kwame, an apparent catch in his own right, did not know what distracted Tranise, but he knew something was there.

"So," Kwame said to her, "here you are at homecoming, looking great and standing here with this great guy—if I'm allowed to say that about myself—who is very interested in you, has had a crush on you since he was a kid…and your mind seems to be somewhere else. I don't know how to take that."

"Oh, no, I'm sorry," she said. "I'm not distracted. I'm just a little overwhelmed. This is my first homecoming since I graduated, and I had no idea how warm it would feel. Seeing old friends and old faces has brought me back in time and has made me feel good."

"That's a great thing," Kwame said. "I can tell already I'll be returning every year. It kind of validates the beauty of going to an HBCU.

"I actually was going to go to the University of Virginia. I got accepted. My parents wanted me to go there. It was expensive, but I got some scholarship money. But you know what sold me on Norfolk State?"

Tranise sipped her cocktail. "What?"

"I was a senior in high school and I came over to Norfolk State for the Battle of the Bay against Hampton," he said. "The game was sold out. The tailgate was amazing. It was like homecoming, there were so many people. The sprit in the air was so festive. I just felt at home.

"I visited Virginia—beautiful campus. Great school. But I didn't quite feel like I did at Norfolk State. It was like the school wrapped its arms around me and hugged me. My cousin, Mike, told me that was the same way he felt when he got to Norfolk State. It's something about the HBCU experience that gives you the feeling of family. We know family can get on your nerves and be a pain in the butt. But we also know family loves you. And in the end, you can rely on your family."

Listening to Kwame made Tranise look at him differently. The way he crafted his statements, the thought he put into his expressions…she saw something in him. He wasn't just talking. He was *expressing* himself. Big difference.

"I couldn't agree more," Tranise said. "I can't believe I haven't been back in five years. But the one good thing about it is being away so long and now being back has made me really appreciate it so much more—the education, the friendships, the experiences. This was home when I really turned from a teenager into a woman."

"You have done just that," Kwame said with a coy smile. "So, you don't have a man waiting for you in Atlanta?" he asked.

Even the way he asked her that made an impression on Tranise. It was strong but not aggressive.

"I'm sure there is somebody there for me, but I haven't met him yet," she said, smiling.

"Well, that means the men down there are not doing their jobs," Kwame responded with no hesitation. "I don't understand it. Are you some undercover psycho or something? Why wouldn't you have a man? I'm glad you don't. But I still don't quite get it."

Tranise had asked herself the same thing more than twice. The men who crossed her path wore an arrogance that she did not appreciate—or would not tolerate. It was as if being in Atlanta spoiled them. The numbers were what they were: women with something going for themselves outnumbered men in the same category by leaps and bounds. And there were enough women who would accept a man who was short of what he should be because they preferred to not be alone.

Tranise was not that way. She preferred her dignity over a warm body. So, when men approached her with too much aggression and too little chivalry, she was turned off immediately. And she had no problem letting them know it, either.

"I had to tell this one guy, 'Excuse me, but I'm not pressed for a man. You seem to think I need you in some way. Wrong.' He looked at me and said, 'No problem. Women are a dime a dozen in Atlanta. I ain't pressed, either.' Then he walked away."

"Are you serious?" Kwame said. "Guys are that rude down there?"

"I would never say all guys," Tranise said. "I can say I have met more than enough of them. And every time I get so pissed because it's insulting. It's like they're saying, 'Take me with all my arrogance and flaws because if you don't, someone else will.' I'm a nice woman. I am. But that gets me going."

"I believe you," Kwame said, smiling. He put his hands on both her shoulders. "Don't get riled up. You look too good to have steam coming out of your nose. You handled those guys the way they needed to be handled. As much as we'd like to, we can't account for everyone's actions. You gotta just pray for them."

"Pray?" she said.

"Yes. I'm serious," Kwame said. "I visited a church in New Jersey one time: First Baptist Church of Lincoln Gardens in New Brunswick, I believe. The pastor said, 'When you pray for those that anger you, it lifts the burden off of you and places it back on them.' I tried it and it works."

Tranise was more intrigued. She was having a real conversation with a man, a conversation of substance. It had been so long that she did not quite recall when it was or whom it was with.

"So, don't you know I'm four years older than you?" she said. "Why aren't you with ladies your age?"

"You don't remember me telling you I had a crush on you from way back, when I met you when I was in high school?" he said. "At that time, I was sixteen, maybe seventeen, I think. You were probably twenty, twenty-one. Age mattered then. I knew I couldn't get anywhere with you if I had the nerve to even say something.

"But I'm just about to turn twenty-two. Age matters much less, if at all—at least as far as I'm concerned. I'm ready for you now."

He smiled the brightest smile she had seen in some time. It was like he amused himself while totally serious. Or that he said something daring, something he wanted to say for years, and he delighted in it.

"You don't really know that," Tranise said. Her smile was bright, too. "As a matter of fact, what do you mean you're 'ready for me now'?"

"I am very clear about that," Kwame started. "I'm ready in the sense that I understand a woman's needs, how to treat her. And I understand who I am, what I can offer a woman. When I saw you when I was in high school, I was just, you know, taken by how you looked. Talking to you now gives me a better sense of who you are. So far, I like you—and want to get to know you better. I'm ready now to hold up my end of a conversation. That's where it all starts. Conversing."

Tranise smiled again. He showed a lot in that statement. One of her pet peeves, especially as a middle school teacher was the use of proper English. She cringed every time she heard someone say, "conversate," as if it were a word, instead of "converse."

She was interested in Kwame. He had a youthful exuberance but did not necessarily look younger than her. But there was an age difference that Tranise did not want to overlook.

And Kwame sensed it. "You're not old enough to be a cougar—and there aren't enough years between us, either," he said. "I saw the movie, *Jumping the Broom*. We're not like those two characters. The older we get, the more age makes less of a difference."

He had a point, but Tranise knew admitting it would relinquish any advantage she had with the young man. "I like the idea of conversing," she said. "What could it hurt?"

"And it could help a lot," he said, smiling.

Before Tranise could respond, she felt the presence of someone behind her. She turned, looked up and saw the smiling face of Brandon, her personal heartthrob.

"Hey, I was just saying good-bye before I leave," Brandon said to Tranise. She was flustered and looked at him.

Kwame introduced himself. He was a little taken aback at first. But then he saw Brandon's wedding ring and relaxed, so much so that he excused himself to go to the bathroom.

Brandon slid into Kwame's position. Tranise gathered herself.

"I heard you married Felicia," she said. The alcohol made her more daring and she just put it out there.

"Yes, you know my wife?" he said.

"I do know her. I haven't seen her in a long time, but we met when we were freshmen," she said.

"So, you know she's pregnant, too?" he said.

"When is she due?" Tranise wanted to know.

"January," he said. "About three more months to go. I'll be glad when that baby pops out. Being pregnant has turned Felicia into a, uh, a…"

"I can only imagine," Tranise threw in.

"Are you being sarcastic?" Brandon said.

"A little," she answered.

"Why?" he wanted to know.

"Well," she started, "your wife and I did not get along in college. In fact, we were like archrivals."

"Oh, my God," Brandon said. "You are the woman she was talking about with so much venom? What happened? You seem harmless to me."

"I *am* harmless," she said. Then she decided to flirt. "Well, I used to be harmless. Now, well, I can show out when I want to."

"So what makes you want to show out?" Brandon said. He picked up on Tranise's flirtation.

"You're a married man," she said. "You don't want to know."

"That could be the reason I really *need* to know," he said.

Tranise smiled. She was having a suggestive back-and-forth with the one man she always admired. It was hard to believe.

"We'll see, I guess," she said. She didn't mean it. Well, she didn't *really* mean it. She abandoned her early thoughts of stepping into the land of a "bad girl" and seducing Brandon as a way of fulfilling a fantasy and earning some level of revenge against her nemesis, Felicia. But talking to Brandon reopened the door on that possibility.

"I guess we will," Brandon said.

Their eyes met for an extended period. Tranise almost had to shake herself out of the mini-trance she could feel herself slipping into.

"Well, you'd better get away from me before someone tells your wife you were talking to me—and flirting with me," Tranise said.

He smiled. "I'm not sure I was the one flirting, but OK," he said. "She actually should be here any minute. She's not coming in, though; she's just picking me up out front. But before I go, you never told me what the problem was between you and her. You seem like a lovely young lady. She's a lovely young lady. I don't get it."

"Well, you have to ask your wife about that," she said. "I'm sure she'll be glad to share with you. I'm surprised she hasn't already."

"It's weird because she made these general comments that led me to believe she didn't like you and you didn't like her," he said. "But she never said what happened."

"What are you doing tonight?" she said. Immediately, she knew it sounded too suggestive, so she cleaned it up.

"You going to the jazz concert on campus?" she added.

"I might," he said, reaching into his pocket. "Felicia said she's not feeling so well today, so I might be out solo. Here's my card. My cell number is on there. Just text me and let me know where you'll be. Maybe we can connect."

"Sounds like a plan," Tranise said as Kwame returned from the bathroom. He and Brandon shook hands before Brandon headed to the exit.

"I thought about you the whole time I was gone," Kwame said to Tranise, making her blush.

"The whole five minutes?" she responded.

"Seemed longer," Kwame said.

"I see you have a verbal gift," Tranise told Kwame.

"That's hard to say," he said. "I think it's more accurate to say that when inspired, the right words come into my head to express what I'm feeling. That's the best way to put it."

Even with that explanation, he charmed Tranise, whose ego was massaged more than she could have hoped for—and homecoming was just beginning.

"So what are you doing the rest of the weekend?" she asked Kwame. "You're so young, you're probably going to the school's homecoming concert in the gym."

Kwame was hardly fazed by her attempt to fluster him. "I might," he said. "I look at it as a positive that I relate to the college student and the more mature world away from school. I take that to mean I'm diverse."

"Good attitude," Tranise conceded. "Good attitude."

"Positive over negative—that was the mantra that my psychology professor at Norfolk State taught me," he said. "And I have been practicing it ever since. And it works. I read somewhere it takes seventeen muscles to smile and forty-seven muscles to frown. And I associate smiling with positive and frowning with negative. So you won't see me frowning often."

A man with a rosy outlook on life… Tranise became even more intrigued. And she was intrigued by Brandon, her teenage crush.

"Girl, this is so crazy," she told Mary when they finally left the party. "I haven't been this popular since I ran for homecoming queen."

"Well, you're not up for Homecoming Slut," Mary said, and she and Tranise laughed long and hard, so much so that Charlene felt left out when she rejoined her crew.

When told of Mary's comment, Charlene bumped into a passer-by as she fell back laughing.

"I could see from the dance floor that she was getting a lot of attention," Charlene said. "I guess that's what happens when you come back to school after five years with some titties and ass for the first time in your life."

And the three friends again laughed.

CHAPTER ELEVEN
THE AFTERMATH

Catherine and Earl

The morning after they made love for the first time, Catherine and Earl did it again before Catherine left the hotel to go home and then to work. It was another passionate experience that further strengthened their bond.

When he walked her to her car, they embraced and kissed deeply. Earl had not been moved to be so outwardly affectionate. But Catherine touched parts of his heart that no one else had.

It was no wonder that he was floating as she drove off. He showered quickly and got dressed in his golf gear so he could be ready when old classmate, Warren Jones, picked him up. They had competed in the Norfolk State Alumni Golf Outing the year before. This time, they and a group of friends decided to play a round at The Signature in Virginia Beach.

They all graduated around the time Earl did and were friends of varying degrees; nice guys that settled into their lives but remained lively and playful. All of them knew Catherine; none of them knew she and Earl was a couple. He was itching to let them know because he was so proud of what they had built over the summer. But he also liked surprises, and all those guys would be at homecoming's biggest and best event, the Best of Friends party Saturday night. That would be their coming-out party.

In the meantime, Earl kept in his exciting news and played golf all day with a smile on his face and in his heart. Never before had he reacted to a bad shot with a grin, but because he loved Catherine, his wayward golf shots mattered less. Even in the breezy and cool morning air, Earl carried a warm feeling.

"What you smiling about?" Bob White, one of his playing partners, said after the first hole. "You just took a double bogey."

"I'm good," Earl said. "We're just getting started."

That attitude helped him hold it together when he usually lacked patience. Instead of sharing the news, he engineered lighthearted banter that started the group to reminisce.

"Jack," he said to the fourth member of his group, "whatever happened to Alana Steele?"

Alana and Jack had comprised one of those always-together couples in college. Some students wondered if they ever went to class. They always seemed to be walking the vast campus, hand-in-hand.

"It's funny you ask about her because I haven't seen her in about twelve, thirteen years," Jack said. Jack was a notorious womanizer, a super-confident former baseball player of significant charisma and humor. "She called me out of the blue about a week or two ago. I told her straight up: Let's get a room at homecoming and do it like it was old times."

"She was like, 'Some things never change.' And I told her, 'You know the deal. Why did you call me if that's not what you wanted?' Man, I have to say what I believe. She goes into this whole 'we could be friends' thing. Then she starts talking about I cheated on her in college.

"I said, 'Alana, I'm sorry. But I was a nineteen-year-old kid on a campus full of good-looking women. You can't hold me accountable for that.' She said, 'Yeah, but it still hurt at the time.' You know me. I said, 'That's long over. But we can go back in time if we spend a night together.'

"She said she wasn't going for it, but I don't believe her. She's here. I will get that before I leave this weekend. You can believe that."

They went on to the No. 3 hole—Earl rebounded from the opening hole to make par on the second—and Jack kept going. "Ah, man, let me tell you this crazy story about Alana," he said. "So, back in the day, she tells me she's pregnant. I'm a sophomore without a pot to piss in or a window…you know the saying. So I told her to get the money for an abortion because I didn't have any money.

"She wants to get a second opinion. So we set up an appointment with a doctor. The nurse tells her to bring a urine sample. So, we go and Alana is carrying this big-ass black purse. At the front counter, she pulls out this huge pickle jar full of piss. I stepped back. The nurse was like, "What's that?' Alana says, 'I was told to bring a urine sample.' The nurse says, 'Honey, a sample is a little. You had to pee three or four times to bring this much.'

"I was totally embarrassed. There were people in the waiting area snickering. But the reality is that she didn't know. She was a country girl and to her, a sample meant a whole jar. It was crazy."

Earl and their playing partners fell out laughing. They all had myriad stories and used the five hours on the golf course to share them.

"What about this?" Bob said. "I saw this girl on campus at the bookstore yesterday. I couldn't place her but I knew she went to school with us. Then it hit me. I remembered her very clearly.

"One night my senior year, after a Norfolk State-North Carolina Central game, we were hanging out at my boy, Rick's house over there off of Brambleton. Rick's girl was over there. I think her name was Tasha. We were playing backgammon and drinking and talking shit. Suddenly, Tasha and Rick get in an argument over something silly.

"But Rick was drunk so he smushed her in the face and told her to get out. He went in the kitchen to get another beer and she went in behind him. So, we're just playing the game—I think Mo Mo was playing against me; you remember Mo Mo, Morris Montey, the fool who got arrested for robbing a professor that time? Anyway, Mo Mo and I hear all this commotion in the kitchen. Finally, Rick comes out with his hand over his stomach.

"He says, 'She stabbed me' and moved his hand. There was blood gushing out of this dude's stomach. We're like, 'Damn. What the fuck?' We rush him to Norfolk General Hospital."

'What?" Jack said. "Get the fuck outta here. I remember when he was out of school for a while. But he played football. I thought it was a football injury."

"Nah, dude, Tasha, sliced him," Bob went on. "It took more than a hundred staples to close the wound."

"Damn," Earl said. "She didn't go to jail?"

"No, because Rick wouldn't tell them who did it," Bob answered. "He kept saying he fell. They knew he was lying. But they couldn't prove it… Man, I was scared as shit. I knew he was gonna die. Blood was everywhere."

Earl said, "The sad part was that—what?—six years later Rick died of a heart attack."

"Hold up," Jack said.

"Yep," Earl continued. "He collapsed playing basketball in New York one day. Apparently he had an undetected heart condition."

"Damn, that is sad," Jack said.

Jack said something else, but Earl did not hear him. His cell phone chimed, meaning he had received a text message. Earlier, he had texted Catherine to tell her how much he had enjoyed their time together and how relieved he was to finally tell her how much he loved her. He was awaiting her reply, and that was it.

"Baby, I love you, too. I really do. Last night—and this morning—were amazing. I'm here at work but I'm not getting much accomplished. All I can think about is you. I look forward to dinner tonight. I hope you are kicking butt on the golf course."

Earl smiled as he read it. For more than four months, they sent each other an average of a dozen or so text messages a day. It was their primary source of communication. Their phone conversations were in-depth and critical. But they used text messaging to reaffirm their interest, attraction and to get to know each other.

"What you smiling about?" Jack asked Earl.

"Oh, man, just a text message from my girl," he said. "She's the text messaging queen."

"And that makes you the king then," Bob said. "I don't get the texting thing. Just pick up the phone and call me."

"I was like that too, at first," Earl said. "But if you use it the right way, it can be effective."

"What's the right way?" Warren asked.

"Well, I'm talking about using it to communicate or express your feelings to a woman," he said.

"Express your feelings?" Jack said. "That sounds like some gay stuff to me."

The men laughed.

"You'd better get with the times," Earl said. "If you think you're supposed to go about your business and not express yourself to a woman, then you're a loser. Women need to hear complimentary stuff, too. Or hear that you are thinking about them. I'm telling you, a properly timed text can make a big difference."

"What is 'properly timed'?" Warren wanted to know.

"When it is least expected," Earl said. He was on the tee box at No. 4, about to hit, but decided to deliver a lesson first. He put the tee in the ground and his ball on it, and then turned to his friends.

"I ain't trying to come off as some expert," he said. "I'm just telling you that we were able to grow our relationship over the last several months through expressing ourselves all during the course of the day when we were working and couldn't really pick up the phone and talk.

"So we would text. And so if I text her at two-thirty in the afternoon saying, 'I smiled just now because I thought about you and how I thought I knew you but didn't really at all. What I am learning, though, is better than I expected.' That's a properly timed text. But it's properly timed only because she wasn't expecting it. It's not contrived. I don't sit around and look at the clock to decide the best time to hit her up.

"And I don't make up stuff to make her feel good. The best part about it is the opposite of that. I texted her because I *was* thinking about her. We've got to, as men, stop with the fake macho stuff. You say in public that you don't have to express yourself to your woman, but behind closed doors, you're probably kissing her ass."

"Looks like you're the one whipped," Jack said. "You can't even get through a round of golf without texting your girl. Golf is an escape from women."

They all laughed again. "Yeah, that's true for you, I guess," Earl said. "See, I'm in love. I'm not in like or playing around. I'm not trying to get away from my girl. I'm trying to get closer to her. So, to spend a few seconds texting her to let her know she's on my mind, well, that's the least I can do. You bamas better get on board."

"I gotta give it to him," Bob said. "I texted my wife one day last week, out of the blue, just to say I enjoyed the dinner she cooked the night before. She texted me back this long message about how much it meant to her. I was eating leftovers for lunch and wanted her to know how good it was. She ended up getting all mushy on me. It made a big difference. It made her day."

"Yeah, women need that affirmation," Jack said.

"And you don't?" Earl asked.

"Hell, no," Jack said. "I'm comfortable in my drawers."

When Bob finished laughing, he said, "You're a fool. But check this out. About a week after I sent that text, one afternoon my wife texted me saying how much she enjoyed the night before in bed. I didn't think I needed—what did you call it?—'affirmation.' But that text sure made me feel good. So I'm more like Earl on this one. If you use it the right way, it has its benefits."

"Only time I text is when I don't feel like talking to that person," Jack said. "I'm over today's world where no one talks to each other anymore. Everyone is sending e-mails and texts. It's impersonal."

"I hear you," Earl said. "If that's the only way you communicate, then, yes, it is impersonal. I'm just saying that sometimes, when you are feeling something and want to express it, dropping a text is not a bad thing. It's a good thing. Plus, most of you numb-skulls can't even communicate what you want to get across. So, it might be better to put it into words."

Just then, his phone chimed, indicating a text message.

"You're not even supposed to have your phone on the golf course," Jack said. "No one else is messing with a phone now—only you."

"Maybe because I'm the only one in love," Earl said, pulling his phone out of the cup holder in the golf cart.

"Yeah, let's see how long that lasts," Warren said.

Earl did not respond. He read Catherine's text: *"You make me smile all the time,"* she wrote. *"I truly am in love with you. I know I just left you this morning, but I miss you. Tonight's going to be another great night."*

He placed his phone back in the cart. "You all can say what you want, but I'm telling you some good stuff," Earl said.

"Okay, Love Doctor," Warren joked. "Will you hit the ball, please?"

That was how their round of golf went—Earl espousing the virtues of love and communication while reminiscing about their college days.

After nine holes, Earl and his group waited at the clubhouse for the second group of friends who was playing behind them. They compared scorecards and talked trash about each other. Earl's pre-round warmup was the worst of the eight friends playing. But he held the lead halfway through the round.

"I figured something out," he said. "I want to play well, but I'm not getting down after a bad shot. I'm just moving on. I'm not focusing on the negative."

"You're playing with that phone so much I don't know how you can focus on anything," Warren said.

Catherine could not focus on anything, either. She had spent much of the morning in a daze. Earl made love to her in a way that freed up her emotions and inhibitions. She had been married before, but, in the end, it became unfulfilling. It, indeed, grew to be exactly opposite of what she always desired.

And after her divorce, the two men she dealt with were less than what she needed. Earl was a revelation. He captured the essence of what she always wanted but never received: a man who was committed to her and who coveted her and made her feel protected and loved and appreciated. She never expected to find it in someone she knew for more than thirty years, but "then again, I always had a good feeling about Earl," she told her closest friend, Starr, the morning after. Because she could not focus on work, she texted Earl while he played golf and called Starr.

"Girlfriend, I'm so happy," she said. "I have never felt like this before. He is wonderful. I feel like a new person. I didn't expect this. But I feel great."

"I'm jealous," said Starr, who was married. "You know I'm kidding. I'm really happy for you. You deserve any happiness he can bring you."

Catherine and Starr were super tight. They were like sisters, only without the sibling rivalry. Each of them had many other friends, but none measured up to their closeness, which started when they pledged Delta Sigma Theta together at Norfolk State. Through the decades, their friendship had grown closer and closer to where they would trust each other with their life. More than that, they would trust their man with each other.

"You have to have one person you can trust enough to know where the bodies are buried," Catherine said. "That's who Starr is for me."

Her excitement about her relationship with Earl prevented Starr from getting much work done, too. It was like sharing their experiences was therapy for Catherine. And Starr was the therapist, eager to hear every detail Catherine wanted to share. Not the intimate details of their passion, but any information that would paint a clear picture of her girl's experience.

"I love that about my girlfriend," Catherine told Earl. "She's genuinely happy for me. And I could talk about you all day and she'd just listen and ask questions. Some people, they would consider it too much. A real friend takes it all in. That's Starr."

Starry-eyed Catherine had no idea how starry-eyed Earl was. While she shared all her emotions with Starr, Earl floated about the golf course, feeling as if he were a refreshed man. That euphoria translated into him playing a solid round of golf in chilly and windy conditions. He had the best score among his seven friends, a fact he was more than willing to share in the clubhouse afterward.

"Seems I recall a lot of laughing and boasting before the round started," Earl said. The guys pushed two tables together and ordered drinks. "Now I look at the scorecards and I'm the one on top."

The conversation would flip to other subjects, and Earl's humility would not allow him to boast on winning at golf.

"Bob," Warren said, "you live in Chicago. Did you hear about the guy from Norfolk State that got shot?"

Warren spoke of Calvin Sutton, a friend of Earl's and Warren's who was killed in the streets of the South Side of Chicago.

"By his wife's boyfriend," Earl said. "I'll never get over that. Calvin was a fun guy. The guy laughed at anything. Even when he was in school, his girlfriend would catch him with another girl and he'd laugh about it when telling you the story. Just a fun-loving guy."

"What happened?" Jack said.

"Well," Earl began, "he was my boy, but Calvin liked women. He was no different from any of us, except he always got caught. So he ends up marrying this woman from Chicago and moving out there. Good woman. Before long, they have all kinds of trouble, but they hang in there, have a son and whatever. But eventually it gets too bad. I spent a weekend with them and saw the drama firsthand.

"So, Calvin moves out and does his own thing. And I guess his wife moves on and gets a boyfriend. One day, Calvin comes over to pick up his mail and to see his son. Mind you, they are doing this but they haven't filed for divorce yet. Anyway, his wife's boyfriend answers the door and they sort of get into it. Apparently, Calvin ends up punching the guy in the face.

"He goes through the house and comes out of the kitchen door, which is on the side of the house and leads to the driveway. When he gets to the front of the house, the wife's boyfriend is kicking his car door. Calvin confronts the dude and he pulls out a gun and shoots him in the chest, right there on the street—in front of his wife and son.

"My man died right there. There was no call for that... Hurt me to my heart."

"Whatever happened to the dude?" Bob asked.

"I got all this information from his wife," Earl said. "And when I asked her that, she says, 'Well, I can't really say because somebody is going to trial for murder.' I'm like, 'I know you're not supporting the guy who killed your son's father.' And she goes, 'I think Calvin had a death wish. I do. Just the way he was acting that day. That's what I think. I swear.'

"It took everything in me to not go off. I said, 'Come on, now. No one enjoyed life more than Calvin. No way he was looking to die. That doesn't make sense.' She disagreed and basically told me that she was supporting her boyfriend."

"Damn," Jack said. "The fact that he killed somebody would be enough for me to say, 'Hey, you gotta go.' I can't believe her."

"No, wait," Earl said. "You won't believe this. I was watching one of those cop shows the other night, the ones when they spend an hour breaking down the murder. Well, I forgot what city in California, but there was a wife, grandmother and three kids shot and killed by the husband.

"Guess who the killer was?"

"Who?" everyone chimed in at once.

"Remember the Que, Vincent Brothers? They called him 'Veech.' It was him," Earl said.

"Dude who went to Norfolk State killed his whole family? Why? Was he crazy?" Warren said.

"Well, considering murdered his entire family, including his kids, I would say the nigga was at least a little crazy," Earl said, laughing. "But can you believe we know someone who killed his whole family?"

"I read the story when it happened," Bob said. "They believe it was about money, that he didn't want to pay child support anymore. But they said he drove all the way from Ohio to California, shot and killed them and drove back to Ohio and then to North Carolina. That's a lot of driving, but after you kill five people, I would think you'd have a hard time sleeping."

"This dude was crazy; he's on Death Row," Earl said. "And I ain't talking about the record label, either."

The recollection of old classmates and old times went on for another hour. The drinks and the stories flowed, with almost each punctuated with uproarious laughter.

"This is why I come to homecoming," Bob said. "This is the only place and the only time a year where you can get these stories that will bring you back to the best time of your life."

Earl, chugging on his third Heineken, challenged one part of Bob's claim.

"You think college was the best time of your life?" Earl asked. "The absolute best time?"

"Yeah, it was," Bob said. "Think about it. You were young, full of life and energy and hope for the future. You didn't have any bills or responsibilities. The world hadn't kicked you in the ass yet. There was a—what?—12-to-1 women-to-men ratio at Norfolk State. It was the best time because we were in college and didn't have a care in the world outside of the classroom. I just felt like I was at a great place, around a lot of friends and not having to scrape and scratch to pay bills made it the best time... Anyone else feel me?"

"Anytime you don't have to pay any bills, that's a good thing," said Bruce Lee, who left NSU after three years, but remained connected to the school.

"Yeah, but you didn't make any money in college, either," Earl said. "I LOVED college. I wouldn't trade going to Norfolk State for anything. I come back for homecoming almost every year because the memories are great. But since I have graduated, I have lived my best life. I have a career, I have traveled and seen a lot of the world—and there are far more women in the world than they were at Norfolk State. And here's the biggest and best part: I have grown.

"College is four years for a reason. It's enough time for you to grow so you can be prepared for the world. The world is a big place. If you go after it, you'll grow even more and you'll be fond of your college and your college days. But, to me, anyway, those days should be the foundation for a great life. Not the best days of your life."

"Both of you make sense, actually," Jack said. "I can honestly say I maximized college from the social aspects of it to the academic to the leadership part of it. It was a blessing for me— especially being at a historically black college. At the time I was at Norfolk State, I didn't think I could have a better time. But then you get out there and live…and you can do more and see more and enjoy it more—even with the responsibilities we all wish we didn't have."

"I wish I could go back to college now, with the knowledge I have," Warren said.

"It wouldn't even be fair," Jack said. "People think I was a terror back then. Let me go back to college now, with all the knowledge on how to deal with women. I'd bang every bad honey on campus."

"So you get to go back to college as a forty-something man in a teenager's body—and that's what you'd use that gift for? To bang every bad honey?"

"Damn, right," Jack said. "What would you use it for?"

"That's exactly what I would do," Earl said, and the groups of men laughed loudly.

As they did, he checked his watch.

"What, you have somewhere to be?' Bruce asked. "He's been checking his watch the whole time we've been here."

"Actually, I do," Earl said.

"He's all in love," Jack said. "Sending text messages during the whole round."

"And still beat all of you," Earl said.

"To who?" Bruce asked. "Who you in love with?"

That was the question that Earl could not pass on. He loved Catherine unashamedly, and this was his moment to say so.

"Catherine," he said. "Catherine Harmon."

Bruce sat up in his seat. "I told you two years ago to step to Catherine," he said. "That girl looks great."

"I know; I remember," Earl said. "But that wasn't our time. Now is our time."

"Are you serious?" Bruce asked. "How? What happened?"

"She sent me an e-mail in June and that was the beginning," Earl answered. He was humble in his remarks, but inside he was bubbling.

"She's my girl now, Bruce," he said. "We've built something."

"I'll be damned. Y'all know she was about the baddest honey at Norfolk State when we were there," said Bruce, whose wife, Holly, was also a prime catch. "I haven't seen her in a while, Earl. She still looking good?"

"Awesome," Earl said, smiling. "You'll see. She's coming with me to the Best of Friends party tomorrow night."

"Oh, this I gotta see," Bruce said. "No wonder you looking at the time. I understand now."

CHAPTER TWELVE

DISPLEASURE IN THE AIR

Jimmy, Carter and Barbara

When Friday evening wore down, Barbara expected Carter to invite her to his room, as he had the previous five years. He didn't. And that angered and hurt Barbara—and made her regret taking the cross-country trip to homecoming.

"I can't believe you're not going to see me tonight," she said to Carter in a text message. *"We talked about this for a whole year. Now you change your mind? Why?"*

She knew, but she wanted him to tell her. Carter and Jimmy sat at their hotel bar, sipping on water to hydrate after a day of drinking. They chatted with more classmates they came across and caught up more on each other's lives. But Barbara's message altered the lighthearted tone of the evening. Carter turned to Jimmy, who was reading a text of his own from his wife, Monica, who remained pissed off about not being at homecoming with her husband.

"We need to have a serious talk when you get back," she wrote to him. *"I have some decisions to make."*

Carter and Jimmy looked at each other with quizzical expressions. They needed each other's advice.

"Go ahead," Jimmy said. "You first. What is it?"

"So, Barbara wants to know why we're not spending the night together," Carter said. "And I don't know what to tell her."

"Well, what would you tell me?" Jimmy asked.

"That I'm not feeling this move to New York," Carter said.

"Well, maybe you should talk to her about it," Jimmy surmised. "It seems like something is missing to me, so it has to feel that way to her, too. You told me earlier today that you all are in love. That was this morning. Now, tonight, you don't want to be bothered with her. That's a big switch. You owe her an explanation."

Carter nodded his head. He knew that answer before Jimmy gave it. He was hoping for something creative that would ease his mind, and Barbara's, too, without having to express his dissatisfaction with her move. But the reality was iron-clad: She and her kids *were* moving to New York and he had to deal with it.

"Yeah, I know," he said to Jimmy. "And I will have a heart-to-heart with her. Tonight. This won't be easy... So what's up with you?"

Jimmy shook his head. "The wife is tripping," he said. "She hit me with 'we have to talk' and she 'has some decisions to make.' What does that sound like to you?"

"Well, whenever I heard, 'we have to talk' or told somebody that, it was about breaking up," Carter said. "I don't know what she means. But the part about having decisions to make doesn't sound good, either."

"Yeah, I was thinking the same thing," Jimmy said. "We've had our issues in the past, but nothing that would threaten the marriage. I never cheated on her. I don't go anywhere, really. For her to trip like this is crazy."

"Maybe you should do like I'm about to do—have a heart-to-heart," Carter said. "It can't hurt."

"You don't know Monica," Jimmy said. "That girl can make a mountain out of a pimple."

They laughed. "Excuse me," Carter said, hailing the bartender. "Can we get a shot of tequila?"

"I don't even want a shot," Jimmy said. "But I'll take it."

They tapped glasses of Herradura Reposada and downed the tequila.

"Okay, man, good luck," Jimmy said as he and Carter walked to the elevators. "I'm going to my room to call my wife. If I'm not too rundown afterward, I might go to the all-black party at the Holiday Inn."

"Same here," Carter said. "I'll let you know when I get off the phone."

The two men went separate ways down the hallway of the eleventh floor. In his room, Jimmy turned on the television and hit the mute button. He always liked the TV on, whether he was watching it or not.

Before he could press the keys to reach Monica, his phone rang. It was Regina Anderson, his college girlfriend that he had seen at The Broadway.

Unfamiliar with the number, he answered anyway. "Hello."

"Why didn't you come and speak to me at the party?" she said.

"Huh? Who is this?" he asked.

"Regina."

"Oh, hi, Regina. How are you?" he said. "How did you get my number?"

"Don't worry about that; I did. Why didn't you say hello to me?"

"I planned to; I did," Jimmy said. "Then some other things happened and when it was time to go, I never saw you again."

"I was there the whole time, with Sharon Prince, Sharon King and Debra Hall," Regina said. "You just ignored me. Eventually we went up to the third level, where the lounge is. But I was so disappointed. I know you saw me."

"Why didn't you just come over to me?"

"I see you're the same old Jimmy."

"Really? How?"

"You've started an argument in less than a minute, that's how," she said.

"You called me with an attitude; not the other way around."

Suddenly, there was a familiar silence and awkwardness for both of them. They'd had an explosive relationship in a good and bad way. Intense passion, intense arguments.

Finally, it hit Jimmy that he had grown and should handle Regina differently.

"So, listen, I'm sorry I didn't get to say hello to you," he said. "But how are you? I did see you and you looked great."

"I couldn't have looked that great; you would have come over," she said.

"Regina, I have apologized and I'm trying to move on," he said, getting exasperated. "You gonna move on with me or am I gonna get the same old Regina from ten years ago?"

"Okay, Jimmy, I'm sorry," she said. "I was just so excited to see you and then to not get a hug and a kiss made me mad."

"That should make you disappointed maybe, but not mad."

"Well, I'm all right now," she said. "Where you staying?"

"Why?" Jimmy asked.

"Because I want to come over and see you," she answered. "Don't you think we should spend some time together? It's been too long."

"I guess it depends on what you mean by that," he said. "I'm married and I hear you're married. So we have some limitations."

"Jim, we have too much history to have limitations," Regina said.

He knew what that meant. One of the reasons he liked Regina was her boldness. When she wanted sex, she asked for it.

"I'm not messing with you, Regina," he said. "We can get together for a drink and to catch up, but that's it."

"Yeah, right; I've heard that before," she said. "Where are you staying?"

"The Marriott."

"Waterside?" she asked.

"Yeah."

"Are you serious?" Regina said. "Me, too."

Jimmy closed his eyes and dropped his head. He did not want that kind of access to Regina. As adamant as he was about not giving in to her, he also knew he could be weak to her. They'd had a hot and heavy past that still burned in his mind, all these years later.

"Well, let's meet at the bar on the mezzanine level," he said. "How's nine o'clock?"

"Okay," she said. "I'll be the one at the bar in the sexy dress. The short, sexy dress. Don't be late."

Jimmy disconnected the call and dismissed thoughts of Regina. His thoughts shifted quickly to Monica, although he did not know exactly what he would say to her. They'd had conversations in the past about one thing or another that put him on the edge. Not the edge of leaving, but the edge of *thinking* about leaving. It was that kind of marriage. They loved hard, but dealt with myriad hard times because of Monica's sensitivity regarding fidelity—or the idea of infidelity. Growing up, she lay awake in bed and listened to her mother and father argue about his late-nights out with "women not good enough to have their own men," as her mother called them.

She never understood how her mom accepted her dad's phil-andering—they remained married, going on their thirty-fourth year. Still, Regina vowed to never let a man treat her as her father had her mother. That position was paramount in her developing what Jimmy called a "psychosis" that made her question anything that seemed out of sorts to her.

More than twice Jimmy underwent a battery of questions and

drama over his actions, questions and drama he found unwarranted. "All men have something to hide," Monica had said. "It's just a matter of where they hide it."

Once, they did not speak for three days because Jimmy arrived home after midnight one Monday night. When he told her he had been at a sports bar with his friends watching a Monday Night Football game, just as he had told her he would, she told him he was "a liar. Men do not hang out this late unless women are involved."

Another time she refused him sex because she read one of his e-mails from a female that said: *"Thanks for walking me to my car."* Monica's position was he walked her to the car after a date with her. His position was she was a co-worker who left the building after dark and he did the gentlemanly thing to make sure she was safe.

Arguments Monica initiated that questioned his commitment and morals ate at Jimmy like acid. He loved his wife but hated some of her positions. And here they were again, at a relationship crossroads for what he deemed a logical choice.

"So, I received your text," he said when Monica answered the phone. "What are you so upset about? And you have some decisions to make? What does that mean?"

"It means, Jimmy, that I'm tired of feeling like I should sit at home while you gallivant all over the place, chasing women," she said. "I just can't—"

"What, Monica?" Jimmy interrupted. "You can't what? You can't trust me? That's a real problem. Let's just put it out there because I'm tired of it. You're one of those women who cannot stand prosperity. I have not cheated on you. Period. And yet all I get from you is doubts. I can't take it anymore. You're going to have to do something or we really are going to have some problems."

In that one tirade, Jimmy put the onus on Monica, who could not get a word in because Jimmy was in a rage.

"There are men who do whatever they like, married or not," he said. "They cheat just because they can. There are men who consider being with other women a sport, as if it's a game. I know these men. I'm not one of them. And here's the crazy part: They get no grief from their wives because their wives trust them. And here I am, being faithful, and I catch hell from you almost every day about one thing or another. Well, I'm sick of it. It's stupid, but mostly it's wrong and I don't deserve it."

"You talking all loud and with conviction doesn't convince me of anything, James," Monica said. "I know what I feel, and I feel like you'd rather be out there among a bunch of women than with your wife. And I don't deserve that."

Both of them were seething, and Jimmy knew that was a conflict that was combustible. But he didn't care.

"Do you like drama or are you just dumb?" he went on.

"You calling me 'dumb'?" she said.

"I didn't," Jimmy said. "I asked if you were 'dumb.' You have to be *something* to ignore what I said to you. But I'm going to take my time and repeat it so maybe you feel me on it: I have not cheated on you. Period. If you don't believe me, if that is not good enough for you, then I don't know what else to say."

Monica did not know where to go with that one. Jimmy had effectively put her in defensive mode. But that did not stop her from firing right back at him.

"I heard what you said, but that doesn't mean it's the truth," she said. "Any man who is proud of his wife would take her to his homecoming. Any man who wouldn't must not be proud of her or must have a reason for not wanting her around. And with a man, that reason is usually another woman."

"Forget talking about what a 'man' would do," Jimmy responded. "Talk about me, about what I do. Not even what I would do, but what I do. What I have done since the day I met you is be available to you, respect you, honor our relationship. I haven't been out there at strip clubs or at clubs partying every night. You seem intent on placing me in a category with any common man, which would be okay if I acted like any other man. But I haven't.

"Like I said, get yourself together, Monica," he said. "I have been good to you. I'm not taking it anymore. One of my friends is here with his wife and he's miserable. She's acting just as I expected you to act—insecure, petty, driving him crazy. You're not even here and you're doing that to me. You can't even be honest with yourself about yourself. You're insecure, baby. You think every woman is interested in me and that I'm interested in every woman I see.

"It's not like that at all. I have been committed to you. You don't see it or believe it, but I have. But—and this is not some kind of threat or anything, I'm telling you because I'm supposed to tell you—I'm not going to take it anymore."

"If that's not a threat, then what is?" Monica said. "I'm the one at home by myself while you hang out and party and do whatever you want to do. I guess I'm supposed to take this, huh? Well, I'm not taking it anymore, either."

"Taking what, Monica?" Jimmy said. "You're unbelievable. I don't go anywhere. I haven't taken a trip by myself before. When you go to wherever—Atlanta, New York on shopping trips—I say have a good time. I look up places online to make sure you have a good time. I trust you. I can't stop you from doing something if you wanted to, and I'm not going to try. If we don't trust each other, what do we have?"

"Well, I don't know what we have. I'm really upset about this homecoming thing, James," she said. "I feel like this all could have been avoided."

Jimmy took a deep breath. He understood her concern about him going to Norfolk alone, but he did not like it. More than anything, he believed it spoke to her belief that he would step outside of their marriage.

"Monica, honey, I want you to really listen to me," he said. His voice was calm and reassuring, almost as if he were trying to seduce her. "I love you. You are my wife. Nothing can break that. No doubt about it: you get on my nerves sometimes. And I guess I get on yours, too. But we're married. It's me and you, no one else. You've got to believe that. We should not have this kind of drama. Life is too short. Let's live it in peace. But you've got to trust me."

Although he spoke calmly, Monica also detected a desperation in Jimmy's voice, like he was giving her one last opportunity to believe in him. And that feeling cooled her like a Gatorade bath. She did not know, though, how to acquiesce after being so harsh.

"Okay," she said, and Jimmy thought his cell phone was breaking up.

"Okay" was a word Monica hardly ever uttered. In fact, Jimmy could not recall a single instance where there was a contentious situation and he made a strong point that prompted her to say, "Okay."

"Excuse me," he said to his wife.

"Okay, James," she said. "I do love you and I want to trust you. I just have to try harder."

Monica surprised Jimmy. He hoped she would come around, but he thought it would take time. Her essentially giving in gave him a euphoric feeling.

"Baby, I'm really glad to hear you say that," he said. "That means a lot to me. I don't want you having anxieties about me. We're supposed to be happy. I want you to enjoy our life together as much as I am."

"I do enjoy our life," she said. "I just have to find a comfortable place with trust."

"I will do all I can to help you," he said. "The big thing is that you want to let go of those issues. That's where it all starts."

They went on to chat lightheartedly about Jimmy's trip, her parents, and life in general. A call expected to become ugly turned out to be something that gave Jimmy hope that he and Monica would live more in harmony. But he had to do his part, too.

And his part at that time meant resisting the aggressive old girlfriend, Regina. She texted him as he talked to Monica: "Let's make it ten at the bar, okay?"

That was fine for Jimmy. It gave him more time to build up his resistance to her. He did not recall much about their college relationship except that it consisted of frequent and intense sex. He used to say of Regina: "If this girl isn't a nymphomaniac, then they don't exist." To which she replied, "Then you must be one, too, because you're right here with me."

Jimmy lived a disciplined life after Regina, though. Entering the Army did not curb his sexual desires, but it did place order in his life. When he met Monica, they blossomed, in part, because her passion level was equal to his. And they thrived despite her obvious trust issues because of Jimmy's patience and commitment to her.

This was his first time away from home without Monica, and there was Regina, ready to pounce.

❂❂❂

When Jimmy got to the mezzanine level, Regina was already there, long legs crossed and extended away from the bar. They were glistening under the short, short dress. Her modest cleavage was exposed and she smelled like fresh daisies. She knew Jimmy's weaknesses and she attacked all of them.

He approached with a smile, but tentatively. She stood up to show that her body remained fit and firm after all the years. Jimmy shook his head. They hugged, and she pressed her body against his and held it there tightly for what seemed like a minute or two.

Jimmy inhaled her perfume and closed his eyes, and her body felt so familiar, so good. Then he literally shook himself out of the daze he could feel coming over him.

"Damn, girl, you still look great," he said. "You actually look better than you did back in the day."

"I feel better, too—figuratively and literally," Regina said, raising her eyebrows.

"I bet you do," Jimmy said.

"I bet you will find out," she snapped back.

"Anyway, I've been drinking all day," he said, looking over the bar.

"Well, it's time to extend it into the night," she said. "And you haven't had a drink with me."

He did not even bother to argue with her on that point; he knew she would never give in to him not drinking with her. So, he ordered two glasses of Pinot Noir.

"So why did you move getting together back an hour?" Jimmy asked.

"I had to talk to my husband for a while," she said. "Good man, but paranoid. Thinks I'm down here going wild."

"Aren't you?" Jimmy asked.

"Not yet," she said. "But now that you are here…"

"I'm not the one," Jimmy said. "You're married, I'm married. We had our day and it's not today."

"Stop being a wet rag," she said. "I'm not saying something has to happen between us. But don't squash the idea of it. Let's just have a good time and see where it takes us."

"Regina, I know where you want to take it," Jimmy said. "To bed. But I can't sleep with you."

"I understand," she said, making Jimmy feel somewhat relieved. But she followed that up with: "But who said anything about going to sleep?"

If he had any doubts about Regina's plan, that comment confirmed it. He did his best to guide the conversation away from her objective. They talked about her life in Delaware and marriage and old friends. They touched on travel and eating right and how awesome homecoming was.

But at eleven-fifteen, after three glasses of wine, Regina's plans for the night were concrete.

"I'm in room 803," she said. "I actually have some wine in the room. Let's go up there."

"Regina, I'm done drinking," he said. "I'm going with Carter to the all-black party. Nothing good will come out of going to your room."

"You must be getting old or losing your memory," she said. "Or your manhood."

Challenging Jimmy's manhood was a route she expected to push him off of his stance. Didn't happen.

"I fought in Iraq against insurgents and the Taliban," he said. "I traveled that desert praying a landmine would not blow up our truck. I lived under duress for more than a year in the Middle East, not knowing if I would ever make it back home…helped raise my little brother when my parents passed in four months apart. I put myself through college. You can say what you want, but you can't challenge my manhood, Regina."

She looked at him for several seconds and smiled. "You have done a lot in your life," she said. "I'm proud of you. You're most definitely all man. I was trying to rile you up to get what I wanted. I'm sorry."

Jimmy was almost taken aback by her sensitivity and willingness to retreat. That was not her style. *Maybe she has grown since their college days*, he thought.

They spent the next half hour laughing and reminiscing about college days. When Jimmy decided it was time to leave for the all-black party in Virginia Beach, he offered her a ride to the event. He was not sure where that notion came from, but he was feeling good—or, at least better—about Regina and could not see the harm.

He sent Carter a text message about going to the party. But Carter was engaged in a heart-to-heart with Barbara that was tough because he was not sure what his true emotions were.

"I need you to be honest with me," Barbara said. "For the last five years you have told me you loved me and that we belonged together. I believed you and I felt the same way. I committed adultery only because I love you and I believed in us. And now I do something for us and you act like, well, like you're not happy about it."

This was Carter's moment to accomplish so much. He could be honest, first and foremost. He could deliver Barbara the words that would offer her so much comfort. He could free himself of the burden he carried.

"I am not happy or happy about it, Barbara," Carter said. "I just wish we had talked about it before you made such a big move. If you say you're moving there for me, then I should have been in the thought process. You're talking about not only changing your life, but changing mine, too. To move all the way across the country, to pull your kids out of school and away from their father…to be with me? That's a lot. That's all I'm saying. That's a burden I have to carry, and I wasn't looking to carry it. Or at least I would have liked to see if I could get prepared to carry it."

Barbara did not say anything, so Carter continued.

"I want you to understand this—I love you. There is no doubt about that," he said. "In the last five years, we have loved so hard over one weekend that it would last me an entire year. I wanted to see you more often, but I was all right because I knew my place in your life. I knew what your life consisted of and we shared enough in our time to hold me. That's saying a whole lot. I hope you don't take that lightly.

"So, now you're coming to New York to live. New job, new city. Big job in the biggest city. And you told me you're doing it for me, so we could be together. You don't think that's a lot for me to handle? No notice. No heads-up. Just 'SURPRISE!! I'm moving to New York to be with you.' I can say that overall I'm glad I'll be able to see you more. I'm sorry about your marriage. As much as I love you and loved being with you, I always felt bad for *how* we were together. I hate that I disrespected that man in that way."

"And that's why I did this, Carter," Barbara jumped in. "I told you I was so sick with myself. I have prayed and prayed for forgiveness. But it just isn't right to keep praying every year, but then come back and do the same thing the next year. I had to make a tough decision. A gut-wrenching decision. My kids love their father. He loves them."

Carter could not hold back a concern about all this that ate at him.

"Don't take this the wrong way, but how could you take them all the way across the country away from their father?" he said. "As much as you love me, those kids have to come first. You can't—well, to me, you shouldn't—just uproot them for your benefit.

"I read years and years ago when Oprah's friend, Gail, got a divorce, she turned down a job making five million a year from Oprah in Chicago because she didn't want to take her kids away from their father. I thought that was admirable. It was unselfish. She had the kids' best interest at heart and turned down money most people never would have."

"So, what are you saying, Carter? That I'm selfish?" Barbara responded. She was not happy. She, indeed, was offended.

"You might want to know the facts before you start calling me names," she went on. "That's how you view me: as some woman so selfish she'd move her kids away from their father and friends to be with a man? To be with you? How arrogant of you. You must really think a lot of yourself."

"Don't get upset," Carter said. "Don't get offended. What do you expect me to think? You haven't told me shit. All—"

"Don't curse at me, Carter," she interjected. "I don't care how mad you get, don't get disrespectful. You know I don't like that."

"I'm not trying to disrespect you," he said. "I'm just making a point. Please don't play the victim role, like you're being attacked. You've told—"

"So you're not going to apologize?"

"I'm sorry, Barbara. I wasn't trying to disrespect you," he said. "What I'm saying is all you have told me is that you're moving to New York and that being with me was a part of the reason. What am I supposed to get out of that? That you did it for the kids? *Please*."

"Okay, okay," she said. "So you do think I'm selfish. I detest selfishness in people and no one has ever said or even intimated that I am selfish. But—"

"Oh, wait a minute, Barbara," Carter said, interrupting her. "Now, listen, I don't want to insult you. But no one could call you selfish because you probably haven't told anyone about what you've been doing with me for the last five years. If a married woman coming to homecoming once a year to have sex with her old boyfriend isn't selfish, then what is? You surely weren't doing it for your kids? Who, exactly, were you doing it for if it wasn't for you?"

Barbara was seething, so much so that tears rolled down her face. She was embarrassed and insulted—plain hurt.

"I did it for my sanity," she said calmly, wiping her face. "I married a good man, but a man who was not for me, a man who did not give me any joy. I know that life is short and we must find the joy in it. To be in a joyless situation was empty and awful. And I needed some small amount of joy to feel better about myself, so I could be the mother to my children that I needed to be and, believe it or not, a better wife.

"I found that joy over two days with you. It was enough to sustain me, to bring me back to a place where I could function with some clarity and feeling something good in my heart. I know that's a conflict because I was so disappointed in myself every time; I knew I was doing wrong based on my marital commitment. There is no way around that. But I was not just out here being a whore. There were times when I really felt depressed and on the edge of insanity, and in those times, I was not what I needed to be to my kids.

"This probably doesn't make sense to you or wouldn't to anyone else. You'd have to go through what I have to understand. So, I'm mad that you think I'm selfish, but I see how you could see that. I don't see it that way. I see me as someone trying to get through life. And here's the important part: I never slept with anyone else. Only with you, once a year during homecoming weekend. I swear.

"And I'm not saying you should be honored or anything. I'm just saying that I chose you for two reasons: I love you and you love me. We were young when we started, but what we had was real. And I know it was real because it has stayed with me all these years. But anyway…"

Carter was not sure what to do or say. Their initial plan, before she dropped the news on him, was for them to go to the all-black party, enjoy seeing old classmates and then spend the night together, as always. But neither of them was feeling particularly romantic after such a heavy conversation.

"So, what's the plan for the rest of the night?" he asked.

"I don't think I'm up to the party," she said. "I think I'll call Donna and we'll get something to eat. Or maybe I'll order room service and watch a movie. I'm kinda drained right now."

"I'm sorry, Barbara," Carter said. "I really am. I definitely don't want to cause you any drama. But I knew you wanted me to be honest with you. And I needed to be honest with you and myself."

"Okay," was all she said to that, a clear indication to Carter that she wasn't feeling him.

"Okay," Carter said. "Well, I'll let you go. Wait, weren't we supposed to go to the parade in the morning?"

"Well, we were supposed to go to the party tonight, too, Carter," she said. "In my mind, we were supposed to be happy and enjoying each other and talking about how wonderful things will be in New York for both of us. But I guess I can't get everything I want, right? I'll just settle for a nice dinner right now. I can manage that without anyone spoiling it."

Carter was troubled by Barbara's state. He had never heard her in distress about him. They always existed in harmony, even as young students on a campus of soap opera drama.

But he did not—or was not willing—to do or say anything to help her feel better.

"Okay, well, have a great dinner," he said.

Barbara did not respond. She pushed a button to end the phone call.

CHAPTER THIRTEEN
DO WHAT YOU KNOW
IS RIGHT

Venita, Jesse and Don

Venita tossed around the idea of seeing her ex-boyfriend, Charles, for dinner and drinks. She *wanted* to see him, to see how he looked, how he was doing, how life had been for him. *It could do no harm*, she thought. She would not go to bed with him, even though her body might say something entirely different.

But Venita was unlike most people. She was honest with herself. She knew that if she spent any amount of time with Charles and the chemistry they had resurfaced, she would be weak against his advances.

She also knew Charles had been divorced a few years and was among the biggest flirts she had ever experienced. It was the reason they did not make it in college. He was sensational in bed, but he liked to be in as many beds of as many women as possible. For a while, being young and whipped was fine. As long as she did not know of Charles' escapades, she was content. The physical feeling he gave her was so good that she abandoned all logic.

As a mature woman of the world, she knew she needed more in a mate. And she knew herself. Given the right time and place, she was subject to have one more go-round with Charles, not out of love, but out of that need for vigorous, intense sex that her husband, a fine man, was not providing.

When she thought of her husband back at home, though, she let go the idea of putting herself in a vulnerable position with Charles. She was not naïve; she knew her being away meant her husband had time to do his thing, if he so chose.

But she decided she should conduct herself as she would rather her husband would when she was away. And so, although heavily tempted, she called her niece, Diamond, instead. And although only twenty, she gave her aunt some mature advice when Venita told her of what she had considered.

"Don't do it, auntie," she said.

And that was that. Diamond and Venita went to California Pizza Kitchen at MacArthur Mall downtown. They ate at the counter, catching up on family news, which always was interesting.

After nearly an hour of talking about Uncle Derwin's death; cousin Paul's third wife in four years, who is a closet alcoholic; and how Aunt Macy had bought a stolen car from her brother, Venita decided to move on.

"So, how are you, really, Diamond?" she asked her niece. "You look great. But I know this is a different experience for you. How do you like it?"

Diamond was the daughter of Venita's brother, Raheem, who had one year left on an eight-year sentence for armed robbery. Raheem was not always a criminal. He, in fact, was once a hard-working mechanic who doted on his little girl. He named her Diamond, he said, "because I like the phrase 'Diamond in the rough.' There will be some rough times, I'm pretty sure. But my baby will always shine."

He was right. He had lost his job behind an insatiable desire for vodka, developed when he couldn't handle learning that his love, wife Saundra, had been diagnosed with the debilitating multiple sclerosis. Diamond was almost thirteen, with a father in prison and her mom becoming less and less able to get around as the disease took over.

At that vulnerable age, the family worried Diamond would crack. And for a minute, she did. She was distraught watching her mother's health deteriorate and dismayed that her "Papa" was incarcerated—he had held up a suburban Washington, D.C., liquor store in an attempt to get money for Diamond to enroll in a summer camp in Maine.

Her attitude changed; she became petulant, which was opposite her sunny nature. She skipped school and sought the attention of boys who walked like ducks because their pants hug below their hips—another dramatic change.

It was not until she finally visited her father in prison that she returned to the Diamond that was the shining light of the family.

Her dad's words were piercing. "Diamond," he said, sitting across the table from her, "do you know why I named you what your name is? Because a diamond sparkles. It can get covered in mud, but when you brush it off, it shines again. It's beautiful. You're beautiful. I couldn't handle your mom getting sick and it got me here. I'm sorry for one reason: I can't be out there with you and your mother. You two are all that matter to me. But since I'm in here, I can't be what I need your mom needs me to be. So, baby, it's up to you. You have to shine now. You have to be the beautiful Diamond we know you are."

Tears rolled down her face as her father spoke. And his, too. They hugged a long hug and all the nonsense that enveloped her life for several months was discarded. With Venita and other family members helping, Diamond went on to graduate from Crossland High in Suitland, Maryland with honors and attended William & Mary.

After a year at the Williamsburg, Virginia college, she decided to transfer to Norfolk State after a friend at rival Hampton University took her to NSU for a basketball game.

"I'm doing great, auntie," she said to Venita. "William and Mary had its place for me. It served a purpose for me—it let me know I needed to be somewhere else."

They laughed. "Don't get me wrong," she added. "I enjoyed the people and the campus is beautiful. But it didn't feel like home. I was away, my daddy was away, and my mom was far away from who she was.

"So I needed to be somewhere where I could feel some love. You know how it is over here; we aren't as organized as we should be. But the administration cares. It's not about getting the money or you go home. It's about figuring out how to keep you in school to get that degree. So, it's been a great change."

"I'm so happy to hear that," Venita said. "It's definitely a shame that there are still long lines at registration and the financial aid office and even housing. I guess we'll never get that right. But the plusses outweigh the minuses because, above all, you feel like a family. Everyone might not get along—like in a traditional family—but there's a feeling of love and caring that you cannot get at a non-HBCU school."

"Having been to a non-HBCU, as you put it, I know clearly the differences," Diamond said. "It works for some people. But it wasn't for me overall."

"Yeah, well, you listed all your reasons for loving Norfolk State," Venita said, "but I ain't heard you say nothing about boys and parties. I know that's a big part of why you're so happy."

Diamond smiled a smile that revealed something. Venita wanted to know what.

"Well," her niece said, "I have been dating this guy. He's great, wonderful, treats me well. I want you to meet him."

"Yeah, well, I want to meet him, too, so we have to make sure that happens," Venita said, sounding like an overprotective parent.

"Auntie, I'm twenty, I'll be twenty-one pretty soon," she said. "You don't have to treat me like some sheltered little girl. Those days are over."

Venita looked over her young niece, who was gorgeous. Diamond was five-foot-seven with curves like a street in San Francisco and flowing mid-length hair, sparkly eyes and a toothy smile. In the vernacular of her peers, she was a "dime piece." But there was so much more to her. The fact that she bypassed the step show and homecoming parties to dine with her aunt said a lot about her.

"I worry about you because you are so cute and innocent," Venita said. "And if you're not ready, college can grow you up in a hurry."

"I know, Aunt Venita," Diamond said. "I'm dealing with…well, something pretty crazy right now myself."

"Really?" Venita asked. "What is it?"

"I don't know if I should say," Diamond said.

"Girl, you better tell your auntie what's going on," Venita demanded as delicately as possible.

"Auntie," she said, her voice low. The expression on her face changed, alarming Venita.

She reached over and grabbed her niece's hands. "It's okay. Whatever it is, it will be okay," Venita said.

Diamond lowered her head and shook it side-to-side. "Well, I'm dealing with a pregnancy issue," she said.

"What?" Venita said loudly, pulling her hands away from Diamond's.

"Diamond, we should have been talking about this all along," Venita added. "Girl, you are just twenty years old with your whole future in front on you. I wasn't naïve enough to think you're a virgin. But how in the world could you get pregnant in this day and age?"

Diamond quickly raised her head.

"Auntie," she said. "I'm not pregnant. How did you get that?"

"How did I get that? You said you have a 'pregnancy issue,'" Venita said. "That sure as hell sounds like you're pregnant to me."

"No, my roommate, Janea, is pregnant," Diamond said. "Pregnant? Me? No way."

"Oh, don't act like it can't happen. It definitely can," Venita said.

"Well, one day I would like to have children. Maybe. But I can't think about that now," Diamond said. "Not for a long time."

"Well, that's a relief," Venita said. "I thought my heart was about to jump out of my chest."

Diamond laughed, but quickly turned serious. "I'm worried about Janea," she said. "She's a great person. Her family is great and has been good to me. She actually wants to have this baby. But she also knows this is not the time for it, too. So, she's totally torn. And it's driving her crazy."

"Well, how far along is she?" Venita asked.

"Almost two months," Diamond answered.

"Who is she talking to for counseling?"

"No one. Well, me."

"No offense, niece, but that's not the best route," Venita said. "She hasn't talked to her parents?"

"No way," Diamond said. "They are nice people. They are in town now for homecoming, in fact. They all are out at dinner. But her father would lose his mind. And her mother, too. Her father is in politics, a city councilman in Fairfax or something. Her mom is the Dean of Women at a small school up there in Northern Virginia. So, appearances matter."

"Well, that might be true to them, but the reality is that she's their daughter and she should feel free enough to talk to them about something so serious," Venita said. "Has she spoken to any adult at all about this?"

"As far as I know, she's only told me about it," Diamond said.

"Well, I'm here, Diamond," Venita said. "I don't know what I would tell her, but she needs to speak to someone older than you to get some perspective. I would be glad to sit down with her and at least encourage her to speak to her parents about it. They might surprise her.

"And what about her boyfriend? Does he know?"

"She hasn't told him yet because she wants to be clear about what she should do," Diamond said. "She thinks he'd want her to have an abortion. She wants to figure it all out first."

"That's a lot to figure and maybe he could help her come to a decision," Venita said. "But I'll tell her that when—or if—I get to talk to her."

"Well, I'll suggest that she talk to you," Diamond said. "I won't tell her that I already told you. I'll tell her that you are a cool old person and that maybe she should talk to you."

"You really think I'm 'cool'?"

"I do," Diamond said. "But that's a little off-subject, don't you think?"

"Wait. Did you say 'cool *old* person'?"

"Auntie," Diamond whined.

The women laughed.

"I would like to be there with Sky if you talk to her, okay?" Diamond said.

Venita took a deep breath. "Sure. Okay. That's fine."

When they got into the car, Venita hit Diamond with some surprising news.

"I was going to wait to tell you this tomorrow, at breakfast,"

Venita said. "I don't know why I picked breakfast over dinner. I think it was because you learn something like this at the start of the day, you have the rest of your day to digest it and by the time you're ready for bed, you can sleep.

"And also—"

"Aunt Venita," Diamond interrupted, exasperated. "What is it?"

"Well, I got a call two days ago from your dad," she said.

"And?"

"And he's getting out early on good behavior," Venita said.

"What? When?" Diamond wanted to know.

"Well, it looks like he'll be coming home next Thursday," Venita told her. Tears immediately welled up in Diamond's eyes.

"I know," Venita said, and then she started crying. "It's been a long time. He's so proud of you. You and your mom are his world."

"I don't know what to think, auntie," Diamond said. "I have seen my friends have their parents visit them and be able to go home for breaks and spend time with them. I haven't had that and sometimes I'm sad about it and sometimes I'm mad about it.

"Mommy is amazing. She stays positive, even as the disease has taken away her ability to walk and, really, take care of herself. Still, she's my biggest cheerleader. I think she stays so positive to keep me up. But she doesn't know that when I'm home and go to my room, I always cry my eyes out. I hate seeing my mother like that. It doesn't seem fair."

"It is horrible," Venita said. "Your mom and I get along like sisters and when this started to happen—what?—nine, ten years ago, I couldn't believe M.S. was so awful. Your mom is a fighter, very competitive. Did you know she played basketball in high school? And could have played in college if she wanted to?

"I knew she was going to fight it. When I read up on M.S., I got so scared. There really is nothing that can be done to stop what it does to the muscle functions. Ultimately, it just takes over."

"I couldn't be my mother," Diamond said. "I'm not as strong as she is. I would have given up. It's too much."

"You wait until you have kids," Venita said. "You're the reason she continues to fight. She wants to see you blossom like that Diamond in the rough they talked about when they named you 'Diamond.' That's what keeps her going. And I think, too, that she wants to see my brother come home and feel him hug her. I know people who say they don't believe in love at first sight or even in everlasting love.

"All I do when I hear that is point to your mom and dad. They met at a Prince concert—have you heard the story?"

"Only a hundred times," Diamond said. "But I love it every time."

"Me, too, because it was real. They both had on purple," Venita recalled. "It rained that night. Your dad's shirt was a deep purple and so was your mom's top. Most people wore a lighter purple, including me. When they saw each other, my brother said—I was standing right there—'that's a nice shade of purple on you.'

"Saundra looked him up and down. 'You, too,' she said. Raheem then said to her, 'We should be together.' Your mom said, 'Excuse me?' But she was smiling. I was with Raheem and she was with a girlfriend. I ended up giving her my seat and they watched Prince together.

"I got the raw end of that deal big time. She watched Prince with him about twenty rows from the front—and found the love of her life. I sat with her mean, smelly girlfriend on the second deck. But the way it turned out, I didn't mind. I got a great sister-in-law. I never saw Raheem taken by a woman like that. I am a huge Prince fan—but I had to help out my brother. I knew he was in love."

Diamond smiled at the story—again.

"Diamond," Venita said, her voice turning serious, "have you gotten over your dad being locked up and away from you for the last seven years?"

"I'm glad he's getting out," she said. "I wish it didn't happen. I thought I knew my father."

"You did know him, honey," Venita said. "But he loves your mom so much, he couldn't handle watching her get more and more sick. He turned to drinking. And when he couldn't provide for you, for you to go to that prestigious camp, well, he felt he had to do something."

"When I think about that, it makes me feel like it's my fault that he turned to robbing someone just for me," Diamond said. "I really wanted to go to that camp and I kept talking about it and talking about it. It made him feel like he had to get that money for me."

"He's my brother and I love him to death," Venita said, "but that was no one's fault but his own. He wasn't raised to take from others. He took an extreme turn—his heart might have been in the right place, but his head was way out of bounds—and he had to pay for it. That's why he didn't even go to trial. He faced up to his crime and it helped his sentence. He had a gun, which means he could have gotten twelve to fifteen years if found guilty in a trial."

"It's been hard for me because people ask, 'What do your parents do?' and I have a hard time answering," Diamond said. "It's been very awkward. I have told them, 'My dad fixes cars.' That's what I remember, what I hold on to—seeing him slide from under a car, all sweaty and greasy, but still wanting me to hug and kiss him. He would say, 'This dirt has nothing to do with your sugar.' What's life going to be like for him? He's a felon. He can't get a job."

"Life is going to be much better because he'll be able to spend time with you, come visit you here next homecoming," Venita said. "And he'll be able to be with Saundra. That's what matters most. But he'll have a job waiting for him. Two of his buddies who learned everything they knew from him opened shops. They're actually competing to get him to work at their place. So, he will be able to step back in and earn a living, which is really important to someone who has been away for seven years. He's going to have to go to school to catch up, but he's so determined that won't be a problem.

"But how you respond to him will be critical, Diamond. You are the second love of his life. He's going to need you to embrace him as your dad. If your mom could, she would. So it's just you who can really be that person to hold him up as he gets adjusted. Knowing his daughter loves him and is not bitter will make everything go so much better."

"Well, Aunt Venita, I love my daddy. Nothing can change that," Diamond said. "I was worried at first because he wouldn't let me come to visit him—just that one time. He writes me and I write him back and send him photos. But he wouldn't let me visit him or send me pictures. He said he didn't want me to have images of him in there."

She wiped her face and took a deep breath.

"I'm getting my daddy back," she said. She looked out of the car window in no direction in particular. And then the tears flowed, like a waterfall. And Venita hugged her.

CHAPTER FOURTEEN
A WILD NIGHT

Mary and Rodney, Kwame and Tranise

By the time they finished off another round of drinks at The Broadway, Mary and Rodney were back in college mode.

"Tranise, we're going to leave and get something to eat," Mary said.

"Yeah, I bet something to eat," Tranise said sarcastically. "Have fun. I'll leave with Charlene."

"Actually, I was hoping we could go do something private," Kwame said.

"Something like what?" Tranise wanted to know.

"I haven't figured it out yet," he said. "Maybe we could go down to the Waterside Mall and sit outside by the water. Maybe we could go back to my place—I live in Ghent Village—and listen to some music."

Tranise laughed. "See, this is where your age shows up," she said. "Listen to some music? That's the oldest—and weakest—line in the book."

Before Kwame could respond, Rodney jumped in.

"We're going to be seeing you fine people later," he said. He hugged Tranise and shook Kwame's hand. "Good luck, partner," he said, and they were gone.

"I'm with Charlene, so even if I wanted to do something, I couldn't leave her," Tranise said.

"You women are funny," Kwame said. "Charlene is over there having a ball. You think she's worried about where you go?"

"Uh, yes, I do," Tranise said.

"Listen, if you don't want to go, just say that," Kwame said. He was smiling but he was serious. "You don't have to use your girl as an excuse."

"Look, she's coming over here now," Tranise said. "Watch... 'Charlene, you ready to go?'"

"Well, can I talk to you for a minute?" Charlene said. She had been dancing with Tyrell Mingus, a former football player who looked like he gave up the game for burgers. He, like Charlene, could have stood to lose a few dozen pounds. But he was a handsome guy who always had a thing for Charlene in college.

Last time they saw each other, which was two years earlier at homecoming, Tyrell misplaced Charlene's phone number and was angry that he did. Seeing her at the party was all the opportunity he needed; he was not going to blow it.

"Girl, I think I'm going to leave with Tyrell," Charlene said. "He lives in Portsmouth and said he wanted to take me over there to that other day party or to his house. Seems to me like I should go. But what do you think?"

"Charlene, you know it doesn't matter what I think," Tranise said.

"No, it does matter," Charlene insisted.

"Well, just like Mary, I think you should go with Ty," Tranise said. "He was a nice guy in college. As long as you feel comfortable and safe, then go have fun."

Tranise and Charlene hugged. "You going to the jazz concert or the all-black party or the Best of Friends reception or...what?" Tranise asked.

"If I'm as lucky as I hope, I'll be seeing you in the morning," Charlene said. "Besides, Mary has the car."

"Damn. That's right. Okay. I guess I should say, 'Have fun,'" Tranise said. Then she turned to Kwame, who smiled at her.

"Well, I guess going down to Waterside won't be so bad for a while," Tranise said. "But I'm going to the all-black party later at the Holiday Inn off Newtown Road."

"Wow," Kwame said. "How ironic. Me, too. I guess I can be your ride—if you want—since Mary has the car."

"Well, let's see how this goes first," she responded. She was all right with Kwame taking her to the event, but only if he understood they were not going together, that she would be free to mingle with her former classmates. She did not know that Kwame had the same ideas.

In the car, Tranise called Mary, who answered, but only briefly.

"So what's the plan for later?" Tranise said. "Or is there a plan?"

"I think your plan and my plan might be different," Mary said, and then she laughed. "I'm probably not going to make it to the party."

"But a lot of people will be there," Tranise said.

"I know. But they'll all be at the tailgate and at the game," Mary said. "So I'm going to catch up with folks then."

Tranise could hear Rodney in the background. "Well, I've got to run," Mary said. "Have fun and call me in the morning."

Mary disconnected the call and immediately contacted Charlene, who was en route to Tyrell's home. "Well, you go right ahead, girl," Mary said. "Tell Tyrell hello for me. I'm in the room with Rodney. So, I'll see you in the morning?"

"Yes," Charlene said. "I'll call before he drops me off."

Mary turned off the ringer on her phone and placed it on the dresser. Rodney had stopped at Total Wine and purchased some champagne. "Why champagne?" he said, repeating Mary's question. "Because we're celebrating."

"Celebrating what?" she asked.

"Celebrating reconnection, celebrating homecoming," he answered as he popped the cork.

The truth was that Mary never got Rodney out of her system. Although they were young when they had met in college, their relationship was something that stuck with her. First loves tend to do that.

The other truth was that at home, Mary had a boyfriend—Clint, a pharmacist that catered to her every whim. He was the catch of a lifetime—financially sound, handsome, smart, likeable and attentive. But there was no magic there, and Mary needed magic—or even the *promise* of something magical.

They were almost three years into the relationship and Mary spent more than half of that time mildly engaged. She found herself envisioning other men making love to her, even as she lay underneath Clint. She was too embarrassed to share that with anyone—or to dare leave a man everyone considered ideal.

When she saw Rodney at The Broadway, her body reacted. It was the anticipation of something magical that made her feel a combination of chills and trembles. She cared about and, in her own way, loved her boyfriend, Clint. But as soon as Rodney professed his long-time interest for Mary, she knew she would be where she was—in bed with him.

"I can't even believe this," Rodney said between kisses on Mary's neck. "I mean, I wanted this, but I couldn't expect it. I feel like this is where we're supposed to be."

Mary's eyes were closed, but her quick-witted mind was not. "In bed? That's where we're supposed to be?" she cracked.

"You say that like it's a bad thing," Rodney said.

"I know it's kinda late to be asking this since we're naked here in the bed, but is this all you want from me? Sex?" Mary said.

Rodney pulled away from her so she could see his face. "Mary, you must not have been listening to me earlier," he said. "I'm still feeling you. I knew I was, but seeing you at the party just confirmed it big time. I'm not playing with you."

With that, he leaned in for a deep, passionate kiss that Mary did not resist. In fact, she creased her lips and let Rodney's tongue enter her mouth. She wrapped her arms around his stout shoulders and was brought right back to her youth, when she was young and inexperienced, but received the pleasure that would stick with her all this time later.

She closed her eyes and enjoyed the kisses Rodney planted on her face and neck and shoulders. When he moved down toward her nipples that were as erect as thimbles, she threw her arms above her head, as if to say, *take me. Do as you please*.

Rodney got the message. He covered her entire body with caresses and kisses, eliciting moans and sounds of pleasure from Mary that she forgot she could make. As she tried to catch her breath, Rodney presented a condom as if from thin air, like a magician. That was Mary's cue to spread her legs, which she did, and Rodney, in two swift motions, applied the condom and inserted his pulsating erection inside Mary's warm, wet crease.

She braced herself at first, but Rodney was gentle, methodically penetrating her, in small increments. Before long, Mary was thrusting upward and pulling Rodney down deeper into her. He obliged her beckoning, pumping harder and deeper the more she screamed. That's how Mary liked it—intense and almost reckless.

Rodney liked it that way, too, so the high-impact loving of their past was just as jarring and pleasing seven years later. The sweat that sat on Rodney's back like standing water was an indication of the work he was doing. And the disheveled hair was tell-tale of Mary's actions.

The first round of passion lasted eight minutes or so, but it was a hot, aggressive, fulfilling eight minutes. Round Two started about forty minutes later, after they lay side-by-side, sipping champagne and reminiscing. It lasted significantly longer, with Rodney flexing his muscles and aggressive nature, flipping Mary to her knees, then on her side, later off the bed and onto the floor. It was the kind of intensity Mary craved in lovemaking.

"Sometimes, you just liked to get fucked," she had told her girls. "Forget being nice and polite. Just give it to me."

Rodney gave it to her. It was not until long after midnight that their frolicking ceased. Mary lay on her back, exhausted and exhilarated. Her body smiled. It was a feeling she needed, but did not get from her boyfriend, Clint.

❋❋❋

"So, is that enough to leave someone over? Sex," Charlene said the next morning, as they prepared to go to the homecoming parade.

"I don't know, to be honest," Mary said. "I mean, it would be awesome if Clint gave me what I needed. He's such a nice guy, a good man. But you know what I think the problem is?"

"He's not endowed enough?" Charlene said, laughing.

"You would think that would be the problem, but that's not it," Mary said. "He doesn't know how to use what he has. He's basically too nice. Rodney handles me, he—now, this might be too much information—but he smacks my ass. He bends me over. He's forceful. It's like he knows what he wants and I, in turn, like what he wants because he's in control. I need a man to be in control and to be aggressive—don't be so respectful that he's treating me like I will shatter.

"I told Clint, 'I'm not fragile.' But that didn't translate into what I wanted. He just doesn't get it and it's hard to tell a man who thinks he's all together that he's weak in bed."

"Well, what are you gonna do?" Charlene asked. "It looks like you won't get what you want. I think it's hard to leave a man just because of sex."

"It's hard to leave a man for most anything," Mary said. "But after last night, I know that if I stay in it, I'm going to be seeing Rodney whenever I can. I'm not saying that like I'm bragging. I'm saying it as a fact. I felt so good that I can still feel it now. That's the way it should be, the way I need it to be."

"Then why stay, Mary?" Charlene said. "Life is too short to be with someone—no matter what his other credentials are—that doesn't really fulfill you."

"That's true," Mary said. "I guess, to be totally honest, I look at all the things the Clint does bring to the table. I look at how all my friends think he's so wonderful and that we're so great together. I look at how my parents feel about him."

"Yeah, well, none of them have to sleep with him," Charlene said.

"I don't want it to sound like Clint is terrible in bed," Mary explained. "Someone else might think he's the bomb. I'm just saying that for me, he's lacking. And his pride and ego would not accept me telling him how to be better. I tried it already and he basically took it like I was crazy and did nothing different.

"Anyway, I don't want to talk about it anymore. It takes away from how I'm feeling right now."

"Just one more question," Charlene said. "Do you feel guilty?"

Mary did not know how to answer. She felt exhilarated. She felt relieved. She felt satisfied.

"I have not allowed myself to feel guilty," she finally answered. "I thought about guilt before we went to the room. But once I decided that I was going to do it, I only felt pleasure. Now that it's over and now that you have asked me about it, I feel sort of sad more than anything. But maybe that's just semantics. I don't know how I feel. I know this: I don't regret it, not the way I feel. I hope that doesn't sound cold. But it's true. Was it the right thing to do, considering I'm in a relationship? No. It was a selfish thing, but something I needed."

Charlene understood. She and Tyrell had enjoyed a night of passion, too. She had not planned on it. It had unfolded.

"Talking about needing it…," she said to Mary. "Maybe that's why I went with Tyrell. It'd been about sixteen months, two weeks and three days since I'd gotten some action."

"I don't know why you put 'about' in that sentence," Mary cracked. "You know how long it's been down to the minute. And you know it's been a long time when you keep a running tab on how long you've been without."

"I know, girl," she said. "I hadn't even had a decent date in eight months. So, I was in need of someone to at least hug me, comfort me, make me feel sexy, make me feel desired. Tyrell did a good job of that. I didn't see stars or rockets taking off. But he made me feel good and made me feel wanted. I needed that."

"I totally understand," Mary said, looking down at her cell phone. It was Tranise. She had texted her to say she was headed to the homecoming parade.

"I'm texting her back to say we're on our way," Mary told Charlene. "We'll coordinate and meet her somewhere. Then we can go to breakfast."

"Breakfast better be soon," Charlene said in a heavy Southern accent. "I ain't some little twig like you. I needs to eat."

The women laughed and headed to the parade. Along the way they put Tranise on the speaker phone of Charlene's cell phone.

"So, how did it go last night? What did you do?" Charlene asked.

"I had fun," she said. She sounded ambiguous, like she was holding back. Then she said, "Kwame and I are almost at the parade."

That explained it. "Can he hear us?" Mary asked.

"No," Tranise said.

"Good. You little slut," Mary said, laughing. "I can't believe you. You just met that guy yesterday."

Tranise laughed, too. "Okay, I will see y'all when you get here," she said. "Bye."

"Can you believe this girl?" Mary said.

"Yeah, I can believe her," Charlene said. "Look at what we did."

"At least we knew the guys we were with," she said. "And Rodney and I have a serious past."

"Well, I'm not gonna judge my girl," Charlene said.

"Me, either," Mary added. "I'm just saying."

When they got close to the school, they called Tranise and coordinated with her so they could meet and enjoy the parade together. When they connected at the corner of Virginia Beach Boulevard and Majestic Avenue, Kwame was not there.

"Where's your man, girl?" Mary asked.

"You are a trip," Tranise answered. "You know that boy is not my man. He just dropped me off."

"So you got with him last night? I'm a little surprised, girlfriend," Mary said.

"Mary, you know me better than that," Tranise said. "He picked me up this morning to bring me here. I didn't get with him. We had a good time last night, though. He was a perfect gentleman."

"See," Charlene said. "Mary was calling you a ho."

"I figured she was, with her jumping-to-conclusions ass," Tranise said. "I, unlike you, remain pure."

They all laughed. "I don't know why you're laughing, Charlene," Mary said. "You fall into the slut category yourself."

"What?" Tranise said.

"Oh, yeah," Mary said. "We'll talk about it at breakfast."

They put aside the banter for a while and enjoyed the parade. Hundreds of people lined the streets. The band from Booker T. Washington High School came through with energy and rhythm. The floats were elaborate. The Grand Marshall of the parade was Derek T. Dingle, a 1983 graduate who worked as executive editor of *Black Enterprise* magazine. Miss Alumni, Lauren Brown, came rolling by not long before the homecoming king and queen.

"Look at how young they look," Charlene said. "Damn. They look like babies."

"You remember being on that float, Tranise," Mary asked.

"I do," she said. "It was so much fun. And you all are crazy. I remember when we got to where you and Charlene were standing. I was waving and smiling and people were waving back at me. And then I saw you two and y'all gave me 'the finger.' I couldn't help but bust out laughing. I was supposed to be poised and stuff and you all made me laugh so hard. And you know I wanted to give you 'the finger' back."

"Hey, what are friends for?" Charlene joked.

They ran into more old classmates, exchanged pleasantries and took photos. Finally, they headed to breakfast at D Egg in downtown Norfolk, during which time they briefed Tranise on their overnight adventures. But Mary and Charlene did not ask about Tranise's night with Kwame until they were comfortable at their table.

"So…," Mary started, giving Tranise a side-eye look.

"So what?" Tranise said, smiling.

"You know what. Don't be cute," Charlene said.

"Do you honestly think I would sleep with a man I just met?" she asked.

"Ah, yeah," Mary said, and they all laughed again.

"No way," Tranise said. "He's really a nice young guy, though. After you hookers left to do God knows what, he took me down to Waterside Mall. We sat in the outside area and literally talked and talked. It's very nice over there with the cruise ships and boats going by. Very nice."

"So, that was it? You just talked?" Charlene asked.

"Look at you, wanting to get some of the nitty-gritty stuff," Tranise said. "Well, there was no nitty-gritty. We stayed there about an hour and guess where we went next?"

"To the all-black party," Mary said.

"We did—but that was later," Tranise said. "We went to the step show."

"Oh, my God," Charlene said. "It's too much going on. I forgot all about the step show. Damn. How was it?"

"It was a trip; that's how it was," Tranise said. "The gym was packed. Some of these students look like they should be in middle school. I swear. They look like some of my students. It's crazy. But the step show has changed over the years. It's almost more about dancing and music than actually stepping, like when we were in school.

"Everyone comes out to music and tries to put on this big production. The Kappas were good; they didn't drop the cane, if you can believe that. The Ques were the Ques—loud and nasty. They had these big buff guys standing guard with no shirts on. They give you what you expect. The Alphas turned it out, though. Those boys did their thing. They had this smoke effect and all of a sudden, they appeared through the smoke. They were in sync. They played to the crowd. They made the best impression. They won."

"I'm not surprised," Charlene said. "They used to win every year with J.D., Ronnie Bagley, Chuck Johnson, Gerald Mason, Randy Brown, Sam Myers, Marvin Burch, Kilroy Hall, Pork and Bean, Harry Sykes, Nick Lambert, Ron Simms, Greg Willis, Frank Nelson, Kelvin Lloyd, Akers, Larry Brown, Maurice Hawkins and that whole crew."

"And every one of those guys you mentioned was there," Tranise said. "I have some photos. They had a huge Alpha section. It was their chapter's fiftieth anniversary, so many of them came back."

"How were the sororities?" Mary asked.

"They were good, too," Tranise said. "The Zetas represented. I was proud of them. The AKAs were hot—they had a lot of girls out there and they did their thing. They were very classy. But the Deltas were equally classy and on point. It was a tie in my mind."

"I can't believe I missed it," Mary said. "I want to see your pictures... So, you went to the all-black party after that?"

"Yep," Tranise said. "I should be exhausted, but I'm not. I'm too excited, I guess. After the step show, Kwame dropped me at my hotel. I showered and changed and he went home and did the same. You have to see this cute little black dress I wore. It was a hit. Kwame picked me up around midnight and we went to the party.

"I thought I was going to have to tell him that I needed my space once we got there," Tranise added, "but he was very cool. It was a lot of people. A great party. I saw more people I hadn't seen in a long time. And I saw Felicia."

"Oh, boy. How did that go?" Charlene said.

"It went okay, I guess," Tranise answered. "She was with Brandon, so I think he was a little awkward because he was clearly flirting with me at the other party. They were standing nearby as people kept complimenting me on how I look. I know that ate her up.

"We never made any kind of connection. Brandon spoke to me for a hot second; he seemed uncomfortable that his wife would see him and say something. So, he kept it moving."

Tranise was surprised at herself. Seeing Brandon with Felicia would have turned her stomach back in the day. Last night, it gave her a thrill, like the challenge to break her man was official. She was a goody-two-shoes chick in college. Maybe breaking out of that comfort zone over the weekend would be a sign of growth for her. At least, that was her twisted thought.

"So, you spent a lot of time with Kwame but you seem excited about seeing Brandon," Mary said. "What's up with that?"

"Kwame is really, really nice; I like him," Tranise said. "He's mature and respectful. But he's also almost four years younger than me. That's getting in my way."

"The older you get, the less his age is a factor," Charlene said. "You get him now, you can mold him into what you want him to be. If you do it right, in a year he'll be good and trained."

"What would you know about training someone," Tranise said, after laughing. "Only thing you've trained is that weave you used to wear."

"That was a *good* weave, I'll have you know," Charlene countered. "Only you and Mary knew it wasn't my hair."

"Anyway," Tranise said, "I like him. I'm not jumping into anything. I'm just getting to know the man. But you know what was funny? It seemed to me that Brandon was a little jealous to see me with Kwame. He saw us together at The Broadway and then again that night. He was a little dismissive of Kwame to me. Kwame noticed it, too. He said, 'I thought your boy was married. He sure seemed agitated to see you with me.'"

"He has no room to be agitated or anything else," Mary said. "His ass is married. Period."

"Don't choke on your biscuit. Damn," Tranise said.

"No, it bothers me when guys think they have territory over us," Mary said. "Not only is he married, but his wife is pregnant. And he knows that you know his wife. Seems to me you need to put him in his place."

"Like you put Rodney in his place last night?" Tranise snapped back.

"All right, now," Charlene jumped in. "We're not getting bitchy with each other. We're all grown folks and can do what we want."

"I wasn't trying to be bitchy, Mary," Tranise said. "I wasn't. I was just saying—"

"You don't have to explain," Mary interrupted. "I will explain this much: I'm not married, so I can do what I want to do. That doesn't mean spending the night with Rodney was the morally right thing to do. It wasn't. I was trying to make the point of how married men, with no shame, approach single women. And even have the audacity to get bent out of shape if he sees you with someone else. That bugs me. I've had a lot of married men come at me, and I think it's such an insult."

Tranise absorbed her friend's words. "I agree with you," she said. "I do. You know I have always had this thing for Brandon, and now he's finally showing me some attention and I kind of like it. It doesn't mean I will sleep with him. That makes me just as bad as him. I have to admit that I like getting attention from him. But going the distance? I don't think so."

That was the ideal way to end their breakfast and head over to the massive tailgate party on campus. "But y'all make sure I'm not alone with him," Tranise said. "I know what I should do. But my body doesn't."

CHAPTER FIFTEEN

LET THE CHASE BEGIN

Jesse and Don

Instead of taking a nap, Jesse had Don take him to Kappatal Kuts next to the 7-Eleven on Brambleton Avenue, across from campus. He did not have time to get a haircut before leaving and Don pointed out that he looked like a "rag-a-muffin."

The barbershop almost immediately became a staple in the community when Junius opened the doors in 1988. He brought in talented barbers Sporty and Kevin Rodgers and it was on. Kappatal Kuts was a fixture, *the* place to get that fade tightened up or to hang out and hear some of the most radical and hilarious social commentary from workers and clients alike.

The Friday night wait was long, which gave Don time to catch up with Bert, who came over to meet him there. And it allowed them to absorb the madness that comes with many urban barbershops.

The DVD man came in offering bootleg versions of the latest movies, followed by the cake lady with a cart of red velvet, pound and chocolate cake slices for sale. Then there was the seafood man, who came in, believe it or not, with frozen shrimp in sandwich bags.

"Being here right now is tripping me out," Jesse said. "I feel like I'm nineteen years old again. The barbers may have changed, but the energy is still the same. And I wish Charlie Wong's was still across the street. That was my Chinese food spot."

On the TV was *Jeopardy*, the game show. Patrons and barbers were struggling to answer questions, which started ten minutes of side-cracking jokes.

"Man, y'all ain't gonna answer none of dem questions," Macho, a barber, said in a deep, deep Southern accent. "You need to watch *Jeopardy For Da Hood*. That's a show you might answer a question or two."

His client egged him on.

"So, what kinda questions would they be on *Jeopardy For Da Hood*?" he asked.

Macho jumped right on it. "Questions like, 'How many rounds does a nine-millimeter hold?"

The packed shop erupted in laughter.

"Or, 'If you have one hundred dollars' worth of food stamps and steal fifty dollars' worth of food stamps from yo baby daddy, how many food stamps do you now have?" another client chipped in.

"How about, 'How many baby mommas does the average drug dealer have?'" another client contributed.

"I got one," another barber shouted. "What is the ratio of baking powder to cocaine in an ounce?"

And on and on it went. Finally, Laurie Hunt, a classy female barber in the shop from New York, jumped in. "You all need to stop," she said. "If you heard white people making these jokes, you'd be ready to kill somebody. Remember last week, when those teachers in Georgia used slaves in a worksheet for math word problems? She could have used anything in the world, and she used slavery with some black kids. And you all were personally offended, as you should have been. So, I know you're joking. But let's joke about something else."

"Ah, Laurie, lighten up," Macho said. "Deez jokes are for present company only. And you know dey funny."

"No, they're not," she said. "They're offensive."

"You rather we talk about women?" he said. "You really would be offended den."

"I'm telling you this feels like college all over again," Jesse said, leaning into Don's ear. "Gotta love it."

After another twenty minutes or so, Jesse got in the chair and out. He and Don went across the street to the jazz concert at the Douglas Wilder Center on campus, where local artists provided a beautiful evening.

When it was over, while standing in the lobby to canvass the women who were leaving, they encountered many friends from their days in school, including Jeff Jones, a former baseball player who ended up in divinity school. Jeff was as affable and funny as anyone on campus, so learning he had become a born-again Christian surprised Jesse and Don.

"I guess we shouldn't be surprised, really," Don said. "It can happen to anyone."

"I know *what* you're saying, but listen to *how* that sounded," Jesse said. "You said it like he got laid off from a job or was stricken with a disease or something."

Laughing, Don said, "I know, right? I guess that was a bad way to put it. I meant that you know someone one way and it's always a surprise when they make a dramatic change. But when I think about it, there was always something spiritual about Jeff."

"Look at that," Jesse said, pointing across the lobby. It was James Granderson, a long-time business professor who retired two years earlier.

"Mr. Granderson can't stay away from Norfolk State," Jesse said. "He taught here, like, forty years or something ridiculous like that. He was my boy, though. I took his classes and he would give me an A as long as I went to the store and bought wine for him."

"What?" Don said.

"Yes," Jesse said. "On top of that, he was banging a lot of the students."

"Come on, man. You lying," Don said.

"No, I'm not," Jesse insisted. "I even caught a friend of mine's girlfriend in his office one day. He caught her cheating on a test and had a 'meeting' with her. She had a look on her face that said, 'I'm busted.' I never said anything to my boy. But it was obvious what was about to go down."

"That's crazy," Don said. "But not surprising, I guess. Wait, look at *that*." He used his eyes to direct Jesse to a young lady who passed by with a can't-miss booty.

"Do you know who that is?" Jesse said. "Hold up. We might have some action tonight."

He left Don standing there confused and caught up with the young lady.

"Excuse me," he said and she turned around. She was a little older, her face was slightly rounder and there was a little bit of a midsection that was not there seven or eight years ago. But there was no mistaking: It was Lynnette Commons, a woman who one night found herself in a sex train at Jesse's apartment when she was a sophomore.

She got there because she liked Jesse and they ended their movie date at his place. She got drunk off of a six-pack of Miller beer with Jesse in his bedroom while some of his friends played Spades in the living room. Having a buzz turned her into something Jesse didn't expect.

She came out of the bedroom, blouse unbuttoned, showing off her ample breasts, and flirting with the other guys. Jesse was taken aback at first but he quickly went with the flow when one of his buddies came to him and said, "We can run a train on this girl."

Jesse didn't respond. He watched as she danced and teased and basically dared the men to do something. Well, they did. She was ushered to the back where one-by-one, the men took their turns. She might have been drunk, but she functioned as if she were coherent.

She passed out about the time the last guy was done. Jesse let her sleep for a few hours. When she woke up, she got dressed and Jesse took her back to her apartment off of Little Creek Road. Neither of them said a word about what had happened.

Jesse drove back home wondering what was wrong with Lynette. Maybe she just got off on pleasing a bunch of men, he'd rationalized. He had been with her alone before that escapade, and she did not seem as lively as she was with the gang bang. But she did not drink that first night, either. In any case, she was forever known among a small group of guys as "The Miller Freak."

"Lynette, how are you? You might not remember me," he said.

She looked at him for a second. "Oh, my goodness," she said, moving in for a hug. "How are you? What's your name?"

"I'm Jesse. It's been a long time," he answered. "You look good. Look like life is treating you well."

"It is," she said. "I live in Connecticut now. It's cold in the winter, but I enjoy it."

Jesse's mind started to race. She did not have on a wedding ring and she was alone. He wanted to get Lynette back to his hotel room. If she was anything like she was at nineteen, he was in for a good night. And she would be good for Don, who was not quite himself. Jesse noticed but had not said anything to him about it.

"So what you up to now?" he asked. "I'm with my man over there, Don. We're talking about going to the all-black party. But we'll probably go to the room and have some drinks first. You're welcome to join us."

"Oh, that's sweet of you; I appreciate the offer," she said. "But I gave up drinking a long time ago. I'm actually going to catch the end of a prayer service at my friend's church somewhere over in Ghent."

"A prayer service? Really?" Jesse said. He was confounded. He did not expect to hear that come out of her mouth.

"Yes, I turned my life over to Christ about two years after graduating from Norfolk State," she said. "It has been the best thing that could have ever happened to me. Earlier this year I was named assistant pastor at my church in Norwalk. God is good."

Instantly, Jesse felt a level of guilt. He was about to proposition one of God's spokespersons.

"That's awesome," he said as Don walked up. "Don, this is Lynette. She was at school during our time."

"Oh, I remember you," he said. "I didn't know you, but you're kind of hard to forget."

Lynette smiled, but was not sure if he was paying a compliment or referring to her notorious drunken sex binges. They chatted for another minute or so before she said her good-byes and walked off. Don and Jesse stood there admiring her substantial ass.

"That's the girl I told you about one time; who came to the house and did four, five guys," Jesse said.

"That's her? Get the fuck outta here?" Don said. "Well, I mean, what's up? Why did we let her get away?"

"Man, you won't believe this," Jesse explained. "She's saved. Not only is she saved, but she said she's an assistant pastor at her church in Connecticut. And—get this: She's going to catch the end of a prayer session somewhere right now."

"Well, damn," Don said. "That's two of Jesus' folks we ran into in, like, ten minutes. Maybe He's trying to tell us something."

"Yeah, like it's time to start drinking again," Jesse said.

"I'll drink to that," Don said, and off they went to the ABC Store.

"Virginia still has these backward-ass liquor laws," Don said. "How you gonna have a liquor store where you can't by beer and wine? And how they gonna make you finish your drinks by two a.m. but your club stays open to four? That's some dumb shit."

"It's because it's a Commonwealth state," Jesse said. "But I'm told they are breaking away from this ABC crap and allowing private citizens to get liquor licenses and open up independent liquor stores. And guess what? All the allotted licenses were purchased in a heartbeat."

"Shit, I wish I had opened a liquor store," Don said. "Good times or bad times, people will drink. I go and open a neighborhood convenience store… It's hard to survive, man. Wal-Mart in particular is the everything store. And our people, well, I love us, but I guess I don't understand us. They'd rather drive ten minutes away to shop at Wal-Mart over walking to the corner to support a black-owned business in their own neighborhood. It makes me sad, to be honest."

"I hear you," Jesse said. "Is that's what's on your mind? You've been having a good time. But you do seem a little preoccupied at times."

"Yeah, well, I'm waiting on a call from my accountant. It should come today or tomorrow," Don said. "I need an investor or my days are numbered. Probably have to go back to stinky-ass corporate America."

"Well, D, let's hope for the best, man," Jesse said. "We're about to do the right thing: Get drunk to get your mind off the situation."

And they did just that. Don slowly drove as Jesse poured Remy Martin. They sipped and talked and wanted to light up a joint, but didn't want to smell like it at the party. Before long, the effects of the cognac started to kick in.

Jesse said, "Do you know it's actually safer for us to smoke weed and drive than it is for us to drink and drive?"

"Ah, shit, here we go," Don said.

"I'm serious," Jesse went on. "There was a study that recently came out. People who drink and drive are three hundred and eighty-five times more likely to have a fatal car accident than those who are sober. At the same time, a study for nineteen years in the sixteen states that have legalized marijuana shows a nine percent drop in traffic deaths.

"And you know why? Because people who are drunk think they are Superman or Wonder Woman. They take more risks. Weed smokers take it easy, drive slower and know when they are too messed up to drive."

"You might have a problem, knowing all this stuff," Don said.

"No, man, I read this online," Jesse said. "The University of Colorado did the study. I'm just telling you what I read. But it does make sense, doesn't it?"

"Yeah, it does," Don said. "And since it does, maybe I should stop drinking until we get to where we're going."

"Good idea, homey," Jesse said. "Don't mind if I keep drinking, do you?"

"You're funny," Don said.

With the liquor loosening his tongue, Jesse talked and talked. "You know, sometimes I drink just to be social," he said. "This is one of those times I'm drinking to be social and to escape my life."

"I'm the one with problems," Don said. "If I don't get the call I need to get, I'm out of business. You're a lawyer in Philly, making good bank—and you're single. Trust me, don't look at not being married as a problem."

"Nah, it's not that. I do miss the good days of marriage—all five of them," he said, laughing. "But I'm worried about my little sister. She got caught up with this guy that from the moment I saw him, I thought, 'He's not right.' I told her that and I told *him* that. About eight months later, she marries this guy. Comes home talking about they eloped. Who elopes these days? It was his idea because he knew I would have talked her out of that dumb shit.

"Come to find out, he's a damn drug dealer. I knew it. He was too flashy and did a whole bunch of stuttering when I asked him what he did. To his credit, he didn't lie. He said, 'I have my own thing, my own business.'

"My sister played the naïve role, claiming she didn't know. Now she's with this guy afraid to leave because he's crazy as hell," Jesse said. "I'm feeling like I want to shoot the guy—if I could get away with it."

"Well, sometimes you hear stuff to make you feel better about your shit," Don said.

"What's going on with you?" Jesse asked.

Don took a deep breath. "I came here for one reason: to get away from all the bad stuff at home," he said. "Business falling apart. Marriage falling apart. This is about the only place I could think of where I could go and feel energized. Homecoming. Any place else, I'd probably ball up in the fetal position and crawl under a desk."

"Man, you need drinks more than I do," Jesse said. "I'm sorry to hear about that. But just as you said, there is always someone worse off than you. And if there's one thing I know about you, you will overcome—damn, I sound like Martin Luther King. But I'm serious. You're a fighter. And anything I can do to help, I will. Just let me know."

Don looked over at his friend. "I appreciate that, man."

Jesse nodded his head. At that moment his mission was to assure Don had so much fun that he went back home feeling better about his plight, even if the circumstances looked grim.

Just before they arrived at the Holiday Inn for the party, Venita called. Her niece had gone to the bathroom, so she took a few minutes to catch up with her boys.

"Are your panties still on?" Jesse said as he answered the phone.

"Shut up, boy," she said. "What's happening?"

"We're about to go to the party. We just got here," Jesse said. "What you gonna do?"

"I might come over there with my niece, Diamond."

"Oh, yeah, the pole dancer. How is she?" Jesse said.

"If I didn't know you were a lawyer, I would think you're an idiot," she said. "As a matter of fact, you're an idiot lawyer… Anyway, her roommate is pregnant and hasn't talked to anyone about it, so I'm hoping to do that tonight."

"You?" Jesse asked.

"Look, I'm not even studying you," she said. "Just text me and let me know how it is."

"All right, baby girl."

"I guess Venita isn't coming, huh?" Don asked as he parked the car in the back of the hotel. "I wanted to see this niece of hers. She said she's cute."

"In the meantime, take a shot of this Remy," Jesse said.

"Make it a double," Don said.

They sat in the car for about twenty minutes, drinking and watching more people—mostly women—go into the party.

By the time they decided to put down the cognac and, indeed, enter the event, they were more tipsy than they realized.

"I guess this is what it feels like after—how many?—six shots of Remy Martin?" Don said.

A cool breeze provided some relief as they made their way from the car to the entrance. The alcohol, though, was in control.

Don's problems were pushed to the recesses of his mind. Jesse was on the prowl for someone to connect with so he could look to close the deal Saturday night.

"That's what tonight is about," he said to Don as they stood in the lobby, checking out the scene, but mostly eyeballing the women. "Meet someone and tomorrow night, go in for the kill. There are enough women who come back here with the same mentality. What happens at homecoming stays at homecoming."

"I'm down with that," Don said. "I just need something to happen to leave here."

Jesse did not hear Don. He was focused on Collette Simpson-Washington with whom he'd had a sexual tryst when they were juniors. As sensual and memorable as it was, there was a problem. There were at least a dozen other guys who had the same kind of sexual tryst with Collette.

"You gotta remember her," Jesse said after he and Collette hugged and chatted for a minute or two. She was with a girlfriend that neither he nor Don knew.

"I'm surprised she's here after what happened three years ago at homecoming," Jesse said.

"Was I here? What happened?" Don said.

"You were here, but you had your wife with you that year," Jesse said.

"Oh, don't remind me," Don said. "I couldn't do anything. I felt like I was in prison... But what happened with her? And why didn't you tell me about it then?"

"Man, I forgot," Jesse said. "But check this out: So, back in college, Collette had this boyfriend as a freshman and sophomore. He wore a high-top fade and she always wore dresses, like she was this Southern belle. She's from Tennessee, I believe.

"Anyway, they broke up and I'm not sure what happened, but

she was like a dude. She was getting it in, one guy after another. She had to have slept with at least ten to fifteen guys—or more—in her last two years. It was interesting because she and I were always cool. We were in the bowling league together and just made a connection.

"She would basically say stuff like, 'I'm just having fun. If men can do it, why can't women?' I'm not sure if she was trying to defy stereotypes or was just some little freak. But with how she looked and with that body, who was going to refuse a chance to get with her? We were so cool that I would tell her who she shouldn't mess with.

"Anyway, she graduates and no one sees her for years. Then she pops up at homecoming three years ago—with her new husband, who was some guy who didn't go to Norfolk State and who had no idea about how she was in college. Not good. So, the way the tailgate was set up then, she had to walk past the Omegas, the Kappas and then the Alphas. She had slept with at least one or two guys in all those frats. These fools were drunk and when they saw her, one by one, they brought up her past.

"Saying, stuff like, 'Collette, are you still easy to get?'

"Cruel, ignorant stuff by some ignorant, drunk guys. By the time I saw her, she had passed all those groups. She had a look on her face that told me she was humiliated. She looked at me with a look that said, 'Please do not embarrass me any further.'

"I picked right up on it. I hugged her and was like, 'So good to see you.' She introduced me to her husband and I smiled at him, shook his hand. I even gave him the two-handed shake, like the President does when he's really trying to make a connection.

"Dude looked at me like he had been through hell. He was waiting for me to say something; he had his fist balled up. I believe that if I had said something he would have swung on me. He had had enough. He learned that his wife was not who he thought she was. It wasn't pretty. I didn't see her the rest of homecoming; they didn't even come to the parties."

"I don't think she has on a wedding ring," Don said. "That's terrible. I hope what happened here didn't ruin her marriage."

"I wouldn't be surprised if it did," Jesse said. "It was that bad."

The party was not bad at all. It fact, it was good. Something about homecoming put everyone is such high spirits.

"And," Jesse said, "you can start a conversation so easily because socializing is what this whole weekend is about. You have an easy entrée into a conversation because you went to the same school."

Don heard Jesse, but he didn't process much of it. The alcohol had him going, and he was sipping on another. There was such commotion at the entrance to the party, with so many converging at once, that Don and Jesse did as they had any number of times: They walked right into the event without paying.

"The key is to keep moving and to not make eye contact with anyone who's working the door," Jesse told Collette when they were inside. "You have to look like you are supposed to be inside. You have to be confident. We were willing to pay. But I didn't want to have to wait through all that drama to spend my money."

"So what's been going on with you?" she said, more interested in Jesse than how he got into the party. "I remember clearly the last time I saw you."

"I remember it, too," he said. "It was kinda awkward."

"Very awkward," she said. "But I should have thanked you long before now, but you saved me from hell that weekend. You treated me and my husband with respect, and that was right on time with all I had been dealing with."

"I can only imagine," Jesse said.

"No, you can't," Collette said. "You can't imagine what it felt like to look into your husband's eyes and see so much pain and disappointment...in you. Those assholes had some pretty mean things to say to me in front of my husband. That was totally unnecessary. What might have happened years ago, when I was nineteen, twenty, twenty-one years old, had nothing to do with who I am today. And there was no reason to humiliate me in front of my husband."

Collette looked and sounded sad. "To this day, I don't understand them. I know they were drunk, but you have to have a mean spirit in you to be that way to someone who was always nice to them."

"Well, I agree with you on almost everything you said," Jesse told Collette. "Remember how close we were and how much you used to share with me. I told you to not deal with certain people. And those people were the same people who turned on you three years ago."

"Really? I can't even count how many years later and you're telling me 'I told you so'?" Collette said, smiling. "I really don't mind them talking about me to my face. I don't mind facing that because that was me at that time. But to try to hurt me by saying those things in front of my husband…?

"If you notice, you didn't see me at any more events the entire weekend. I didn't want to go anywhere else. I just knew someone was going to make it worse for me and my relationship. We didn't even go to the game. We watched on television—him not even speaking to me. Finally, we had a heart-to-heart.

"He wanted to know why those guys were so vulgar and mean toward me. I told him he had his chance to ask them himself, that I couldn't account for anyone's actions but my own. He asked me what my relationship was with them; I told him we went to school together and that some of them I knew, some I didn't. Then he finally came out with it: He said, 'Did you fuck all those guys?' I just looked at him.

"Here's the thing, Jesse: From what I could tell, I didn't sleep with any of the idiots making comments. They were just drunk and talking shit. So I told my husband, 'No, I didn't, which was the truth.' He didn't believe me and kept asking me questions about why they would act the way they did.

"Finally, I had it. I told him, 'You just stood there and let them say things about me and you didn't say a word; you got mad at me. That's not how it's supposed to be. You're supposed to protect me and if it came down to it, take an ass-whipping defending me. But you didn't. You didn't say one damn word."

"Ah, man," Jesse said. "I'm sorry it got so ugly."

"Me, too," she said. "But I learned he didn't have my back. I would have pulled some bitch's eyes out if they had disrespected him in front of me. Or I would have at least tried to. That whole episode wasn't the reason we broke up, but it was the beginning of the end."

"I'm sorry, Collette," Jesse said.

"It wasn't your fault. And I'm fine now," she said. "I guess I learned two things; if you're not going to be proud of it later, don't do it. In college I wanted to experiment; I wanted to test the waters. I guess when a woman does that, she'd better be ready to get labeled."

"The double standard is true," Jesse said. "What's the other thing you learned?"

"Oh," Collette said, "don't bring your spouse to homecoming."

They both laughed.

"Come on," Jesse said, "let's dance."

"You were always really nice to me," she said. "I always appreciated that about you. Even as I was going through my wild stage, you never judged me or looked at me differently. That's a true friend."

CHAPTER SIXTEEN

THE TAILGATE, PART I

Catherine and Earl

Earl and Catherine skipped the step show, the jazz concert and the all-black party on Friday night and the parade on Saturday morning. They were in the homecoming spirit, but more into their own world. Elevating their relationship by making love on Thursday night (and Friday morning), had created an insatiable desire that was hard to harness.

Those displays of passion grew their affection into the stratosphere, and so, after Earl played golf and hung out with friends in the clubhouse, he and Catherine spent Friday evening over dinner at Catch 31 on the Virginia Beach oceanfront. There was time to make the all-black party afterward, but they bypassed that opportunity for a chance to spend more intimate time together.

"What's so special about what I'm feeling right now," Earl said to Catherine, "is that I expected you to be so wonderful and special just based on what I knew about you in college, from being around you and observing you. But you're better than I even imagined."

He leaned over and kissed her waiting lips, another show of public affection that surprised him. He considered himself a romantic, but the women of his past hardly appreciated his actions. If they did, they did not let him know it, which made him vow to hold back displays of thoughtfulness until he had a confident grasp on the person he was seeing.

Earl never felt as comfortable and confident with a woman as he did with Catherine, but he still told himself he would hold back. And yet, he could not. There was a magnetic force between them, and so trying to play coy simply would not work. They were drawn to each other, like human magnets.

"Thank you for saying that, Earl," Catherine said, blushing like a schoolgirl. "That means a lot to me. And I hope you know the feeling is mutual. I knew you as Earl Manning, a gentleman who seemed serious about his career. I had no idea about who you really were. And the more I get to know, the more I like, the more I love.

"You do know I love you, right? Can you feel it? I hope you can feel it."

"I can feel it—when I'm inside you, when I'm close to you and even when we're apart, which really speaks to our connection," he said. "We're good together. And I think we can be great together."

The passion they shared was almost touchable. There was a mutual respect, admiration and attraction. They could not mask it if they tried; making their impending appearance together on campus something that would send the gossipy folks into a craze.

They planned to go to the tailgate and the game separately: Catherine with her girlfriends and Earl with his fellas. They would no doubt see each other there, but it would not be obvious they were in a relationship. But the Saturday night Best of Friends party was the big capper to a phenomenal weekend. Alumni came out by the hundreds, dressed beautifully and in wonderful spirits. It also was the last opportunity for those looking for love (or sex) to close the deal before the close of homecoming. So, the drinks flowed and people danced and mingled all the way beyond 3 a.m.

"You know this is going to be news when we show up together at that party," Earl said.

"You think so?" Catherine asked, which was typical. Her spirit was so pure that she seldom made assumptions. She took a moment or an occasion for what it was. She certainly did not expect that a buzz would be created because of her and Earl's hook-up.

So, Earl had to break it down for her. "It's human nature for people to whisper and spread the word when two people they did not expect to be together become a couple. In our case, you were thought of as among the finest one or two women during our era at Norfolk State. I can tell you that with one hundred percent confidence. That's what men thought then and, baby, it is amazing, but you look better now, almost thirty years after graduating. So, if you showed up at the Best of Friends party with *anyone*, it would be gossip.

"But you're showing up with *me*. People knew we knew each other but they would not put us together. I can't say how I was regarded in college. I do know I have a lot of friends from Norfolk State—and gained even more through Facebook. And we're pretty much here today because of your friends and how they regarded me. I'm grateful to them because I know your girls, but only on the surface. I didn't know any of them in-depth. So, for them to encourage you to reach out to me says something about how people looked at me.

"Us together? At the Best of Friends party? That's going to be the subject of much discussion. I can promise you that."

"Well, I guess you're right, huh?" Catherine said. "You said something about people not expecting us to be together. I understand your point, but being with you, really knowing you now…it makes sense that we would be together.

"I'll tell you a secret," she added. "I didn't reach out to you a year ago when you sent me a friend request on Facebook because something in me told me that you were wonderful and I wasn't ready for you. I was in a relationship and I don't see more than one man at a time. Shoot, I haven't dated but three or four men since college. But my point is I felt something about you a long time ago. I wasn't sure what it was. But the last time I saw you before September was ten years ago. And I was married and I had to walk away from you. There was something about you that made me know I needed to leave. So I did.

"This summer, my girls kept saying, 'Catherine, Earl is such a nice guy.' This went on for a while until I promised I would e-mail you... That was the smartest thing I have ever done."

They smiled at each other. "Thank you," Earl said.

"For what?"

"For saying that. For e-mailing me. For being who you are. For loving me," he said.

They spent the rest of their dinner eating and sharing loving thoughts. When it was time to go, Catherine suggested they go back to her place to relax. That sounded great to Earl.

At her place, she pulled out a bottle of Vueve Cliquot and a slice of brie with apricot topping. She lit candles and turned on Sade as Earl popped the champagne. She pulled out a pair of flutes and Earl filled the glasses with bubbly.

Catherine stood in front of Earl, in five-inch heels and a luxurious silk dress, with champagne in hand. Earl looked down into her eyes.

"You are my baby," he said.

"You are my baby."

They sipped champagne and then kissed.

"I adore you," he said.

"I adore you."

They sipped champagne and then kissed.

"I love you," Earl said.

"I love you," she repeated.

They sipped champagne and then shared a long, sensual kiss.

"This is the best homecoming ever," she said. "And we haven't even been a part of it yet."

They took a seat on Catherine's couch. Earl had her put her legs in his lap so he could take off her pumps. "You should be comfortable."

Catherine sat up and sliced the brie and served it to Earl. And he served some to her. They were experiencing another fairy tale-type night, culminating with another lovemaking session that lasted well into the early morning.

Afterward, they lay on their backs, breathing heavily and mesmerized by their connection.

"I'm not going to cry this time," Catherine said. "But my heart is so full. I am in love with you and I want everyone to know it."

Earl did not say anything. He just pulled her to him, and she rested on his chest and they fell asleep together.

That morning, Earl was awakened to kisses from Catherine, starting still another heated, passionate expression of love and affection. It was not even 7 a.m.

"It's going to be a beautiful day," Earl said, "if what just happened is any indication… Amazing."

They fell asleep for another hour or so before Catherine got up and made them breakfast. They sat at her bar and enjoyed the meal and smiled at each other like kids in love for the first time.

Their plan was to meet on the Yard during the tailgate following Catherine's Delta Sigma Theta brunch. She drove him back to his hotel room, where Earl contacted his Alpha Phi Alpha brothers and let them know he would meet them at the fraternity's set-up at the tailgate. The weather agreed with the occasion: seventy-two and sunny. Earl wore jeans and a frat T-shirt—the first time in two decades he wore Alpha paraphernalia. It was the fiftieth anniversary of his chapter, Epsilon Pi, and brothers came back in resounding numbers wearing the colors.

After checking e-mails and making a few more calls, Earl walked from the Marriott Waterside a few blocks to the Light Rail, a train commuter system that recently began operation. It was a quick and smooth ride through downtown, past the minor league baseball stadium and just outside of campus.

The train was packed with Norfolk State supporters ready for a good time. The football game mattered, too—the Spartans were challenged by Howard University—but not as much as the fun to be had at the tailgate. Or as much fun as watching the outstanding NSU band, the Mighty Spartan Legion.

Earl could see the massive gathering of people already on campus from the train's platform, and a sense of pride rushed through his body. When he was a student, Norfolk State did not have an on-campus stadium. The Spartans played their "home" football games at Old Dominion, so there was no remarkable mass of more than ten-thousand supporters at the tailgate. Throw in the thirty-five thousand that pack the football stadium and there were upward of forty-five thousand people on the NSU campus for homecoming. It was a spectacular sight with the feel of an enormous family reunion.

Earl made his way across Brambleton Avenue and onto the campus, a pep in his step that came with the energy he felt once he set foot on the grounds. He knew where the Alphas set up and headed directly to that location. Along the way, however, he encountered many friends and former classmates. His close friend and frat brother, Myron, called. "Yo, where are you?" Myron asked. "We're over here near the new library."

Earl headed that way and ran right into Myron and a legion of brothers. It took him two minutes to greet and give the grip to Sam, Randy, Davenport, Nick, Ron, Marvin, Kilroy, Pork & Bean, Ronnie Bagley, Gerald Mason, Chuck, Greg Willis, J.D. Freeland, Ronnie Akers, Jacques, Steve Butler, Kelvin Lloyd, Frank Nelson, Brian White, BJ, Slick, Sykes, Fred and Steve Nottingham, who captured homecoming weekend as well as anyone through pictures.

So, Earl and the crew posed for photos, all the while laughing about one thing or another. They monitored every woman in sight. Davenport passed out cigars. Younger brothers distributed the so-called "Alpha Punch," a concoction that amounted to a little bit of juice and a whole lot of liquor.

Older brothers in their sixties set up the tent and handled the massive, L-shaped grill that was covered with chicken, burgers, hot dogs and fish. There was mashed potatoes, beans, macaroni and cheese, salad, coleslaw, corn on the cob. Earl grabbed a plate and went down the buffet line. "I need to coat my stomach with something if I'm going to be drinking this early in the day," he said.

"I can't believe how grown these young girls' bodies are," Myron said.

"Must be all the hormones in the food," Earl said.

"So how you been, man? Where you been?" Myron said. "Everyone was looking for you last night at the step show and the all-black party. A couple of honeys were looking for you."

"Man, I wanted to be there, but I had a date," he said. "I couldn't be in two places at once, so I had to be where I wanted to be."

"I hear you," Myron said. "But a date with who?"

"Catherine," he answered. "Catherine Harmon."

"Wait—Catherine Harmon who went to school with us?" Myron said.

"Yeah. That's my girl," Earl said, smiling. He took a bite out of his hot dog and continued, "We've been communicating for four months. Now it's official. It's on."

"Damn," Myron said. "How's she doing? She still looking good? I guess so, if you're messing with her."

"She looks great and is doing great," he said. "She should be over here at some point."

"You're serious about her; I can tell," Myron said.

"How?" Earl asked.

"Because when I told you honeys were asking about you at the party last night, you didn't even ask who they were," he answered.

Earl laughed. He could feel someone behind him and turned around to see an attractive woman with a huge smile. "Heeey," Earl said.

"Hi, Earl. It's been a long time," she said. "You look so good."

"Thanks, so do you," he said. "Where are you now?"

"I live in New Jersey, south Jersey," she said. "I actually have been there the last ten years. After graduation I moved back home to New York. But I got tired of the city life and needed something a little more calm. Shoot, I think I could move to Norfolk now. Downtown is so nice now. And I hear the other cities—Virginia Beach, Hampton, Chesapeake—are all blossoming as well."

"I know," Earl said. "I am impressed. It seems like a place I could live now."

The small talk went on for another two minutes or so.

"Are you coming to the game?" she asked.

"Oh, definitely," Earl said. "But I probably won't make it there until the second quarter."

"Are you coming to Best of Friends tonight?" she asked him.

"No doubt," he said.

"Good. I want a dance," she said. "A slow dance."

"We'll have to see about that," Earl said.

They hugged and she moved on. Earl turned to Myron. "Who the fuck was that?" he said.

Myron almost choked on his food. When he gathered himself, he said: "You mean you didn't know who that was?"

"Hell, no," Earl said. "She obviously knew who I was. I couldn't say, 'Who are you?' So, I engaged her, but I had no idea who she was. That was crazy. Damn."

Myron and Earl finished their food and traded stories with their frat brothers for a few minutes.

"I remember when I was on line pledging and the first day I saw you I was standing outside a classroom in Brown Hall," Earl said to Davenport, a brother who lived in Houston. He told the other brothers to listen to his story, so they gathered around.

"So I'm standing in Brown Hall my first day as a Sphinxman and here comes Davenport. And I was like, 'Oh, hell.' So you come up to me and say, 'Good to see you on line. You have any candy?'

"I said, 'Yes, big brother.' And you said, 'Put it in your mouth. Your breath stinks.' And walked away."

The Alphas fell all over each other laughing. The stories continued, one brother after another sharing a comical experience from their college fraternity days. Finally, Myron pulled Earl to the side. "Let's take a walk and see who we see," he said.

And they did, along with Sam, Randy, Marvin, Bagley, Gerald and Pork. They made their way to the Omegas' area and saw the same crews that hung together decades earlier still together. "Look," Myron said, "there goes Dave Brown, Rainbow, Bootsy, Ronnie Palmer, Conrad, Tim Lamb...Let's go holla at these fools."

And the Alphas and the Ques embraced and briefly caught up on one another's lives. Earl expressed his condolences about the death that summer of Donnie Ebanks, an Omega who was in school with them. Some guys looked younger than others. Some looked better than others. All of them were glad to be there, to be alive.

Nearby, a group of AKAs released pink and green balloons into the air in memory of one of their sisters, Parish D. Percell Grimes, who died years earlier from a rare bone disease. Her soror, Marsha Lewis, pulled out her camera and it was like a photo shoot. The Alphas and Ques posed with AKAs Leslie LeGrande, Sybil Savage, Sparkle, Linda Vestal, Wanda Linnen and Sandra (Beasley) Barrett.

The Alphas and Ques whispered among themselves how proud they were that the ladies—all either fifty or close to it—looked good.

Earl stepped away from the crowd when Catherine called him. It was hard to hear because every tent set-up had its own music blaring. There was hardcore rap in one area, R&B in the next, old school jams next to it. All of it loud. But he was able to find a place that was not so loud.

"Hi, baby, he said. "Can you hear me now?"

"I can," she said. "How are you? How's it going?"

"It's going great," he said. "It'll be going better for me when you get here."

"Aww, baby, I don't think I'm going to come," Catherine said. "I was going to go to the brunch but Starr isn't going; she has some things to do. So I'm just going to stay home and relax, clean up a little and catch up on my rest. You wore me out."

"You sure?"

"I am. You go ahead and have fun with your friends. I need to rest," she said. "Let me know who wins the game. And call me later so we can coordinate for tonight. I'm definitely going to the party."

"All right, dear," he said. "If you change your mind, call me. Otherwise, I'll hit you later...love you."

"I love you, Earl."

They ended the call and Earl paused before rejoining the fray. He wanted Catherine to be a part of the tailgate with him, which was another sign that he was truly taken by her. Any other time, he would have been okay with being able to roam and hang with his boys and enjoy all the hijinx that came with that.

But they were up late on Thursday when Catherine had to work Friday morning. And Friday night they were up equally late. So he accepted her position for what it was and reimmersed himself in all the goings-on.

At home, Catherine took up residence on the couch, put on some music and sipped on a cup of coffee. She was tired and figured she would see all her friends at the party. The day was left for her to relax and reflect.

She was in love with Earl, truly in love. She had felt that emotion several weeks before he told her of his feelings, but did not want to share it over the phone. Being in love was a place she did not expect to be.

"Starr, I have never experienced anything like this. Never. He is a man who communicates with me so well," she said. "I totally trust him. He cares about me. He loves me. I know it. I can feel it."

"I'm so happy for you," Starr said. "You deserve to be happy."

"Thank you," Catherine said. "It's a nice day out and I almost want to go to the tailgate and the game just to be with Earl. I really do. But that party is tonight and I can't have tired eyes. So I'm going to take advantage of this quiet time and relax. This is exactly what I need."

A minute after ending her call with Starr, Catherine's phone chimed, letting her know she had a text message, from Earl.

"Baby, you are all over me. I am enjoying all of this, but I cannot shake you. It is not the same without you. J"

Catherine smiled. She loved and appreciated that he consistently let her know that she was special to him. Best of all, she loved that he made her feel free enough to express her heartfelt emotions.

"I love you, baby," she texted back. *"You make me feel so special. Please know you are special to me. Very special."*

Earl was reading her text message when he and his boys came along some of Catherine's Delta sisters. He, Sam, Myron, Randy and Co. held court with Felita, Sheila Wilson, Donna, Shelia Harrison, Adrienne James, Cheryl Boyd, Wanda Brockington and Susan Davis-Wigenton, who was a judge in New Jersey, among others. They shared stories of the old days and caught up on each other's lives. Only Sheila, Donna and Susan knew of Earl's romance with Catherine. And they were not sharing that information with anyone.

"Where's Catherine?" Myron asked. He looked back at Earl. Susan, Donna and Sheila knew, but said nothing. Finally, Sheila said, "I think you'll see her at the Best of Friends party tonight."

"Sounds good," Earl said with a smile. "We will see you all later."

The men negotiated the huge crowd at the tailgate, running into old friends along the way. "You know what?" Sam said. "It's a good thing we didn't have all this when we were in school. I would have lost my mind."

Before Earl could come up with a joke, he ran into a flurry of old classmates that made him feel good: Keith "Blind" Gibson, Kerry Muldrow, Jeff Jones, Zack Withers, Bruce Lee, Val Guilford, Laura Carpenter, Tony Carter, the twins from New York, Darlene and Darlynn, and Barbara Ray-Jackson from D.C.

"Our era is representing," Jeff said. "We might feel like we're fifty, but at least we don't look it."

"And I'd rather feel it than look it," Laura said.

"Look at all this," Darlene chimed in. "To see how much the school has grown can make you feel older. But when I look at these students... Did we look this young?"

"Not only that, but I was over here yesterday," Tony said. "Have you all been around the campus? I haven't been back in a while so this is shocking me. You see the cars these kids are driving. BMWs, trucks, Acuras, Infinitis. It's crazy."

"I know," Val said. "And there are ATM machines everywhere. When we were in college, there was no need for ATMs because no one had any money."

They all laughed.

"Exactly," Earl said. "If I got twenty dollars in the mail, I had to live off of that for damn near a month."

"I had a car, but I ran out of gas probably eight times because I used to put seventy-five cents' worth of gas in it; two dollars at the max."

"I ate so many Whoppers in college off the two-for-one coupon in *The Spartan Echo* that I haven't had one since I graduated," Blind said.

"Well, I had a gym bag full of Oodles and Noodles," Zack said. "I would doctor those bad boys up with so much seasoning to make one package taste different from the next. It was crazy, but it built survival skills. I wouldn't trade it for the world."

"Me, either," Darlene said. "We had a struggle, but we had fun. It was truly an adventure."

"Let me tell you," Val said. "I literally didn't have money to eat. So I went to the guy in the cafeteria and struck a deal with him. He'd let me eat a few days a week if I cleaned up and did some work in the café. So that's what I did. I had to broker something to make sure I got fed. And I don't know if you could do that at any place but a black college. The guy understood where I was coming from and he wanted to help me. He related to me. But he didn't want to just give me the food. He was teaching me about earning what I wanted way back then. I didn't see the lesson then but I did years later."

"Any honey I met who even *looked* like she *might* have money, I was on her," Sam said. "You had to be resourceful to survive in college."

"Not many of these kids today," Darlynn said. "So many of them have credit cards and bank accounts and much more of a financial support system. Parents, aunts, cousins, godmothers can just go to a bank and deposit money into their account. Or they can use your cell phone to transfer money to someone. It's a different day."

They told a few more stories and started the ten-minute walk from the tailgate to Dick Price Stadium. But Earl wanted some more Alpha Punch, so he, Sam, Randy and Myron broke off from the group and retreated back to the Alpha section.

Nearby, they encountered the Davis brothers: Kent, Kevin and Hank—Kappas who were among the more respected guys on campus during their time at NSU. As they dapped each other up, over came more Kappas: Tony Starks, Bob White, Bob Z, Tony Sisco, Darryl Robinson and Kevin Jones.

They shared more stories and laughs before they all finally decided to head to the game. Earl had seen many of his friends who would be surprised that he and Catherine were together. That thought made him wish the day would go by quicker.

CHAPTER SEVENTEEN

THE TAILGATE, PART II

Jimmy, Carter and Barbara

"Man, I am tripping," Jimmy said to Carter. "Look at this. I could not even imagine this. This is awesome."

The size of the tailgate threw Jimmy. Carter and others had told him about it. Actually seeing it jolted him.

"We had to park about fifteen minutes from here over there off of Ballentine Boulevard," he told former classmate, Lonnie Knox from the Bronx. They came upon each other just as they reached the heart of the activity. "It used to be nothing over there. Now there are these nice houses, a nice community. I had no idea."

"You've been away too long, son," Lonnie said. "But I bet you'll be back next year, though. Won't you?"

"No doubt," Jimmy said. "No doubt."

"Look," Lonnie said, pointing. "Look at your boy."

It was Joe Cosby, one of Jimmy's close friends from New Jersey that he'd lost touch with for years. The two men shared a warm greeting and caught each other up on their lives. Carter broke away from a group of "friends" he didn't quite remember to join Joe and Jimmy.

Jimmy surveyed the scene as Carter and Joe chatted. He tried to figure how many new buildings had been constructed in the decade he had been away. "I'm thinking it's about twelve," he said. "Maybe more. I haven't even been on the other side of campus yet, by the stadium."

"Well, the game is about to start. I'm gonna catch up with Jones and 'em and head that way," Joe said. "I'll catch you guys up there."

"Ah, shit," Carter said.

"What?"

"There's Barbara," he said.

Carter went with Jimmy and Regina to the all-black party the night before, expecting to relax, party and get his mind off of Barbara. Only Barbara showed up at the party, too, after dinner with her friend Donna.

He noticed her while he was on the dance floor. Something about her presence always captured him, and from a distance he knew it was her. Barbara saw him, too; she stood there for a minute or so and stared at him as he partied with another woman. She waited to see how Carter would react, if he would end the dance and come over to talk to her.

Carter did not. He danced another two songs, throwing his hands in the air and conversing with his dance partner as if he did not see Barbara. She was offended, and stepped into the lobby area, where old classmates gave her attention and conversation.

Several minutes later, Carter made his way out there. Their eyes met and she turned away.

"Yo, did you see Barbara?" Jimmy asked Carter.

"Yeah, she's right there," he answered.

"Look, I couldn't talk about it much with Regina in the car, but you should go and talk to her, man," Jimmy advised. "You gotta focus on the bottom line. And the bottom line is that she's your girl. If you really love her, then you shouldn't be over here and her over there."

Carter marinated on Jimmy's words and then made his way over to Barbara, who was standing with Donna and Cynthia Kirby. Sadness marked their faces.

"What's wrong?" he asked, hugging Cynthia.

"We were just talking about our friends who are not here: Madinah and Ladina," Cynthia said.

Madinah Aziz Grier was a classmate who had succumbed to bile duct cancer the previous summer after nearly a two-year battle. Ladina Stevens had passed a year earlier to breast cancer. Both ladies were classy and smart, well-liked and fun.

"I know," Carter said. "It's hard to believe they're not with us anymore. You know them: They'd be on the dance floor right now, dropping it like it's hot."

They all smiled at the thought. Carter asked if he could buy them a drink. Only Donna and Cynthia responded. "Barbara, can I get you something?" he said.

Again, she looked at him and turned away. She was being stubborn; every instinct in her body told her to hug and kiss Carter. The way he eased that tense moment was one of the traits about him that she adored. But she was so disappointed in how he received her news of relocating to New York that she could not bring herself to even say anything to him.

"Ohhhh…kaaay," Carter said to Barbara's silence.

Two gentlemen asked Donna and Cynthia to dance before Carter went to the bar, leaving him alone with Barbara. "Would you please talk to me?" he said.

"What's there to say, Carter? I mean, really," she said. Her voice was low, but the tone was sharp. "You saw me in there and you just kept dancing."

"Why did I need to stop dancing because I saw you?" he said. "That's not a big deal. You're focusing on the wrong thing."

"Oh, am I?" she said. "Well, let's forget about that. What about New York? I'm moving there and you don't want me there. That's the bottom line. If it were anything different, we wouldn't be going through this."

Carter took a deep breath and made a decision: He was not going to talk about her moving to New York. He was going to enjoy the night.

"Can you do me a favor, please? Just one favor?" he asked.

"You want me to do you a favor?" she said. "Wow. I guess I shouldn't be surprised. What is it, Carter?"

"Let's have a good time tonight," he said. "Let's forget about everything else and focus on drinking and mingling and dancing. That's what we always did and we had a great time. That's what we need to do now to turn this thing around."

As mad and disappointed as Barbara was, she was able to fight through those emotions and see the upside to Carter's plea.

"Okay. Fine," she said.

"Thank you," Carter said. "I'll start off our fun time by saying that you look beautiful. I did see you when I was on the dance floor and my heart stopped for a second. You look great."

Barbara agreed to put aside the issue at hand, but it was not easy. She did not crack so much as a grin at Carter's compliment. "Thanks," she said as flatly as possible.

Carter smiled. "You're something else," he said.

"What about you? What are you?" she said.

"Me? I'm horny," he said. "Horny for you."

That drew a smile from Barbara. "Well, I'm not," she said.

"Give me some time," he said. "I will definitely change that."

"Oh, you think you got it like that?" she asked.

"I sure the hell do," he said in a high-pitched voice, and they both laughed.

Just then, Jimmy came over. "I'm glad to see you all smiling," he said. "Now, I feel better."

Barbara felt better, too. She had traveled across the country to attend homecoming. The least she could do was have a good time. And so she and Carter danced and flirted, trying hard to disguise their relationship. At one point, though, he hugged her after a dance so long that Barbara had to nudge free of his grasp.

"I think you need to sit down," Barbara said. Carter had been drinking all day and was downing shots of vodka seemingly every fifteen minutes. His eyes became a little glazed over and his voice a little hoarse.

"I hope you know you have to drive when you all leave," Donna said to Jimmy when he came over to the table. "Your boy is feeling pretty good right now."

Carter heard the talk. "I sure am feeling pretty great right now," he said. Then he slid his chair so he could get into Barbara's ear. "Baby, we should spend the night together," he said. "I know you have Donna with you. But drop her off and come over to my room. We should be together."

Barbara embraced the idea with little hesitation. So when it was time to go, Jimmy and Carter walked Barbara and Donna to their car. "I see why you didn't bring your wife with you," Donna said to Jimmy. "Lots of single women here."

"It is, but it doesn't matter," Jimmy said. "I know how to behave myself."

"Oh, okay," she said. "If you say so."

"I'm faithful to my wife, Donna," Jimmy said. "Not that you care, but I just wanted to make that clear."

Carter chimed in. "He's one of the good guys," he said. "They don't make many like Jimmy anymore."

"What about you?" Barbara said.

"Me? I'm a different cut," Carter said. "You know the mold was broken when God finished with me."

"God or the devil?" Barbara cracked.

"Somebody gag me," Barbara said.

"Glad to," he said. "What time will you be at my room?"

"You're so crazy," she said. Then she looked to make sure Jimmy and Donna were not listening. "In about forty minutes," she added.

Carter gave her the room number and he and Jimmy found Regina and headed back to the hotel.

"Seems like you got things back in line," Jimmy said in the car.

"Once I do this business tonight, then it'll be all the way back in line," Carter said.

"You probably can't even get it up," Regina said. She, like Carter, was buzzing pretty good, which made for a loose tongue and lively ride back to the hotel.

"Can't get it up?" Carter said. "She better worry that I can't get it *down*. I don't play, girl. When I go to work, I bring an extra hard hat for the woman because she's liable to be banged right through the headboard."

They all laughed.

"Let me tell you, Regina," he went on, leaning up from the back seat, "I'm gonna go so deep that when I pull it out, oil gonna shoot up from between her legs."

Regina screamed and Jimmy almost lost control of the car. "You about the silliest guy I know," he said after wiping tears from his face. "Just sit back."

They made it back to the hotel and Carter unsteadily made his way to the elevator. Regina tried one last pitch at getting Jimmy to let down his guard.

"So, Barbara is married and coming over here to get with Carter?" she started. "I understand. It's not like it's going beyond this weekend. She lives in California. What happens at homecoming stays at homecoming."

"Can I tell you a secret?" he said. Jimmy was about to reveal that Barbara was divorced, making her case totally different from his. But he decided that it was her business and not his to broadcast. "Never mind."

"No, go ahead," she insisted.

So, Jimmy made up something else to say. "Sometimes at home, I think about you and the times we had and it makes me feel good," he said. "More than ten years later, I still remember a lot of what we did while here in college. But that was then, Regina. I'm married. If I can't honor that, then what does that say about me? If you can't honor that, what does that say about you?"

A look of embarrassment covered Regina's pretty face. "You're right," she said. "I wouldn't want anyone pressuring my husband for sex. And I wouldn't want him to give in to it, either. I'm sorry. I guess I just got caught up on memories."

Jimmy did not say anything. He just hugged her. They walked to the elevator and to her room. He hugged her goodnight and she kissed him on the side of the face.

"See you tomorrow," he said.

By the time Jimmy got settled in his room, Barbara had arrived at the hotel after dropping off Donna. Carter had given her his room number, and so after leaving her car with valet, she made the journey to his room. She felt good, as if Carter was beginning to settle in with the idea of them being together.

She knocked a happy beat on the door. It went unanswered. She knocked again, only louder. Nothing. She called Carter's cell phone, but it rang and rang. She put her ear to the door and could hear voices. She heard a female's voice and chills went through her body.

She banged and banged on the door, but Carter did not answer it. In a full-blown panic, she hurried downstairs to use the house phone and call his room. The line was busy. "He took the phone off the hook?" she said aloud. Now she was not only hurt, but also furious.

There was no one at the front desk. Her mind was racing. She didn't know what to do. But she was not leaving—she knew that. Then an idea came to her. She went to her car that was still in front of the hotel and put her purse in the trunk.

Then she went to the front desk and called out for some assistance. A male worker came from the back, and Barbara went into her plan. She explained that she had left her room key in her purse in the room with her husband, who was not answering the door or his cell phone, and that the room phone was off the hook.

"I'm praying he's all right," she said, looking petrified. "He had a lot to drink, but I hope he hasn't fallen and hurt himself. Could someone please let me in?"

The front desk person asked for the room number, which she gave him. She told him when "they" had checked in and Carter's address that was on the reservation. Finally, he gave her a duplicate key. "I hope he's all right," he said.

Barbara was relieved that her plan worked. She hurried to the elevator and down to Carter's room. Then a moment of trepidation occurred. She knocked once, twice. No answer. She called him on his cell phone. No answer. She pressed her ear against the door and again heard voices. And that's when she lost all apprehension. How could he be in the room with another woman, knowing she was coming over?

Her heart beat so fast and so hard it felt as if it were going to burst out of her chest. She slid the key card into the slot, and the light turned red. "Shit," she said. She tried it again, and this time it lit up green, releasing the lock. Barbara opened it slowly at first and then quicker. She stepped in and was shocked by what she saw.

Carter was sprawled out across the bed, stark naked with a beer in his hand. The room phone was knocked onto the floor. And the television was playing.

As bizarre a scene as it was, it was still a relief to Barbara of gigantic proportions. She put one hand over her heart and the other over her mouth. The relief that came with seeing him in the room by himself—albeit it pissy drunk and passed out—made her lightheaded. She sat on the edge of the bed, her elbows on her knees, shaking her head.

She could not believe how emotional she got when it seemed Carter was in the room with another woman. When he did not answer the door, her mind raced to the darkest places. She just *knew* there was someone in that room and that he was ignoring her at the door and her calls.

It took her about five minutes, but she finally got herself together. She wiped her face, as if to discard the awful thoughts that ran through her head. She pulled the comforter over Carter, took the beer out of his hand and placed it on the nightstand, picked up the hotel phone and placed it next to the Heineken and turned off the TV. She decided she would stay with Carter and help him get over what looked to be a certain hangover.

So, she slipped out of her elegant dress and hung it up in the closet. In her bra and thongs, she slid under the covers next to the man she wanted to be her man. Before she could get settle under the sheets, she heard Carter's phone chime, alerting him of a text message.

"Who the hell is texting him at almost three in the morning?" she asked herself.

So, she went on a mission to find the phone. And under his shirt, which was on the floor near the window, she found his BlackBerry Torch. Remarkably, Carter did not have a security code on it. She paused but then rationalized that him not having the phone locked was some sign that she could go through it, that she *should* go through it. Anything to make acceptable something she knew she should not do.

And so, Barbara took a seat on the bed next to a snoring Carter and went through his text messages, call log and e-mails as if she were conducting a CIA investigation. She saw text messages from a few females; nothing out of the ordinary, except one from Marlena that read: "I know you're having a good time. Be safe baby."

"Baby?" Barbara said aloud. She looked back at Carter, whose snoring sounded like a lawnmower. "Baby?" she repeated. And like that, anger filled her bloodstream. She threw his BlackBerry on the bed and retrieved her dress from the closet. After slipping it back on, she stood over Carter, who had curled into a fetal position. Finally, she shook her head in disgust and left.

So, when Carter saw Barbara at the tailgate, he wasn't sure to be upset that she did not come to his room or what? He had called her that morning, but she did not answer or return his call.

"Hey, you," he said to her. "How you doing?"

Barbara did not know what to say. Her weekend was going drastically opposite the way she envisioned. But over a cup of coffee, she decided that she was going to get some concrete answers from Carter.

"I'm okay. How are you? You had a lot to drink last night," she said.

"I know," he answered. "I feel okay. I think if you drink quality liquor you minimize a hangover. I had some water and coffee and I'm feeling pretty good right now.

"But tell me," he added. "What happened last night? I thought you were coming to my room."

Barbara smiled and shook her head. Before she could answer she noticed friends from her college days, sisters Avis and Tracy Easley, and exchanged hugs with them. "You all look great," Barbara said.

"How's your family?" Tracy asked, staring down at Barbara's hard-not-to-notice ring.

"Overall, the family is good," she said. "We're moving to New York, though, in a few months."

"I love New York," Avis said. "But I don't know about living there."

"It's going to be a big adjustment, but I'm ready for it," Barbara said.

"But the people are totally different," Avis added. "People in New York are cutthroat."

"But Carter lives there, don't you, Carter?" Tracy asked. "If he can make it there, I'm sure you can."

"What you trying to say, Tracy?" Carter said. "I see you still got jokes. Some things never change—even if they should."

"I'm just joking," Tracy said. "We know you're *almost* all man."

The group laughed and Carter playfully put his arms around her neck. "If I didn't know your lesbian lover would miss you, I'd choke you right here."

Tracy laughed off Carter's joke—"My husband would kick your butt," she said—and she and Avis moved on, leaving Barbara and Carter to resume their discussion.

"Carter, I did come to your room last night," she said.

"No, you didn't," he said. "I did see where you called me a few times."

"Who you think put the comforter on you?"

"You didn't have a key to my room, so how could you have gotten in?" he asked.

She went on to tell Carter the story of how she got into his room, and he could not contain his laughter. "Are you serious? I was laid out, naked and snoring with a beer in my hand?" he said. "Wow. Wow. That is crazy. I musta been more messed up than I thought. I don't remember any of that.

"I just got up at some point and stumbled to the bathroom and got back in the bed. But you know what? I *do* remember thinking that I smelled your perfume when I came from the bathroom. But I thought I was just trippin'."

"I could have done anything to you and you wouldn't have known a thing," Barbara said. "It's pathetic to be that drunk."

"I know I had a buzz, but I wasn't, like, wasted," he said. "I have been wasted before and that wasn't it. I think the drinking all day at the day party, then all night, too. I was just fatigued and drunk. It all caught up with me."

Barbara did not tell Carter about what she saw in his text messages. She decided she would wait, but having it hang over her did not allow her to freely enjoy the festivities.

They made their way to the NSU Alumni tent, where alumni director Michelle Hill gave them wristbands so they could eat from the pretty significant spread that was laid out. Jimmy had wandered off with E. Franklin, a graduate of Virginia Commonwealth who got hooked on Norfolk State's homecoming a few years earlier. He and Jimmy had met at Nordstrom, where E. Franklin was a manager in the men's department.

E led Jimmy to a tailgate area where a boisterous man with a grease-stained apron manned the grill. "That guy right there," E said, pointing to Reverend Davis Wilson, a 1973 graduate of Norfolk State who was on the flight with him to Norfolk. "He is a trip."

Rev. Wilson was in the first-class section of the plane, across the aisle from E. Franklin, dressed in a lavender suit, black shirt and matching lavender tie. A flight attendant noticed him from television, and asked, "Who are you going to save on Sunday, Reverend?"

"This weekend I'm doing my saving on Friday and Saturday," he said. "I'm going to my homecoming, and there will be a lot of people there in need of God's grace."

The flight attendant and others laughed. Before the plane backed out of the jetway, Reverend Wilson broke out loudly in prayer, startling E. Franklin and others.

"God, we ask that you guide this plane directly and safely to our destination," he began. "We know you can shift any storm out of our path, any issues to the side, and elevate us up off the ground and down softly in Norfolk, Virginia. I ask that you do that for us today, and that our homecoming weekend be a blessing to many. In the precious name of the Son of God, we pray. Amen."

At sixty-something, "Rev" was a fixture at homecoming. He was proud of his school and he was close to the dozens and dozens of old classmates and the dozens and dozens of new friends he'd met over the years over the sacred weekend.

What he enjoyed most was that he was not looked at by most as mega church pastor Davis Wilson. Rather, he was "Rev," a spirited man who financed probably the biggest and most lively tailgate party of the weekend. It was one of his contributions to the occasion. He spent more than three thousand dollars on a deejay, alcohol, soft drinks, supplies, chicken, burgers, cole slaw, beans, salmon, chips, beer, hot dogs, condiments—whatever was required to have a full-fledged cookout…for whoever came by.

All that, and he spent hours on end at the Saturday tailgate behind a huge grill, sweating and talking to anyone in front of him. He got off on not only providing the food, but cooking it, too. A huge football fan, he eschewed attending the game and instead cooked food all day and mingled with the tailgaters.

"I love this school," he said, placing a chicken thigh and leg on Jimmy's plate. "This is where I became something. I came here a seventeen-year-old from Rock Hill, South Carolina without any idea of what was going to happen for me. I was snotty-nosed and scared. This school held me together. It hugged me my entire five-and-a-half years here. Yeah, it took me a while to get out. When it let me go, I was a man who knew where I was going."

"Same thing happened to me, sir," Jimmy said. "This is my first homecoming, and I graduated ten years ago. Now that I'm here, I feel embarrassed I haven't been back before now."

"No need to be embarrassed; you here now," the reverend said. "Where you live? And I see you have a wedding ring on. Where's your wife?"

"I live in Washington, D.C.," Jimmy said. "My wife? She's at home mad at me because I'm here without her."

"I see," Rev said. "Well, I understand both your points. I wish your wife were here so she could see how wonderful it is. It's always good when you can show off your school, you know? But my wife is at home, too. She came with me two years and had enough. She saw what it was about and now she's fine. But we had a few arguments back in the day when I told her she didn't need to come.

"I gave in after several years—and that was it. She was amazed at the number of people, the spirit of the people and the spirit that covered the whole weekend. She actually had a good time because she knew a few women, so she was able to get away from me for a time and do something on her own. That's what worked for me. You might want to think about that. But know that she could get here and have a ball and want to come every year. I don't know if you want that."

The two men laughed.

"She doesn't get that I'm not here trying to get women—although, I must say, there are plenty of cute ones here," Jimmy said. "I just need some time for myself. Plus, she'd be bored here. She wouldn't know anyone."

"This is no secret, I'm sure," he said. "Women, us men don't quite understand. And I can't pretend to know all the dynamics of your relationship. And you aren't asking for my advice. But I'll just say this: you will have moments that you're glad she's not with you, and you'll have moments when you wish she were here. That's just how it is."

And "Rev" was right. Throughout the tailgate, as Jimmy maneuvered through the thousands of couples, he wished Monica were with him. He saw married couples enjoying the day: Tony and Erika Sisco, Susan and Kevin Wigenton, Leroy and Sybil Savage, Kevin and Hope Jones, Hadley and Sharon Evans, Sheri and Rodney Dickerson, Leigh and Ed Hughes, and Carla and Andre McManus.

But their cases were different: They all met while at Norfolk State. So, they were attending their own homecoming and knew many people.

"My wife would enjoy some of it, but once she started to feel out of place, she would have made it miserable for me; I know it," Jimmy said.

Thinking about her prompted him to call her. He felt much better after their previous conversation and he wanted her to know that he was thinking of her. She would not be entirely over the situation for a while, he realized. But staying in touch with her would accelerate the process, he believed. He hoped.

"What's going on, Mrs. Hamilton?" he said when she answered the phone.

"Not much, Mr. Hamilton," she said. "I'm sitting around watching movies. I've cleaned the house, eaten lunch. So, I'm just here."

"Well, there's something to be said for quiet time, right?" Jimmy said.

"It sure doesn't sound quiet there," Monica shot back. "Where are you?"

"I'm at the tailgate, which is basically a big outdoor party for thousands of people," he said. "There are—I don't know—seventy-five, a hundred—different parties out here. Each one has its own grill and its own music and its own food. It's pretty crazy. I'm about to find Carter and walk down to the game. But I'm told thousands of people don't even go into the game. They just hang out and eat and drink and mingle for hours."

"You telling me all this like I've never been to a tailgate before," she said.

"Well, excuse me," Jimmy said jokingly.

"You know what?" he said, getting serious. "I must admit that there's a part of me that wishes you were here with me."

There was silence on the phone. Monica did not know how to respond. The cynical part of her wanted to say, *"Yeah, well, it's kind of late for that now, isn't it?"*

But the rational part of her, the part she did not show often when she was emotional, took over. After all, she loved her husband and she realized, in honest moments with herself, that he put up with far more from her than she did from him. She even contemplated counseling on her trust issues. But she never took the step.

"That's really sweet of you to say, Jimmy," she said. "I wish I were there, too."

They talked about him getting back in time on Sunday to watch the Redskins game and then taking her to dinner. "That's the least you can do," she said.

"Oh, I'm going to do more," Jimmy said. "You can believe that."

"Promises, promises," Monica said.

"Okay, you wait until I get home," Jimmy said. "I got something for you."

CHAPTER EIGHTEEN

LET THE GAMES BEGIN

Tranise, Mary and Charlene

"I can't believe they are selling those giant, deformed smoked turkey legs," Charlene said as she, Mary and Tranise walked the concourse of Dick Price Stadium just as the game began. "I like to eat—make that *love* to eat—but I wouldn't mess with that. If a turkey was big enough for that leg, he would be able to post up Shaq."

"And look at that line," Tranise said. "I guess folks are hungry."

There were a lot of hungry folks in the bowels of the stadium for the homecoming game between Norfolk State and Howard. There were thousands of people who remained at the tailgate and did not even attend the game. And there were more than thirty thousand at the game. Most were in the stands, but many people made their rounds walking the concourse. It was a prime opportunity to see even more former classmates.

Most people, especially women, attended the game only to reconnect with old friends and to see the band perform at halftime. They wanted the Spartans to win, but it was not that important to sit there and see *how* they won.

"Oh, I just got a text from Joi Edwards," Tranise said. Joi was a friend she had met in Atlanta at a Jill Scott concert at Chastain Park two summers ago. They complimented each other on their hair and learned that they went to the same place, Like

The River The Salon in the Inman Park section of Atlanta.

"Who's Joi?" Mary asked.

"She's my girlfriend from Atlanta," Tranise explained. "She's a dentist. She went to Howard, but I don't hold that against her."

"She came here just for the game?" Charlene asked.

"Yes," Tranise answered. "Her cousin plays for Howard and she hadn't seen him play in person this season, so she picked this game. She told me she was getting in this morning. We've got to connect with her. She's a sweetheart."

The ladies backed away from the center of the concourse, away from the wall-to-wall foot traffic. "I can't believe this many people are here," Tranise said. "This is so great."

Steven Nottingham came up and pointed his high-tech camera toward Tranise. "Hello, ladies," he said. "Strike a pose." And they did. Before they could break up, Marsha Lewis, the AKA, asked them to stay there for another picture.

Steve and Marsha were special in that way. Seemingly every other person had a camera and took photos. But those two loved to capture the weekend in pictures. They did not ask for money to receive the photos or even a donation. They did it because they enjoyed doing it.

They inspired Tranise to pull out her camera. "I have been so overwhelmed that I forgot I even had my little Canon," she said. "Come on, ladies, pose."

She took photos of her friends and then anyone who passed by them. "It just feels good to be here," she said. "I am embarrassed to admit this: I went to a homecoming at the University of Georgia last year. I hadn't even come to my own but this guy who went there invited me."

"How was it?" Mary asked.

"It was good," she said. "But it wasn't *this*. He was a nice guy and made sure he introduced me around. But the bond I see here wasn't what I felt there. This is like one big family reunion, one big community. There, it was the few black people among ninety-thousand white people making their one little spot on a huge campus. The people I was with were great and they were happy to see each other. It just was on such a smaller scale and nowhere near the passion I see here."

Indeed, they stood by and watched old classmates reconnect over and over and over, with a few of them shedding tears. "I cried when I saw you, Mary," Tranise said. "When I think about it, you and Charlene and other people we were close to—and Norfolk State—represent a special time in my life. By the time I left, I was more proud of being a black woman than I can even tell you. I believed I could do anything. That pride has stayed in me, made me stronger when I could not get the job I wanted out of college.

"That's why I wear this Norfolk State T-shirt with so much pride. I have about five of them. I wear them in Atlanta. I tell my students about NSU. I have told my students about the both of you, how the friendships I developed in college mean so much and last a lifetime."

"Damn," Mary said, "and she ain't even been drinking yet. Already into her sentimental speech mode."

"You just want to play hard all the time, but I saw you crying, too, when we first saw each other," Tranise said to Mary.

"Ain't nobody cry when you saw me," Charlene said in mock disgust. "That's some bullshit right there."

"Awww, you know we love you," Tranise said, hugging her.

"Speak for yourself," Mary cracked. "I ain't liked this bitch since she ate my Pop Tarts junior year."

"Must we go back to that?" Charlene said, laughing. "I was

hungry. And I replaced them with some fresh Pop Tarts. The ones I ate were dried out."

"This is what I'm talking about," Tranise said. "The memories."

"I also remember you stealing my TV out of my room and putting it in the living room to entertain some guy," Mary said.

"Damn, right," Tranise said. "You were sleep and the TV in the living room was broken because you tried to do a cartwheel and banged into it, remember? So, it was your fault it was broke. I needed a TV."

"Oh, yeah, I remember that," Charlene said. "She was mad as hell. She was being all selfish about her little-ass TV. Thing couldn't have been but about fifteen inches."

Playfully, Mary said: "You had no right to steal my TV. I should have called the police. I—"

BOOM!!!! came a sound from inside the stadium.

The ladies jumped.

"What the hell was that?" Mary said. "Scared the shit out of me."

"Oh, that was the cannon going off," said Jimmy, who was walking by with Carter and heard Mary's question. "It means Norfolk State just scored. The cannon goes off every time we score."

"Well, damn," Mary said. "They need to warn you before they do that. Somebody's gonna have a damn heart attack."

Jimmy laughed. "Well, the good news is that Norfolk State is in the lead," he said.

"And that I have a strong heart. Thanks," Mary added as Jimmy and Carter walked on.

"Maybe we should go into the game and see what's going on," Charlene said. "I happen to like football. And my damn feet are starting to hurt."

"No one told you to wear heels to a tailgate and football game," Tranise said.

"That's okay," Charlene added. "I got my flats in this bag, so when it gets too bad, I'm changing. But I need heels to give the illusion of a slimmer me."

They laughed and made their way up the ramp on the home side of the stadium, where the stands were packed with students and alums. Charlene heard someone call her name. She looked up to see Aundrea "Inky" Johnson, who waved her to come up to where she was sitting. There were some available seats on her row three-quarters of the way up the stands.

They greeted Inky and slid their way past fans and plopped down on the aluminum bench. Just behind them were the Alphas, and they were in a celebratory mood.

During breaks in play—dozens of them clad in black and old gold led by Colonel Ronnie Bagley, Sam Myers and Randy Brown—chanted, "You, you, you know the story... Tell the whole damned world this is *Alpha* territory. Oh-six, mother-fucka, oh-six!"

In the next section, the Deltas, wearing red and white, made their "ooow ooop" sound signifying they were in the house. And that made the Alphas address them with another chant: "The Ques are your brothers but the Alphas are your lovers. Say what? Ha ha ha ha ha ha ha ha...this situation is serious!!!!"

The band, stationed in the north end zone, rocked ESPN's theme song and a series of hits, current and old school. The dancers shook what their mommas gave them, creating a sort of huge party atmosphere. On the track on the perimeter of the field, the alumni cheerleaders—some of them looking more exuberant than others—tried to summon their youth. On the other end, the current cheerleaders, perky and spry, did their thing. And Mr. Norfolk State—an elderly gentleman who had attended NSU games for decades—pranced around the stadium with a green umbrella clad in an all-green suit, shirt and tie. After halftime, he would change into an all-gold ensemble.

"I feel like I'm back in college," Tranise said. "I forgot how great it felt to be a Spartan. Homecoming is the best thing ever. I've got to go over to my sorors' section for a while. I'll be back."

And off Tranise went to convene with her Delta sisters, many of whom were surprised and delighted to see her after so long. She pulled out her iPhone and programmed the numbers of several friends—the experience inspired her to be committed to keeping in touch with her sorors.

At halftime, Joi texted her again and asked to meet. But Tranise insisted on doing so only after the band, the Mighty Spartan Legion, performed. "I know y'all band at Howard sucks," Tranise said. "But ours is awesome. You should stay and watch a band give a great halftime show."

"Whatever," Joi said.

Seeing the homecoming court walk onto the field touched Tranise, who watched alongside her soror Felita Sisco Rascoe, who, at fifty, looked so much younger. "It seems so long ago," she said to Felita. "But you inspire me to take care of myself so I don't have to look my age."

"Aww, you're sweet to say that," Felita said. "But you're off to a great start. You look beautiful."

Tranise smiled and thanked her. "I can remember so clearly what it felt like to walk onto that field as Miss Norfolk State University," she said. "It was one of the proudest moments of my life. I know just how that young lady feels right now: happy, nervous, proud."

After the coronation, Tranise stood with Felita—and the entire stadium—to watch NSU's band put on another awesome show that ended with long-time public address announcer James Stanton declaring, *"Behold…The Green and Gold."* Nearly the entire stadium recited the Norfolk State calling card with him.

Tranise then sent text messages to Joi, Charlene and Mary,

asking them to meet her at the stadium entrance near Joe Echols Arena. When Joi arrived, wearing a Howard University sweatshirt, Tranise shook her head. "I should have known you'd come in here wearing the enemy's garb," she said.

"Don't hate," Joi said.

They hugged just as Charlene and Mary arrived. Tranise introduced Joi to her old roommates and the ladies immediately clicked.

"I've been to Howard's homecoming," Mary said.

"It was great, right?" Joi asked.

"Well, I had a good time," Mary said. "It wasn't quite the same as ours, you know? For starters, we couldn't even get into the game. The stadium is like a high school stadium. Or smaller."

"This is nice," Joi said. "Y'all do a nice little job. But it's not like a Howard homecoming."

"Everyone thinks theirs is the best," Tranise said. "My friends in Atlanta, Jewel Rowell, Kathy Brown and Toni Tyrell—they swear by Tennessee State's homecoming. Petey Franklin, William Mitchell and Jeri Byron would bet on Morehouse's and Spelman's. Venus Chapman and Len Burnett, they will fight you if you say your homecoming is better than Florida A&M's. Michelle Lemon and Tinee Muldrow will put A&T's up against anyone's. My friends from Virginia Union—Dixenn Toliver, J.B. Hill and 'Trouble'—they stand by their school. D.J. and Mischa Davis would go with Clark. Deborah Johnson and Eileen Stokes went to Virginia State and believe in their school. Monya Bunch and Marty McNeal are Hampton Pirates all the way. I have never been to Maryland Eastern Shore, but my friend Tim Lewis will let you know in a minute how good their homecoming is. So will Xavier Rogers about St. Augustine's.

"So, Joi, you swearing by Howard is the same as anyone else."

"Well, that may be true," she said. "But only at Howard could you get the experience I got in 1995."

"Really?" Tranise asked. "What happened?"

"I'm telling you I can remember it like it was yesterday. It was October 25, 1995," she began. "I was in my dorm—Slowe Hall. I heard this commotion outside. I went to my window and it was like a scene from the movie 'X.' There were dozens and dozes of brothers, Fruits of Islam, dressed in black suits, white shirts and black bowties. They were calling the men of Howard to come with them. It was the Million Man March.

"They were gathering the brothers and I was mesmerized. I hadn't showered. I hadn't even brushed my teeth. But in my sweats, I went right out there with them. I wasn't processing that there would be more black men, but there were more—lots more. So we start the march, down Fourth Street, I believe. We meet with Marion Barry, who was the mayor of D.C. at the time. There's this police escort leading the way. We got to Founder's Library and I had a decision to make: Do I make a left and go back to Slowe? Or do I keep going?

"I was feeling the energy. It was in the morning. The sun was rising. I was feeling it all. So I just kept going. I was with them but by myself. I didn't know anyone, but I met people and talked as I went. Before I knew it, we were all the way down on the Mall. It was an amazing thing.

"I met so many people. I stayed for all the speakers and walked all the way back up to Howard with the crowd, meeting more people. It was an amazing day, something I will never forget. All that and I hadn't even showered or even brushed my teeth. It was so powerful that it just carried me right with them. So, y'all's homecoming is great—I mean, it really is great—but you could only get that experience unless you went to Howard."

"Wow. Well, you got us there," Tranise conceded. "That had to be awesome."

CHAPTER NINETEEN

HAPPY HOMECUMMING

Catherine and Earl

Homecoming for Catherine was not as much about seeing the many friends from her college days as it was about falling deeply in love. It was a liberating feeling for her, an entirely new feeling. After a twenty-five-year marriage collapsed and the subsequent two relationships fell short of what she desired, Catherine did not give up hope on true romance. But she was not that optimistic, either.

Finding Earl aroused emotions in her that were either dormant or had gone untouched. He inspired her, amused her, uplifted her. He *changed* her. At the core, she remained the lovable, sweet, genuine woman many knew and adored. But he altered how she felt about love, how she felt about being in love, how she felt *being* loved.

"Where did you come from?" she said to him half-jokingly. "I mean, really. The things you say to me, the open communication, the way you make me feel... This is not normal. I don't mean that it's abnormal. It's unique. It's no ordinary love."

It surely was not. Earl could not pinpoint the moment he knew he loved Catherine, but it came around the time he created a new word to describe how he felt: "loke." He never explained it to Catherine when he texted It to her, but she knew right away it signified a combination of like and love.

The feelings he had for her inspired him to lengths neither of them had ever experienced, lengths of romance from a bygone era: Earl wrote her letters. He sent her gifts to her office, he held her hand, he kissed her often.

There were times when he was unable to pull himself off of his couch because he was so caught up in imagining himself with her. Not sexually, either. Just enjoying her presence, her effervescent demeanor, her warm and true spirit. He felt good being around her, which helped him make her feel good about being around him because he always was in the best mood. Basically, he aimed to please.

That he was not consumed with making love to her was the ultimate indicator of how he felt about Catherine, that he, indeed, was in love. He had been in love before, or so he thought. Compared to what he felt for Catherine, the past relationships were child's play. It all seemed so run-of-the-mill.

It was different with Catherine. For him to fall in love with her—and her with him—before ever making love told their rare story. His feelings translated into giving Catherine the kind of thoughtful attention she had never before received.

During her visit to Charlotte, more than a month before homecoming, he presented her with a "care package" that included items that showed he paid attention to her. She spoke at some point about enjoying the beach; he included a seashell in the package. She spoke of being a Starbucks fanatic; he included a gift card to the coffee shop. She liked inspirational quotes; he gave her a beautiful book of motivational quotes from famous African Americans. She said she enjoyed fresh scents; he included an aromatic Voluspa candle. She loved music; he added a custom-made CD of all the songs they listened to that espoused love and togetherness.

Catherine was surprised and honored. That "care" package showed Earl cared enough to be in tune with her. It was extremely romantic. Still, she was cautious about taking that relationship-changing step of making love.

"If we ever do make love," she started saying to Earl one evening. He cut her off.

"Let me let you in on a little secret—we've already made love," he said. "To each other's mind. That is the most pure and lasting kind of intimacy two people can share."

Catherine was blown away. "You're right," she said. "This romance we have had has been awesome. I feel like we have grown so much together. I love the way you communicate with me. I love the way you listen to me. I love the way I feel when I talk to you or hear from you or even think about you."

"The other part to that," Earl said, "is that there is no 'if' we make love physically. It is an eventuality. With the passion we have and the emotions we have and the connection we have, there is no way it will not happen. It's just a matter of when."

That time came at homecoming. And by the time Saturday morning rolled around, they had made love four times in one-and-a-half days. Earl partook of the tailgate and football game, feeling revived and buoyant from their intimacy. He hung with his boys and had a beautiful time. But every pause allowed him to think about the passion they shared—and would share that night.

He could not contain his glee, so he called his closest friend, Raphael, in California, Friday before his round of golf. "I know it's early out there; sorry," he started.

"I'm good; what's up?" Rafael said.

"Slim, I'm caught up," Earl said. "My girl and I…"

"I know what you're saying," Rafael said.

"How?" Earl asked.

"I've been knowing since before you ever had sex," Rafael answered. "You have talked about Catherine for the last five months like you've never talked about a woman before, like you and she have the magic that it takes to be something special. So, you call me in the morning and I don't hear any distress in your voice. I hear excitement. I hear fulfillment. I hear joy. That's how well I know you. You and Catherine christened the relationship, so to speak, and I am not surprised."

"Well, I'm a little surprised," Earl said. "I didn't count on it and I wasn't expecting it. It sort of happened."

"Not sort of happened; it *did* happen," Rafael said. "And I'm gonna tell you something that you might be surprised I know: That woman adores you. You have taken her to a place she's probably never been. And she's done the same with you. I can hear it."

Raphael took Earl's silence as confirmation of his instincts, so he continued. "You have proved my theory," Raphael said, "which is that women are a virgin twice in their life. Once when the hymen is broken in the very first encounter...and again, later in life, when she falls in love with the right man and experiences intimacy in a way that she had never even imagined."

When Earl told Catherine of Rafael's theory, she thought about it for a second and said: "He's right. Being with you is like nothing before you ever happened."

As Earl recalled her response, he altered his plans for Saturday night. In the two weeks between their Richmond rendezvous and homecoming, he did something he had considered "over the top" and "almost silly": He wrote a poem for Catherine. After he finished it, he asked himself: "Is this too much?" He even questioned if he should give it to her. But the romantic in him prevailed.

He had planned to give her a printed version of it after they returned from the Best of Friends party, when they were back at her place, alone, sipping champagne. But it struck him as he walked to the football game to e-mail it to her at that moment. She was at home resting; it was a great time for her to hear from him in this way, even as he was enjoying homecoming. That's what being in love with Catherine inspired. He consistently sought ways to surprise her with expressions of his affection.

He called the poem, "What You Do." He had e-mailed it to himself, so it was easy for him to forward it to her from his BlackBerry. It read:

I heard your voice and my spirit was replenished
Soft, strong, assured. Sweet.
It moved me, made me smile.
Made me walk to the rhythm of your words

I saw your eyes and your soul was revealed
Warm, genuine, pure. Kind.
They made me look beyond the obvious
Made me see the magnificence in you.

I kissed your lips and I felt your heartbeat
A scintillating cadence of anticipation. Hope.
They were soft and irresistible, delightful
A lasting, tasty pleasure

I held your hand and you touched the center of me
Gentle, firm, sensitive. Delicate.
In it, I felt life and joy.
And an unbreakable connection of like and "loke" and love.

He knew the words would mean a lot to Catherine, a woman who loved being loved by him. But as soon as he sent the poem to her, he could not shake the feeling that he might be moving too fast, doing too much. Not even forty-eight hours had passed since he'd told her that he was in love with her, which she reciprocated. Two days since they had made love for the first time. That was a lot. Plenty. Maybe the poem should have come later, much later—or not at all, he pondered. He started to feel anxiety about it. *What if it turned her off, made her feel like I'm moving way too fast, that I needed to back off?*, he thought. *What if she thinks it's corny and too mushy?*

His head was spinning for the first time about something negative as it related to Catherine. It finally occurred to him that she did not check her e-mails often. She had access to them from her iPhone, but she infrequently checked her e-mail account. Maybe she would not get the poem right away. Maybe she would not get it until he was back home in Charlotte—or later. Those counter thoughts allowed him to go on and enjoy the rest of the day on the Yard and at the game without much consternation.

Catherine, meanwhile, was reflective. She rested on her couch a significant amount of Saturday. She put on a Norfolk State T-shirt and a few times she wished she were at the tailgate with her sorority sisters and with Earl. But those thoughts were fleeting. Her life had come together in a remarkable way, and she was thankful for the opportunity to rest and think. Catherine liked to think, to get her thoughts clear before she proceeded. That's why she was resistant to sex with Earl, even though they had "dated" for nearly five months and grew to become the closest of friends with a strong physical attraction.

"Sex changes things," she told him. She coveted the relationship they built so much that she did not want to risk losing it or even it being one iota off what it had been. But the connection they had was combustible. They lived apart, but the depth and transparency of their communication brought them together.

Earl said, "It *will* change things—for the better. It doesn't have to be a change that pulls us apart or makes things awkward. With us, the change will make us even closer. I'm going to leave it at that because I don't want to sound like I'm trying to convince you to do anything. I want you when you are ready for me to have you."

She appreciated his patience and his calm. He respected her caution and concern. And that was a key to their happiness: there was mutual admiration and consideration.

Catherine poured herself some cranberry juice with a little water to dilute it, put on her sunglasses and took a seat on her seventh-floor balcony, basking in the sun and in her romance. Her mind raced to various places, all of them with Earl. She wondered how they had the same major and took several classes together for four years of college and yet never had so much as a memorable conversation. If they had, maybe they would have changed the course of their lives.

"You can't really question that," said her friend, Starr, whom she called from the balcony. "This is your time now. You can't question God's plan. It could be that if you all started something back then, it wouldn't have lasted. This is the right time for you."

"That's what Earl says," Catherine admitted. "He says that he wasn't ready for me back then. Well, I tell you what: He's ready for me now."

Starr knew what that meant—that sex with Earl was one of those fireworks occasions. He had told her their connection was "combustible," and he was right. There was a synergy to their passion. Every touch was in the right spot. Every kiss was delicious and sensual. Every movement was as if they were dancing. Catherine smiled when thinking about their passion.

"A woman without passion in her life is living an incomplete life," she said to herself. Starr had long since hung up the phone. Catherine was left with her thoughts and emotions.

Suddenly, though, like a supernova, a thought streaked across her mind: How would Earl handle their appearance at the Best of Friends party that night? It was the awesome close to a special weekend, and their classmates would be there in big numbers.

Catherine pondered how Earl wanted their classmates to view them. Would he want to show up at the Best of Friends party that night together? Would he want to meet her there? Would he be attentive or would he leave her for long stretches to socialize?

Earl had not shown her anything but a caring and respectful nature. *But sex changes things*, she told herself, and since they actually had experienced it, was that enough for Earl? Was that his entire mission? Was she the proverbial "notch on his belt"? She sipped her juice and came back to her reality: Earl had never, not once, shown himself to be that way. He was forthcoming and generous and kind. And when she got past that flash of insecurity, she was embarrassed to even consider he pursued her only for sex.

She called Starr back. "I'm sorry to bother you, but I want to make sure I'm not crazy," Catherine said. "You're riding with me to the Best of Friends party tonight, right?"

"Yes," Starr answered.

"Okay. Earl and I never really discussed how we would do the party, whether he would go with his boys and meet me there or if we would go together, as a couple," Catherine said. "Would I be thinking something into it if he decides he wants to meet us there instead of walking in with me?"

"I'm willing to bet that he wants to go there with you," Starr said.

"That's why I love you, girlfriend," Catherine said. "You always have my back. You're always positive...I'll be at your house around ten to pick you up. Hopefully you are right and Earl will be with me."

Catherine moved from the balcony and back onto the couch. She flipped channels on the television, but found nothing that captured her interest. She got up and washed dishes and put a load of clothes in the washing machine. She changed the linen on her bed and took garbage to the trash chute. She was piddling around, doing things to pass time.

By the end of the Norfolk State easy victory over Howard, she realized she had not determined what she would wear to the party. So she searched her closet, pulling out and trying on a number of elegant dresses before deciding on a violet number that draped just above the knees. It had a low back and hung off the edge of her shoulders.

It was made of spun wool and with a crochet covering, providing a see-through effect on her arms. It was sexy and classy. Content with her selection, she pinned up her hair and finally drifted off to sleep.

Earl sent her a text message later, saying, "We won, baby. Hope you had a peaceful day. We're going to get something to eat. Call me when you have time."

Around seven, Catherine woke up to Earl's text message. She smiled while reading it, and then called him. He was at Captain George's all-you-can-eat seafood buffet with a host of fraternity brothers. She could tell he was having a good time.

"I don't want to interrupt your dinner," she said.

Earl left the table and found a more quiet place near the entrance.

"I'm good, baby," he said. "We got here before the big rush. I figure I should be back at my hotel room by eight. That'll give me some time to rest before the party."

That was Catherine's moment and she seized it. Well, sort of.

"Do you want me to pick you up? You can ride with me and Starr to the party," she said. "Or do you want to go there with your friends and meet me there?"

For Earl, that was a peculiar question. Why would he not want to go to the party with his woman? Why would he want to go with his boys that he'd been hanging with all day? The question threw him. In an instant he had to process whether she was simply giving him an option or whether she wanted to meet him there instead of walk in with him.

He finally told her, "I will figure it out after we leave here and call you back, okay?" Catherine offered a cheery "okay," but it was not okay. *Why doesn't he know*, she questioned.

Now, she was back in a tailspin, analyzing and overanalyzing everything to the point where she actually started to feel sad. She hadn't eaten much, so she put together a salad and baked a piece of salmon with her "world famous" cabbage. She ate most of it, but she did not enjoy it as she normally would because of Earl's indecision.

In the shower she worked on her response to him, saying he would meet her instead of going with her to the party. None of it sounded genuine. She decided she was going to go with what he wanted. They would meet there and have a great time and how they got there wouldn't matter. That's what she tried to convince herself of. Until he called her back with his decision, she was on edge. It was a little thing, but it was a big thing, too. If they walked in together, among their friends, it would announce to them all that they were together. It would show that he was proud of their relationship. If they did not, then maybe he wanted to temper Catherine's expectations, she surmised.

Earl continued to devour the crab legs and other items on the lavish buffet and he continued to laugh and share stories with his friends. But he could not shake the thought that Catherine would rather meet her at the party instead of arrive with him. He dared not share the question with his boys. Many of them would be surprised to learn he and Catherine was a couple.

Then he figured that she received the poem and thought it was too much, so she started the backing-off process by suggesting they meet instead of going together. *I knew I shouldn't have written that damned poem*, he said to himself.

He caused himself all kinds of inner tumult that he could not take any more. He rode with frat brother Ronnie Bagley from Captain George's to his hotel. Halfway there he placed the call.

"Hey, how are you?" he asked.

"I'm great, baby," she answered.

"I'm almost at the hotel," he said. "I decided that I'd like to ride with you to the party."

He was relieved to get it out. Catherine was relieved to hear his words. Her heart fluttered. "Great," she said. "I can pick you up first and then we can go get Starr."

"Cool," he said. "I will call you a little later from the room."

Behind the wheel, Ronnie smiled. Then he looked over at Earl. "Smart choice," he said.

CHAPTER TWENTY

REVELATIONS

Carter and Barbara

Barbara was at her wit's end. Hardly anything she hoped would happen at homecoming had happened for her. Worse, she got the feeling that Carter did not want her to move to New York because he had a girlfriend there.

After masking her discontent through the tailgate and the game, she asked Carter the question of the weekend:

"Do you have a girlfriend in New York?"

"Why would you ask me that?" he responded, which was not a good one.

"Just answer the question, please," she implored him.

"No, I don't," he said.

"Carter, please, the least you can do is be honest," she said. "We're at a critical point right now."

"We are?" he said. "When did it become critical?"

"It has been critical ever since I told you I was moving to New York," she started. "Since then you have been distant, like you're either mad at me or that you don't want me being close to you. And then there is Marlena."

Carter had been looking away as she spoke, but he turned when Barbara called that name.

"Marlena who?" he asked.

"Marlena 'baby,' that's who?"

"What?"

"While you were snoring like an animal last night, you received a text message from Marlena. And she called you 'baby.' That's the Marlena I'm talking about."

Carter stared at Barbara. He was fuming. They had not argued since their college days, but there were some memorable, loud arguments. This had the potential to be another blow-up. Because they were among the thousands after the game marching with the band up Presidential Parkway—which led from Dick Price Stadium, behind the old gym and the prodigious new Lyman Beecher Brooks Library, through the massive tailgate area, past the president's house and into Park Avenue—Carter controlled his voice level.

"So now you're reading my text messages?" he asked rhetorically. "You can't invade my privacy. Do you see me doing that to you? Do you think that's okay? And now you want me to answer questions about something you read on my phone? Well, that's not happening."

"Carter, I am sorry," she said. "I agree; it was stupid and I am really sorry. It will never happen again. But I can't forget what I saw."

"Well, I can't help what you saw and I can't help that you can't forget it," Carter said. "But I'm not discussing it. You had no right to violate me in that way. That's not cool. This isn't the first time I have had this happen and I guess it won't be the last. But I'm not taking it like it's a small thing."

When Carter got that way, she knew breaking his position was virtually impossible. So she let it go. Barbara was desperate for a turn of emotions, so she tried a different approach.

"I am really sorry, Carter. Do you forgive me?" she asked.

"I do," he said sternly. "But…"

"I promise, it won't happen again," she said. "I promise."

Carter didn't respond, but he lowered his shoulders, indicating he had relaxed at least a little bit.

"Can we spend tonight together?" she said. "I came here thinking it would be like it always has been with us. But it hasn't been that way so far. I am finally not married and can enjoy you without a black cloud hanging over me. I hope we can make these last hours special. Seems like we might not have many in New York."

There was a sadness in her voice when she spoke that last sentence, and Carter picked up on it. As salty as he was about her going through his phone, he could not deny his heart. He had feelings for Barbara that were more than casual.

"Yes, definitely," he said. "Listen, I want us to have a good time, too. I love coming to homecoming, but the main reason to come was to see you, to spend time with you. New York is going to be all right. We just have to figure it out."

Barbara lit up. It was the first time Carter expressed any notion that her move could be a good thing. She did not want to over-react to his comment, but she did want to acknowledge it…gently.

"Thank you for saying that; it means a lot to me, Carter," she said.

"And you mean a lot to me," he said. Something came over him. All the posturing and frustration melted away. Carter had a revelation: Enjoy Barbara.

"I'm not sure where this came from, but just now, it hit me," he said. "Life is short. You're a beautiful person. Embrace it. Embrace you. I sometimes get too serious. You're moving to New York and I have to accept that and make sure we make the most out of it."

Barbara smiled. "I'm so glad to hear you say that," she said. "That's all I ever wanted to hear. And I am sorry for not dis-cussing my divorce and move with you. I just thought it would be a surprise, a good surprise, and not a shock. But, thinking back on it, if it were reversed, I would have the same issues you had. I would have felt like I should have at least had some heads-up about what was going on.

"Part of my thinking was that I didn't want to bury you with all that was going on with my divorce. It wasn't ugly or anything, but it was taxing."

Carter was empathetic. "I'm sure it was," he said. "I've broken up with women and that was drama. I can only imagine what a divorce is like, and with kids involved... How are your kids?"

"I don't know," she said. "I'm a little worried. At the tailgate I saw Lisa Godley—remember her?—and she was with someone who seemed sad. I asked her if she was okay and she said she was. But after a few minutes, she started talking about being single again with two kids. The transition can be harder for the children than the parents."

"Well, you're going to have to really put in the time and effort to make sure they are okay," he said. "That's why I questioned you about moving so far away from their father."

"I was so mad when you said I was selfish I just didn't even bother to tell you that my husband—ex-husband—and I picked New York together," she said. "He's an artist and can live wherever he wants. He wanted to go to New York to open a studio. I felt the least I could do was to move there, too, so he could be close to his children. So I had my job transfer me.

"Pretty selfish, huh?"

Carter felt like a fool. He had made leaps about Barbara's character that were insulting. Turns out, she was the opposite of selfish when it came to her kids.

"Wow, baby," he said. "I guess I owe you a big apology. I'm so sorry. I should not have gone there with you. And I should have known better. That's pretty awesome of you. Come on, let's go get some dinner."

They had gotten back on course. They spent their dinner at The Bistro downtown, across from Nauticus, gossiping about what and whom they had seen at the tailgate and the game. The tension that enveloped them was released.

"I tell you what, Ramona Detrick looks crazy," Carter said.

"*Carter*. That's not nice," Barbara countered. "It's not like she didn't look crazy in college. She just looks like herself. Hairstyle from the '70s, clothes out of place. Even her glasses were not up to date. I don't get it."

They laughed.

"What about Peter? Did you see him?" Barbara asked.

"Pete Lomax?" Carter said. "Yeah, I saw him. I talked to him. And you know what he was talking about?"

"Women," Barbara said.

"Every word he had to say was about getting with a woman," Carter said. "I don't like him so I will say this: He told me that last night he banged Wendy Minor."

"You lying? Wendy is in a relationship with Andrew...I can't remember his last name. The guy who is the TV anchor in Hampton."

"What? No, that's not right. Andrew Blackwell is his name," Carter said. "Andrew Blackwell is tight with Jimmy's home boy, Rocco, who said Andrew was involved with Dylcea, the cheerleader who fell from the top of the pyramid that time and broke her ankle. She's looking great. Did you see her? She looks better than she did in college. She's the vice president of marketing at Norfolk Southern or some big company."

"Well, I talked to Myron, the Alpha, and you know how crazy he is," Barbara said. "He thought I was married. We stood there as I waited for Donna to come back from the bathroom at the game, and in five minutes, he pointed out three women that he had slept with in previous homecomings. One of them was Audrey Jackson; one was Judy Richie; and the third was Stacy Bridges. He was proud of it. I said, 'Myron, who you sleeping with this weekend?' He said, 'I got two offers already. I'm holding out for a third.' And he was dead serious."

"Well, he isn't married, right? So, technically, he can do whatever he likes," Carter said. "The thing about all those women you named is that they are all married."

"Well, Myron was married three years ago," Barbara said, "so some of his dirt was done when he was wearing a wedding band… But who am I to judge."

"The difference between you and them is that we are in love," Carter said. He had held back his feelings about Barbara the entire weekend. He poured her another glass of chardonnay from the bottle he had ordered. "They were doing their 'What happens at homecoming stays at homecoming' thing. It was for simple gratification or to just be bad. We are connected out of love. I ain't judging them for what they do; they have to do what they have to do. But I know we are on a love thing."

Barbara smiled. "See, this is the Carter I know and love. I don't know who that other person was."

Carter pulled out his cell phone to check for calls, raising Barbara's awareness that there appeared to be someone else in Carter's life. He sensed it and quickly generated another conversation.

"So, Jimmy," he said, "he had to put Regina in her place last night. Apparently, she pretty much threw herself at him."

"Really?" Barbara said. "And he turned her down? That's surprising. I'm not saying anything about Jimmy. I'm just saying a man has an opportunity to have sex and there is no way his wife will know about it—Regina is married and lives in another city—and he turns it down? That's not the norm. Plus, we used to spend a lot of time with them in college on double dates. They have a serious past. Why would he not do it? His wife would never know."

"Because *he* would know," Carter said. "Some of us—a very few of us—are built differently. We don't have to screw anything that is in front of us. I admit: There are only a handful of men who have those kinds of standards and those kinds of morals. This guy is one of them. I have known him since he was nineteen, maybe twenty.

"When he was with Regina, he had plenty of chances to cheat on her in college. I was with him when he was propositioned by, uh, shit, what's her name? She was the SGA vice president one year. From North Carolina."

"Oh," Barbara said, "we, the women, called her 'Booty Girl' for obvious reasons. And we know it was real because they weren't even doing butt injections back then. Anyway, you're talking about Melissa."

"Yes, Melissa. But I thought she was from Staten Island," Carter said. "Anyway, when he was dating Regina and we were living off of Azalea Garden Road, I remember Melissa coming over the apartment. It was a Friday night and Regina went to a party at Hampton with her girls. I don't know how Melissa ended up at our place, but I opened the door and there she was. She liked to show off her body—and her booty. We weren't mad at her, either."

"Yeah, I bet you weren't," Barbara said.

Carter smiled. "Anyway, I was surprised to see her there," he said. "Before I could even ask her anything, Jimmy came from the back and walked her in. I just stood there..."

"Watching her butt, right?" Barbara cracked.

"Can't lie, yes. That girl had the best body—other than yours, of course—I have ever seen," Carter said.

Barbara curled her lips and looked at him sideways. "Anyway," he continued, "I stayed in the living room—hey, come to think of it, where were you that night? It was a Friday and we spent every Friday together. Who were you off seeing on the side?"

Barbara curled her lips again and looked at him sideways. "Anyway, a few hours later, they came from out the back. He walked her out, to her car. When he came back, I was like, 'Dog, what's up?' He said, 'Nothing. I couldn't do it. Good girl. Phat ass; oh, my God. I *did* squeeze it. I had to. And it felt like it looked—luscious. But I couldn't do that to Regina. I told her about Regina. And this girl said, 'I know about you and Regina. I *know* Regina. I'm not trying to take you away from her. We're just here in the moment.' I don't know, man. I would have to look Regina in the eyes tomorrow. I don't want that on my conscience.' I said, 'Dude, you're better than most.' "

Barbara wondered about Carter. Was he "better than most"? As a woman, she knew Marlena calling him "baby" meant he had been intimate with her. Or they had built something that was headed that way. In a sense, she could not blame Carter; she was married and felt trapped, as if there was no way out. She even told him that because of the children, "I can't go anywhere."

And the fact that he was having a once-a-year-affair with her meant that he was not above doing the unscrupulous, even if they declared their relationship special.

At the same time, Carter wondered about Barbara. Because she had declared she would stay in her marriage for the foreseeable future, what made her change? He wanted to know.

"I know we have to leave soon to get ready for the party, but I have to ask you something," he said. Barbara braced herself. She was not sure where Carter was about to go, but the set-up to the question made her tense.

"You told me more than once that you would not get a divorce because you had kids and you wanted to keep the family structure for them," he said. "I don't think you were lying. I think you meant it, and you had your reasons for saying it. So what happened? Why now are you divorced?"

Barbara was prepared for that question. She had expected it sooner, much sooner, but Carter never got directly to it after she shocked him with the news.

"You might laugh at this because it's funny. Not comical funny, but ironic funny," she said. "I found out that he was having an affair—a long, drawn-out affair. Here I was the one feeling guilty and upset about breaking our vows, and he was doing it, too, only longer and more elaborate."

"Wow," Carter said.

"Wow is right," she went on. "We were married for almost nine years. He had been seeing this woman for seven years. They traveled together. He even had her in our house, probably in our bed. I was so shocked. I almost couldn't believe it. But when I started thinking about it, all the signs were right there."

"How did you find out?" Carter asked.

"It was the eeriest of things," she said. "We were home. The kids were asleep. It was a Thursday night. We were flipping channels and he stopped at *The Real Housewives of Atlanta*. I said, 'Keep going. I cannot poison my brain with that nonsense.'

"He said, 'Barb, you need to open your mind.' He'd never said anything like that to me before. I said, 'Open my mind? That show is an affront to black people. It goes against everything our culture really, truly stands for.' He said, 'Loosen up, woman. It's just entertainment.'

"You've got to understand: My ex-husband detests nonsense. For him to defend that show threw me off. Then he said, 'Well, did you watch *Good Times*? That show was silly and an embarrassment.' Oh, I hit the roof. I said, '*Good Times* is an iconic show. It represented the times. It had two parents struggling to make it for their family. Each show had a moral lesson. Was J.J. a buffoon? Yes. But the show was a comedy. It was one of the few places where we could turn on the TV and see brown skin. And you're calling it an 'embarrassment'? Who has gotten into your head?'

"He didn't say anything. So I said, 'Who have you been watching that trash with?' He turned the TV off. He got off the couch and went over to the steps to make sure the kids were asleep. When he came back over, he put his head down and put his hand on my leg.

"Then, he said, 'Barb, I'm sorry. You've been a good wife to me and a great mother. But…I have been seeing someone else.' I moved his hand off of my leg. I was totally, totally shocked. I did not see that coming. And then he gave me the details. He was painting at Jack London Square in Oakland, on the dock by the water one day when this young woman came by. She admired his work and they started to converse. Before long, they were going on dates and the affair began.

"She knew he was married and was okay with seeing him only when he was available, which, as it turned out, became more and more as time went on. So, when he traveled to Mountain View and San Jose—towns not far from where we lived—to paint, she would go with him. And when I went back home to Ohio with the kids, she spent the weekend with him at our house. He gave me so many details to where I just told him to stop. I had heard enough. Although I had been unfaithful to him with you, I was still devastated. I was not going to leave him. I was going to stick it out because of the kids. But when I heard that, I knew I couldn't."

Carter did not know what to say. "Damn," he finally uttered. "I'm sorry. You've been through a lot. But you could have told me about this. You should have told me. Trust me, it would have saved me—saved us—a lot of drama."

"The way my life has been, I figure you're going to run into drama as soon as you step out the front door," she said. "It's just a matter of how much."

CHAPTER TWENTY-ONE

EEENIE MEENIE MYNEE…NO

Tranise, Mary and Charlene

When the cannons erupted following the game, signifying the Spartans' victory, Tranise did not jump. This time, she was ready.

"I didn't watch much of the game," she said, "but homecoming is a little better if we win. Now, *everyone* is in a great mood. I love it."

Walking out of the stadium, she hugged Phyllis Simms, an NSU graduate whose book, *In the Name of Sisterhood*, was one of Tranise's favorites.

"I knew it was you as soon as I saw you," Tranise said. "I really enjoyed your book. It reminded me of my friendships I made here at NSU."

She posed for a photo with Phyllis. "We have some really talented authors from Norfolk State: Nathan McCall, China Ball, Regina Southall—those are three more I can think of off the top of my head," Tranise said. "I'm so glad I got to meet you."

Phyllis hugged her and they departed. Tranise was torn about what she should do that night. Another friend, Kayrn Shepard from Maryland, was encouraging her to step back in time and attend a party called "The Sweatbox."

It was a concept a group of Norfolk State students had developed in the late 1980s at the old Student Union Building's ballroom. Students would pack the place and jam until they sweated out their clothes. It was all about one thing: dancing. Dancing hard and long. It was not unlike The Garage in New York way back in the day, where party-goers would show up with a backpack full of a change of clothes. Then they would throw down until the sun came up.

"The Sweatbox is an experience," Tranise said. "I don't think you ever went. They said it's down at the Crowne Plaza in Virginia Beach. Artie Jarrett, the Alpha, is hosting it. Three floors. Food on the lower level. You just pack a bag of clothes so you can change and get your groove on. They expect three hundred people there."

"Well, I won't be three-oh-one," Mary said. "I went to the salon on Thursday. You think I'm gonna undo what I paid ninety-dollars for in ten minutes of dancing like I'm some fool? Not gonna happen."

"Ninety dollars?" Charlene said. They were walking down Presidential Parkway behind the band and a massive group of people.

"My hair is natural. A press and a trim is ninety. I got off the 'creamy crack' two years ago," Mary explained. "Relaxers serve a purpose; I ain't mad if you get one. But I got tired of them."

"Well, you have a manageable grade of hair," Tranise said. "Me? If I don't get a relaxer, I'll be looking real crazy right about now."

"Your hair is fabulous," Mary said. "You got it done in Atlanta?"

"I tried at least four, maybe five different salons down there until I found one that I love," Tranise said. "It's called Like The River. Beautiful, professional, no waiting. And my stylist, Najah, is the owner; she's the bomb. In fact, her sister, Madinah, went to Norfolk State.

"But your point is well-taken. How I look sweating out my hair at a party? Shit, I don't even like to sweat at the gym."

"The gym?" Charlene said. "If I set foot in a gym, I think the alarms would go off."

"We're laughing, but you're my girl so I've got to keep it real with you," Tranise said. "I'm really glad you said you are starting to watch what you eat. We have to be mindful of how much weight we put on now while we're still relatively young. We've got to make it a lifestyle choice. If we get it under control now, it will be the way we live and we'll be able to manage it. A lot of teachers in my school—or shoot, just look at some of our classmates—have blown up. It's not healthy. And it's easy to put on but very hard to get off."

"You're not even as big as Jennifer Hudson was and look at her now," Mary chimed in. "I want you to be healthy because here's the thing: We're not just talking about having a stroke or a heart attack and dying. Just as common are illnesses that come from weight problems. You don't want to be on medication all your life. I have a co-worker who is thirty-two years old and she's taking all kinds of pills every day—cholesterol, blood pressure, so on and so forth. It ain't cute, honey."

"Damn," Charlene said. "I was about to say let's go to the all-you-can-eat seafood place."

Mary and Tranise punched her in either arm.

"No, I hear you and I appreciate you," Charlene said. "Looking at you little cute bitches inspired me even more to do better. Seriously. I looked at both of you yesterday and I was like, 'I've got to come down.'

"So, I'm giving up my butter pecan pint of ice cream three times a week before bed. I'm giving up my double-pattie burger and fries every Saturday. I'm giving up fast-food altogether."

"That sounds like a lot, Charlene," Tranise said. "Maybe you should be a little more gradual about it."

"I don't know," she said. "But I'm serious. This is how serious I am: After Tyrell and I finished our business last night, he passed out as if someone took a hammer to his head. I got on my phone and looked up diet and healthy choices. I basically developed a strategy on how I'm gonna attack this."

"Which is what?" Mary asked.

"Well, I will start my day with an apple for breakfast and oatmeal," she said. "They are both great for you. For lunch I will eat fish, chicken or turkey and vegetables. For dinner I will have a salad with salmon or chicken and occasionally steak. But no white starches. No white bread or French fries or white rice. It said I could have dessert a few times a week, but I'm going to let fruit be my desserts. And I'm going to walk three or four times a week. This is the vow I made to myself this morning.

"Oh, and the other thing I read was there are a lot of health benefits to sex. So I'm having it at least twice a week. And that means, since I didn't get none last week, I'm hooking up with Tyrell again tonight."

The women fell all over each other laughing. "You are a sho-nuff fool," Mary said.

"Does Tyrell know this?" Tranise asked.

"You saw when I talked to him at the game, didn't you?" Charlene said. "I told him then."

"What did he say?" Mary said.

"Nothing. He just smiled and smacked me on my ass," Charlene said. "I took that to mean he is down."

"Well, anyway, I am glad you have made a smart decision—about changing your eating habits, not Tyrell," Tranise said. "I'm going to be calling you every week to check on you."

"Yeah, right," Mary said. "We might not see your little cute butt for another four years."

"After these two days?" Tranise said. "I'll definitely be back. As a matter of fact, we should get together in the summer somewhere. Maybe you two should come to visit me in Atlanta."

"Give me until the spring; by then you will see a difference in me," Charlene said. "How about April? That's—what?—five months? Oh, I'll be light in the ass by then."

"You're already light in the head," Tranise said.

"I don't know about you, but I'm hungry," Mary said. "You want to get something at the tailgate or go to a restaurant?"

"The game is over; the tailgate isn't?" Tranise asked.

"Girl, I've never been here when it was over," Charlene said. "I always end up leaving at some point while they're still going, even out there in the dark cooking, eating, drinking and partying."

"Well, let's go back there and see how it is, at least for a little while," Tranise said. "Maybe I'll see Brandon down there."

"Umm-hmm," Mary said. "I thought you had gotten past that puppy love from afar with a man who didn't know you existed until yesterday."

"That's funny," Tranise said. "I'm good. I know how to handle Brandon. Don't worry about that. But Kwame could be another story. He's putting the moves on. This young guy has more on the ball than most of the guys my age that I've met. I gotta give it to him."

"Give him what?" Charlene asked. "The booty?"

"Just because you let Tyrell get it and Mary opened them legs for Rodney doesn't mean I need to do the same thing," Tranise cracked.

"Actually, you probably do need some," Mary said. "It'll loosen you up some."

"I am loose enough, thank you very much," Tranise responded.

"Well, see if you're loose enough to handle Brandon, because there he is right there," Mary said.

Sure enough, standing across from the baseball stadium with a plate of food in his hand, was Brandon, looking as distinguished and pleasant as ever.

"I gotta admit," Charlene said, "That's a tall glass of chocolate milk right there. I'm lactose intolerant, but I'll be damned if I wouldn't sip him up with a straw."

Mary laughed, but Tranise did not. She did not even hear her friend's comment. She was focused on fluffing her hair and applying lip gloss and generally getting herself proper for a talk with Brandon. They made a direct line to him, cutting from one side of the street to the other, entangling themselves with people along the way.

"Did you even go into the game?" Tranise asked him.

"How you all doing?" he said. "Yes, I did go in. I stayed until I knew we had the game won. Then I came out here to get something to eat."

"That plate looks like you're eating for two," Charlene joked. "I thought it was your wife that's pregnant, not you."

Brandon laughed. "Well, I'm a growing boy, you know? We need our nutrition to keep our energy up," he said.

"I'm sure that ain't all that gets up," Charlene whispered into Tranise's ear.

"So what are you doing tonight?" Tranise asked.

"I'm going to the Best of Friends party at the Holiday Inn," he answered. "Have you been to one of their parties before? It's actually a crowd that's a little older than us, but they party. Really nicely done, everyone dresses up. I'm sure you have a sexy dress you're dying to show off."

"How did you know?" she said, smiling.

"It just made sense," he said. "I'm sure I'll appreciate it."

The conversation among the four became all about Brandon and Tranise, which was Mary's and Charlene's cue to move on. "Girl, we're going over to the Ques' tent," Charlene said.

"Okay, I'll be there in a minute," Tranise said.

Brandon smiled. "I thought they'd never leave," he said, smiling more. He was coming on to Tranise. If there ever was any doubt, there wasn't anymore.

"Why did they have to leave?" she asked.

"Oh, where are my manners?" he said. "You want to get a plate?"

"I actually have a ticket to the buffet at the alumni tent, so I'm going to head over there," Tranise said. "But you didn't answer my question."

"I was joking, but when I think about it, it is good that they left," he said, "because I was interested in talking more to you. It would be rude to leave them out of the conversation when we're all standing here together."

"That's true," she said. "And it is good that they left because I have a question I want answered."

"Go," he said.

"Are you flirting with me?"

Brandon finished off the potato salad on his plate and tossed it in the trash can behind him. "Do you want me to flirt with you?" he asked.

"I'm not ashamed to say I have wanted you to flirt with me since we were in college," Tranise admitted. "I just don't know if I'm finally getting what I wanted."

If he thought that because he was tall and handsome and charming and smart and popular that he was going to get somewhere with her, well, he was right. Tranise was weak to him. It was only when she reminded herself that he was married that she put up any real resistance.

Before he could answer, none other than his wife appeared from a group of people to Tranise's right. The look on Brandon's face said she should go away.

"Honey, you remember Tranise?" Brandon said.

Felicia just looked at her husband. He turned when someone called his name. "Honey, I'll be right back." He was off, leaving Felicia and Tranise standing there frowning at each other. Nothing was said for about ten seconds, before Tranise decided to take the mature approach.

"When is your baby due?" she asked Felicia.

"When is yours due?" Felicia responded.

"I'm not pregnant," Tranise snapped back.

"Then stop staring at my husband as if he's something you're craving," Felicia said.

"Already that baby is making you crazy," Tranise said. "And I thought you couldn't get more crazy."

"You can deny it all you want; I saw it for myself just now," Felicia said.

"As usual, you are way off base," Tranise said. "Why would I want someone who has had you?"

"Because you haven't had anyone," Felicia said.

Brandon returned before it got really ugly. Felicia grabbed his hand and led him away from Tranise before he could ever say anything. They both were heated. When they got out of Tranise's line of sight, Felicia went off on her husband.

"Brandon, what the hell are you doing entertaining that...that silly little woman?" she said. "I have told you how I feel about her. That's not acceptable. She's grinning in your face and you're grinning back at her. What's that about?"

"Calm down," he said.

"Don't tell me to calm down," she snapped. "That was totally disrespectful. And I'm not having it."

"Baby, it's homecoming," he said, remaining calm. "All I did is what all these thousands of people out here are doing. There was nothing out of bounds about speaking to Tranise."

"I don't even want her name to come out of your mouth," Felicia said. "What is it, because I'm fat, walking around with your baby, that you're looking to other women? Of all people... not her. You know how I feel about her."

"If you saw, then you saw her come over to me," Brandon said.

"And I saw you smiling and laughing with her," Felicia said. "You haven't even been doing that with me. And from what I saw, it looked like you were flirting with her. I know you, Brandon Barksdale. I know you from your body language, and what I saw was a man enjoying the attention of a woman he knows I detest."

"Why is that?" Brandon asked. "I don't understand. You never told me why there's such animosity."

"Does it matter?" Felicia said. "Does it really matter? Bottom line, you knew and you didn't care."

Brandon kept his composure. He felt like people were always looking at him, so he refused to be pulled into a blatant argument with her right there at the tailgate.

"Felicia, I love you," he said, holding her shoulders while looking into her eyes. "You are my wife. I don't care how it looked—we were just having a conversation. You can't be carrying our child and getting upset about any little thing. That doesn't help the baby."

He knew what cards to draw to get Felicia to throw in her hand. Talking about the health of the baby was it. Felicia immediately calmed down. "Well, I was going to stay home tonight, but I'm going to the Best of Friends party," she said.

"You don't have to do that."

"You don't want me to be there with you?" she asked.

"Of course, I do. As long as you're up to it, that's great."

"Well, if I wasn't up to it I am now."

✪✪✪

Tranise was up for whatever might come her way with Felicia and Brandon. That encounter with her arch-nemesis had sent her into a fury. She was not planning on sleeping with Brandon, but that underexposed devilish part of her psyche had emerged. "I'm gonna make her so mad, she will have that baby right there on the damned dance floor," she told Mary and Charlene.

"It's not time for that baby to come, so maybe you shouldn't wish for that," Charlene said. "The baby could die. *She* could die."

"Well," Tranise said, "I would never wish harm on a baby. But that bitch...."

"*Tranise*," Mary said.

"Well, okay, I'm sorry. I don't want her to die," Tranise said. "How about close to death?"

"That's not good," Charlene said. "You're putting bad karma out there. You get back what you put out."

"I don't believe that," Mary said. "I mean, she shouldn't want anyone to die. But even if she really did, that doesn't mean she's going to die."

"She *is* going to die," Charlene said.

"Yeah, but not because she wished death on someone else," Mary countered.

"You don't know that," Charlene argued. "That bad karma could come right back and she could die right on the spot."

"Wait, wait, wait," Tranise finally interrupted. "Why you two heffas talking about my inevitable death? Really? Seriously? Can we talk about something else. *Damn.*"

They made it to the restaurant in the lobby of the Airport Hilton, and enjoyed a nice dinner before resting for the weekend's closing event. There was a Chuck Brown concert, but, while they appreciated "go-go" music, they were not in love with it like most everyone from Washington, D.C. The Sweatbox was unanimously ruled out. There were other parties, including one hosted by the Ques in downtown Norfolk. But the buzz about the Best of Friends party was too loud to ignore.

"What are you going to wear?" Mary asked her friends.

"I actually went to MacArthur Mall before I went over to campus yesterday and found something so nice at Nordstrom," Tranise said. "It's a little black dress—simple but elegant. And sexy. It's fitting all my new curves."

"Showoff," Charlene said.

"I have a nice dress, too," Mary said. "I started to bring a black dress, but I'm glad I didn't. We'd be looking like we dressed together."

"Remember when we used to do that, though?" Charlene said. "I remember going to The Broadway for some party and we all had on jeans tucked in our boots with polka dot shirts."

"With different color polka dots," Mary said.

"We were cute," Tranise recalled. "Turned it out. And tonight I'm going to turn Brandon out. And turn Felicia into a basket case."

CHAPTER TWENTY-TWO

A NIGHT NOT REMEMBERED

Jesse, Don and Venita

Neither Jesse nor Don enjoyed the tailgate or the game as much as they should have. Jesse was working on a hangover that took him until after the game to shake. And Don was missing his wallet, so drunk that he did not remember what he did with it.

"What the fuck happened to the car?" Venita said that morning when they went to the hotel parking lot to go to the tailgate.

"Oh, shit," Jesse said. "Don. What the fuck?"

"Man, it was a bad night. Well, it was a good night that turned bad," Don said. "I don't know what happened, man. I was driving along Interstate 264 and all of a sudden I felt the car vibrating. I woke up and we were running up against the median wall. Jesse, I'm sorry, man."

His 2009 BMW 745i was damaged all the way up the right side, as if someone had taken a giant piece of sandpaper and wiped it down. Another kind of man would have been beside himself. Jesse viewed cars as necessary to get around. Nothing more. He was more concerned that he did not even realized what had happened.

"How in the hell could I sleep through that?" he asked. "Are you telling me I didn't even wake up?"

"You don't remember?" Don said. "Ah, man, you were *really* ripped. I woke up and was scared as hell. I stopped the car and we both got out and looked at the damage. You said, 'Damn. You all right, D?' I apologized. You turned away from me and threw up. I got panicked because if a trooper had seen us and stopped, our homecoming would be over. Our asses would be in jail."

"Jesse, look at your car," Venita said.

"I can't be worried about that," he said. "It's messed up, but that's why we get insurance. As long as we survived it, I'm good. We can still drive it and can still get home... But it's scary that I don't remember any of that shit. Nothing. Last I remember I was grinding on Collette on the dance floor. And—"

"Collette, who slept with everybody at Norfolk State when we were there Collette'?" Venita asked. "You were grinding on her?"

"Damn right, I was," Jesse said. "She felt *good*—I remember that. And she looked great. I can't hold against her what she did in college. I mean, she was out there, no doubt about that. It would be hard for me to marry her knowing what she was like. But she doesn't have the Plague. She and I were always close. I'm still her friend."

"Well, can the passenger door open?" Venita said. "Matter of fact, I'm not sure I can even be seen in this car."

"Well, lay down in the back seat then," Jesse said. "We're rolling."

"I guess I can't even ask if the party was good or not; you bums can't even remember what happened," Venita said. "And by the way, that's pathetic."

"Was it pathetic when I saw you at the CIAA Tournament walking the streets of downtown Charlotte with your shoes in your hand and eyes all gazed over, draped over some dude who was feeling you up the whole time?" Jesse asked. "What was that? At least no one saw us messed up. You were on display for any-one on that street."

"That night was an exception for me, not the rule," she said. "I was messing with my girl who had some guy buying us shots of Goldschlager. That shit had me twisted up. I can't even try to fade that. I was done. Never again."

"Can we just go?" Jesse said. "I don't feel so great right now. If I threw up last night, I should feel better than I do now."

"Venita, you have to drive," Don said. "Jesse can't drive in this silly-ass state and I shouldn't be behind the wheel. But I guess we have to give you the whole rundown of what happened last night."

"There was more? Ah, shit," Jesse said. "What the hell else could have happened?"

"Do you remember going to breakfast with these two women at IHOP?" Don said.

"Come on, man. You lying now," Jesse insisted.

Don did not flinch. He went into his pocket and pulled out a receipt from their meal.

"You paid for everybody's food," he said. "I kept the receipt just in case you hit me with exactly what you're doing now."

Jesse reviewed the credit card receipt. "I left the waitress a twenty-five-dollar tip? What the hell, Don? Why didn't you stop me?"

"Well, as a matter of fact, I did try to get you under control, but—Venita, you know how he can get," Don said. "I said, 'That's way too much.' You said, 'My daddy ain't here and neither is my momma. I ain't got no wife to make me miserable. So I can do whatever I want.' It would have been crazy for me to try to stop you. You were in top form—aggressive, belligerent, funny, wild."

"So who were these two honeys?" Jesse wanted to know.

"We met them at the end of the party," Don said. "You walked Collette to her car—and y'all kissed, too. A tongue kiss."

"What? She musta been drunk, too," Venita said, laughing.

"I'm not even going to address you," Jesse said. "I guess we're to believe you stayed in your room on a Friday night at home-coming? By yourself?"

"I will tell you what I did, but let's finish hearing about this night that you don't even remember."

Throughout their day of eating, taking pictures, greeting old friends and watching the game, Don gave them snippets of a mostly forgotten night for Jesse.

"Okay, see that girl right there," Don said, using his eyes to point out the woman instead of pointing at her. "Watch what happens when she sees Jesse."

"Come on, man, tell me what I did so I know how to react," Jesse pleaded.

"It won't be as much fun if I tell you," Don said.

"Well, tell me," Venita said.

Don put his arm around her and whispered into Venita's ear. When he was finished, she stepped away from him. "Don, you are lying."

"I wish I was lying," he said.

"You," Venita said, pointing at Jesse, "are crazy."

"That's messed up that you won't tell me, Don," Jesse said. "But that's all right. I got something for your ass."

"What?" Don said.

Jesse did not bother to answer; the young lady noticed him and came over. She was totally unfamiliar to Jesse, although she was tall and pretty.

"I'm glad to see you today," she said. Jesse smiled and glanced over at Don.

"Really? That's good to hear," Jesse said.

"I'm glad because I was sure you might die of alcohol poison-ing," she added, and Don and Venita burst into laughter. Jesse had a look of indifference on his face.

Don introduced her to Venita. "I believe you said your name is Rochelle, right?"

"Good memory," she said. "You were done and this guy right here... Jesse, you're a piece of work."

Jesse did not know how to take it because he didn't know what the hell he did. Finally, he let it be known he was out of the loop.

"I hope I didn't offend you," he said. "I apparently had too much to drink. But since there was no Breathalyzer that wouldn't stand up in court."

"You actually offended the Holiday Inn ballroom more than you offended me," Rochelle said.

"Huh?" Jesse was puzzled.

"Are you going to tell him, because I'm not," Rochelle said. "Call me later, after you find out. I put my number in your phone. Do you remember that?"

Jesse lied. "Yes, I do," he said. "I will definitely call you."

Rochelle smiled, said her goodbyes and walked away, and Jesse stood there admiring her.

"Whatever I did, it must not have been that bad because I think she's feeling me," he said. "But what the hell did I do?"

"Should I tell him, Venita?" Don asked.

She nodded her head.

"Okay, well, you met her in the lobby after Collette left," Don began. "She was walking by and you said, 'I remember you from school.' She said, 'No you don't.' You said, 'OK, you're right. But I should have.' And a conversation started from there. You all danced. You bought her a couple drinks. Then one of her friends came up from nowhere. Then all four of us were dancing, having a great time.

"You and Rochelle sat down way in the back to the side of the dance floor. The girl I was dancing with went to the bathroom or someplace and you and I went to the bar. You said, 'I like this girl. She's a lawyer, too.' I bought us more drinks, and you went back in there with her. Well, about fifteen minutes later, your girl finds me in the lobby. 'You need to go check on your boy.' I looked up and you were staggering to the bathroom.

"I asked her what was wrong. She said, 'We were talking at the table. I knew he had a good buzz—it showed up in his eyes. But he was still coherent, so I didn't think much of it. Then all of a sudden, in mid-sentence, he puts up one finger to mean 'just a minute,' turns away from me and throws up right there on the floor. I was so shocked I couldn't move. Then he reached on the table and knocked over his drink to get the napkin under it and wiped his mouth. And believe it or not, he turned around and looked at me and continued the conversation as if nothing had happened.'

"I laughed so hard everyone in the lobby turned and looked at me. I couldn't believe it."

"Oh, my God," Jesse said. "The sad part is that I actually remember some of that. Didn't you come and get me out of the bathroom?"

"Yeah," Don said. "I let you stay in there for about ten minutes to get yourself together. Finally, Rochelle said, 'You might want to go check on him.' So, I go there expecting to see you washing your mouth out. Yo ass was in the last stall, sitting on the toilet, knocked out, face pressed all up against the wall."

Venita and Don laughed so hard. Jesse shook his head.

"Oh, shit," Jesse said. "So I threw up twice in one night?"

"Well, yes, you did because after you got up, you seemed to be together," Don explained. "You put some water on your face. I gave you some eye drops. You downed about ten mints. We got back out there, Rochelle and her friend—I can't remember her name—were standing there waiting.

"You held it together. You were walking straight, talking straight. You said you were hungry. Rochelle's friend said she was hungry, too, so we went to IHOP on Military Highway. The place was packed. And you put on a show. You were funny and obnoxious and silly and engaging. And Rochelle seemed to eat it up.

"And you paid for the meal because I reached for my wallet and it wasn't there. I called the hotel and no one turned it in. So I have some issues."

"Did you cancel your cards?" Venita said.

"Forget about his wallet for a minute," Jesse said. "That woman, Rochelle is bad. I've got to get with her."

"You know how much drama losing your wallet costs you?" Venita said. "Listen, you'd better cancel your cards. My aunt lost her wallet and in two hours she had charges on her card from London, Miami and New York. They ran up about twelve-hundred dollars' worth of stuff. She got her money back, eventually. But who wants to go through that hassle?"

"Yeah, you're right," Don said. "I checked my accounts online and there was no activity. But that doesn't mean nothing will happen."

Jesse smiled. "What you grinning about?" Venita asked.

"Before you make those calls, let me tell you about this fool," he said. "I might have been messed up, but Don was, too. Do you remember taking your drink on the dance floor and spilling it all over this woman to your right? She was with her husband and homeboy was not happy. It was all on the front of her dress, all up in her cleavage."

"Oh, yeah, damn, I do remember that," Don said. "That was messed up. I think her husband was trying to fight me."

"He was," Jesse said. "But he quickly realized he would have gotten double-teamed, like we did those guys that time from ODU. Remember that?"

"I don't remember that," Venita said.

"We went to a party over there one night," Don said. "I think it was a Delta party. Yep, because Donna Scott invited me. And you were invited by Tawana Turner. She wasn't a Delta, but she went to Old Dominion. Anyway, some chick said I felt her on her ass when she walked by."

"You *did* feel her on her ass, Don," Jesse said.

"Yeah, but she couldn't have know it was me," Don said. "There were four other guys right there."

"Anyway," Jesse continued. "So Don denies it and we go on and stay for another hour or so. It was winter and I forgot that I had put my coat on the back of a chair. Don went to get the car and said he'd meet me in the front of the building. On his way, the chick has her boyfriend confront Don just before he gets to the car. I can see this as I'm coming behind them, so I start running to catch up. The guy gets aggressive and Don pushes him away from him—right into my arms. I threw him on the ground and, well, it wasn't good for him after that. His girl was screaming as we beat and kicked his ass."

"Needless to say," Don added, "that was our last party at ODU."

"So you are a lawyer and you're an entrepreneur and all these years later, you were going to gang up on a guy last night? After you spilled a drink on his wife?" Venita said. "Seems to me you all would be overly apologetic."

"I was," Don said, "but he wasn't hearing it. He wanted to show off for his wife or something."

"So I just eased over and said, 'Don, you cool?' But I was staring at the husband," Jesse said. "That ended the drama."

Venita shook her head. "I had more adult conversation last night with my niece than I'm having right now with you grown-ass men," she said.

"Well, wait. It ain't over," Jesse said.

Don started to call his credit card company. "Hold on one more minute," Jesse told him. "You want to hear this."

Don had a smirk on his face, but he waited…and listened.

"So, I woke up this morning, and the room isn't spinning or anything, but I just feel totally drained. I make it to the shower and feel a little better when I get out. I go through my pants pockets and guess what I found?"

"What, nigga?" Don asked.

"Two wallets," Jesse revealed. "I opened them up and one was mine; the other had this driver's license photo that looked like Sammy Davis Jr."

"Ah, man, gimme my damned wallet," Don said, snatching it out of Jesse's hand. "How you get this?'

"You asking me?" Jesse responded. "It's *your* wallet."

"It was in *your* pocket," Don shot back.

"I can't take you two anywhere," Venita said. "Just be glad you got the damn wallet back."

"You know the anxiety I felt this morning thinking I lost my wallet?" Don asked.

"You *did* lose it," Jesse said.

"No, you must have taken it," Don said. "Yeah, you must have taken it when we went to the bar that last time. That's the last time I remember seeing it. Your drunk ass grabbed it off the bar and put it in your pocket."

"And your drunk ass didn't realize you didn't put it back in your pocket," was Jesse's retort.

Then he said, "Listen, you crashed my car, I took your wallet. Both were accidents, so we're even."

"If you call your car being damaged the same as taking and returning his wallet 'even,' then you're still drunk," Venita said.

"Venita, whatever," Jesse said. He pulled out two more Excedrin

Migraines and threw them back. "What did you do last night after hanging with the pole dancer?"

"That's the last time you're going to call my niece that," she said. "She's beautiful and smart. And you'll see for yourself because she's on her way over here. She was at breakfast with her roommate's parents. And her roommate is pregnant. That's just a bad mistake when you're young and doing well in college."

"Well, that's true but it can be overcome," Don said. "Look at Jamayah. Remember her?"

Venita said, "That was the girl who was doing everyone's hair in the Twin Towers. I wondered how she had time to have sex—she had those girls lined up. She was good, too. She did my hair a couple of times."

"If she made your hair look good then she was better than good," Jesse said. "She was *real* good!!!"

"You know what?" Venita said, ignoring Jesse's joke. "She had that baby at the end of her junior year. She delivered in Petersburg, I think, and came back three weeks later and took her final exams. She didn't bring the baby, but she brought pictures.

"She never did come back to school, though. Never got her degree, as far as I know."

"But she did open a hair salon, I heard, that is doing very well," Don said.

"Where did you hear that?" Jesse asked.

"I heard it from her," Don said. "She was at the party last night. You don't remember that? We talked to her right after they played the third or fourth line dance song in a row."

"What's up with that, anyway?" Jesse said. "I vaguely remember us talking to somebody, but I do remember the whole dance floor packed for about thirty minutes as everyone did these 'Electric Slide'-type dances. Who comes up with this stuff? And who has time to learn four different line dances?"

"I can't even believe you," Don said.

"What?" Jesse responded.

"You were out there with Collette learning how to do them last night."

"What? Well," Jesse said, "it's official: I was drunk as hell. I ain't even trying to do that crap. At least not when I'm sober."

"Are you going to drink tonight?" Venita said. "I'm just asking because I'm not letting you all get wasted like that again. You're at homecoming but you don't even remember you're at homecoming."

"Right now," Jesse said, "I don't want to see a beer bottle, much less have a drink. Are you kidding me? I feel like I've been in the spin cycle of a washing machine."

"Venita, you still haven't told us what you did last night," Don said.

"Oh," she started, "well, I had a great time with my niece. Then she went on to the gym to the homecoming concert and some other parties. So she dropped me at the hotel. Charles called me again, sweating me about seeing me because he's traveling today and won't be here. So, he came over Waterside. I met him at Hooters and we talked for a while."

"And?" Don said.

"And that's it," she said. "Look, I know there's a whole lot of sex going on this weekend, most of it by married people who just want to do their thing for the weekend and go back to their lives on Sunday. But I'm not participating in that. Did I want to? Not really. He looked good and we had a good time. But some things from college days need to stay right where they were. And he is one of them."

She looked to the right of Don and could see Diamond approaching. "And here comes my niece. Don't even think about it, either," she said.

Diamond came over with Janea and Teri. They were all attractive with beautiful bodies. And they looked like babies.

"So, you're Diamond?" Jesse asked. "Good to meet you. Your aunt has spoken very highly of you."

"She has? That's my auntie," Diamond said.

"So what's homecoming like for you as a student?" Don asked.

"It's fun because, first of all, no classes on Friday," Diamond said.

"And my parents came to town so I get to eat really good food for two days," Janea said. "The rest of the year, it's not cute. But we're not starving or anything. We have an apartment, so we put together and get groceries and we cook. We even have people over."

"Yeah," Teri added, "but only when we cook something like spaghetti, where there is so much that we can share. We've got to be smart about it."

"Homecoming also is great because we get to see people like you," Janea said, "old people who have been here and come back every year because they have so much pride in the school. I graduate in May, but I know I'm going to be a part of this every year. Look at this. It's amazing."

"Did she say 'old' people?" Jesse asked.

"Yes, she did," Venita said. "Diamond gave me a compliment last night but messed it up by saying I was old. You girls are so young that you don't know. Old does not come for a very long time, and I'm nowhere near it."

"Do you call your parents 'old,' Janea?" Venita wanted to know.

"My parents *are* old—they are both fifty," Janea answered. "They're so old, but both of them are on Facebook. They are so funny. I go to their pages and they post stuff about politics or fundraisers. I'm like, '*boring*.' I tell them it's a social media thing and they tell me they are socializing. But because they are old, they don't get it."

"That's why you think your parents are old? Fifty is not old, young lady," Don said. "Does your father golf? Does your mother dance? If they can still participate in that kind of physical activity, they are not old."

"Do they have all their teeth is what you should ask," Jesse chimed in.

The girls laughed. "You all are funny," Diamond said.

"What entertainment did you all have at the concert last night?" Jesse asked.

"Okay" Diamond said. "If I tell you and you can't name one of the songs of the artists, that means you're old. Okay?"

"Bet," Jesse said.

"Wiz Khalifa," Diamond offered. "You heard of him? Gimme a song by him."

"First of all, that's a stupid name; I'm just saying," Don said. "His real name is probably Albert Jenkins. How you get Wiz Latifa out of that?"

The girls laughed again. "It's not Latifah. It's Khalifa," Janea said. "And his real name is Cameron Jibril Thomaz."

"Yeah," Jesse said, "I know who that bama is. He's from Pennsylvania. They love him up there. He's from Pittsburgh, I think. Lil boney bastard got tattoos all over his body. Look like a wall somebody bombed with graffiti."

"Oh, wow, I'm impressed," Teri said. "But what about a song? If you don't know a song you owe us twenty dollars each."

"Okay, here comes the hustle," Jesse said. "I ain't mad at you. Struggling college students trying to get some money in your pocket. It makes sense. But if I get it right, what do we get?"

"*Jesse*," Venita shrieked.

"They're gonna have to do something—get me a plate of food, wash my car...something."

"Okay, we'll get you a plate of food if you know a Wiz Khalifa song," Teri said.

Don, Venita and Jesse huddled as if they were on the *Family Feud*. The girls found it humorous.

"Okay, we have our final answer," Venita said. "'Black and Yellow.'"

"Oh, my God. Who knew that?" Diamond said.'

"I did because there was some special on him the other night," Jesse said. "His name is Arabic and Khalifa means 'successor' and 'wisdom.' So he shortened 'wisdom' to 'Wiz.'"

"My mouth is open," Diamond said.

"Mine is, too—so go get me a plate so I can close it," Don cracked.

"And bring me a chair," Jesse yelled as they embarked on getting food.

"And don't forget some napkins and something to drink," Venita threw in.

Within minutes, the girls came back with plates of food. While they were gone, the adults decided they were going to give the kids twenty dollars anyway.

"Because you all are cute and seemingly smart and were good sports, we decided to let you have the money anyway," Jesse said. "But don't go around calling young people old anymore. We're not as young as you, but we're not old, either. Not yet."

Diamond and her friends thanked the "old people" with hugs and ran off to the football game.

By the time Don, Venita and Jesse finished tailgating and watching the game, they felt old. "I tell you what, my body doesn't feel right," Jesse said. "My head feels better. I might even be able to drink tonight. But I think I need to get a nap. I might just order room service instead of going out. What do y'all think?"

"You know, I didn't feel that great when I woke up this morning," Venita said. "My mind felt good because I'm here. But I think I had one too many drinks with Charles. That last one took me down. I was asleep so fast last night, it wasn't funny."

"Yeah, because I called you after we hit the wall in Jesse's car, but you didn't answer."

"Didn't even hear it; and I always hear my phone," she said.

"I can have a burger and a nap and I'll be fine," he said. "Let's do that. I want to be fresh for the party. It's the last night. Gotta make it happen."

CHAPTER TWENTY-THREE

IT'S GETTING HOT IN HERE

Jimmy, Carter and Barbara

J immy spent his first several minutes at the Best of Friends party talking to Tony and Erika Sisco, a delightful couple that met in college and were married for twenty-two years. They were with another married couple, Mo Pryor, who attended Norfolk State, and Bonita Pryor, who did not.

Jimmy was amazed at both couples: the Siscos for their longevity; and the Pryors because Mo and Bonita were enjoy homecoming, even though she did not attend NSU.

It made him feel funny about not inviting his wife and the strife it caused. The last two years of their marriage were turbulent. But they steadied things and, save for an occasional insecurity flash by Monica, they enjoyed being together. Despite loving her as he did, at times he wondered about how long they would last because of her insecurities.

When Jimmy encountered Maurice and Eula on Friday, his concerns about having Monica with him were confirmed. Maurice, an NSU alum, seemed miserable, as did his wife, Eula, who was not a Spartan. She felt left out, wanted to do something else and basically wished she were anywhere but there. That's exactly what Jimmy expected from his spouse.

In the end, though, his dominant feeling surprised him: He wished his wife were there to experience homecoming with him—

especially the Best of Friends party, which was a massive coming together of friends that felt like family. Seeing couples having a fun, romantic time made him miss his wife. He would be home the next day, he rationalized, so he was able to put aside that feeling and bask in the spirited feeling of the evening.

People came in looking great and feeling vibrant, as if the toll of all the drinking, sex, flirting, socializing and partying was minimal. Ladies arrived in their best—sexy dresses that turned heads. Men came dapper—suits that displayed a sense of style they did not have in college. It made for a classy, fun event. Most everyone served as paparazzi, with flashes going off every few seconds. Facebook would be overwhelmed with photos posted on alumni pages and countless individual pages.

Jimmy and Carter arrived relatively early, around nine forty-five, so Carter could greet Barbara when she got there with her friend, Donna. Being among the first at the party had its benefits: They could get glimpses of everyone before the place got packed.

"Oh, my goodness," Jimmy said. "That's Shorty Kev. He used to push that weed."

"What's up, boy?" Jimmy said as he and Kevin embraced. "Man, it's been a long time."

Kevin was short with an ever-present smile in the center of a round, over-sized head and the most unlikely demeanor for the campus' biggest drug dealer. He only dealt with weed, though. He did not sell the infamous and debilitating "Lovely," a more potent drug laced with embalming fluid that was popularized in D.C. "You know what?" Kevin said, "I was thinking about you not that long ago. My son goes to Virginia State. You remember what happened when we went up there back in the day?"

Jimmy surely did recall. He was a sophomore when he rode with Kevin to VSU. Kevin was visiting his sister, who was enrolled there, and Jimmy was visiting his girlfriend, Deborah Johnson, who was a freshman. They went up to see the school's football teams play that afternoon and stayed until well after midnight.

But just before it was time to go, Kevin's sister's dorm room got raided by campus police. And with Kevin being a drug dealer, there was marijuana all over the place. Jimmy had walked Deborah to her room and went to another dorm to get Kevin so they could get on the road. As he was walking down the hallway, searching for the room, he witnessed the police go in and Kevin come out in handcuffs.

"That was a crazy night," Jimmy told Kevin. "I'm still amazed they let you go. What did you tell them? I asked you then, but you gave me some bull. You had to negotiate something. They had you dead to rights."

"I didn't tell them anything," he said. "When they got me away from everyone, I said, 'What will it take to make this go away?' One cop was like, 'What you got?' I said, 'I got about six hundred dollars.' I told them I went to Norfolk State and I wouldn't be coming back. Man, they took the money, gave me my product back and said, 'Don't let me catch you on this campus again.' They drove me back to my car. You were standing there looking at me like, 'What the hell just happened?'"

"Wow, all these years I had no idea you bribed those guys," Jimmy said. "But it makes sense. You were only gone about fifteen minutes, maybe thirty minutes. You had the keys to your car. I had no money to bail you out. I was standing there thinking, 'How the hell I'm gonna get back to Norfolk?' Crazy night."

"I'm guessing you got out of that business," Carter said

"Yeah, long time ago," Kevin said. "I run a rec center in Kenilworth in D.C. But it's good to be back here."

Carter got the text from Barbara that she and Donna were coming in. He paid their admission and greeted them at the door. Donna looked happy and pretty, her hair pulled up. Barbara was stunning: a long red dress that fit her curvaceous body like a pair of panty hose. Her cleavage was pronounced, but not so much that it looked like her breasts were going to spill out.

Significantly, she took off her wedding ring. She decided there was no need to not be up-front about her divorce or her love for Carter. He noticed her naked ring finger almost immediately, but did not say anything. He hugged the women and led them through the hotel lobby into the ballroom area.

Barbara broke away for a few minutes to greet some old classmates outside of the ballroom, including Anna Burch, who was from New York but made her home in Norfolk. Anna worked Saturday so she missed the game and the tailgate, important parts of the festivities.

When they finished chatting, Carter led Barbara to a table on the right side of the ballroom. That was another reason Carter had planned to arrive early; he wanted to assure Barbara a seat.

"You've gone from being distant with Barbara to kissing her feet," Jimmy said. "You all right?"

"Yeah, I'm good," Carter said. "I have some heavy stuff I need to share with her and I need to do it before we leave tomorrow."

"Really? About what?" Jimmy asked. "About how you feel about her and her moving to New York? Not trying to be nosey, so don't feel pressured to say."

"Well, that's it in a nutshell," Carter said. "We need to talk about it, *really* talk about it, before she gets there."

"I hear you, man," Jimmy said. "Good luck."

Jimmy sat for a few minutes with Donna, who took a few classes at Norfolk State but graduated from Old Dominion. "So, how's this weekend been for you?" he asked. "You look great, by the way."

"It's been good," she said. "And thank you. I have met a lot of people, a lot of fun people. You Spartans are pretty live. I'm feeling it. How has it been for you? I'm *sure* you've had a good time."

Jimmy smiled. But he detected something in Donna's delivery that he didn't like. "You say that like you think I've been chasing women," he said. "Why do I feel that?"

"Well, I wasn't trying to convey that, but that's what men do, right?" she said. "Especially when they leave their wife at home for the weekend."

"You seem pretty…won't say obsessed, but interested in my wife not being here," Jimmy said. "That's at least the third or fourth time you've alluded that point. Why's that?"

Donna said, "No, I wouldn't say that. I'm just giving you my observations."

"What is it?" Jimmy asked. "You like me?"

He was surprised that he asked her that, but he was not in the mood for innuendo or hints.

"Yes, I do," Donna said. "You asked me and I told you. Now what?"

Jimmy was again surprised. He considered himself a keen judge of people and certainly could tell when a woman was interested in him.

"You sure haven't shown me that you like me," he said. "I'm flattered that you do. Trust me, I am. But…"

"But you're married?" she said. "You're married, but you chose to come here without your wife. You did that for a reason. Weren't you looking for something? Someone?"

"I'm married," Jimmy said. "I didn't come here to find something or someone. I came to see my old classmates, enjoy my time away from home—"

"Blah, blah, blah," Donna said. Jimmy was taken aback. She had been very quiet the whole weekend, observing without commenting on much. Suddenly, she was open and direct.

"Do you like me, have an interest in me?" she said. "Aren't you leaving tomorrow, going back to your wife? Aren't you looking for a highlight of your weekend?"

"I'm going to go get a drink," he said, "because I need one. Not too many times in my life I have needed one. After surviving being attacked by locals early in my Iraq tour, I needed a few drinks. This is the first time since then."

"You thirsty? Or are you hot?" Donna said.

Jimmy didn't answer. He just got up and went to the reception area outside the ballroom. He chatted with NSU national alumni president Butch Graves for a minute before he found Carter coming from the bathroom. "Yo, this is crazy," he said.

"What?" Carter asked.

"Your girl's friend, Donna; she's coming on to me stronger than any woman ever has, well, except for Regina. She basically just asked me to hit it. I can't believe this."

"You can't believe she did or you can't believe you're considering it?" Carter said. "Look, man, I don't care what you do. I don't. In fact, I know you won't hit it. That's who you are. You're one of the few good guys who would turn it down. And that's great. But I do need you to occupy Donna a little bit, dance with her, talk to her. I need to spend some time with Barbara and she's worried about Donna being by herself. You see these guys in here; most of them out here in the lobby talking and laughing instead of in there with tables full of women."

"All right, I got you," Jimmy said. "But I need to get her under control."

After getting a shot of Absolut, Jimmy went back into the ballroom. He did not even sit down. He grabbed Donna's hand

and took her to the dance floor. That gave Carter the space he needed to talk to Barbara.

"Barbara, I really want to share some things with you about you moving to New York," he said. "We can try to find someplace more quiet."

"This is okay," she said. "No one is here right now. We have some privacy."

"Okay," Carter said. "I really want to tell you about Marlena, the woman whose text you read… She's…she's my wife."

The music was loud and Barbara was not sure she heard him correctly. He just couldn't have said what she thought he did. "What?" she asked.

"She's my wife," Carter said.

Barbara heard him clearly that time and her poise and elegance were shattered. She was flustered and confused. "Your wife?" she said. "What the fuck are you talking about, Carter?"

Barbara hardly ever used profanity, but she was incensed. Carter took a deep breath and looked down at his shoes. Then he raised his head and looked into her teary eyes. His heart was pounding and a queasy feeling arrived in his stomach.

"We got married almost three months ago," he said. "We—"

"How in the fuck could you get married and not say anything to me?" she said. "How in the fuck could you call yourself loving me and marry someone else? How in the fuck could you try to condemn me for getting a divorce? What the fuck is wrong with you?"

That was the most he had ever heard Barbara curse in all the years he had known her—combined. He literally was scared because he had no idea where she would go with her anger. There was a drink on the table and he picked it up and moved it far away from Barbara.

"I'm sorry, Barbara. I am," he said. "This was not about love. I, uh, we decided it was the right thing to do considering the circumstances."

"What fucking circumstances?" she yelled.

"She was pregnant," Carter blurted out. "Her period comes like clockwork and when it didn't, she took the test. She's a Seventh Day Adventist and premarital sex is forbidden. Her parents are staunch in their religion. She said she was going to be ridiculed and basically catch so much hell if she was pregnant before marriage."

"And you fell for that shit?" Barbara said. "You are a very smart man. You telling me you fell for the dumbest, lamest trick in the goddamn book?"

"It wasn't a trick," he said. "I know her family. It was real. It would have been messed up for her if they found out she had premarital sex. And I couldn't let her go through that. I was trying to protect her relationship with her family."

Barbara seethed. "Oh, so now you're Mr. Save-a-Ho? You're Mr. Morals? You get married because someone is pregnant? And that's supposed to be something I should believe?"

Carter was in unfamiliar territory. He had never seen Barbara in such a rage. Worse, he did not know how to handle it.

CHAPTER TWENTY-FOUR
COLD TRUTHS

Tranise, Mary and Charlene

T rue to her word, Tranise showed up looking beautiful, sporting a little black dress that plunged in the front, displaying a set of breasts she did not have as a college student, and a chiffon back. She knew Brandon's attention would be hers. But she did not expect to see Kwame there.

"There goes your young suitor," Mary said. "Did you tell him you were going to be here?"

"I must have; I can't remember," she said. "I haven't talked to him since I saw him at the game. We didn't talk about tonight. But it's cool. I'm fine."

"This is a little older crowd, but it's sophisticated," Charlene said. "Maybe we can learn something. Or teach a few things."

"To who?" Mary said. "You on the prowl?"

"It's the last night. Damn right I am," Charlene answered. "Tyrell is a nice backup plan."

"Is Rodney coming?" Tranise said.

"Of course, he is," Mary answered. "After what I gave him last night, how could he not come back for Round Two?"

"I'm scared of you," Charlene said.

"Y'all so freak nasty," Tranise said. "I don't even know if I should be hanging with you hookers."

The ladies laughed as Kwame came over. His youthful energy was apparent. His interest in Tranise was, too.

"So this is our last night together, huh?" he said to her. "I feel kind of sad about that. I'm thinking we should extend the night."

Tranise smiled. She knew what he meant but she wanted him to say it. "Extend the night?' she asked coyly. "What does that mean? Go to breakfast after the party?"

"Actually," Kwame said, "no. I was thinking about my place. It's small. But it's clean and it's cozy."

"Are you open to learning?" Tranise said.

"Teach me everything you know," Kwame eagerly answered.

"Here's your first lesson," Tranise said. "Understand who you are talking to. If you understood me at all, you know I would not go back to your apartment. You would know, in fact, that I could be offended that you asked me that after meeting me yesterday."

Kwame was thrown. He had not been rejected much in his young life—indeed, he had his way with women—and so he did not know how to respond. Tranise was as interested in educating him as she was getting to know him.

"You are a good catch," she told him. "You're smart. You have charisma. You're handsome. You obviously know a good catch when you see one since you are interested in me. Sorry, I couldn't help it. Seriously, though, you have to be able to discern a woman from a 'trick.' A trick would go to your apartment tonight to 'extend the night.' I know you don't think I'm a trick. You probably have used that same approach to others and it worked. But it won't work and shouldn't be used on everyone. You have to be able to discern how you should be with individuals based on that individual. I know I didn't give you any indication that I would go home with you. So…"

Kwame felt awkward. The competitive gene in him wanted him to continue to go for it. Maybe he could turn her. The conscious side of him felt like a little boy in class, admonished by the teacher he admired.

"Thank you for telling me that," he said to Tranise. "I'm sorry. I hope you know I would never try to offend or disrespect you. I don't know. I guess I just wanted a chance to see you in private before you left tomorrow."

He's good, Tranise thought, *especially to be so young*. There was an innocence and genuineness to him. "Let's just have a good time tonight," she said. "I like you. I think you're cool. And I gave you my number, so we can keep in touch."

"I'm good with that, Kwame," he said. "I'm good with that. Let's hug it out."

They embraced and he kissed Tranise on the side of her face. She smiled. "Seems like you're trying to do more than hug, Kwame," Tranise said as she pulled back.

Kwame smiled and pointed to the bar. Tranise nodded her head and they walked together for the first round of drinks for the night. The bartender made them cranberry and Belvederes with a twist of lime. They toasted to "meeting new, wonderful people," Kwame said.

They tapped glasses and took a sip of their drinks. "Good for you?" he asked Tranise. "If it's not, I will send it back and demand that whoever made the inadequate drink be fired."

Tranise laughed and her spirits were lifted. But just as quickly as she smiled, the sight of Felicia on the arm of Brandon gave her a queasy feeling. Kwame noticed.

"What's wrong?" he asked, looking over his shoulder and spotting Brandon and Felicia walking into the ballroom.

"Nothing," she said. "Just saw something that made me sick."

Kwame did not feel good about that. He had been trying to earn Tranise's interest and yet she clearly had something for Brandon. Not minutes after receiving a lesson from Felicia, he delivered one to her.

"Don't take this the wrong way, but I don't understand something," he said. "You obviously have something for this guy. It's obvious. And that's the problem. I have told you and shown you that I really like you. You have been lukewarm with me, but very hot about this guy. That's cool. But he's married. You gave me some good advice a minute ago and I will take heed. I think you ought to take this advice: If you are in the presence of someone who is interested in you, it's pretty rude to constantly show interest in someone else. I tried to ignore it yesterday, two or three times. And now I see that this man's wife is pregnant... And you talk to me about someone being a trick and someone not? Maybe I'm young, but I do know that he is not a good catch.

"Have a good time."

And then he walked away, leaving Tranise standing there, somewhat shocked, definitely embarrassed. He had eloquently put her in her place. And in doing so, her level of respect and interest in Kwame soared.

She walked into the lobby area, looking for him, but found Mary and Charlene. "What's wrong?" Mary said. "Where's Kwame?"

"I'm not sure," she said. "I'm looking for him... How's it going?"

"It's going great," Mary said. "The men look like men. It's sort of a receding hairline convention, but I don't mind that. They are mature and confident. You can tell they have done things in their life by how they walk and talk. And I love just standing here and watching friends see each other for the first time in years. There's something really nice about that. You can see how genuinely happy they are to see each other. I love it."

"I also saw a couple folks whose greeting was not all that enthusiastic," Charlene said. She lowered her voice. "This woman behind me," she said. "She hugged this other woman and when she walked away, she came over here and said to her friend: 'You believe she had the nerve to speak to me? When we were in school, she didn't pay her rent for three months and then just moved out. I got evicted because of her. And she never apologized.' Her friend said, 'What year was that?' The girl said, 'Ah, 1982.'

"So she's been holding that grudge for thirty years. Wow."

Tranise listened, but her head was on a swivel; she wanted to talk to Kwame, to apologize. Instead, Brandon walked up. Charlene and Mary spoke and left.

"You look great, Tranise," he said.

"So do you," she said. "So does your pregnant wife."

Brandon smiled. "Has homecoming been good for you?"

"It's been amazing," she said. "I feel like I will never miss another. I feel more connected to the school. I left and stayed away, but never again. This weekend has been inspiring, in more ways than one."

"Same here," he said. "I am inspired to visit Atlanta."

"Don't you think you should be focused on your wife and your baby that's coming in—what?—two months?" Tranise said. She was angered because Mary and Kwame were right—he was married. That college crush was good for college. The reality of today meant a different set of emotions.

"I can multi-task," he said, and offered his captivating smile.

Another time it was a smile that would have overwhelmed Tranise. This time, it flat-out angered her.

"You know, Brandon, I am glad we got to talk and really meet after all these years," she said. "But you are married. I know your wife. But you seem to think it's okay to flirt with me. You're being very discreet about it, but it's flirting. And that makes me think you don't think highly enough of me. To think I would see you, date you, sleep with you…whatever, is a real slap in my face and I don't appreciate it. I don't get any pleasure out of saying this because at one time in my life—several years ago—I had a serious crush on you. But that was then. You're married, Brandon. You should act like it."

She turned to walk away and Brandon reached out and grabbed her arm. Tranise looked down at his hand on her and he let go. "I'm sorry," he said. "I apologize. That's really all I can say. I'm sorry."

He was really sorry because Felicia arrived at that moment. "I thought you were getting me some water," she said.

"I am. Come on," he said.

"You go ahead," Felicia said, looking at Tranise. "I'm coming."

Brandon walked on and Felicia walked up to Tranise. The number of people milling in the reception area outside the ballroom had increased exponentially, so Felicia remained poised as she spoke.

"What is it about staying away from my husband that you don't understand?" she started. "You hate me? Fine. I hate you, too. But you don't interfere in my marriage. I might be pregnant, but I can and I will bust you upside your head with a bottle. Now you can hate me and look at me crazy like you are right now. But you gonna respect me and my marriage."

Tranise was about to tell her that her husband had come on to her, that she needed to check him and not her. But at that moment, Steve Nottingham emerged with his camera, asking the ladies to pose.

"Don't move; stay right there and smile," he said.

Neither of them wanted to, but they did. He flashed the photo. "Beautiful," he said. "Thanks."

Tranise turned to Felicia to tell her off, but saw only the back of her head. She walked away.

Charlene and Mary came over. "Okay, so what the hell was that all about?" Charlene said.

"Nothing worth talking about," Tranise said. "She hates me and thinks I'm trying to get with Brandon."

"Well, aren't you?" Mary said.

"At first, it was very, very flattering that I even met him and he was talking to me," she answered. "But you were right about what him flirting with me meant. And Kwame was, too."

"Kwame said something about it?" Mary asked.

"He did," Tranise said. "I've got to talk to him."

She scanned the reception area and then went out into the hotel lobby seeking Kwame. She caught the attention of Greg "Night Hawk" Cook, Val Guilford, Curtis West, Jon Aponte and Mark Conrad—friends from their Norfolk State days in the early 1980s.

"Excuse me," Curtis said politely as she walked by.

Tranise was pleasant by nature, but she was rattled by the events of the night and came off rather snobbish with her response: "I'm really not interested in talking right now," she said.

"That's fine," Curtis responded. "I just wanted to tell you that you have toilet tissue stuck on your shoe."

She looked down and was embarrassed about what she saw—and how she responded to him. "Thank you," she said. "I'm really sorry. I'm really a nice person. I just have something on my mind."

"We understand," Val said. "Just don't let it happen again."

They all laughed and Tranise was on her way.

CHAPTER TWENTY-FIVE
CHIT CHATS

Jesse, Don and Venita

Don and Jesse entered the party feeling better than most—they had smoked two joints before leaving the room and had two beers en route to the party in Jesse's scraped-up BMW. Venita got high, too, but she stayed behind to connect with her cousin, Diamond, and her pregnant roommate, Janea.

"I need to have a buzz," Venita said. "I'm about to advise this child and I'm not sure what my advice should be."

"Just tell her what makes sense to you," Jesse said. "In the end, she's going to do what she wants to do. That's how people are. You can only give her something to consider."

Don actually considered bypassing the party and staying at the hotel. But the call from his accountant came and it was encouraging: Don's finances were not as bad as originally thought and he had a commitment from an investor, a builder in Richmond who had notions of supporting small black businesses.

"This guy will put you on another plateau," Don's accountant said. "We have to work out the terms. But we have an agreement in principle. He will be a silent partner and you will go on functioning as you have. Without bogging you down with the details right now, you will be in a position not only to succeed, but to expand."

That half of his life saved, Don was pumped about hanging out with his old friends at the party. He, in fact, became the most jovial person.

"You sure have a burst of energy," Jesse said.

"Well, that's what happens when your life gets saved," Don said. "You feel like you have a new reason to live, like you have a second chance. I was suffocating. You know, if a man can't earn a living, he can't do much anything else without feeling some kind of way about himself. My accountant identified a potential investor and dude is committed to putting a half-million dollars into my business. It's an investment for him and I'm told he will get special tax benefits because I'm a small, minority-owned business. I don't care what the benefits are for him. For me, it moves me to another level and frees me up to do the strategic marketing I need to do to help the business to thrive, not just survive."

"Man, I'm happy for you," Jesse said. They were standing outside the ballroom, sipping cognac and watching women. "I know that's got to be a relief. And not that we *really* need a reason—as last night showed—but we should drink to that."

"A can't even believe you have the slightest interest in drinking after all you had last night," Don said. "You have some crazy tolerance or something. The last time I was as drunk as you were, throwing up and shit, I didn't drink for two weeks."

"I don't know what it is, but after the game, I started to feel better, like myself," Jesse said. "At first my head was pounding and I felt sluggish. That nap really helped. Now I feel almost like new. Not quite one hundred percent, but much better. Good enough to party tonight."

Rochelle, the woman Jesse hardly recalled meeting on Friday night, came over. She was drop-dead, wearing a metallic dress that fit the contours of her body, drop earrings with rhinestones and metallic heels that accentuated her shapely legs.

Jesse's bald head was shining and his thick eye brows and mustache caught Rochelle's attention. "You look good," they said in unison.

He called her after the game as she requested and they talked law and life and laughed and created an interest in each other. They found a table in the ballroom and sat close together.

"So why would you be talking to me after you saw the condition I was in last night?" Jesse asked. "I'm glad you're here; don't get me wrong. But I know I was out of it. Wasn't being that drunk a turnoff?"

"Well, it wasn't a turn-*on*," she said. "But there was something you said—and you obviously don't remember—when we talked last night that stuck with me, made me think that you were interesting enough to get to know."

"Oh, Lord," Jesse said. "What did I say?"

"I asked you why you came back to homecoming," she began, "and you gave an answer I never heard before. You said: 'Because I like to be around courage.' I found that so interesting. I asked you what that meant and do you remember your answer?"

Jesse remembered. "I said, 'It is not easy, in the face of drugs and crime and economic struggle and peer pressure and family dynamics to push on, to strive for a higher education. That's what I see when I see young students. I don't see the sagging pants—well, I do see them and it bothers me, but I can see beyond that. I see that they want something better for themselves. It takes courage to ignore the trappings—and there are more trappings for them than there were for us—and press on. So I like to be around courage in a place where I was lifted up to become a good citizen, to become a lawyer."

"That's a great closing argument," Rochelle said. "And that's why I'm here with you now—because I like to be around a man who has more than surface thoughts."

"Who knew?" Jesse said. "Sometimes you get drunk and you're a babbling idiot. And sometimes, the truth comes out coherently. Anyway, I appreciate you being here and what you said."

Rochelle also liked that she and Jesse had similar tracks out of NSU. Jesse went to law school at New York University after graduation and Rochelle, three years later, enrolled in law school at Columbia University to become a corporate lawyer.

"So, I'm sure you hear this a lot, but what is it like to be a defense attorney?" she asked. "Do you feel like you're getting guilty people off?"

"I feel like I'm doing my job," he said. "That's how I keep my sanity and commitment to it. My client is not guilty. Period. I have to think of it that way. If I don't, well, as a human, it would be hard for me to do my job effectively. I have had cases—murder cases—where our client was not the most upstanding citizen. But before accepting the case, we had the firm's private detective to snoop around and we went in believing he did not kill his wife. I was lead on one particular case—and he was found not guilty. I was happy with the jury's verdict. But I felt better two days later when the real murderer was found—a co-worker she had an affair with. I didn't think he was guilty but I under-stood why he was arrested, so I had some inkling that he might have done it. Finding out he didn't do it meant a lot to me."

"Well, corporate law is not as exciting, which is fine for me," she said. "The emotion of both sides of the family in a murder case would be a lot for me to stomach. So I do my boring job, which I actually like, and go home and not have images about broken families because of a heinous crime."

Jesse studied her. "You know, north Jersey where you live is not that far from Philly," he said. "I've got this big event coming up two weeks from today. I need a date. It's the 100 Black Men of Philadelphia. I'd like you to come with me."

"I'm assuming then that you do not have a wife, mistress, girlfriend or stalker," she said, smiling.

"No to all that," he said.

"Well, have your people contact my people and we'll see what we can do," she said.

"I'm going to take that as a yes," he said.

"As you know, counselor, I reserve the right to change my mind," Rochelle said.

"Under what statute?" Jesse said.

"U.S. Code I'm-a-woman-and-I-can-change-my-mind-if-I-want-to," she cracked.

Jesse smiled and nodded his head slowly. He was feeling her wit and charm. "I like you," he said. "And I'm going to enjoy getting to know you."

Across the ballroom, Don found old college friend Renee. They'd had a serious attraction to each other but somehow never crossed that line. He respected her so much that he actually was afraid to broach romance with her. It was truly a case of not wanting to ruin a friendship that was pure and real.

She got married years before Don, and he made sure he was at the wedding to support his friend. A part of him, though, wished he were standing across from her when the vows were read. He got over that feeling and eventually married Nona, a registered nurse with a love of sports and cigars. He called her "a man's dream."

"So, Don, you've been having fun this weekend?" Renee asked.

"I have," he said. "And I needed it. I needed to come back to the campus, see my old friends, like you, and just get away from it all. I was telling Jesse, I don't know anywhere else other than homecoming I could go and feel the love I feel this weekend— not all directly aimed toward me, but the love of everyone around me for their old classmates and our school. There's an unbelievable spirit, a spirit of family and community."

"I know," Renee said. "I teach at Norfolk State, so I'm over there every day. And it feels like a college. But when homecoming comes around, it transforms itself. It becomes a big home and all the family comes back to visit. Like any family, some of them you'd rather not see. You know what I'm saying? But you deal with them."

"Who don't you want to see, Renee?"

"Well, let's start with that Henry Molden," she said. "Did you see him at the game? This man, who never said two words to me in college, comes approaching me all friendly about joining some multilevel marketing scheme."

"What?" Don said. "Selling what?"

"I don't know; you think I was listening to him?" she said. "I was just waiting for him to take a small pause from talking so I could excuse myself. I wasn't going to be totally rude, but don't come to me with that mess any time, but especially at homecoming. I'm trying to enjoy the band and he's talking about selling whatever."

Don laughed a good laugh. "He's here; I saw him from a distance," he said. "I'll be sure to *keep* him at a distance."

"And the other person I don't want to see is that damn Jessica Dennis," Renee said.

"What did Jessica do to you? She's sweet," Don said.

"She *is* sweet," Renee said. "But you know what else she is? A pain in the ass. She will talk about herself and her children all night if you let her. And I'm talking about the most minute, inane, silliest detail about something they said or did. I've met her kids; they ain't that spectacular. But if you let her tell it, one is about to be an astronaut and the other one built the spaceship."

"Girl, you are a trip," he said. "I'm glad I'm on your good side."

Renee joked: "I'm just saying. What do the little kids say? 'I'm keeping it one hundred.'"

As funny and brash as she could be, Renee also was smart and sensitive. She expressed joy when he told her of his new business prospects. And she could see in Don's expression when she asked about his wife that he was hurting.

"Well, Don, can your marriage be saved?" she asked.

"Here's the amazing thing about getting your life saved— you're able to look at things clearer," Don said. "With all that shit swirling around me, everything was blurry. Now I can see that the problem wasn't my wife. It was me. I was borderline depressed. The last few months have been so stressful, trying to make the business go, not knowing if I would have to close my business, hoping and praying I wouldn't have to go back to a nine-to-five.

"I wasn't a good husband. I was moody and petty and hard to be around. But you know what I really was? I was scared."

"Of failing?" she asked.

"Of not being able to provide for my family," he said. "For a man, that's it: being able to take care of your family. I'm blessed that I have been able to do that all these years. But when it looked bad, when it looked like it was over, I was lost. I felt my manhood slipping away. It was hanging on by a string when I got here. I got stronger the longer I was here. Now, I'm ready to get home and explain to my wife why I have been so crazy lately."

"That sounds like a good idea," Renee said. "And don't forget to apologize while you're at it."

Don smiled. Then he felt a vibration in his suit jacket. It was a text message from Venita. *I'm on my way. How is it?*

He leaned over and hugged Renee. "This is my girl Venita. I've got to give her a call."

Don excused himself and stepped into the reception area outside the ballroom. He dialed Venita's number. She did not answer. She was preparing to speak to Janea, even though she was unsure of what to say. Diamond and Janea came over to her hotel around nine-thirty, smiling and laughing. But Venita was serious. So she got to it right away.

"I'm glad you came to talk to me," she said. "I understand how you can be wary of talking to your parents. But the first thing I will suggest you do is to talk to them. They love you more than anyone. And they might not be happy at first. They might be mad. But that won't last. And it's the right thing to do.

"But let me ask you: Where are you right now in your thought process?"

"Well, everything is scary, really," Janea said. "I'm scared to have a baby and I'm scared to have an abortion."

"And you should be," Venita said. "It's a serious thing—both options. I'm going to tell you a story. Only three people know this story—a man named Gary and my friends you met today, Don and Jesse. But I'm going to tell you in the hope that it helps you. You have to decide what to do. I can't do that for you, Diamond can't, your parents can't and the young man who got you pregnant cannot.

"Anyway, there was this young lady about twelve, thirteen years ago who was in college like you, who had dreams of becoming a human resources manager and consultant. She identified her career early and did the things necessary to make her dreams a reality. She had a 3.8 GPA and had done internships between her sophomore and junior, and junior and senior years. She had done all she could to put herself in prime position. Bank of America called and offered her a job after graduation.

"She knew better, but she began to have sex with her boyfriend without a condom or any protection. You—Janea *and* Diamond— have to be adamant about safe sex. Please... So, it's two weeks before finals and a month before graduation and her cycle does not come. She's pregnant. She's scared. Her whole life is out there waiting for her and now there's this very real situation."

The sadness on Venita's face scared Diamond.

"She does not talk to her parents, does not talk to the boyfriend. She tells her two best friends—two men—and they try to get her to listen to reason and to talk to her parents. Well, she didn't. She had her two friends go with her and she had an abortion. It was the saddest day of her life.

"She went on to achieve what she wanted, but she has been unfulfilled all her life."

With tears streaming down her face, Venita looked at her niece. "To this day, every day, I wish I had made a different decision."

Diamond came from the other side of the bed and hugged her aunt, and they cried together.

CHAPTER TWENTY-SIX

INTRODUCING...

Earl and Catherine

C atherine, Starr and Earl arrived at the Best of Friends party at the height of the night. There was congestion at the table, people pulling out money to pay their admission and others displaying tickets. They continued walking into the party.

Earl had carte blanche. He was among a group of guys who founded the Norfolk State Best of Friends group, along with Kent, Kevin and Hank Davis, David A. Brown, Kevin Jones, Kerry Muldrow, Keith "Blind" Gibson, Sam Henry, Troy Lemon, Kris Charity, Ron Payne, Joe Cosby and Gerald Berry. Most of them lived in the River Oaks apartment complex down Princess Anne Road, near Military Highway.

For twenty-five years they put together an upscale event that grew into the must-attend occasion of homecoming. On this night, it was rocked by the appearance of Earl and Catherine together, hand-in-hand.

By the time they settled into a table on the left side of the ballroom, Earl's frat brother Myron had been approached by a half-dozen women asking about Earl and Catherine. It was a couple that made sense, really: two good people deserved to be together. But it still was shocking to see because hardly anyone was clued in that they were so close, much less in love.

Catherine could not sense the interest in their arriving together. Earl could. Even his friends who knew but had not seen them together stared. Catherine looked as beautiful as advertised, and she and Earl, who wore a chocolate brown suit, looked ideal together.

When he went to the bar to get drinks, he was virtually attacked by friends who wanted to know the deal.

"You're with Catherine?" "How did this happen?" "When did this happen?"

Earl smiled and carried on without saying a word.

"Boy, you and Catherine have this place buzzing," Myron said. "Honeys are tripping me out. I'm telling them, 'It's obvious they're together. Why you asking me?' Listen, forget that. I know her from school but I want a formal introduction."

"All right," he said. "We have a table in the back left. Just come on back there."

When he got back to the table, Catherine introduced him to some of her friends he did not know and some he did. "Earl and I are together," he heard her say to some old friends Mike and Brigitte Booker-Rogers, who also knew each other in college and reconnected many years later.

"You threw me off when you asked me if I was going to ride with you to the party," Earl told Catherine at the table. "It made me think you didn't want me to."

"Oh, I'm sorry," she said. "I wasn't sure how you wanted us to be seen to our classmates. So, that's why I asked."

Earl said: "Well, I finally said, 'If she doesn't want me to go with her, she's just going to have to tell me."

"Well, I'm glad you did, baby," Catherine said, holding his hand. "That's what I wanted. I want the whole world to know that we're together and that I love you."

Then she leaned in and they kissed, and it seemed the entire ballroom was looking. They posed for photos and danced and enjoyed each other as they always had. They were having their own little private party within the party.

One by one, their friends made it over to their table, interested in saying hello and confirming with their own eyes that they were together. Earl was reserved and subdued in how he dealt with their friends. Catherine was direct: "This is my man, Earl," was how she introduced him.

Their relationship was hardly a secret, but not many people knew. This was their coming-out party, and they did it with a bang.

"We've got to talk," Leslie, Earl's friend, said when they connected for a moment. She and Earl kept in touch, but had not spoken in several months, so she was surprised to see him with Catherine.

Earl went outside the ballroom and admired what he saw: Alphas and Ques and Kappas convening, as one; Deltas and AKAs posing for photos; women complimenting each other on how they looked; brothers laughing and joking; old cliques still together, twenty-five years later; cameras flashing all over the place.

"Eddie," Earl called out and Eddie Keith turned around.

"Oh, shit," he said loudly when he saw Earl. They had not seen each other since 1981. They hugged and laughed and recalled going to the closed-circuit viewing of the Sugar Ray Leonard-Tommy Hearns welterweight championship fight at the Scope.

"It was September 16, 1981, to be precise," Earl recalled. "I had thirty dollars to my name. That's it. It cost twenty-five dollars to go see the fight. It was a Wednesday night. I left myself with five dollars. I wasn't going to miss that fight."

"That's a hell of a college memory," Eddie said. "Sugar Ray won in an epic fight. Great night."

Catherine had not been to homecoming since her divorce, although she lived in the area. Many of her old classmates had not seen her over that time, so it was especially nice for her to see familiar faces, especially so many of her sorority sisters.

But as nice as that was, it was all about Earl for her. And it was all about Catherine for him.

Earl's friends joked with him about all the attention he gave Catherine. And he didn't care.

IT'S GOING DOWN

The Whole Damn Gang

"I'm glad to hear that," Jimmy said to Maurice, who brought his wife to homecoming. Their issues of Friday were resolved and Maurice and Eula were having a great experience. "It makes me feel like maybe I can bring my wife next year... Maybe."

They sat at a table sipping Cosmos when Maurice excused himself, leaving Jimmy with Eula. "I'm glad it got better for you; you didn't look happy yesterday," he said.

"Now that I'm here, I see why he would want to come alone," Eula admitted. "It's not really *for* me since I don't know anyone and didn't go here, but I'm glad I came. I like seeing him so happy with his friends."

They chatted for a few more minutes before Jimmy felt the presence of someone standing over him. He turned around and looked up to see Donna. He had ditched her when she went to the bathroom. It was his protective mechanism.

"I thought you were going to wait for me," she said.

"Donna, this is Eula, my friend Maurice's wife," he said. Identifying Eula took the edge off of Donna.

"You want to dance?" Donna asked Jimmy.

"Actually, sit down," he said. "Let's talk."

They sat on the other side of the round table, away from Eula. "Look, I don't want to sound presumptuous, but it seems like you are interested in me," he said. "And that's flattering. But I'm married. That means something to me."

"What does it mean?" she said.

"It means I'm going to say bye to you right now," he said. "It was nice meeting you."

"Wait," Donna pleaded. "I have to tell you something…met you before yesterday."

"What? When?" Jimmy said.

"At Monica's family reunion two years ago," she said. "Monica is my cousin."

Jimmy looked at Donna hard. "Family reunion? In Houston?" he said.

"Yes."

"There were so many people there. I don't remember you," he said. "So what was all this about? You trying to come on to your cousin's husband?"

"No, I would never do that," she said. "I was…was…"

"You were testing me?" he said.

She nodded her head, somewhat embarrassed.

He looked at her. Finally, she said, "When I saw you on Friday at The Mansion, I immediately thought I knew you, but I couldn't place where. Then I heard your name and it hit me right away. I was waiting for you to say something, but you never did. I hadn't talked to Monica in about a month. Last time I talked to her you all were hanging out at 14th and U Streets. You remember that night?"

"Damn. I do," Jimmy said. "I remember her even asking me to remind her to call her cousin in Virginia when we left. But why didn't you say something to me yesterday?"

"I don't know," she answered. "I was, and then I thought I would just see what happened."

"You mean spy on me?" Jimmy said. "Worse than that, tonight you get all aggressive to test me? I knew it was strange you came on so strongly all of a sudden. I have one question."

"No, Monica did not ask me to spy on you," she answered. "I'm surprised she didn't call me to tell me you were going to be in town. She still hasn't called me back from my last call to her."

Jimmy was a little angry and a lot relieved. He was angry that Donna had taken it upon herself to test his commitment to his wife. And he was relieved on two fronts: he resisted the advances of Donna; and Monica was not behind Donna's actions. That would have sent him into an emotional, angry tailspin.

"Donna, I will get over your little shenanigans at some point," he told her. "But not right now."

He got up and left her sitting there.

He wanted to check on Carter, but Carter was outside the hotel, pleading with Barbara to let him explain why he was married. "Please let's go to the car just for a minute and talk in private," he said.

She didn't answer, but she walked with him. He opened the door for her and she got in. Carter rushed to the other side and began his spiel.

"I'm sorry this is coming out like this, Barbara," he said. "You knew I dated and I had been dating her for about a year. What I was trying to say is that she is a Seventh-day Adventist, and they are forbidden by the religion to have premarital sex. Well, not everyone abides by it, but when you don't, you'd better make sure no one knows.

"Her brother and sister both had children before they were married, and it was ugly. She told me the story of her brother writing their father a letter to tell him his girlfriend was pregnant. She intercepted it and gave it to her mother, who read it and then told her father. But this was after the baby was already born.

That's how nervous her brother was about telling his parents. It was a really big thing. They love the child, of course, but it took them a long time to get over him not being as devout as he was supposed to.

"And her sister had the same situation: pregnant but petrified to tell her parents. I'm telling you all this to give you some background and some idea about how devout this family is about its religion. So, my, uh…"

"Go ahead and say it, your *wife*," Barbara said angrily.

"Marlena, that's her name," Carter said. "Marlena is the baby of the family, the jewel, the innocent one. In your family, you told me your sister was the one everyone expected to be perfect, to be so wonderful. Well, that's Marlena to her family. That reputation means everything to her. I have been around long enough to see how they cherish her.

"I couldn't refuse her when she asked me. In fact, to be honest, she didn't ask me. I asked her. I asked her because I care about her and I didn't want her to crush her parents. She found out she was pregnant really quickly. She was only a few weeks. So we hatched a plan to get married within the month and so when the baby came, it would look like she got pregnant as soon as we got married.

"You can call me a fool or whatever you want. But it really was about helping preserve the reputation of someone I care about a lot. It meant a lot to her and so I did it."

Barbara did not say a word. She stared straight ahead. So, Carter went on.

"The other reason I did it is because you told me more than once that we didn't have a future," he said. "You told me you were not leaving your husband. And you actually told me, now that I think about it, that you would be friends with me if I ever got married. You told me that last year, here at homecoming."

"And you think I meant that?" she said.

"Yes, I did, because you are married—or, were married. So why would you care?" he countered. "Anyway, if you had given me any indication that we had a chance to be together one day, I would not have married Marlena. I'm not blaming you for this. It was my choice. But part of my decision was based on what you told me."

Barbara, as angry and hurt as she was, had no retort. She had been adamant with Carter about not expecting anything more than their once-a-year-homecoming rendezvous. He even talked about them meeting somewhere for a weekend in the summer, but she declined. When she played back those scenarios, she softened.

"So, damn, Carter—I'm single and now you're married?" she said. "This is crazy."

"I know," he said. "I know."

"What are we going to do?" she asked. "And don't say meet at homecoming once a year."

"Oh, that was good when you were married, but not when I'm married?" Carter said. He did not disagree with what she said, but he attacked it on principle.

"Carter, what are we going to do?" she repeated.

"I don't know," he said. "When you told me you were divorced, my mind got jumbled immediately. I didn't know how to respond. But I was going to tell you this weekend about Marlena. I tried to figure out how and when, but just couldn't. When I got to the party, I realized I couldn't hold it in any longer... I'm sorry."

"Maybe when your child gets old enough, my kids can babysit them," Barbara joked. She laughed, easing the tension in the car, which had gotten stuffy.

"All I know is, I love you," he said. "I love my...wife, but it is different. You are the love of my life. You are. And to not have you like I want you hurts. Above all, it speaks to the power of communication."

"If I had told you what I was doing, maybe you wouldn't have gotten married," Barbara said.

He hugged her and wiped the tear that ran down her face. "What we have on our side is love," Carter whispered into her ear. "Love never loses."

"We will see," Barbara said.

They stayed in the car another half hour, hugging and comforting each other.

Inside the party, Tranise located Kwame and apologized. He readily accepted. "You're a good guy and I want to get to know you," she said.

Kwame looked distressed, but not at what Tranise had said. Venita arrived at the party with her niece Diamond and Diamond's pregnant roommate, Janea. They were dropping off Venita, but decided to at least come into the lobby. Almost immediately, Kwame's and Janea eyes met.

"Excuse me a minute," he said to Tranise. He was trying to separate himself from her before Janea got to them.

"What's wrong? Tranise said.

"Hold on," Kwame said. He walked a few feet away from her to greet Janea. They hugged. "I didn't know you were going to be here," Janea said.

"I didn't know you were, either," he said. "I went to the concert first and then came here."

"Miss Venita, this is my boyfriend, Kwame," Janea said.

Venita could see something was amiss by the expression on Tranise's face. "How are you?" Venita said. "Nice to meet you. Handsome young man."

"Thank you," Kwame said. The cool he possessed all weekend was gone. He was obviously uneasy.

"Tranise, this is…Janea," he said, "and Diamond and…I'm sorry; did she say Venita?"

Tranise shook everyone's hand. But there were a few awkward moments of silence. Janea wondered who Tranise was; Tranise wondered who Janea was to Kwame. Venita picked up on it and broke the silence.

"Tranise, you're a Spartan?" she asked. As Tranise answered, Venita walked over to the other side of Tranise so she would have to turn her back to Kwame and the girls to respond. And as soon as she started talking, Kwame tapped her on the shoulder. "I'll be right back," he said, and he and Janea and Diamond walked off.

Tranise could only nod her head. "If I'm wrong, I apologize," Venita said. "But it looked like you are with Kwame. Is that right?"

"I'm not *with* him," she said. "We met yesterday and have been getting to know each other. Why?"

"Oh, well, I'm certainly not trying to get into anyone's business," Venita said. "I just want to say this: that young man's girlfriend is Janea. I don't know if he told you he had a girlfriend or not. But they are in a delicate situation and he might not be coming back here after they talk."

"His girlfriend? She looks like a college student," Tranise said.

"She is," Venita said, "a senior."

"Interesting night for me," Tranise said.

"Tell me about it," Venita said. "You want a drink. Or, if you indulge, I have a joint."

"Shit, how about both?" Tranise said, and they laughed and headed to the bar.

They became fast friends, laughing and joking about the weekend and their college days. Tranise told Venita she needed to go to the bathroom before they went outside to smoke the weed.

She stood in the mirror applying lip gloss when a stall door opened behind her. It was Felicia.

Tranise looked at her through the mirror. Felicia saw her and frowned. She made her way to a sink next to Tranise, who was preparing to let her know all about how her husband, Brandon, had come on to her.

"Why do you hate me?" Felicia said.

It was a fair question, an honest question. Tranise was stumped.

"Well, I remember all the things you did to me in college," she finally said. "And you slept with my boyfriend, Michael Jennings."

"Tranise, I didn't do anything to you in college," she said. "Your friends told my friends that you said I thought I was cute and that I was snobby. My response to them was: 'I am cute. But if she said it, she's wrong about being snobby.' That's all I ever said."

Tranise said: "My friends said you said, 'Damn right I'm cute and cuter than her. And I have a right to be snobby to her. And she's not AKA material.' "

"I did not say that," she said. "Why would I? I didn't even know you."

"Well, what about the attitude?" Tranise said.

"I had the attitude because you had an attitude," Felicia said.

They smiled about how silly it all sounded. "But what about Michael, Felicia? You didn't have to go there," Tranise said.

"No offense, but Michael was not my type," she said. "I never slept with him. In fact, I knew him, but that was the extent of it. He never even came on to me."

"I asked him about you and he said, 'I'm sorry. You don't want me to say it, do you?' He led me to believe you all had something going on," Tranise said.

"No, girl," Felicia said. "No."

They both felt even more silly. Two of the most dynamic women on campus were arch-enemies for...nothing.

Telling Felicia about Brandon's advances became something

she just could not and would not do. She was about to apologize when she noticed Felicia again frowning, but this time from pain. She held her stomach.

"Oh, my God," she said. "Oh, my God."

Tranise rushed to her side, holding her up.

"What is it?" she pleaded.

"Sharp pain in my stomach," she said.

"It's okay, I got you, girl," Tranise said. "Just breathe. But don't have that baby right now. I ain't ready for that."

Even in her pain, Felicia looked into the mirror, where their eyes met and they shared a brief laugh. "Me, either," Felicia said.

Holding her up, Tranise kicked open the stall behind her and slowly eased Felicia into it and sat her down on the toilet. "You've got to sit down. I'm calling 9-1-1," she said. "And what's Brandon's number?"

She poured out the contents of her black clutch on the counter and retrieved her phone. Between grunts, Felicia got out his number. Tranise reached someone at emergency.

"Listen, we're in the woman's bathroom by the ballroom at the Holiday Inn off Newtown Road," she said. "My pregnant friend is having pain and I see some spotting. You've got to get an ambulance here right away... What? She's seven months' pregnant, so it's not time yet. How long before they get here?"

Holding her stomach and holding onto the stall's wall, Felicia looked up at Tranise. "Your 'friend'?" she said.

Tranise froze. "Yes, my friend, as of two minutes ago," she said. She then grabbed a paper towel, wet it and dabbed Felicia's face.

"Shit," Tranise said. "Brandon's not answering. He probably can't hear it. How you feeling?"

"Like there's pressure on my stomach," she said. "What's going on? I've never felt this before."

She held her hand with both hers. "It's going to be okay. They'll be here any moment. I'm not going to leave you."

"Our friends would die if they saw this picture: you in a stall on a toilet and me holding your hand," Tranise said, and they shared another laugh.

"Let's meet them at the front," Felicia said. "I can walk. I don't want them busting through the party, making a scene coming all through the lobby. That's not a good look for me to be wheeled out of here on a stretcher."

"How vain is that?" Tranise said. "And I *totally* understand, girl."

They laughed once more. She helped Felicia to her feet. She teased her hair to get it back in place. Felicia held her arm as they gingerly exited the bathroom. But they stopped at the last of a series of mirrors and fixed themselves up even more.

"I get the feeling, ironically enough, that we're a lot alike," Felicia said.

"Me, too," Tranise said.

They made it to the reception area outside the ballroom and moved slowly through the crowd. "Don't make eye contact with anyone; they'll want to stop and start talking," Tranise said.

When they made it to the lobby, Tranise saw Charlene, who could not believe Tranise and Felicia were arm-in-arm. "Charlene, don't say anything. Just go get Brandon and tell him to come to the front of the hotel now," Tranise said.

Off Charlene went. When the automatic doors to the front of the hotel opened, the ambulance pulled up. They got Felicia on a gurney, put an oxygen mask on her and lifted her onto the vehicle.

The paramedics were ready to get her to Sentara Leigh Hospital, but Brandon was not there. "Well, I'm going," Tranise said, and she hopped in the back. "I'll call him again." They shut the doors and took off.

As the medics asked Felicia a series of questions, Tranise called Charlene. "I didn't see him until just now," she said. "Wait, he's here."

"Tranise, what happened?" he said into the phone.

"I don't know. I'm in the ambulance with her now. We're going to Sentara Leigh. In the bathroom she started feeling pain and bleeding a little. Brandon, you just need to get to the hospital."

"What's going on?" Tranise said to the paramedic.

"I can't tell right now," she said. "But the baby's heartbeat is good. We'll be at the hospital in a minute."

"Thank God," Tranise said.

Tears flowed under Felicia's mask. There were tears of fear. Tranise reached over and grabbed her hand. "Hey, girlfriend, I'm here," she said. She was smiling. "It's going to be all right. Probably something minor. Your baby probably was upset that we were acting like fools to each other for no good reason."

Tranise could see a smile on Felicia's face through the mask. Tears started to flow down Tranise's face.

When they pulled up to the hospital, Tranise ripped off her pumps and jumped out of the ambulance first. The workers swiftly got Felicia off and hurried her into the hospital, Tranise running behind them with her shoes and purse in her hands.

Several minutes later, Brandon arrived to the waiting area, looking totally disoriented. "What's going on?" he said.

"I don't know," Tranise said. "We just have to wait."

Brandon did not say much. He shook his head. Tranise left him and went outside to make some phone calls.

"Thank you, Tranise," Brandon said before she walked away.

BRINGING IT HOME

The Whole Damn Gang, Part II

J immy pushed aside his discontent with Donna long enough to let her apologize. "I'm really sorry," she said. "It was a stupid thing to do. But I am glad to know my cuz has a real man as her husband. I wish I were so lucky."

"I appreciate that," he said. "Other than being crazy, you seem like a together sister."

She laughed and extended her hand. "Forgive me?" she asked.

He looked at her hand and then clutched it. "Okay, cousin," he said. "Forgiven."

On the other side of the ballroom, Carter pleaded with the DJ to play a slow song—"What's that about? Used to be there were slow songs throughout the night. Damn." The DJ obliged him and the dance floor was packed.

He and Barbara shared a slow dance. She buried her face in his chest and wept. He held her firmly and rubbed her back. Their lives were in flux. He loved her but was married to Marlena. She had gotten a divorce with the expectation of having him, but had no one.

When Janea decided she was going to have the baby, Kwame soon after learned he was going to be a father. He was floored and no longer in a partying mood. She was floored, too, with the finality of the decision. "You'd better not even think about abandoning your dreams," Venita had told her. "A baby should enhance your life, not stunt your growth. At times it won't be easy. But you have family and a great friend in Diamond and a new 'auntie' in me for support."

Janea hugged Venita. "You okay?" she said to Kwame.

"No," he said. He looked at Janea. "But I will be."

"I won't be all right until I tell my parents," Janea said.

"I'll be there with you," Kwame said.

Mary and Rodney made a pact: They would not have sex again until she ended her relationship back home. It was a tough decision for her; she craved his touch and passion. But she was shrouded in guilt for having spent Friday night with him knowing she had Clint at home.

It would be a difficult conversation. She knew Clint loved her. Breaking his heart was something she never anticipated or wanted to do. Further, her family and friends saw them as an ideal couple. She loved some things about Clint, but she was not in love with him. And she wanted true love in her life—needed it—and believed she could have it with Rodney. At minimum, she was willing to seek it with him on the *promise* of true love.

Charlene was looking for love, too, but mostly a love of self. She used jokes to suppress her displeasure with her body. And Tyrell picked up on it. "You talk about your weight a lot," he said as they left the party. "That tells me it bothers you. And that's okay, if you are willing to do something about it. If not, then you should stop talking about it."

For a moment, Charlene was upset. But the truth is strong. She told Tyrell of her plan to make a lifestyle change. "Well, if you are okay with it, I will adopt the same plan," he said. "We can do it together. I could stand to lose some pounds myself."

And so, they vowed to become each other's inspiration in their lifestyle adjustment. That commitment took their homecoming reconnection to another level. "You know," Tyrell said, "sex is great exercise."

Said Charlene: "Well, I guess we know where to start then."

Don took Renee's advice and called his wife right there, from the party. "Baby, I have a lot of making up to do, and I'm willing to do it," he said. "Something happened to me down here at homecoming. I found myself—and I want us to rediscover each other."

His wife was shocked—and happy. "I thought I had lost you, baby," she said. "Don't you know, no matter what, I'm your wife. Our love is stronger than any business or any situation. You're my man. And I'm your woman."

Don, the man who deemed crying as weak, was moved to tears. He wiped them quickly, before anyone saw, especially Jesse or Venita.

But Jesse's focus was somewhere else: on Rochelle. "There are a lot of women out here," he said to her when explaining why he was not in a committed relationship. They sat at the same IHOP from the previous night. Only this time, he was sober. "But it's about quality, not quantity. There's a real sorting-out process that leaves you drained. You can't just accept anyone because she is available. The fact that she is available might even be a red flag."

"Oh, so I have red flags?" Rochelle said.

"You have red, black *and* green flags," Jesse cracked. "But I'm willing to make an exception for you."

"Kiss my you-know-what," she said. "That's why I'm gonna stand you up at that event in two weeks."

"You do and I'll sue you," Jesse said, laughing.

Earl and Catherine took photos together with friends and left the party the way they came in—hand-in-hand, with a group of friends looking on pleasantly surprised by their coming together.

"Baby," she said, after they dropped off Starr and headed to her place, "we are a true love story."

"That's true," Earl said. "And after tonight, I think we're going to be the source of a lot of gossip. But I don't care."

Jimmy was tempted to tell his wife, Monica, about her cousin Donna's "test" but he didn't. "Why won't you?" Donna asked.

"Because she should already know who I am and what I would do," he said. "I prove it every day. That should be enough for her."

"I hear you," she said.

Tranise stayed at the hospital with Brandon until the doctor came out with his prognosis of Felicia: pre-term labor, meaning the baby was trying to come out. It was not an uncommon event, but one that required Felicia to minimize her activities until the baby was delivered. Any more drama and she would be restricted to total bed rest.

"It was meant to be that you were in that bathroom when I was," Felicia said, resting comfortably in her hospital bed. "How could it be that you, of all people, are a hero in my life?"

"I don't know about hero," Tranise said, "but I do know this has been an unbelievable weekend. And I'm glad I was in that bathroom at that time. Amazingly enough, I gained a new friend."

"Two friends," Brandon said.

On Sunday morning, as he stood in front of the hotel waiting for his car to come up from valet, Jimmy embraced several friends and old classmates and wished them safe travels home.

He and Carter had a talk over breakfast, where he learned his boy was married but in love with Barbara. "I don't envy your position," Jimmy told him. "I'm not sure what I can do, but I'm willing to help any way I can."

"Pray for me," Carter said.

Jimmy called Monica as he tipped the valet and settled into his vehicle. "Hi, wife," he said.

"Hi, husband. How was everything? What's next on your agenda?" she asked.

"It's been an awesome weekend," he said, putting on his dark sunglasses. "People told me, but now I know for sure. It will take a few days to recover. Homecoming was great. But, baby, it's time to come home."

"Am I coming with you next year?" Monica asked.

"Yes," Jimmy answered.

"No," he then said after a few seconds. Monica did not say anything.

He put on his dark sunglasses and smiled.

"Well, maybe," he said, finally, driving off.

ABOUT THE AUTHOR

Curtis Bunn is a national award-winning sports journalist who has evolved into one of the most critically acclaimed authors of contemporary fiction about relationships. His novel, *Baggage Check*, ascended to No. 1 on the *Essence* magazine and Cushcity. com bestseller lists. He has been featured in national magazines (including *Essence*, *Black Issues Book Review*, *Uptown*, *Black Enterprise*, *Rolling Out*) and local Atlanta media outlets (*The Atlanta Journal-Constitution*, Fox 5 Good Day Atlanta, Fox 5 Good Day Xtra!). He has written for *Black Enterprise*, *Honey* magazine, *ESPN The Magazine*, *Hoop* magazine and others. A native of Washington, D.C., Bunn covered the NBA, NFL, Olympics, college basketball, pro baseball, professional boxing and wrote columns for *The Washington Times*, New York *Newsday* and *New York Daily News* and *The Atlanta Journal-Constitution*.

In 2002, he founded the National Book Club Conference, which has developed into a premier annual literary event for readers and authors. This bolstered his connection to hundreds of reading groups around the country. His website is www.curtisbunn.com and he has more than 4,600 friends on Facebook.

ALL HAIL
THE HBCU
HOMECOMING
EXPERIENCE!

"I remember my high school guidance counselor exalting all the virtues of the HBCUs. He told me I wouldn't be just another student, a number. He told me that I would get personal care from my professors— and he was right! At Norfolk State, I became a part of a huge family that included professors, administrators and an eclectic group of friends from all over the US.

There are 10 federal holidays in 2012. For me, you would need to add two, maybe three more days for homecoming weekend. Homecoming at NSU is a must on my calendar. It is a necessary part of my year."

—SAM MYERS, NORFOLK STATE UNIVERSITY, CLASS OF 1984

"My great-grandfather, Henry C. Baker, was a friend and confidant of Booker T. Washington (founder of Tuskegee Institute) and George Washington Carver (the school's first president). Naturally, when it was time for college, Tuskegee was the only place for me. In fact, I always envisioned myself one day being a learned scholar and being so proud to see my grandmother's face as I was one of the many well-known former students who passed through town to participate in events at Tuskegee Institute. As a freshman, what I remember as my most impressionable moment was my first day. The most memorable and life-molding person I encountered at Tuskegee was my ROTC instructor, Major Neal,

the polished, impeccable intellectual man I had ever met. He was a man who had traveled the globe. Major Neal was intimidating but also humorous, and I gravitated to him. He would often tell me "Whatever area you choose to pursue, always put your best foot forward." It was a simple but lasting message that I held on to...was at Tuskegee when Dr. King was there discussing the Rosa Parks bus boycott. I was there when my grandmother and I were thrown off a Greyhound bus to make room for a white family. All in all, being at Tuskegee gave me the gumption to start an international corporation that has worked across the globe. I take my time at Tuskegee as my history lesson not only by which I live by, but as the rich cultural history I have tried to shape the lives of my children and grandchildren."

—TED BAKER, TUSKEGEE UNIVERSITY, CLASS OF 1962

"When I think about my time at FAMU, I then think of how that was a period of my life that I could live over again and again. Being surrounded by like-minded people who shared my goal of achieving success and mostly looked like me...my HBCU experience was amazing! Going back to Homecoming allows me to put aside everything, and go back to a place where I had the best time of my life and made my forever friends!"

—VENUS CHAPMAN, FLORIDA A&M UNIVERSITY, CLASS OF 1994

"Attending TSU was the greatest decision I ever made. The friend-ships I made during those four years are still with me today. Homecoming is like walking on hallowed ground. With 2012 as TSU's 100th anniversary, we know it's going to be even more special than ever, and 'off the chain' experience... TIGER4LIFE!!!"

—JEWELL ROLLEN, TENNESSEE STATE UNIVERSITY, CLASS OF 1972

"When I graduated from Bethune Cookman, I felt good about myself and the education I gained, but I also felt a strange sense of sadness. Part of me was ready to go; another part of me felt a pull to stay. Then, it dawned on me: I had grown accustomed to this place. In essence, I was leaving my home."

—JANELLE THOMAS, BETHUNE COOKMAN COLLEGE, CLASS OF 2005

"My Spelman experience has given me the strength and tools I need, as a woman of color, to exist in a world that is not designed for me. Having lived abroad for over eight years, I find I value my HBCU experience even more! How I have missed attending homecoming and reunion celebration that provided me with a sense of belonging and connectedness that I haven't found any other place. Though now I can only be a part of this event through social media, it continues to empower me to keep on keeping on."

—JERI BYROM, SPELMAN COLLEGE, CLASS OF 1987

"Going to Clark Atlanta University or, as I know and love 'the school on the hill,' basically raised me. The nurturing of the professors and the camaraderie of my classmates reside in me to this day. As for Homecoming, the fun usually begins Thursday evening (if you're lucky) and doesn't end until Sunday afternoon on your way to the airport. It will take a day or two to recover, depending on how hard you roll."

—DARRYL (DJ) JOHNSON, CLARK ATLANTA UNIVERSITY, CLASS OF 1983

"Attending North Carolina Central was truly one of the best decisions I made as a young adult. I cherish the friendships that I developed there and they will last a lifetime. Homecoming at an HBCU, specifically

NCCU, is a great experience that is hard to put into words. You reminisce about your college experience, tell 'tall tales' and school some of the young students that are still wet behind the ears. The camaraderie is indescribable. However if you ever walked on our yard during homecoming, you would feel the love, joy, excitement and the common bond that is shared among ALL EAGLES!!!! We soar very high. EAGLE PRIDE!!"

—DEBORAH MCCLOUD, NORTH CAROLINA CENTRAL UNIVERSITY,
CLASS OF 1997

"Graduating from North Carolina A&T was a major milestone. It meant a lot to me to study in Martina and Gibb Halls, same as A&T alums, the late NASA astronaut Dr. Ronald McNair, The Greensboro Four and Jesse Jackson, among others. Our homecoming is not called the best in the world for nothing. I get to be a teenager all over again and reminisce while sitting on the steps of Holland Hall with my dorm mates from fall 1986. It's the best time!"

—MICHELLE LEMON, NORTH CAROLINA A&T STATE UNIVERSITY,
CLASS OF 1991

"The first day on campus at Virginia State felt like the beginning of a four-year vacation. It was the only time my wonderful parents invested thousands of dollars on me to go on a vacation. It was challenging academically, but I mostly recall how much fun I had. After years of growth, returning for homecoming means more than crowning a king and queen, attending a parade, football game or homecoming dance. Above all it's a cherished time for uniting the past and present."

—DEBORAH R. JOHNSON, VIRGINIA STATE UNIVERSITY,
CLASS OF 1984

"We were fortunate to grow up with exposure to HBCUs so the biggest decision I had to make was choosing one. Shaw University not only provided an excellent education but the nurturing that we needed. The faculty and staff were surrogate parents and many of my schoolmates were like siblings and we still maintain those relationships over 30 years later. No matter where you came from or needed it or not, you were taught how to walk among Presidents, Queens. Homecomings are just that—coming home to the place where you did so many firsts or met people who will remain in your life forever. The stories get a little fuzzy and sometime more colorful but that's what makes Homecoming so cool!

—ELEANOR AND DAVID LINTON, SHAW UNIVERSITY, CLASS OF 1980

"I visited tons of colleges as a high-school senior, but no place stood out like 'THE HILL.' The difference in environment and student atmosphere was astounding. It was like a home away from home, but with an edge. It wasn't just the hype of homecoming, but every single function was one you never wanted to miss. The fashion, the Greeks, the band and the many festivities were all just another representation of our African heritage. No matter what side of THE HILL you lived on, everyone came together as one during almighty homecoming. And no matter how many years have passed, it's every HBCU's family reunion. It's like seeing your long-lost cousins and being introduced to the new additions to the family. 'A-M, A-M, A-M, A-M-U, whooooo ah booty bootaayyyy!!!!'"

—ERIN SHERROD, ALABAMA A&M, CLASS OF 2001

"Homecoming, freshman year (1972) was like going to the best party ever and having Earth, Wind and Fire on campus and this young group called The Commodores throw down off campus. There was a comfort level attending HI (now HU) that made the maturation transformation from high school to college seamless. And accompanying this growth was the country's finest collection of intelligent sisters. It ain't braggin' if it's true."

—MARTIN MCNEAL, HAMPTON (INSTITUTE) UNIVERSITY, CLASS OF 1977

"My HBCU experience was great! I actually turned my life over to Christ during college. The love & friendship through Campus Ministry was the best thing ever which really helped me through. Every HBCU needs a real Down-to-Earth Christ Rocking Ministry!"

—ARTICULITE POETRY, MISSISSIPPI VALLEY STATE

"Other than the birth of my children and my wedding day, Morehouse College has been the best thing that ever happened in my life! Morehouse took a scared and naïve boy from Buffalo, New York and shaped and motivated him into a man. Relationships that I've developed during my college years are still my closest friends today. They were my groomsmen, godfathers to my children, business consultants and confidants. Seven years ago I started to rent executive coach buses for homecoming for a few reasons. First, it was an opportunity for us to fellowship and laugh at the hair we were losing and the weight we were gaining. Secondly, this was a way for us to have our children meet and get to know each other in a wonderful environment. Finally, it was the best tailgate party in the history of football! One of the best days I had last year was when I hosted a lunch with 10 Spelman and Morehouse freshmen and sophomores. They were all sons and daughters of friends that I attended college with. It was great to see our sons and daughters becoming successful men and women. This is just another blessing from Morehouse College."

—WILLIAM MITCHELL, MOREHOUSE COLLEGE, CLASS OF 1984

"They say college is when you're supposed to 'find yourself' so I chose an HBCU to make sure I would find myself among my people. And I instantly felt at home. All of my wildest, funniest, craziest and all-around greatest memories of college are from homecoming. There's nothing like a Howard homecoming. It's something every young person should experience at least once…or more than once if you can handle it."

—Naeesa Aziz, Howard University, Class of 2006

"I will never forget my first homecoming experience and the genuine love and happiness amongst the CSU family. The atmosphere of the whole day was one that had me in a trance and there was no question that CSU was the place for me. Each day on campus was a learning experience and when you're obtaining knowledge and culture in an educational environment, it's always a step in the right direction."

—Franklin White, Central State University

"Every fall I look forward to the Virginia Union homecoming celebration. I enjoy going to the 'hole,' which is the Kappa frat room on campus in the basement of Storer Hall. Gathering with the brothers from Alpha Gamma, reminiscing on the days gone, reminds me of the things I wouldn't want my son to do, but I sure had fun doing them. Homecoming weekend at VUU gives me the opportunity to reconnect with my extended family and rejoice in the lifelong education I received in the classroom and hanging on the 'yard.'"

—J.B. Hill, Virginia Union University, Class of 1990

"As a native of Detroit, MI., I didn't know what to expect as I passed through red clay roads encompassed with livestock, blue jays and red robins en route to my freshman year at Alabama State University.

Turned out, a 'newbie' like me could not have asked for a more rich in culture steeped Hornet pride with the most passionate educators and administrators. My HBCU experience enriched my life tremendously through education and by instilling African-American pride and reminding me of the struggles of others before me. Our homecoming, The Turkey Day Classic, fills your heart with pride and joy, as alumni return from all ages and walks of life. And those Mighty Marching Hornets... lifetime impressions. A. S. A. S. A. S. A.S. ...U!! Clap clap clap, clap clap clap!"

—TAMELA ALLEN JONES, ALABAMA STATE UNIVERSITY, CLASS OF 1997

"I am proud that I went to an HBCU. I always knew that I would attend Morgan State University because of the way it gave back to my community. Morgan State made me feel like extended family. The school laid the foundation for me for the importance of community service. Homecoming is a chance to catch up with old friends and to celebrate the success of their lives because of this great institution."

—ANGELA BELTON, MORGAN STATE UNIVERSITY, CLASS OF 2006

"When I think of our homecoming at Morris Brown, I hear the drumline and see the drum majors high-stepping onto the yard ahead of Bubbling Brown Sugar, the dance team. This scenario always stirs up nostalgia: hanging on the yard between classes; chilling in the dorm social areas for hours; talking trash over Spades; Greeks stepping; going to football games. It's a special time of reminiscing and catching up. Although Morris Brown has had its financial and accreditation issues, the spirit of the Brownite Alumni remains strong. The large number of graduates converging on the yard from all over the country showed

that at homecoming. We continue to have pride in the purple and black of dear 'ole Morris Brown. I would never trade my experience of going to Morris Brown for anything. Go Wolverines!!"

—SHERLINE TAVERNIER, MORRIS BROWN COLLEGE, CLASS OF 1994

"I'll never forget the feeling of love, support, and pride I experienced when I entered Winston-Salem State University (WSSU Mighty Rams!) as a freshman. The valuable life-lessons I received from caring faculty, staff and my fellow students impacted me in a powerful way, providing a nurturing environment that allowed me to grow into adulthood with a greater sense of purpose. Ask anyone who has attended an HBCU and they will tell you that it is an experience like no other—and in particular, homecoming! Every year I look forward to this special and time-honored tradition at my school. What's homecoming like at an HBCU? Imagine a joyful family reunion held during Thanksgiving, Christmas, Easter, and the Fourth of July wrapped into one! Beautiful black people coming together in this spirit of love and fellowship to reminisce, support, celebrate, and give back to the community while supporting our treasured academic institutions. I will forever be grateful to WSSU and all our sister HBCUs!"

—TRICE HICKMAN, WINSTON-SALEM STATE UNIVERSITY,
CLASS OF 1991

HISTORICALLY BLACK
COLLEGES AND UNIVERSITIES

Alabama A&M University
Normal, AL

Alabama State University
Montgomery, AL

Albany State University
Albany, NY

Alcorn State University
Lorman, MS

Allen University
Columbia, SC

Arkansas Baptist College
Little Rock, AK

Benedict College
Columbia, SC

Bennett College
Greensboro, NC

Bethune-Cookman University
Daytona Beach, FL

Bishop State Community College
Mobile, AL

Bluefield State College
Bluefield, WV

Bowie State University
Bowie, MD

Central State University
Wilberforce, OH

Claflin University
Orangeburg, SC

Clark Atlanta University
Atlanta, GA

Clinton Junior College
Rock Hill, SC

Coahoma Community College
Clarksdale, MS

Concordia College–Selma
Selma, AL

Coppin State University
Baltimore, MD

Delaware State University
Dover, DE

Denmark Technical College
Denmark, SC

Dillard University
New Orleans, LA

Edward Waters College
Jacksonville, FL

Elizabeth City State University
Elizabeth City, NC

Fayetteville State University
Fayetteville, NC

Fisk University
Nashville, TN

Florida Agricultural and Mechanical University
Tallahassee, FL

Florida Memorial University
Miami Gardens, FL

Fort Valley State University
Ft. Valley, GA

Gadsden State Community College
Gadsden, AL

Grambling State University
Grambling, LA

H Councill Trenholm State Technical College
Montgomery, AL

Hampton University
Hampton, VA

Harris-Stowe State University
St. Louis, MO

Hinds Community College–Utica
Utica, MS

Howard University
Washington, D.C.

Huston-Tillotson University
Lorman, MS

Interdenominational Theological Center
Atlanta, GA

J F Drake State Technical College
Huntsville, AL

Jackson State University
Jackson, MS

Jarvis Christian College
Hawkins, TX

Johnson C Smith University
Charlotte, NC

Kentucky State University
Frankfort, KY

Lane College
Jackson, TN

Langston University
Langston, OK

Lawson State Community College–Birmingham
Birmingham, AL

LeMoyne-Owen College
Memphis, TN

Lincoln University
Jefferson City, MO

Lincoln University of Pennsylvania
Lincoln University, PA

Livingstone College
Salisbury, NC

Meharry Medical College
Nashville, TN

Miles College
Fairfield, AL

Mississippi Valley State University
Itta Bena, MS

Morehouse College
Atlanta, GA

Morehouse School of Medicine
Atlanta, GA

Morgan State University
Baltimore, MD

Morris College
Sumter, SC

Norfolk State University
Norfolk, VA

North Carolina Agricultural & Technical State University
Greensboro, NC

North Carolina Central University
Durham, NC

Oakwood University
Huntsville, AL

Paine College
Augusta, GA

Paul Quinn College
Dallas, TX

Philander Smith College
Little Rock, AK

Prairie View A&M University
Prairie View, TX

Rust College
Holly Springs, MS

Saint Augustine's College
Raleigh, NC

Saint Paul's College
Lawrenceville, VA

Savannah State University
Savannah, GA

Selma University
Selma, AL

Shaw University
Raleigh, NC

Shelton State Community College
Tuscaloosa, AL

South Carolina State University
Orangeburg, SC

Southern University and A&M College
Baton Rouge, LA

Southern University at New Orleans
New Orleans, LA

Southern University at Shreveport
Shreveport, LA

Southwestern Christian College
Terrell, TX

Spelman College
Atlanta, GA

St. Philip's College
San Antonio, TX

Stillman College
Tuscaloosa, AL

Talladega College
Talladega, AL

Tennessee State University
Nashville, TN

Texas College
Tyler, TX

Texas Southern University
Houston, TX

Tougaloo College
Tougaloo, MS

Tuskegee University
Tuskegee, AL

University of Arkansas at Pine Bluff
Pine Bluff, AK

University of Maryland Eastern Shore
Princess Anne, MD

University of the District of Columbia
Washington, D.C.

University of the Virgin Islands
Charlotte Amalie, Virgin Islands

University of the Virgin Islands–Kingshill
St. Croix, Virgin Islands

Virginia State University
Petersburg, VA

Virginia Union University
Richmond, VA

**Virginia University
of Lynchburg**
Lynchburg, VA

Voorhees College
Denmark, SC

**West Virginia State
University**
Institute, WV

Wilberforce University
Wilberforce, OH

Wiley College
Marshall, TX

**Winston-Salem
State University**
Winston-Salem, NC

**Xavier University
of Louisiana**
New Orleans, LA

IF YOU ENJOYED "HOMECOMING WEEKEND,"
BE SURE TO CHECK OUT

A COLD PIECE OF WORK

. A NOVEL

BY CURTIS BUNN
AVAILABLE FROM STREBOR BOOKS

CHAPTER 1
LOVE TO LOVE YOU

The force of his thrusts pushed her to the edge of the four-poster bed. She was lathered as much in satisfaction as she was in sweat, exhilarated and weary—and unable to hold herself atop the mattress against his unrelenting strikes. A different kind of man would have postponed the passion; at least long enough to pull up her naked, vulnerable body.

But Solomon Singletary was hardly one to subscribe to conventional thinking or deeds. He always had a point to prove and always was committed to proving it—with actions, not words.

And so, Solomon thrust on…and on, until they, as one, careened onto the carpet together, she cushioning his fall from beneath him. So paralyzed in pleasure was she that she never felt the impact of the tumble. Rather, she found humor that they made love clean across the bed and onto the floor, and she found delight that the fall did not disengage them.

Solomon lost neither his connection to her nor his cadence, and stroked her on the carpet just as he had on the sheets—purposefully, unrelentingly, deeply.

"What are you trying to do?" she asked. "Make love to me? Or make me love you?"

Solomon did not answer—not with words. He continued to speak the language of passion, rotating his hips forward, as one would a hula-hoop. Her shapely, chocolate legs were airborne and his knees were carpet-burned raw, but hardly did he temper his pace.

His answer: Both.

She finally spoke the words that slowed Solomon. "Okay, okay," she said. "Okay." She gave in, and that pleased Solomon. She would have said the words earlier—before they tumbled off the bed—but he never allowed her to catch her breath. All she could make were indecipherable sounds.

"I mean, damn," she said, panting. "We're good together… Damn."

Solomon kissed her on her left shoulder and rolled off her and onto the floor, on his wide, strong back. He looked up toward the dark ceiling illuminated by the single candle on the nightstand, so pleased with himself that a smile formed on his face.

Then he dozed off right there on the floor. She didn't bother to wake him. Instead, she reached up and pulled the comforter off the bed and over both of them. She nestled her head on his hairy chest, smiled to herself and drifted off to sleep with him, right there on the floor.

That was the last time she saw Solomon Singletary. And he only saw her a few times, but only in dreams that did not make much sense.

"I wish I knew what the hell it meant," he said to his closest friend, Raymond. He and Ray became tight five years earlier, when they got paired together during a round of golf at Mystery Valley in Lithonia, just east of Atlanta. They had a good time, exchanged numbers and ended up becoming not only golf buddies, but also great friends.

Ray was very much the opposite of Solomon. He was not as tall but just as handsome, and he was charismatic and likeable, in a different way. Solomon was sort of regal to some, arrogant to others. Ray was more every man. He had a wife of seven years, Cynthia, and a six-year-old son, Ray-Ray. He was stable.

Solomon knew a lot of people, but only liked some and trusted only a few. He really only tolerated most; especially the various women who ran in and out of his life like some nagging virus. "In the end," he told Ray, "the one person you can trust is yourself. And even with that, how many times have you lied to yourself?"

Ray figured there was something deep inside Solomon that would bring him to such feelings, and he figured if Solomon wanted him to know, he would have told him. So he never asked. Ray and Solomon coveted each other's friendship and had a certain trust. And they shared most everything with each other.

Ray's way was to provide levity when possible, which, for him, was practically all the time. His upbeat disposition seldom changed. If the Falcons lost a football game, he'd show disgust and disappointment for a while, but he'd let it go.

Solomon Singletary was not that way. He could be solemn at times, even-tempered at others and occasionally aggressive. Above all, he was quite adept at pulling people close to him. He had a unique ability to be open but remain private. He could be disinterested but still engaging. And those unique qualities made people open up to him; especially women.

"You're so interesting," Michele told him that last night together. "We've dated for six months. You try to act like you don't love me, but you do; I can tell by how we make love. Why won't you say you love me?"

"Come here." Michele came over to him, to the edge of her bed. "Don't get caught up on what I say to you or don't say," he said. "Worry about what I do to you; how I make you feel."

"Is everything about sex with you?"

"See, I wasn't even talking about sex. I was talking about how you feel inside, when we're together, when you think of me," Solomon said. "That's more important than what I say. Right?"

Before she could answer, he leaned over and kissed her on the lips softly and lovingly. "What does that kiss say?"

"It says you want to make love," Michele said sarcastically. "Some things can get lost in translation. That's why you should say it. Plus, sometimes it's just good to hear."

"Hear this." Solomon kissed Michele again. This time, it was not a peck, but a sustained coming together of lips and tongue and saliva. He leaned her back on the bed, and she watched as he pulled his tank top over his head, revealing his expansive chest and broad shoulders.

He smiled at her and she smiled back and the talk of saying "I love you" ceased.

"Whatever happened to that girl?" Ray asked Solomon. "You regret not having her now?"

"Regret? What's that? You make a decision and you stick to it. No looking back. But a few years ago, I saw a woman briefly who reminded me of her, and it made me think about calling her."

"You thought about it? Why didn't you call her?" Ray wanted to know.

"Hard to say. Young, dumb. Silly," Solomon answered. "What would've been the point? I got a job here with Coke and wasn't about to do the long distance thing. So what was the point?"

"Well, did you at least break up on good terms?" Ray asked.

"The last time I saw her, she was on the floor next to her bed, sleeping. I got up and put on my clothes and left. The next day, the movers came and I drove here, to Atlanta."

"Wait," Ray said, standing up. "She didn't know you were moving out of town?"

"Nah," Solomon said, looking off. "Nah."

"How can you just roll out on the girl like that?"